FIVE LITTLE BITCHES

A NOVEL BY
TERESA MCWHIRTER

Other Books By Teresa McWhirter

Some Girls Do
Dirtbags
Skank (YA)

What the critics had to say about McWhirter's previous books:

About *Some Girls Do*

"Before approaching this book you have to decide if you are interested in reading about people who are pimples on the ass of society. ... Twenty-something alcoholics and druggies do not or cannot read, and people who can afford books do not want to read about them." –**W.P. KINSELLA**, author of *Shoeless Joe*

"Some Girls Do is a sharp, poetic glimpse into the yearning but hopelessly unfocused lives of a group of marginal urbanites...surprisingly, McWhirter makes them touching rather than alienating." –**ELLE CANADA**

About *Dirtbags*

"McWhirter is a mistress of momentum. ... Dirtbags will take its place in any sensibly constructed future Canadian canon. This is a great book and a funny, moving and entertaining read." –**THE GLOBE AND MAIL**

"These are not the young, hip, irony-driven quipsters from Douglas Coupland novels, biding their time, hoping for elevation into a higher level of consumerism; McWhirter's generation of urban drifters are jumping over the edge of despair into pits of self-destruction. Romance is a luxury they can't afford."
–**ABC BOOKWORLD**

A NOVEL BY

TERESA MCWHIRTER

Vancouver | 2012

Anvil Press Publishers Inc.
P.O. Box 3008, Main Post Office
Vancouver, B.C. V6B 3X5 Canada
www.anvilpress.com

Library and Archives Canada Cataloguing in Publication

McWhirter, Teresa, 1971-
Five little bitches / Teresa McWhirter.

ISBN 978-1-897535-90-5

I. Title.

PS8575.W484F59 2012 C813'.6 C2012-901151-7

Book design & cover photo: Derek von Essen
Author photo: Bronwyn Absalom
Back cover photo: Jade Fawkes

Represented in Canada by the Literary Press Group

Distributed in Canada by the University of Toronto Press
and in the U.S. by Small Press Distribution (SPD).

The publisher gratefully acknowledges the financial assistance of the Canada Council for the Arts, the Canada Book Fund, and the Province of British Columbia through the B.C. Arts Council and the Book Publishing Tax Credit.

Printed and bound in Canada

To my mom,
SHARON
AND
ADDIE, AMBER,
BRONWYN,
JADE, LYNN,
and SANDRA
–the FUCKIN'
little bitches!

ACKNOWLEDGEMENTS

i would like to thank Brian Kaufman and Anvil Press for their continued support;

Derek von Essen, for the sick book design;

Chris Hutchinson, Billeh Nickerson, and Meghan Martin for their editorial input;

The Real McKenzies, for letting me tag along on tours;

chef Todd for the use of his menus in this book;

Aron McKenzie for the skull tattoo;

Mike, Heather, Terry, Rachel, Logan, Ellery, Ashley, Kathleen, and Sophie for their love and encouragement;

imon, Jamie, and Fe, my favorite Jaks;

My Berlin family: Demonica, Muttis, and Frieder

and Mark "The Bone" Boland for making me laugh every single day.

TABLE of CONTENTS

BIO

NAME: Maxine Micheline AGE: 35

OCCUPATION: Frontwoman, Wet Leather

BIRTHPLACE: Mission, BC.

PREVIOUS BANDS: Death by Rollercoaster

INTERESTS: Musicals, French cuisine, gangbangs

EARLIEST MEMORY: Hochtaler wine commercials

QUOTE: "Rock 'n' roll is in my blood!"

MAXINE MICHELINE

As soon as Maxine walks into the party, she knows it's a mistake to have come. It's at the Nation of Fuckers clubhouse, and the men are loud, greasy, and drunk. A few rough-looking girls stand in clots around the living room. None are friendly.

She finds a bathroom and gulps water from the faucet. At thirty-five, her face shows the character lines of an aging party girl. With her long neck, short bleached hair, and thin nose, she gives the impression of an exotic, weak-chinned bird. Maxine hitches her leather pants over her burgeoning pot belly. The booze takes a downturn, and she digs into her fringed leather purse to apply more powder, mascara, and another layer of red lipstick with a practised hand. She leans back and checks her reflection, satisfied.

Maxine goes out to the deck to find Jesse, her so-called date. Jesse is also her pot dealer, and since there'd been nothing else going on when he'd invited her, she'd agreed to go. It's been the same long party for the past ten years, and somewhere, there's more booze. Maxine never stays home on a Friday night, and over the years she's dated her share of NoF boys and their uniforms of greasy denim vests with poorly sewn patches.

In the living room she sits down on the couch, and is joined at once by a slurring drunk guy in a T-shirt ringed with sweat. "Hey Tits."

Maxine shoots him a sour look.

"Oops. Looks like I'm goin' downhill."

"I have a feeling you didn't make it too far up the hill before you started to slide back down." She blows a grand cloud of smoke in his direction. The booze she'd drunk at home has worn off and she needs a beer.

"You're a feisty one," he says, pushing closer. "Wanna go do a bump in the can?" She's considering it when Jesse walks into the living room, assesses the situation, and glares in her direction. Maxine sighs. For years she and Jesse were casual friends. He made her laugh and usually had good coke. A few weeks ago she'd ended up at his place following a rock show after-party. Despite his beer gut and ironic mustache, she'd fucked him. The sex had been bad and in the morning both were on the verge of a puking hangover. At the door Maxine had stood awkwardly, pondering how a few hours earlier she'd had his balls in her mouth, and now it felt too intimate to kiss goodbye.

She gets off the couch and walks over to Jesse. "What's up?" she asks. He's drinking a beer and has one more in his pocket he doesn't offer.

"Not my dick," Jesse says, looking her up and down. It's obvious the minor undercurrent of attraction between them, once explored, left a faux friendship that easily disintegrated. Maxine turns on her heel and walks into the kitchen. She knows the deal. Around the kitchen table, guys with lit cigarettes and jailhouse tattoos play poker, while looking like they might have a gun in the waistband of their pants. Their greedy eyes dart over her before turning back to their cards. She wonders if she'll have to fuck someone just to get home.

Then she notices a small woman in a leather jacket wedged in at the table, a messy pile of chips in front of her. It impresses Maxine to find a tiny rocker right in the middle of this criminal element, tearing it up. Everything changes. "Haw HAW Randy!" the girl crows, throwing down her cards. She reaches for the pile of chips in the centre of the table.

"Simmer down, Squeaky."

"Fuck you," she squeals. "You just got bitch-slapped by some ovaries!" Maxine laughs, but it's clear the disgruntled men do not like losing. Squeaky beams up at her.

"Hey girl," she says. "You want in?"

That's the beginning. It's that simple to start.

Maxine Micheline was born to be a rock star.

Her father played saxophone for a bar band that had weekend gigs at a roadside tavern. One Saturday night, after her mother had served her father his third cocktail, they'd screwed in the parking lot. Maxine was conceived in the back of a van between forty-minute sets. As an infant the only thing that soothed Maxine's cries was Fleetwood Mac albums and TV jingles.

When Maxine began to walk, she would climb onto the coffee table and perform along with the radio. She roared, "Hot child in the city! Lookin' wild feelin' prit-ty!" with such passion and intensity, it made her parents, who were often stoned on pills and grass, slightly uneasy. They did not understand that Maxine believed the songs were about her. She couldn't wait to be a teenager and wanted to change her name to Sweet Sixteen.

When Maxine was four, her father went on the road. A month later he called home from a pay phone to say he'd fallen in love with a woman he'd met in a Chicago jazz club and was never coming back. During a frenzied two weeks, her mother sold off everything that belonged to him: a bass guitar, a banjo, stacks of samba records, even his wing-tipped shoes. "Women are the slaves of the slaves," her mother told her. "Men will leave you with nothing." The memory of Maxine's father became more fractured over time: his mustache and yellow fingers; thin, sweet-smelling cigars; his grey fedora with blue feathers in the band.

One afternoon Maxine came home from school and found most of the house packed up in boxes. She trembled on the edge of a tantrum and began to wail. "It's a lesson you're going to have to learn," her mother sighed, hauling up their bags. "Nothing good lasts and money always runs out." Their new home was in a suburb of Vancouver. Maxine's grandmother owned the house and was dying of emphysema in a bedroom upstairs. She had begun to look, in Maxine's opinion, like a very large onion.

In the new city where they lived it always rained. Maxine hated umbrellas and rubber boots. She was an excitable blonde child with thin pigtails who got into trouble at school for not staying in her seat. Instead of homework, she performed song and dance numbers for her row of stuffed animals. Bigger productions were staged in the living room. Maxine never invited friends from school because the house smelled like baby powder and shit. Usually she made a plate of graham crackers with honey and watched TV alone. Her mother cleaned an office building, and began to gain a lot of weight. She kept her hair pulled back in a tight bun, and always had a disappointed look on her face.

Maxine had bad judgment and a lopsided smile that got her in and out of trouble. Her daydreams involved motorcycles and speeding cars, intercut with big showgirl song and dance numbers. Over the years, she got the best parts to sing in music class. She loved talent contests and surprise parties and cultivated a taste for menthol cigarettes. Sometimes she had to fix her grandmother dinner, which consisted of instant potatoes and creamed corn with a mashed banana chaser. When Maxine was forced to sit with the old woman, she got a panicky feeling that she was missing out on something important.

Her partner in crime was Rosie Stone. They went to the same high school, and met one afternoon in detention—Maxine for smoking in the bathroom and Rosie for cutting class to go shopping. They became instant best friends like teenage girls can. By the following weekend they were siphoning booze from grandma's liquor cabinet, and trying out an assortment of pain killers pilfered from the medicine cabinet.

Everyone noticed Rosie first. She was a stunning, curvaceous girl with amber doe eyes and a gentle voice that could get away with saying the most crass or ludicrous things. Rosie did not get along with Elsa, her mother, whom she referred to as the "Money-cunt Swede." Rosie's father was from Ghana and had gone to medical school in London, where he'd met Elsa, a Swedish catalogue model. He had died three years earlier of a rare blood disease. Rosie never talked about her father, except to say it had taken an entire year for him to die. By then he was separated from Elsa and lived with a Sri-Lankan veterinary student who put herself through school by lap dancing.

Elsa often travelled to Europe, where she imported a line of skin care products from Hungary, and had various affairs. She thought nothing of leaving her teenage daughter alone for weeks with the house keys and a credit card. Instead of buying what they wanted, the girls went to the mall and shoplifted. Rosie would walk into a store, pick up the biggest item she could carry, and stroll casually out. Maxine had watched her take a floor lamp, a rubber dingy, even a giant Crock-Pot for Elsa's birthday, which Rosie found amusing since her mother never cooked. They palmed earrings, layered jackets, switched old bras and shoes for new, and dropped tubes of makeup into their bags or false pockets. Then they'd go to Rosie's and try out the new lipsticks and powders, crowing at each other in the mirror.

The day Maxine got expelled from school she found her best friend in the library, poring over a style magazine. Rosie got three spares a week because of a phony note that excused her from gym class for life. They commiserated over their sour stomachs. "I'm only fourteen," Maxine grumbled. "I'm not supposed to get hangovers like this. *Am* I?"

The night before, they'd taken the long bus ride into downtown, applying thick makeup in the back seats to go with their gigantic hairdos, huge earrings, and teetering heels. After trying three different bars, Rosie had found a bouncer who'd let them in. "If the cops come, get the fuck out," he'd barked, crossing his enormous arms. His eyes had lingered on Rosie. "I'll take YOU out back." Once inside, the drinks had been cheap and there'd been lots of men buying. The girls couldn't wait to return.

Across the library, Maxine spotted her nemesis, the teacher's pet. "Watch this." She turned the 63 on her paper into a bold 88. "We just got our tests back. Hey Kimmie, what did YOU get?" Kimmie scowled and moved her ample ass to the other side of the library.

"What's *her* problem? God, I feel sick," Maxine moaned. "AND I have math next and haven't done my homework. Mrs. Charleston is going to eat me like I'm one of her young!"

"Sounds like time for some paperwork." Rosie flashed Maxine her smile, the one that charmed bills and coins from stranger's pockets. They went out to the faculty parking lot to smoke up.

Maxine wasn't the greatest student and skipped a lot of classes. She was in danger of failing Grade 9 but didn't much care. When the joint was done, Maxine chugged a cola and then barfed. The bell rang and they ran to the washroom, leather purses bulging with cosmetics. Maxine crept into her seat at the back of class and realized she had no pencil. She took one from the cup of extras Mrs. Charleston kept on her desk. "Maxine Micheline," the teacher snapped. "First you come to class late and then you have no pencil. Is that correct?"

Maxine's stomach heaved. "Yes."

"That is *disgraceful*."

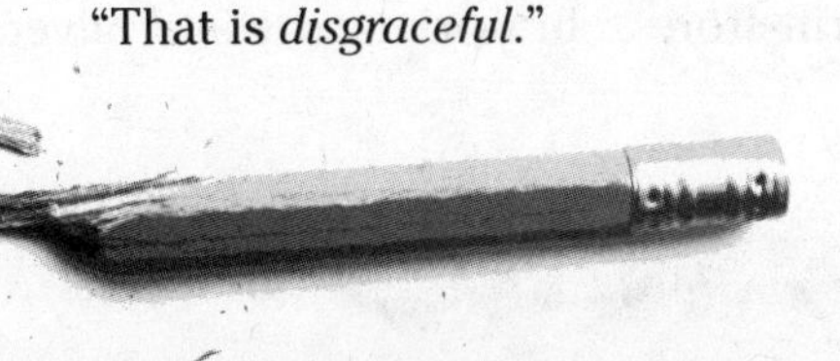

She wiped her mouth. "Fuck off," she said under her breath. But it wasn't soft enough. The teacher screamed, "Go to the principal's office IMMEDIATELY!"

One more suspension meant she was likely to be expelled. Maxine felt something wild break loose inside her. Going to the bar last night was the most fun she'd had in her life and now she was reduced to this boredom, this horrible silent tedium, and she tried, she tried so hard to go along with their stupid little rules. Her ears burned and her eyes began to throb. She didn't give a shit about math equations. It was such an outrage that Maxine grabbed a pencil from the cup and tapped Mrs. Charleston in the centre of her forehead, yelling, "Here it is, Mrs. Charleston!" She tapped her on the forehead again. "HERE'S my pencil!" Mrs. Charleston's face formed a wide O of surprise.

Maxine walked out of the classroom, but instead of running away she opened the door wide and hid behind it. She peeked out as Mrs. Charleston peeled down the hallway, butt cheeks grinding in her polyester slacks. Then Maxine strolled back in the room. The class was in hysterics. She sat down in her desk and waited.

After looking at her file and teacher comments, the principal informed her she was not the type of student they wanted in their school.

"As per your absentees and poor academics, Miss Micheline, if you don't want to be here, then we certainly don't want to have you."

"Well, I DON'T want to be here."

"Okay," said the principal.

"Ookay," said Maxine.

Two weeks later she was transferred to another school. She showed up in a thrift-store zebra print coat and silver

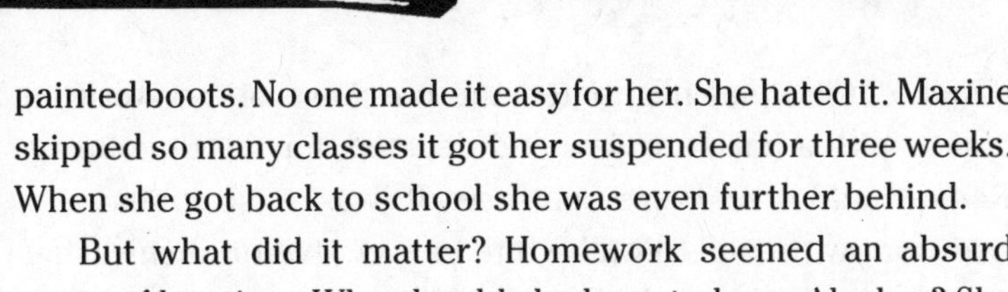

painted boots. No one made it easy for her. She hated it. Maxine skipped so many classes it got her suspended for three weeks. When she got back to school she was even further behind.

But what did it matter? Homework seemed an absurd waste of her time. Why should she have to learn Algebra? She was never going to use it. The novels she read at home were more challenging than the ones assigned in class. Boys in school didn't even have hair on their nuts and she and Rosie were in nightclubs with men, real men who paid for their drinks and packs of cigarettes. The DJ even let them sit with him in the booth above the common crowd.

The dim light of a bar meant excitement to Maxine. It was the only place anything good ever happened.

Maxine's hips grew bigger but her bra size didn't. Each night she prayed her boobs would grow. It was like waiting for an invitation to a party that never arrived. To distract from this, she bleached her hair white and always wore red lipstick and black-rimmed eyes. Super-short skirts showed off her long legs. Various rumours started, but Maxine couldn't help it if guys liked her. She took birth control at her mother's insistence, but was a spontaneous girl with a head full of music, and continuously forgot to take her pill.

When Maxine got kicked out of school again for missing too many classes, she decided not to go back. For a while her mother cried and yelled, then went back to her TV programs and romance novels.

So began many years of short-term jobs: a grocery clerk, telemarketer, counter girl at a cheap-slice pizza joint. At times it puzzled her to feel so tired at seventeen.

Elsa came back from a vacation at an adults-only resort for swingers, and felt unusually generous toward her teenage

daughter. She had negotiated the purchase of a waterfront condo with a harbour view and decided, for the time being, Rosie could live there rent-free. It was a spacious one-bedroom with wall-to-wall white carpet, even a dishwasher and fireplace. "Jeezus," Maxine said, standing on the balcony for the first time, "Look at this place! How can you say your mom doesn't love you?"

"Big deal," Rosie shrugged, twisting her long, caramel-coloured locks. "To her, it's just a real estate venture." She looked out over the water while Maxine looked at her. Rosie had an incredible body, beautiful skin and perfect teeth, but the saddest brown eyes. Most people never noticed.

"We're best friends," Maxine said. "You'll always have *me*."

18 Without rent and bills to pay, Rosie lived on her allowance. Elsa was willing to foot the expenses and keep her voluptuous teenage daughter away from home. For a while, Rosie got into ecstasy and house music. During this era, the apartment became a place for club kids to gather. Boys in colourful hats would dance to their reflection in the sliding glass doors. Slowly, the white carpets turned grey.

When she tired of techno, Rosie dumped the latest DJ for a fetish model and the tedious pursuit of arm-cutting and vodka-fuelled laments. Maxine worked in the fishy-smelling gift shop at the aquarium and slept around. The idea of love just didn't make sense to her. There was always a moment, alone with a cigarette in the middle of the night, when she knew it wouldn't last. Maxine expected to be alone, as if set on a course her heart could no longer control.

Then, suddenly, Elsa cut her daughter off. The skin care line was losing money, and Elsa could no longer afford to pay for Rosie's rent or give her a monthly allowance. The girls moved into a cheap place in East Van. The neighbourhood was full of kids who, like Rosie and Maxine, couldn't afford to live anywhere else. In their rundown apartment, cockroaches came out of the oven and cracks in the counter. One morning Maxine even found one on her toothbrush. Rosie adapted to her new life quite well, and soon stopped letting out blood-curdling screams each time she saw one scuttle across a wall.

Luckily there was a dive bar down the street. The Sewer offered refuge, and punk rock became the soundtrack to the manifesto they forged on those long days of empty bellies. It meant the abandonment of material conventions, the joy of chaos. Filth was the new aesthetic. When Maxine and Rosie got together, they were impossible to control.

A swarm of admiring males constantly buzzed around Rosie, including the Australian pot dealer downstairs who gave them free bags of weed. Maxine smoked a lot. It was lovely without the noise of questions, criticism, and the unavoidable knowledge that every one of them wanted Rosie, not her.

Over the years, Rosie cultivated non-sexual relationships with infatuated men. She treated it like a job. They gave her rides, took her for dinner, loaned rent money she'd never repay. Rosie ran up huge tabs on their bar bills, borrowed their credit cards. They accepted this because she was beautiful, and she and Maxine reasoned that if males were going to be that stupid and shallow, why *not* take their money? Eventually one would become too persistent, and when Rosie refused his advances he moved off into the next unhappy stratosphere. Another rapidly took his place.

The dealer had gone back to Sydney, and left the acid as a parting gift. It kicked in just as they got to the bar and they headed straight to the counter for booze. The bartender served their drinks and winked, “That’s eight dollars, please.”

Rosie put a bill on the counter, smiling. “How about five bucks?”

Maxine installed herself in the corner while the bartender chatted with Rosie. Rosie didn’t join her, and Maxine was too afraid to walk across the room. It felt like she teetered on the edge of a staircase that didn’t exist. Focusing her attention on the music fully absorbed her—the notes hit the bottom of her feet and travelled through her body before popping out the top of her head. Finally Rosie appeared. “There’s a table over there.”

“I’m not going *anywhere!*”

Rosie took her by the hand to the table, propping her up on a stool. Maxine screamed, “This group is *AMAZING*.”

Rosie looked at the stage skeptically. “Meh.”

“I’M gonna start a band, too.”

“Great idea! You should. Now, how are we going to get more drinks?”

Maxine was still too high to move. Someone brought her a glass of ominous looking liquid. Everyone in the bar danced like they were in an aerobics class. A guy near the stage wearing a sun visor seemed capable of murder. Ordinarily, this would be enough to make the acid take a dark turn, but tonight, none of this bothered Maxine. She was too consumed by her vision of absolute stardom.

Patsy Cakes played drums. A half-Dutch and Japanese lesbian, she held sex toy parties for a living and gave Maxine and Rosie free dildos and more lube than they could ever use. She also had a rehearsal space, a cement block room in a storage facility with a smelly couch in one corner. Patsy recruited a skinny art school graduate named Kirk to play guitar. Kirk was a musician, a painter, and a lover of obese women with cocaine-covered tits. He recalled contentedly how he had put himself through art school as a gigolo.

Things happened in the band with a natural ease. They picked their band name from the headlines of the newspaper: DEATH BY ROLLERCOASTER. Maxine worked as a hostess in an overpriced seafood restaurant and funded rehearsals by skimming off the till. The owner and head chef was a sweaty redhead with a gap between his front teeth. One night after closing, he fucked Maxine on the kitchen cutting board, inspiring the song, "Dirty Mr. Deenie," with a schoolyard refrain: *"Dirty Mr. Deenie/don't wanna see your weenie!"*

Kirk booked their first gig at his old art school, playing at an opening of an exhibition made entirely of coat hangers. The room didn't even have a stage. The crowd stopped talking when the band plugged in. No one introduced them. Maxine's voice cracked and hit one wrong note after another. They played their best three songs: "Don't Wanna Puke (Your Love Away)," "Purring like a Sonofabitch," and "Hats n' Flaps," a song Kirk wrote about his love for large women and cocaine. When they finished there was a smattering of applause before the crowd resumed their chatter.

Death by Rollercoaster had another gig a few months later, this time at a squalid dive bar with two other bands. It was a punk rock crowd with an art-fart element, and as Maxine strode across the stage she felt a new kind of energy. The lights were hot and this time they didn't hit as many sour chords. Maxine belted out song after song. The room filled with the sound of her voice, and she loved it. When the set was done, the audience roared with applause. Maxine, who'd been terrified to play and drank whisky throughout the set, lifted up her skirt and slapped her ass. The boys in the crowd went wild.

They got another gig, then a bigger one. Rosie was a loyal fan at every Death by Rollercoaster show. More bands wanted to play with them. Word spread around town about their crazy live performances. Boys sent up shots and doubles for Maxine. The more she drank, the more clothing she removed. Soon their sets were crowded with boys who had heard about the hot, train-wreck-of-a-singer, and the ex-gigolo who played guitar.

The band borrowed money from friends and relatives for studio time and recorded their album in three days. The sound was shit but they believed it lent a crude charm. *Must be This High to Ride* got peddled to a few record companies. No one showed much interest. One label head told Maxine he'd consider it if she got rid of Kirk and "the ugly drummer." The band decided to release the album on a small hometown label. It didn't make any money, but was a huge local success.

Patsy Cakes was also an actress, and won a small role in a short-lived series as a loveable crack whore. She quit the band and they were still looking for a replacement drummer when Kirk fell in love with a woman fatter than all the others. Soon after, the fat woman became pregnant with Kirk's child. He moved in with her and her three dogs, two birds, plus turtles in an aquarium. The woman lived way out in the suburbs and Kirk almost never made it to practise. Death by Rollercoaster officially broke up.

For some time, Rosie had worked in a retro-themed nightclub as a coat-check girl for ridiculous tips, and got Maxine a job there serving drinks. They had all the same shifts. It didn't hurt that Rosie was fucking their boss. Julian, tall and good-looking, had a pompadour and cultivated sideburns. He motivated his staff with cocaine. Rosie developed an interest in his drugs that quickly became a problem. It started with drinks and lines after work to wind down, then key bumps at midnight to get through the last few hours.

The girls crammed together in the front booth: Rosie in lingerie, high and chatty; Maxine with aching arches, rubbing her swollen feet as her friend worked a lollipop in a way that was particularly off-putting.

"I'm in love."

"With who?"

"Don't be sarcastic. With *Julian*."

Maxine found this profession of love laughable, since their boss paid minimum wage and Rosie made her money by collecting tips for her revealing outfits and strategic tongue flicks. She and Julian had officially dated for all of two weeks.

"Oh, he's a dream. I especially like how whenever we hang out at his place after work and do a few lines, he starts bugging us to make out."

"Julian likes to watch me with other men."

"Hot," Maxine said with little enthusiasm. "Nuclear hot."

The coke had loosened Rosie's tongue and she told Maxine of other co-workers—a waitress and aging bartender—who were often involved.

"I guess in an orgy you just take whatever comes your way," Maxine concluded dryly.

"It's such a relief to tell you this."

"Why did you hide it from me?"

"I don't know, I thought you'd judge me or something."

"Of *course* not. I'm mad I wasn't invited."

But it occurred to Maxine that she really didn't know her best friend anymore. Between all the coke, caps of GHB, ketamine, pills, and whatever else she was doing, Rosie seemed content to walk around in a half-dressed, lubed-up haze.

Julian asked Maxine to come to his office, and she sensed something was up. It was mid-shift with tables waiting, and Rosie was at home sick. He'd been giving her looks all evening. His office door was wide open, and he sprawled in the leather chair at his desk. Behind him were large glass panels that showed a wide expanse of the dance floor.

"You wanted to see me?"

"Close that behind you." Maxine shut the door, muffling the loud thump of bass drifting up from the club. She made a move toward the couch but Julian patted the desk in front of him. It was too close and she perched awkwardly.

Julian was handsome, and Maxine couldn't deny that she was attracted to him. Without saying anything, he grabbed her hips and pulled her in front of him. His hands pushed up her skirt and slid off her thong.

She grabbed his hair and grinded against his face. It was wrong, she knew, but she and Rosie weren't really getting along and at that moment Maxine didn't care. Julian yanked up her T-shirt and bra. She'd always been embarrassed by the small nubs of her breasts and long purplish nipples, but Julian sucked them noisily. Then he turned her over roughly and fucked her from behind. It took less than a minute. When Maxine turned around he pulled up his pants and checked his watch. She rinsed off in the employee bathroom, and they never spoke an unnecessary word again.

Julian made a lot of money as a successful promoter, and was always taking Rosie away on trips to Maui or Las Vegas or the Bahamas. Julian liked his girlfriend well-dressed and bought her entire wardrobes for these vacations. Shortly after the incident with Maxine in his office, Julian moved Rosie into his penthouse downtown. Maxine hadn't been seeing her at home much over the last few months, but it was still a hard adjustment when the last box was packed. They'd gone through broken hearts, STDs, evictions. Maxine moved into a dumpy room in Chinatown and tried not to resent her best friend.

There were always new developments in Rosie and Julian's elaborate dramas. Maxine endured them all. Rosie could be high maintenance, and as a cokehead, she was monstrous. Her story constantly changed—she and Julian were getting married and wanted a baby; the next time Maxine spoke to her they were through, only to be madly in love a week later. Though the girls still partied together on occasion, Maxine never got high at work like Rosie, who made a game out of hiding her habit from Julian. Maxine had never known anyone, besides herself, who had such a problem with rules.

It was a Tuesday evening and Rosie kept calling. Finally Maxine picked up.

"Where were you? I really need someone to talk to. Come over."

"Rosie, it's my day off. I'm tired."

"Plee-eease?" It was pointless to refuse. Rosie would keep phoning until Maxine agreed. Maxine picked up some hot and sour soup and took the bus to Rosie's penthouse. The doorman tipped his hat and held the door.

"He's fucking someone else," Rosie said, letting her in. She sat down on the edge of the couch, rocking back and forth. "I know it for sure this time."

Rosie looked terrible. She was thin and anemic, and though still beautiful, there were blemishes on her skin and blackish-purple circles under her eyes. Maxine had a guilty flash of the episode with Julian.

"Where's he now?"

"Julian's in New York. He forgot to leave me any money and I lost my goddamn bank card. Can you lend me some cash?"

Maxine walked through the apartment noting the stacks of

takeout containers, clothes in dirty piles, layers of chocolate bar wrappers over everything. Flowers long dead in a rusty jar. The place smelled like perfume and cat shit, and Rosie didn't even own a pet.

"You know if I lend you forty bucks you'll just do rails with it."

"Sounds good," Rosie brightens. "We'll have some drinks. It'll be fun, like old times." But she never did a couple of lines—if Rosie had one, she wanted ten more.

"I'm broke," Maxine lied. "Besides, do you think Julian gives you drugs because he cares, or because he doesn't care at *all*?"

"I hate you."

"Shut up," Maxine said mildly, and dug a mop and bucket out of the closet.

Rosie followed, pulling her hair. "I HATE you!"

"No, you don't. Jeezus, how can Julian not notice that you're completely fucked *up*?"

Rosie panted in anger. "I'M SICK OF YOU! Always living off me! You're a goddamn pimp! GET YOUR OWN FUCKING LIFE!" She hurled a heavy glass ashtray at Maxine that missed and shattered a lamp.

Maxine pitched the mop at Rosie, who screamed with rage. They rushed across the room at each other, teeth bared. Maxine spun Rosie around then launched her onto the couch.

"STOP IT!" Maxine pinned her down as she thrashed. Maxine's arms were strong from carrying heavy trays every night.

"Do you really think I don't know Julian fucked you? I ASKED him to do it. I felt *sorry* for you, tit-less freak!"

Maxine let go of her arms and slid off. She couldn't tell if Rosie was lying, but it didn't matter anymore. Their years together came over her with sudden, bitter tears.

"I'm done with you," she said. "For good."

There was just enough money in her pocket for a bottle of vodka and the bus fare home. Between furtive gulps, Maxine thought in disbelief of what Rosie had done. Her ex-best friend was a malicious fucking cunt.

She didn't know what she wanted or expected out of life, but for now there were plenty of her own mistakes to contemplate. At home she sat on the toilet, drunk, head bobbing. The last drops of vodka spilled from the bottle. Maxine took off her clothes and stared at her reflection in the mirror. She felt as pale as the moon, and starless.

As she turned, her feet slipped on the spilled vodka. Maxine fell, smashing her face on the edge of the porcelain sink. Her chin split open and her front tooth broke; pain shot through her face like a bullet of ripped nerves. The curtain of blood running down her neck shocked her. After Maxine waited hours in the emergency room, the doctor put three stitches in her chin. They looked like small whiskers.

Maxine quit her job to avoid seeing Rosie at work and decided to move back home to the suburbs. She could no longer afford her dumpy room, and most of her stuff was still in her mother's basement. It had been years since she'd lived there.

Each time Rosie phoned, Maxine ignored her. She felt a hard pit of satisfaction replaying then erasing the apologetic messages. It grew considerably when she ripped up photographs or marked letters "Return to Sender." Finally Rosie stopped calling. By then, Maxine had very little energy and slept for long periods of time. Mostly she stayed in bed, watching TV. Girls were too cruel, Maxine concluded, and vowed to never have a best friend again.

HATE YOU!

WET LEATHER

FIVE LITTLE BITCHES

When the poker game breaks, Maxine and Squeaky move out onto the deck. It's close to midnight and a siren wails in the distance. The girls give each other a sideways glance.

"Hey, I'm Maxine."

"Hiya. I'm Squeaky." She cracks a beer and slurps the foam.

"Squeaky, eh?"

"I will also accept 'Tabletop Rocker' and 'Midget Bardot.'"

"Any chance you've got another one of those?"

Squeaky opens her knapsack and hands over a beer. Then she fishes a crumpled joint out of her back pocket. She lights it, takes two massive hits, and passes it on. Squeaky's long hair is in braids, with Frankenstein bangs clearly cut at home, and she wears a mini-sized leather jacket with sleeves that are too short.

Maryse Ladeucer, also known as Squeaky, looks like a little doll with glossy brown hair and big brown eyes. Growing up, she'd proudly watched her three delinquent brothers rule her small town. They'd nicknamed her Squeaky because of her high-pitched voice when excited, and she played enthusiastically rough. Since the age of fifteen, there has been a pair of drumsticks in her back pocket.

"Who did you come to this party with?" Maxine takes a small puff and hands the joint back, cradling her beer.

"I didn't come with anyone," Squeaky answers. "I had to drop something off for my brother and got sucked into their game. I've known these guys forever."

"Jesse brought me here but I don't think I'm getting a ride home with him."

"You came to the Nation of Fuckers clubhouse with Jesse?" Squeaky grimaces then corrects herself.

"Instead of nice guys, I go for interesting jerks," Maxine says. "I fucked him once and stupidly thought we could be friends."

Squeaky laughs. "Jesse's a joker. You can't date him. He's in clown college."

"Actually, he's going to culinary school."

"He should do both," Squeaky says, passing the joint back to Maxine. "Then he could make stuff that tastes funny."

"Ha!"

"But I'm not one to talk." She hoists herself easily onto the railing. "I used to date Rocket. They call him that 'cause he runs fast but doesn't think too quickly."

"Rocket? Was he in that cover band, Rocket and the Retards?"

Squeaky's stomach twists when she thinks of that blonde, dirty-knuckled boy. "You know him?"

Maxine taps the ash from the joint. Her hands are rough and her makeup heavy, but there's a gracefulness to her movements. She knows Rocket from the same party circle of loosely connected acquaintances. He's a short loudmouth, the kind of guy who tips strippers with guitar picks. Despite having just met her, Maxine can tell Squeaky could do much better.

"This is a small town masquerading as a big city. I know him, just from around. Did he act like a dirtbag?"

"Well, he wasn't the kind of guy you'd get an ear-candling with."

Maxine giggles. "How long ago did you break up?"

"Put it this way, the trail is not exactly cold."

"What happened?"

"Hmmm," Squeaky replies, and tamps out the roach on the wood railing. "I guess it went bad when he stopped wanting to be my boyfriend and didn't tell me."

"Oh yeah, that's my favourite—when they're too chicken shit to break up with you and start being a prick so you'll do it for them."

"A real classic manoeuvre."

Until recently, Squeaky and Rocket were in the middle of a prolonged break-up. Once every ten days or so, Rocket came over and she made food and they watched a bit of TV and fucked. Or else she went to his place with a six-pack and they played video games, drank beer, and *then* fucked. Other than that they didn't see or call each other. It had been going on for almost six months and neither had the guts to end it.

"My advice is stay away from musicians." Maxine gives a self-conscious laugh. "I should know—I used to sing for Death by Rollercoaster."

"Maxine *Micheline*. That's IT! I thought you looked familiar. My brother Andre had *Must Be This High to Ride*."

"That was our only record."

"Yeah, and epic! I'm a drummer. I played in The Druggies but we broke up. The last show was Halloween. I went as Artimus Pyle from Lynyrd Skynyrd, but ended up just looking like a tiny, creepy dude."

Maxine is impressed—she'd never seen The Druggies, but heard praise for their heavy stoner rock. "Man, I love it when girls play drums. I'll bet you kick ass!"

Squeaky demurs and jumps down, zipping her jacket. "Well, I'm heading off." She takes a ball cap from her knapsack and pulls it low. "Nice meeting you."

"I'm *stuck* here," Maxine says. "And I don't want to stay."

"I'm going to a party that should be pretty decent. You can come with me if you want. I'll leave my bike here and grab a cab."

"Sign me up. Wait, I'm gonna go back in that party an' steal some booze."

"Don't do that," Squeaky warns. "Not here."

Maxine walks to the street to hail a cab and stands on the corner, hip jutted with authority. She doesn't bother looking for Jesse to say goodbye.

The Party on Punk Street

The noise of the party gets louder as they walk down the street. It's an odd pairing—tomboy Squeaky with no makeup, board shorts, skate shoes, and Maxine towering over her with bleached out hair, red lipstick, leather pants, and tottering heels.

Packs of girls saunter around a yard littered with beer cans. "I'm getting drunk tonight," Squeaky declares. "But then again, a shot of Bailey's get me *shittered*."

"We need to think of aliases in case we get into trouble."

"I'll be Gretchen Van Token."

"And I am Princess Fridge-scum."

"No, change that. My new handle is Piss Whisky."

"Damn," Maxine slaps her forehead. "I just remembered I have to start work early tomorrow."

"Where's that?"

"Freudian Slips. I'm supposed to be there at nine."

"Do you still want to go to this party?"

"Of *course*."

At the front door the hostess passes out chocolates made with magic mushrooms. Squeaky bounds up the front steps, puts a chocolate in her mouth, then considers and throws in another. Maxine sees some people she knows and disappears on a booze reconnaissance mission.

The first beer goes down easy. Squeaky hangs out in the kitchen and listens to an acquaintance complain about how her alcoholic boyfriend keeps falling through coffee tables. A man wearing an oven mitt calls himself "DJ Soft Touch" and begins to freestyle, badly. Then the mushrooms start to work—Squeaky's teeth feel strange and her thigh muscles weak, a sure sign she's getting high. She moves to check the action outside.

A group of skateboarders film tricks in the driveway. Harassing them is Squeaky's friend, Kitty Domingo. When Squeaky had dated Rocket, Kitty dated Rocket's best friend, Jasper. It had been a brief but intense period when the two couples hung out together. Then Kitty dumped Jasper and took off. Squeaky and Rocket's own break-up soon followed. The girls haven't seen each other in six months.

"Man up and land it," Kitty hollers from the sidelines. "What's wrong with you? Stop being a pussy and make it happen! What, are you afraid of the bail? You're trying to get sponsored, dipshit!"

Kitty's jagged black hair is cut short. It frames her angelic face and blue eyes. Though only twenty-one, she has numerous tattoos: bluebirds on her shoulders and stomach, a pirate ship on her bicep, an anarchist symbol on her ankle she'd done herself, and two devils behind each ear. Kitty's vibrating, manic energy is unaltered since Squeaky last saw her—scarred knuckles and chipped blue polish on roughly bitten nails.

Kitty jumps up when she sees her and screams with glee, “Oh my god, you fucking BITCH, I love you!” They hug each other and then Kitty does an exaggerated jive walk. She still has the absurd habit of abbreviating any possible word.

“Where you been muhfuh—?”

Just then one of the skaters, a shaggy blonde in a fedora, comes over to Kitty. “Hey, my friend wants to meet you.” He points to one of the boys in the driveway.

“Meat? I don’t want any meat,” Kitty says.

“He likes you.”

“Who, him? That guy looks like he has worm bum. I’ll bet he smells like goddamn dog shit!”

The boy backs away with apprehension. Squeaky sneaks him a sympathetic look.

“Do you think that was a bit harsh?”

Kitty smirks. “NO.”

“It’s nice to see you haven’t changed.”

“Nevs! Hey, remember that night I got fucked up on crystal meth and shaved off a big patch of hair then tried to hide it by rubbing glitter onto my scalp?” Kitty makes a motion for Squeaky’s beer and takes a large gulp.

“Me and Rocket finally broke up.”

Kitty nods. “After Jasper, I was dating this really nice guy.”

“Yeah?”

“It only took two weeks to break THAT toy.”

“I don’t miss Rocket at all, anymore.” Kitty

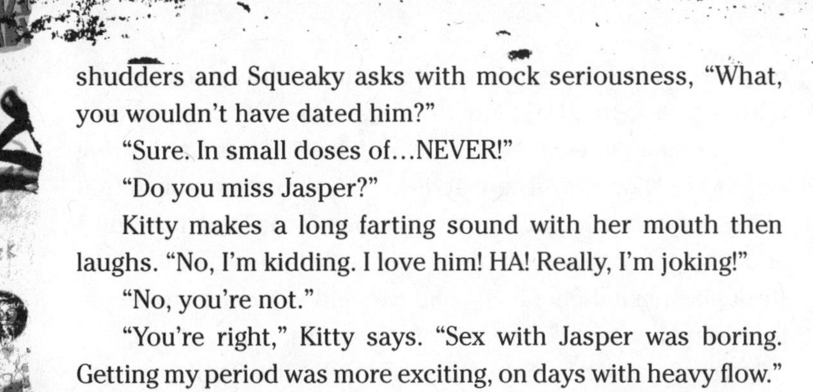

shudders and Squeaky asks with mock seriousness, "What, you wouldn't have dated him?"

"Sure. In small doses of…NEVER!"

"Do you miss Jasper?"

Kitty makes a long farting sound with her mouth then laughs. "No, I'm kidding. I love him! HA! Really, I'm joking!"

"No, you're not."

"You're right," Kitty says. "Sex with Jasper was boring. Getting my period was more exciting, on days with heavy flow."

Squeaky goes in the house for another beer, still chuckling. She can hear Kitty continue to heckle the skateboarders. Inside the party has swelled. Squeaky gets lost easily in crowds because she can never see over anyone. She takes a quick detour through the kitchen: one man sniffs cocaine off the back of his hand while another hovers anxiously; two girls cackle in the corner; a barely dressed blonde talks loudly to three boys while a nearby woman frowns; and a girl with a shaved head looks out the kitchen window and smokes. Squeaky manoeuvres into the middle of the living room dance party, where she throws down a few slippery hip swings.

Squeaky's roommate, Paula Grubler, jumps in the circle and busts out an array of lewd moves, grinding into Squeaky's ass. Then she acts surprised that people are watching and runs off. Squeaky attempts to follow her through the crowd, but gives up. She has begun to realize her roommate is a definite weirdo.

A couple squeezes in beside Squeaky as she twists a joint on the kitchen counter. "It is only just a misunderstanding," the girl says, with a thick Eastern European accent. She is much younger than her companion.

The man glares at the girl, who falls silent as her lip ring trembles. "I'm not interested in your miscommunication today, understand? Go take your headache and fuck off." Squeaky takes note of his motorcycle helmet and walks through the kitchen. Maybe she can find someone interested in helping her take the air out of a few tires.

"Hey Squeaky! Li'l Squeak. SQUEAKY!" Kitty Domingo holds an enormous pan of what looks like a greenish brown sludge and leans against the fridge. Squeaky makes her way over.

"What IS that?"

"Weed brownies," Kitty giggles, tipping back. "Oh fuck. Poo-schwag. I'm so fucked up."

"Kitty, I thought you didn't even like weed."

"I DON'T. But I said I'd help pass out these brownies and I didn't know they had weed in them. I ate a really big one." Her face contorts. "Oh god, I hate this feeling. I need to hide under the table. Jesus! Jesus! Jesus!"

"Relax," Squeaky commands with authority. "Go outside and get some air."

Kitty puts the pan on the counter, and windmills through the crowd, bellowing, "Get out of my way! I'm totally FREAKING out!" Squeaky debates then cautiously eats a small spoonful of brownie. On the way to the bathroom, she becomes hyper-aware of her back molars with her tongue. The lineup of impatient girls for the toilet goes all the way down the hallway.

When Squeaky comes out of the bathroom she sees Maxine Micheline in the living room. She is entertaining a small circle of drunken boys with talk of a bacon festival held every year in Croatia.

"Squeaky!" Maxine gasps and hugs her like they haven't seen each other in years.

“Let’s go outside,” Squeaky whispers. “You’ve got too many Klingons and I’m almost out of weed.” On the back porch she pulls out the joint. From their vantage point they watch a guy hitting on a girl who abruptly barfs into a planter.

“This is a good party.” When Squeaky kicks her stubby little legs, Maxine finds it adorable. “Hey, did you ever play in any bands after Death by Rollercoaster?”

Maxine gulps the remains of her drink. Then she’s silent, rubbing her blonde hair so it stands in rumpled spikes. Just as suddenly, she flings her plastic cup across the porch. “I *miss* having a band,” she wails. Fat tears well up in her eyes. “I miss playing so much.”

“Start a new band,” Squeaky encourages. She hates to see drunk girls cry. “We should jam sometime.”

“Yeah,” Maxine brightens, wiping her eyes. “YEAH!”

“My friend Kitty Domingo plays bass,” Squeaky says. “We used to kinda jam together. She’s here right now, freaking out on the weed brownies.”

“How is she?”

“I’m gonna go check on her in a minute. Oh, is she a good bass player? Yeah, pretty decent. She’s young and kind of unreliable, but also really enthusiastic. She’s got lots of natural energy to channel. As long as Kitty’s bass isn’t in the pawnshop, she’ll be into it.”

“Has she ever been in a band?”

“Nah,” Squeaky answers. “Sometimes we’d fool around on our boyfriend’s gear when they left rehearsal to buy drugs. We had this joke band called Dong Side of the Tracks, but it’s not like we played gigs.”

When Rocket had begun scoring heat with Jasper, his relationship with Squeaky declined at a rapid pace. She’d watch him frenzied at practise, thin with bad skin and bloodshot eyes too big for his face. Squeaky had tried meth

only once. After snorting a line, she'd gone home and written out a will, convinced she was going to die.

Squeaky and Kitty had cemented their girl mafia while commiserating with each other at the rehearsal space, still covered in sweat from their rock and roll boys. Kitty would play a riff while Squeaky added the drum beat and they traded off back and forth. Kitty had ADD, but could focus enough to learn pieces of her favourite songs. During this period there was a dockside bar the boys liked to party in, with an upstairs room that had bloodstains on the floor and a filthy mattress for blackouts only. The two girls clung to each other in that sea of troubled boys. They would always be friends after surviving those strange and rough times.

Squeaky begins to get excited about the possibility of jamming with these girls. Her four on the floor rock drumming compliments Kitty's jittery, relentless bass. Not only could they get a band together, it might actually be a good one. She knows Maxine has a lot of presence as a frontwoman.

"We could book a room at Powder Keg Studio, maybe on Sunday. It's twenty an hour, drums and PA included. Cans of beer for three bucks each."

When Maxine is wasted she makes a lot of plans she forgets sober. She takes a cider out of her purse and cracks it. "This isn't just drunk talk, right? Because I'm really serious about this. Oh my god," she interrupts herself. "Squeaky, what size is your waist? The perfect thing came into Freudian Slips yesterday." She describes in detail a tiny sailor suit, making her promise to stop by and try it on.

When the song changes Maxine chugs her cider and then wails, "WU-HUH, HUH-HUH." She thrusts her fist and bangs her head, open-mouthed. "CRANK it *UP*," she booms, flinging herself off the porch onto the lawn to dance. After a few minutes she stops, panting, and lights a cigarette.

Suddenly Kitty lurches outside, looking green-skinned. "Air, gimme air." She heaves in the bushes beside the house, and then takes a long swallow of beer. Wiping her mouth she announces, "Out with old, in with the new!"

"Kitty, are you okay?"

"I wrapped myself in a comforter and wouldn't get off the bed. It took a really long time to even leave the closet."

"This is Maxine."

"I know you," Kitty says. "I tried to pick a fight with you once."

Maxine arches an eyebrow. "Oh, really?"

"No."

They look over as someone smashes a beer bottle against the back fence. Two ranting men shove each other around and everybody makes a big deal.

"My brother told me the best way to get out of a fight," Squeaky volunteers. "Throw cayenne pepper in your opponent's eyes."

Kitty snorts. "I'm not walking around with cayenne pepper in my pocket. I ain't some goddamn hummus!"

A boy with a six-pack goes into the house and she trails after him.

"I hate fights," Maxine says, grumpily. "They ruin the party and then no one gets laid." She says goodbye and takes off to find the guy who'd offered a ride earlier.

The party has peaked and begins to wind down. Squeaky goes in the house to pee, then has a random conversation with two dudes involving the dangers of cougars versus grizzlies. A scowling white girl with dreadlocks asks for a rolling paper. Then Squeaky wanders back outside. Someone beats on a pair of bongos. It pains her because they clearly lack rhythm. Squeaky sees that it's her roommate, Paula Grubler, in the shadows of the porch. She sits down beside her.

"Hey Paula, I haven't seen you all night."

"I thought you were avoiding me."

"No way," Squeaky laughs. "Why would I do that? You weirdo."

Paula's shrill voice cuts through the quiet yard. "Don't call me that!"

"O-*kay*. Sorry." Squeaky takes a swig of beer and has a feeling the end of the night is not going to be as smooth as the beginning. She looks back at her roommate, who begins to work the bongo drum again.

Paula Grubler has brown hair and tiny, square teeth beneath a large nose. She also has a mustache, pronounced enough to seem in contrast with her hyper-insecurity. She also smokes copious amounts of weed that only serve to make her more socially awkward. Once, Paula had an asthma attack while talking to a boy she liked.

Squeaky changes the subject. "Me and this girl Maxine might be starting a band. Isn't that great? Man, I miss playing my drums." Squeaky had set them up in the apartment once, and within minutes their landlord had been on the phone complaining.

Paula asks, "Can I be in your band?"

"Well, do you play an instrument...that isn't the bongos?"

"No."

"Can you sing or write music?"

"No."

"Well..." There is an awkward silence.

"Maybe I should just shut up." Squeaky feels a pang of guilt. Her roommate has an uncanny ability to make her feel that way.

A short-haired rocker in wrist cuffs sits down on the porch and offers Squeaky his bottle of Newfoundland Screech. He's from Halifax and says when he got to town someone stole his fiddle. They have a conversation about trailer parks and East Coast beer. He says he's going into business for himself and when

Squeaky asks what kind he answers, "Creative gardening."

"I'm familiar with that line of work."

The boy winks and says, "You're damn cute." He looks over at Paula and says nothing. Squeaky sips the god-awful rum and passes the bottle to Paula, who takes a long swallow. The boy and Squeaky keep talking, and then he gives her a kiss, soft and salty.

"I'm falling in love," he says. Squeaky rolls her eyes, but considers taking him home. One-night stands aren't her style, but it's been a while. She goes in the house for a pinch of toothpaste and scavenges more liquor. When she returns to the porch, Paula and the boy are kissing noisily. It's even more insulting when Paula starts to moan.

Squeaky stumbles down the stairs then around to the front of the house. She's drunk and doesn't feel so good. Paula is always bringing strange boys home for sex, and Squeaky has sat through numerous strained breakfast scenes. Someone chucks another bottle and it smashes on the road. She's relieved to find Kitty drinking a beer on the front steps, and sits down to join her. Inside, the party has fully died down.

"I kissed this boy on the back porch."

"Woot-Woot!"

"It's no deal, but he's real cute. Then I went to get a drink and when I came back my roommate had snaked me. Plus, she was giving him a wiener cup!"

"WHAT?" Kitty jolts upright. "Where is that *CUNT*?"

Drunk or sober, she is rowdy and ready to fight. Squeaky attempts to calm her down. "Forget it. I just met the guy."

"Let's go throw a bucket of water on 'em!"

They creep around the side of the house. Squeaky falls down and Kitty chortles, moving with the exaggerated movements of a clown caper. "Oh grossies," she says, peeking around the corner. "They're in the backyard. I think she's RIDING him."

Squeaky pushes past to look. Sure enough, the boy is splayed on the grass while Paula straddles him. Her head is thrown back, knees grinding the dirt. There are a few murmurs from the porch, and laughter. "Get a room," someone says.

"No, get the hose!"

"I just got pink eye from seeing that," Kitty says, ducking back. "I gotta ask—does your roommate swallow fuck-paste for a living?"

Squeaky takes a swig of warm beer and her stomach churns. A stellar evening, she reflects—getting to meet Maxine Micheline, seeing Kitty again—a fucking amazing night up until now. She goes back around the house and decides to walk home. It will be hard to forget the sight of Paula's open mouth, gleaming with spit in the darkness.

Freudian Slips

The day after the party, Maxine Micheline viciously pulls a Mexican wrestling mask over a mannequin head in the front window of Freudian Slips. Her head is pounding, but her mood elevates when Squeaky rides up on her skateboard. Maxine bangs on the window. Squeaky kicks the board into her hand and opens the door.

"Hello Your Wee-ness!" Maxine jumps down from the display with a flourish.

"Hey Maxine…" Squeaky's voice trails as she spins in a slow circle. "Holy butt cheek. I've always wondered about this place."

The store is crammed with racks of vintage slips, crinoline, '80s prom dresses, fake furs, sequined sweaters. Ornate bird cages hang from the ceiling above a bin of roller skates, shelves of board games, and glassware decorated with mushrooms. A display case holds exquisite costume jewellery that looks like the real thing.

"Try on anything you like," Maxine encourages.

Squeaky's usual attire is jeans, sneakers, and a denim vest with *Squeaky* embroidered over the pocket. Buying and trying on clothes has always bored her, and her favourite shirts were hand-me-downs from her brothers. Still, she notices a row of leather jackets with a red one that might be small enough to fit. She props her skateboard against the wall and takes a look.

Maxine's bleached hair is sculpted with pin curls. Her bone structure and elaborate updo contrast with the scar on her chin. She wears large silver hoops and dark cuffed jeans with a rolled blue work shirt. "What do you think of this outfit? I'm going for Madonna circa True Blue meets Rosie the Riveter." She struts down the aisle, then unbuttons her shirt and yanks it down over one shoulder. Her mouth falls open lasciviously.

"It's working," Squeaky approves.

"Hold on, I'm gonna go grab my smokes. Take a look around. There's a bunch of new stuff in. Maybe later you could try some outfits on for me. Honestly, how do you feel about Lycra?"

Outside, Maxine lights a cigarette with great satisfaction.

Squeaky asks, "How long have you worked here?"

"I guess about two years. The last owner left the business to become a full-time nudist. No, really. So Fanta and I took over the lease. When my grandmother got put in a nursing home she sold her house and I got a little money. So for the past eight months it's been *our* store. But it's not like I want to sell prom dresses to bitchy teenage girls for the rest of my life."

Squeaky has been in kitchens for most of her life. Now she works at a bakery full-time. It amazes her when people she knows have actual careers and do things like building houses or running dairy farms or fixing sailboats. She flips open her wallet and checks her bus transfer. Maxine spots a photo tucked in the plastic. "Ooooh, is that you?"

"Yep," she laughs. In the photo, she and her brothers stand in the driveway of their house, each holding a fish-speared stick. Only Squeaky, tiny, wild-haired, and pinching her nose, is empty-handed.

"I always wanted a brother. And you've got three! What was that like growing up?"

"Hmmm...*loud.* And really hard getting a table in a restaurant."

"They're so cute!"

"Growing up I didn't notice. But they definitely had hot friends."

"It was just me and my mom. Well, my grandmother, but.... she was always sick. You must have had so much fun." Maxine is intrigued. "What are they like? What do they do?"

"You really want to hear about my brothers?"

Normally Squeaky doesn't talk about her brothers' business, but she succumbs to Maxine's enthusiasm. "Leon has a bad temper," she answers. "It gets him into trouble. He looks like an Allman Brother on steroids and hangs out with bikers. I don't really ask a lot about what he does. You know? Anyway, he's the oldest. Then there's Andre. He's real smart but likes to act dumb. He put himself through university by writing term papers for rich kids—"

"Rich people are stupid," Maxine interrupts. "I do *all* my reading on the bus."

"—and now he works in construction. He's into hockey and his pickup truck. Oh yeah, and he lives with an ex-stripper. And I have a younger brother, Louie, a little badass. He's all about hip-hop and video games. We skateboard together sometimes. He just moved here from the Island, where our folks live. Him and his big-mouthed skater friends kept getting beat up by rednecks."

"Wow, you're really lucky, I always wanted other kids around. I used to imagine my stuffed animals were a big family and we all slept together in this giant bed."

Squeaky doesn't say that when Leon's first grow house burned down, the bikers he worked for threatened to kill him so he joined the army. When Leon came home after being kicked out of basic training he looked like a stranger without his long hair and mustache. Other than that, the army hadn't cleaned him up much at all.

"Who's your favourite brother?"

"JESUS! I couldn't figure that out. And I wouldn't even try."

"Hey, are we still gonna jam tomorrow night?"

Squeaky twists her ball cap, considering. It might be interesting. Maxine is a girl full of distractions. "Yeah, I'll get ahold of Kitty about it."

"I know someone who plays guitar," Maxine says, "but it'll be hard to convince her."

She steps on her cigarette butt, and they return inside. From the back of the store a steamer hisses. Maxine says, "Fanta has gone through a *mountain* of clothing. It's amazing how much ironing that woman can endure. Hey Fanta! Take a break for a minute."

Squeaky hears a voice say, "A break? How bourgeois."

"C'mere! I want you to meet someone."

A woman comes slinking up the aisle from the back of the store. Maxine introduces Squeaky to a bony redhead of sharp edges and angles. Her green eyes, ringed with yellow, burn beneath the long fringe of her red bangs. She looks chronically malnourished. Sharp metal studs in her belt and bracelets, and her uncomfortable-looking boots give the impression of someone who can withstand a tremendous amount of pain. She wears striped pants and a man's suit jacket over a *Kill City* T-shirt. Her fingernails are practical, short.

"This is Fanta Geiger. Fanta, meet Squeaky."

"Squeaky," Fanta answers. "Now, is that your *real* name?"

"Maybe. How's it going?"

Fanta ponders the question for a moment. There's a pinched look on her face. "How is IT going? IT is going very slow."

"Cool, cool," Maxine says nervously.

After a long pause Fanta turns and walks to the back of the store. The steamer begins to hiss again. Maxine looks at Squeaky and shrugs. Then she turns the stereo louder and shouts, "I fucking love this Cramps song!"

She bobs her head violently, and then does the can-can followed by a series of jumping jacks. Despite being thirty-five, Maxine has the same overabundance of natural energy she did as a fidgety kid in school. "Let's do some paperwork," she chants, beginning to scissor kick. "Paperwork! Paperwork!" Fanta emerges from the back and sighs, searching through various piles of clutter around the cash register for rolling papers.

They crowd in the back office and Maxine lights a long stick of incense. "So Squeaky, did *you* get lucky last night at the party?"

Squeaky declines to mention the incident with Paula Grubler. "Nope. And I'm way happier on my own."

Maxine cheers. "That's right, little sister." She passes the joint to Fanta, who takes a small hit. "Squeaky used to date this guy named Rocket, but wisely cut him loose."

"Yeah, the problem was we broke up but kept hanging out—"

"—fucking—" Maxine interjects.

"—so it was always that last-time-forever sex. But forget looking for the one," Squeaky says, and bangs her tiny fist on the coffee table, "I AM the one."

"I need to start screening my dates better," Maxine says. "I was thinking of coming up with some kind of questionnaire. Like, Question 1: Have you ever done so much coke your nose started bleeding?"

Squeaky joins in. "Question 2: Do you enjoy your food with a frank in it?"

"Question 3: Do you eat it prison-style?"

"Herm," Fanta nearly laughs. "Herm-herm." Squeaky can tell a smile from her is a rare and bright thing. There is gravity to Fanta that makes her seem like a woman difficult to impress, but they both sense a common understanding from working years alongside the cooks and busboys that secretly run the city. They are not the kind of girls who carry tiny dogs to brunch or discuss celebrity divorces.

"This is a great record," Maxine says, pointing in the air and cocking her head. "Poison Ivy is my favourite guitar player. Besides you, Fanta," she adds, giving Squeaky a wink.

"There are about two hundred songs that informed my entire social fabric," Fanta says. Squeaky admits she grew up on heavy metal and once wanted a tit tattoo that said *Born a rocker, Die a rocker.* Maxine cracks up.

"If I like a record, I listen to it over and over and then never play it again," Fanta continues. "I detest sentimentality."

"Bullshit! I've seen your apartment." Maxine changes gears. "Squeaky's a drummer. We're gonna jam tomorrow night. All we're missing is a guitar player. Why don't you come and join us?"

"No thanks."

"Why not? We need you, Fanta."

Maxine would beg if it wasn't pointless. Fanta Geiger never does anything she doesn't want to do.

"I'm not interested." They soften a bit when she says, "I wouldn't even know how to…*jam.*"

"It's simple. I'll give you a beat like, *Buk-tak-a-bukka-tak,*" Squeaky says, hitting an imaginary snare and kick drum. "Then you throw together a simple rock riff. When Kitty hears it she'll know what to do."

Fanta looks back and forth at them—Maxine is practically uncontainable. "Let's just try it out and see what happens," she urges.

"I haven't jammed since The Druggies broke up," Squeaky says. "And if Kitty Domingo plays bass, that makes it strictly chick and no dick."

The weed slows everything down and Maxine relays a story she heard about a celebrity airhead in California who was trying to bury her goat in a funeral plot beside Marilyn Monroe. She gets her news from an armload of tabloids each week, which she claims to detest, yet never fails to read. Fanta goes back to the steamer.

The bell rings and some girls come into the shop. Maxine shows them a variety of dresses. She is organized and efficient, having learned from her mother to never make a trip empty-handed. Squeaky tries on a jewelled figure skating costume for kicks. Maxine screams in delight.

"Damn, I gotta go." Squeaky checks the time. "I'm getting a tattoo at King City."

"You are so little and ferocious," Maxine says, tucking in her shirt. "You're getting a tattoo today? Of what?" Squeaky describes a skull with flowers and diamonds, and a pair of crossed drumsticks behind it. She shyly tells Maxine the three diamonds represent her brothers.

"Definitely don't be late. You don't want to piss off the guy jabbing needles into your skin for the next three hours." Squeaky scurries into the dressing room to change.

When she comes out Maxine walks her to the door. "What time should we meet tomorrow night?"

"I don't know, let's say six? I'll call and book a room."

"I'm gonna work on bringing Fanta," Maxine says, but looks skeptical. She bends down and grabs Squeaky in a goodbye hug. "I'm so glad you came by today." Squeaky finds that because of her tiny size, people often want to pick her up or pat her on the head.

As she pushes off on her skateboard Maxine yells, "Bye sweetie!" Squeaky throws deuces and turns her ball cap backwards, rolling down the street. Fascinated by Maxine, Squeaky realizes girls always know the secret things her brothers could never teach her.

BIO

NAME: Maryse "Squeaky" Ladeucer AGE: 28

OCCUPATION: Drummer, Wet Leather

BIRTHPLACE: Trois-Rivières, QC

PREVIOUS BANDS: Mud Love, The Druggies

INTERESTS: Punk, metal, classic rock

EARLIEST MEMORY: in pajamas with feet, drumming wooden spoons on boxes

QUOTE: "Stink washes off."

SQUEAKY LADEUCER

The shop smells like sweat, antiseptic, and apprehension. A skate video plays on the wall-mounted TV and screaming metal thrashes out the speakers. A muscle-head lying on his tummy winces through a calf tattoo. Squeaky rubs her palms against her knees and does a quick sniff of her armpits.

"Squeaky Ladeucer," Tony booms. "Are you ready?" Tony King is stocky with a hard-lived face, silver stubble and ink-covered arms, busted teeth in an easy grin. He shows Squeaky the drawing he came up with based on her idea and she loves it.

She admits to being nervous. "It's my first tattoo."

"If you need a break just say so. But I'm pretty gentle."

"That's not what I heard," pipes a guy in the back with stretched-out earlobes. "I heard he'll *rip* through your pooper!"

"Cretin."

"What's that?"

From the way the guys who work there joke around, Squeaky can tell she'll be comfortable. She learned growing up with her brothers how to share her space with men. Their behavior was generally predictable. They liked to be fed and

comfortable and adored, just like anyone, and are drawn to what is easy and in front of them. Her brothers were a rough crew but always watched out for her. When Squeaky decided to move to the city at twenty-one, her brother Leon told her if she ever had any trouble, for fifteen hundred dollars he could have a man killed.

After Tony King disinfects and shaves Squeaky's arm, he applies the transfer. The black outline is okay but when he moves onto colour it seems to hurt even more. She grits her teeth and shifts in the seat. Tony glances up and says, "It's gonna look really good."

"THANK YOU!"

At another chair, the last of large dragon wings are being tattooed on a young girl's back. She turns the pages of her Fantasy novel and cracks her knuckles with a bored look. Squeaky's own arm has begun to feel like she has a sunburn being rubbed down with sandpaper.

"So you play drums? Is that the reason for the sticks?"

Squeaky nods. "My brother Leon had a set and I'd sneak down to the basement to play when he wasn't home."

"Leon?" He stops and raises an eyebrow. "Leon Ladeucer?"

"You know him?" Tony shrugs and goes back to her arm. She says nothing else. Everyone has heard of her brother Leon.

The pain of the needle keeps on. Squeaky wonders what her mom, a devout French-Catholic, will say about the tattoo. Her mom is into bingo too, but mostly Jesus. She never had much control over Squeaky's brothers, who were always on the edge of the crowd, causing trouble. Leon spent a year locked up, for possession of a firearm and insurance fraud, and before Andre got his bipolar meds, he was a notorious street fighter. Little Louie is a loudmouth horror-show, though, Squeaky concedes, that's part of his style.

Between short bursts of the tattoo gun, Squeaky's thoughts drift: Leon in the basement, wildly hitting the drums with wild teenage rage, long hair flying, Southern rock cranked on the stereo, his motorcycle jacket with ripped lining; icicle-crowned forts and pelting cars with snowballs; little bratty Louie doing backflips off the porch so they'd pay him some attention. On the poorly paved road in front of their house they rode their bikes and tried to skateboard. Each finished fights the other lost. When their mom was at bingo, Squeaky made dinner. She knew what she was doing in the kitchen and when she bossed the boys around, they listened. Her brothers had taught her how to set up a drum kit, take apart an engine, and roll a perfect joint. Squeaky was only five feet, but stood very tall in the world.

"I have a sister," Tony King says, bringing her back to the whining, tight pain. "We used to throw knives at each other

and fistfight. She kicked my ass all the time." He chuckles at the memory. "When we got older, we got along. I went after one of her boyfriends with a baseball bat once." The needle hits a spot that makes her whole arm tingle.

Squeaky's first boyfriend was Dante Russo. He was seventeen, two years older. Her family lived on the outskirts of town and Dante would steal his mom's car to come and pick her up. Besides hanging out at the arcade, their social scene consisted of bush parties at the reservoir, heavy metal, and trucks parked in a half-circle shining their lights. Teenagers would pair off and screw in the forest. Other kids got lost on stoned missions. At one of these parties, Dante coaxed Squeaky into the woods. She lost her virginity lying on the ground, dirt in her ass crack and bleeding on leaves. Afterwards, staring at the bonfire, she saw Dante and his friends slap palms. A few days later, Dante came to school with a broken nose and a sling on his arm. Neither he nor his friends spoke to Squeaky again.

She blurts, "My brothers kicked the shit out of my first boyfriend and no one ever dated me in high school again."

"Well, you gotta understand," Tony says. "They know what guys are like. And you're their *sister*."

He wipes the blood off her arm. She grimaces.

In high school Squeaky rarely knew the correct answer in class, but because she was well-mannered and helpful, the teachers passed her. One by one her brothers had left home, and she couldn't stand to be alone with her school books. After graduation her mother pleaded, so for one year Squeaky agreed to go to community college, but her heart wasn't in it.

College seemed much like an extension of high school. Squeaky met her friend Sunshine there, an upbeat girl with kinky black hair, who smelled like lavender and cinnamon gum.

They both took Communications and volunteered at the campus radio station. Sunshine's family ran a bakery at the ferry terminal and she played acoustic guitar for the passengers waiting on the docks. A few times Squeaky joined her with a set of bongos. The well-heeled bohemians loved that. One sunny afternoon they made nearly a hundred bucks.

When Leon left home he'd passed his drum set onto Squeaky. Long ago their father, the foreman of a construction company, had soundproofed the basement. The girls got together and played at Squeaky's a few times a week. One day, Sunshine brought her friend Nicole, a pretty French girl with stubby fingers and a sarcastic nature. Nicole could really sing. Despite Squeaky's protests, they named the group Mud Love. Sunshine and Nicole liked the earthy imagery, but it made Squeaky think of adult diapers. She knew Mud Love and their folk harmonies weren't very good, but she was playing drums. All year long she lived in her parent's basement, dragged herself to class, and made music every chance she got.

When the final term ended, Squeaky moved to Victoria, the biggest city on the island, and a mecca for film students and aging hippies. Sunshine had lived on one of the tiny Gulf islands all her life and couldn't wait to leave. The girls found an affordable apartment in a cinderblock complex. One weekend Andre painted their kitchen and laid down new laminate. Leon came in and out of town. On one of his trips he gave Squeaky a DVD player and on the next, a can of bear spray. It was an exciting time in her first apartment. Buying a mop or putting ice cream in the refrigerator was a big deal. She missed her mom and called home to get recipes for tourtière and Quebec sugar pie.

Squeaky worked in one minimum-wage dish pit after another. The following year she and Sunshine moved into a house with Nicole and her boyfriend, setting up their equipment in the living room. Many nights the girls drank cheap wine and played music until dawn. Nicole's boyfriend had a lot of friends that came over. One night Squeaky met Curtis, a twenty-three-year-old drunkard who lost his skateboard as often as he lost his job.

They fell for each other, hard. Squeaky rode a BMX, didn't wear makeup or a bra, and Curtis dug her style. He was funny and sweet, also from the Island, a wild kid let loose on the cityscape. There was always a point in his drunkenness when Curtis stripped down naked, no matter his location. He shimmied up drainpipes, challenged strangers to wrestle, crouched in his seat and screamed like a monkey on the bus. Curtis was odd and interesting, with the heart of a poet and liver of a drunk. They were inseparable for years. Whenever he drank whisky he wanted to fight, but he was a thin boy with small fists and almost always lost. One night he flipped his bike while riding drunk and broke his jaw. When they finally unwired his jaw and took off the braces Curtis decided to quit drinking.

It was around this time Squeaky was invited to try out for a band called The Druggies. The badass guitar player was the pastry chef in the restaurant where she worked. No one in the band really did that many drugs, except for smoking a ridiculous amount of weed. Squeaky could really get behind The Druggies' fast, stoner rock, which was very different from Mud Love's coffeehouse crap-folk. Lately, whenever Squeaky played drums with them, it seemed as interesting as making sandwiches.

The Druggies had a trial show with Squeaky on drums. Halfway through the gig she threw up, but kept playing. The band voted her in unanimously. After a few months The Druggies decided to relocate to Vancouver for a bigger music scene. Curtis didn't want to move. He and Squeaky fought over it. They'd been together for three years and had a deep fondness, but it didn't feel like love anymore. Squeaky went

ahead and gave her notice. Sunshine was planning to travel through Southeast Asia with her boyfriend and didn't mind. Curtis, on the other hand, minded very much.

It was a difficult breakup. For weeks Curtis wrote love poems for Squeaky in the park underneath the sad willow. In the middle of the night he screamed obscenities at her window. When he calmed down he helped her pack and, for a few months, made occasional trips to the Mainland to see her, which usually resulted in arguments outside of bars. His visits petered out.

Squeaky lived in the basement of a band house amid buzzing amplifiers. Most days she played drums with her earphones on and worked nights in a kitchen for an intense master chef. When the chef wasn't working he shopped for women shopping for vegetables. He called Squeaky his G-Force and from him she learned how to clean tenderloin and duck, make a soufflé, French a rack of lamb, and perfectly blanch green beans. Her brothers had needed an enormous supply of food and drink and she knew how to get things done in a kitchen.

There were other boyfriends after Curtis: an overweight pot dealer with giant muttonchops and a stutter; an illiterate jackass who rode in a BMX gang and had a missing front tooth. Squeaky had never been into pretty boys. A few months after dumping the jackass, she stopped by a skate shop where Rocket happened to work. Rocket knew she played drums for The Druggies, and invited her to smoke a joint in the bathroom. A week later they were at the same bar, and she burned a doobie with him in the alley. They ran into each other at a party the following night. It was on.

Rocket was a hardcore rock 'n' roller, obnoxious when drunk, but endearing sober. He was similar to Curtis, who, she'd heard, had since married a yoga instructor. She and Rocket were both into seeing live bands and searching for

vinyl. The Druggies had the occasional gig and played a few memorable shows, but then the singer quit to go to India and study meditation with his bitchy girlfriend. Squeaky moved into Rocket's band house, where roommates were always coming and going. Their relationship was one long eighteen-month after-party.

Not being in a band made Squeaky restless. Rocket, in turn, was drunk and high most of the time. Theirs was a friendly breakup and Rocket admitted he'd been a terrible boyfriend. They got back together. They broke up again. Squeaky put her drums in storage, then moved out for good. She was twenty-eight years old and refused to spend her thirties with these boys.

For a while it's just a grey space and the needle drilling into her arm. Just as Squeaky begins to feel an intense dislike for Tony King, he says, "That's it, we're done." Her arm is rubbed down a final time.

"Whoa," she admires, and forgets the pain when she sees the finished tattoo. It twists across her bicep in the mirror. "Tony, I love it. It's fucking great!" Black branches, flowers, and blue diamonds are a bold landscape around a grinning skull. It looks tough. Tony spreads Vaseline on her tattoo and wraps her arm in plastic, giving her instructions on its care.

"Man, I'm glad I held up."

"You didn't even flinch," says Tony. She's so happy it's over she reaches up and hugs him. There's a strange kind of intimacy with the person who inks a first tattoo.

Out on the street she runs a few steps and jumps on her skateboard. It's the end of the afternoon, shadows beginning to stretch. Her arm throbs and she pushes off toward home, carving the streets in long arcs, real slow.

Kitty Domingo

There is no answer when Squeaky calls Kitty Domingo late Sunday morning. Her arm is still pounding. She tries again later and gets Kitty's mother. "Hi Jewel, it's Squeaky. Kitty said she was staying with you." They chat for a minute and then Jewel gets her daughter.

"Hello," Kitty answers sleepily.

"Hey, I know it's early for you and everything, but we're jamming with Maxine Micheline tonight. Don't forget."

"Huh," Kitty croaks. "Maxine Micheline?"

“You met her at the party the other night. She’s the old singer from Death by Rollercoaster.”

“Oh yeah,” Kitty says, waking up. “Now I remember. Yeah. Yeah. Yeah!“

“So, you’re gonna come?”

“Okay. But I don’t have any money. MY MOM WON’T GIVE ME ANY MONEY,” she shouts down the hallway at Jewel.

“I’ll pick you up and we’ll go together.”

“Fuck,” Kitty complains. “I’m so fucking broke right now. I hate living at my mom’s. I cry all the time. I’m so depressed.” The conservative government had instated a three-month wait for welfare, and all the punks from Montreal are starving. Squeaky has never known Kitty to have money, or actually work.

“If we start a band, you won’t be depressed. Maxine wants her friend to play guitar. I don’t know if she’s any good.”

“Who IS she?”

“Her name’s Fanta. I met her at Freudian Slips, you know, that weird looking store? She’s a redhead and kind of stood in the corner and scowled.”

“Hey, remember your skanky roommate at that party, doing that guy in the backyard?”

“Uh...*yeah.*”

“They were, like, RUTTING.”

“I haven’t seen Paula since then. It’s kind of a relief.”

“No shit,” Kitty says with her usual crude charm. “The only thing going near that girl is the flies.”

“I’m glad your bass isn’t in the pawn shop.”

“Nah, my mom got it out for me. She’s been keeping my stuff. I was...uhhhhhhhh...*kind of*...fucked up for a while.”

Squeaky knows what that means and lets it hang in the empty space of the phone line. They both knew that Kitty still craved the jab of a needle in her arm, and the warm rush of her troubles floating away.

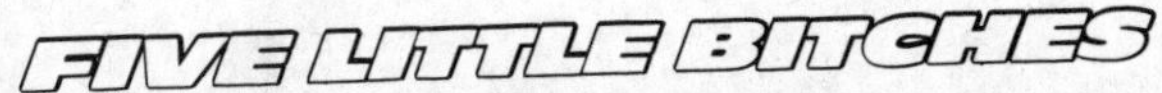

NAME: Kitty Domingo AGE: 21

OCCUPATION: Bass player

BIRTHPLACE: East Van loce!

PREVIOUS BANDS: Dong Side of the Tracks

INTERESTS: Gettin' rad

EARLIEST MEMORY: i forget

QUOTE: "Some days i just want to climb up to the top of a mountain and spread my ass cheeks so the whole world can get a taste of raisin."

kitty Domingo

Kitty Domingo could break anyone's heart.

Everyone thought they knew something about her: she'd been junkie street trash; she was a hot chick who turned her boyfriends crazy; she was a hard, messed up girl who got around.

A Gemini with a wild streak and dark eyebrows in a thin arch, Kitty's appetite for drugs was insatiable. She had short black hair she cut herself, big blue eyes, and fair skin that easily burned. Her mouth curved in a perfect, pink-lipped smile. Kitty gave out sly flashes of attention that made old farts randy and unloved boys obsess. Over time, she learned it was not in her best interest to be kind.

It was generally accepted as fact that Kitty was the mean and beautiful sister and Nadine, two years older, was the smart, nice one. Their mother, Jewel, a voluptuous flower child, had been duped most of her life by unworthy men. Kitty and Nadine's father was a musical prodigy who'd gone back to London when they were just young enough to remember. Jewel took them to live on a commune in Oregon. Kitty and Nadine thrived on lentils, mung beans, and tofu. Then Jewel met Santana Domingo at a farmer's market where she sold homemade candles. They married that winter. Santana was a handsome man with a drinking problem. A year later, he died of a massive heart attack while shovelling the driveway and Jewel was no longer a carefree love child. She realized she couldn't rely on anyone else to support her and the girls. They moved back to East Vancouver and into a one-bedroom apartment in a poor neighbourhood with few green spaces or trees.

Nadine went to grade two and Kitty was sent to kindergarten. One day in September Nadine came home after school with her glasses broken. Her lip was puffed and swollen from some kids in the neighbourhood. Kitty couldn't do anything but sit outside the door to the room she shared with Nadine and listen to her cry. That sound made Kitty feel hopeless and scared of the world in a way she would never forget.

Jewel worked part-time in a health food store while she went to nursing school. They lived in social housing and had a plot in the community garden. Jewel dated a nurse from the hospital where she had her practical training. He was an older, grey-haired man who wore glasses, and babysat the girls when Jewel worked double shifts. At night he went into

Kitty and Nadine's room and put his hands on them under the blankets. Kitty always fought him. Nadine lay terrified with her eyes squeezed shut, believing that if she stayed small and quiet it would be over sooner. They didn't tell Jewel. Even at a young age they knew she was different from other mothers. She'd have another breakdown like she'd had once before, and they'd be sent to stay with strangers again.

When Jewel graduated from nursing school she began to work in the trauma unit at a crosstown hospital. Money was tight, and she took extra shifts. In grade school, Kitty wore ripped jeans and Doc Martens, and dyed her hair purple with Kool-Aid. She and Nadine refused to have babysitters and scared each one away. Kitty stayed out late in the park with her friends. She was enrolled in an alternative school but rarely went. Instead she hung out downtown with the punks begging for spare change. At thirteen she quit going to school at all and spent the afternoons drinking cider in the park with the crusty hippies and runaways. Kitty knew the city in ways much different from other kids her age. Men offered her booze, pot, ecstasy, PCP, acid. She liked drugs and wanted them all. Sooner or later, one of them gave her heroin.

She did her first line off the back of a toilet and barfed right away. But it wasn't a gross feeling; there was an oozing in her stomach that warmed every muscle. She was so warm she walked around outside for hours with no coat on, high and intense. It felt like true love, falling into a waking dream, a beautiful bubble where no pain or fear could penetrate.

She disappeared from home for weeks. On heroin, the future seemed a glorious thing. Men liked Kitty and she went home with them to take their money. She stole from anyone who came into the house—strangers, friends, relatives—whenever she could. Kitty stole everything of value from her mother and then, after a while, Jewel wouldn't let her come home.

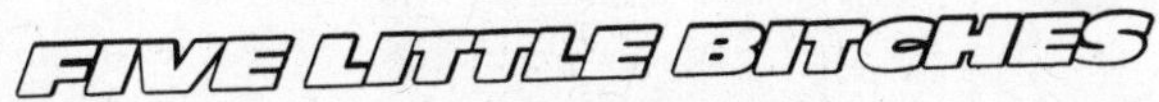

Nadine had a schizophrenic boyfriend named Ashtray, and they took off to Montreal. She disappeared for nearly six months. Nadine was a skinny, sensitive girl not hard enough to deal with the ugly realities of street life. When she came back home she was on antipsychotic medication and had spent time in a Quebec mental institute. Nadine never seemed right after that, always paranoid and depressed. She refused to talk about what had happened to her in Montreal. Kitty wanted to quit heroin, and checked into detox over and over—dope-sick with that familiar dry cough that made her puke, freezing and boiling in the same second, the painful goosebumps like her skin was being stretched. It took many long years of relapses and piss tests and methadone to do it. At the end of it all she was the hardest eighteen-year-old girl you ever saw.

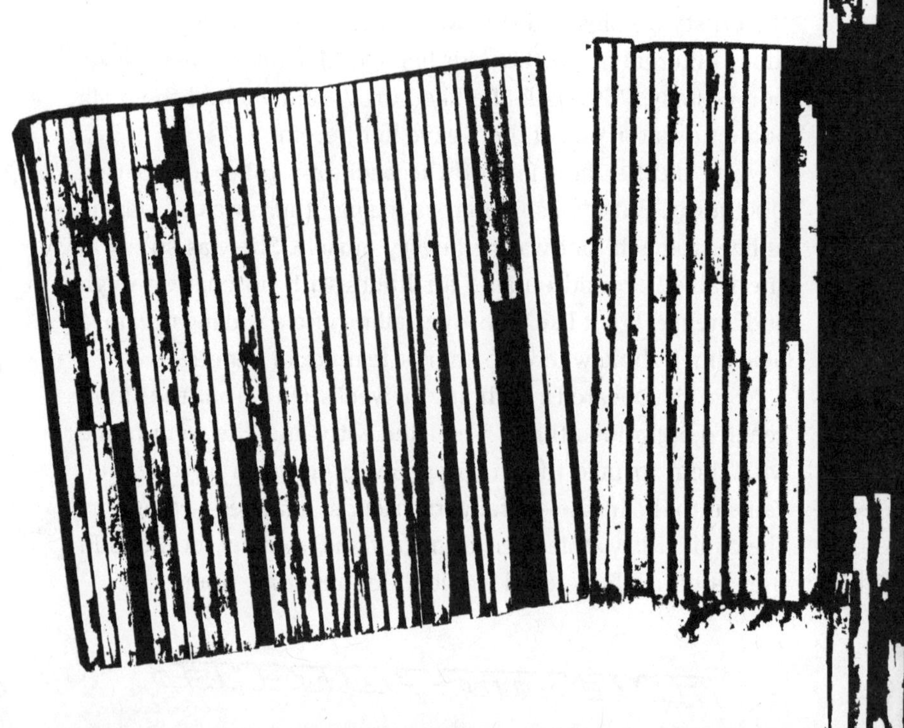

Maxine stops by Freudian Slips late Sunday afternoon with a coffee for Fanta. It makes her nervous to ask again if she'll join them for practise. "Any plans tonight?" she begins, but some customers come into the shop and Maxine leaves, unable to endure the laser beam gaze of Fanta's green and yellow eyes. She decides to try by phone later at home. After work she keeps calling and Fanta finally picks up, irritable. "Hel-*lo*?"

"Fanta, it's Maxine. We're gonna jam tonight at Powder Keg from six to nine."

"Have fun."

"You said you'd think about it."

"I did *not*."

Maxine exhales loudly. "What's the big deal? You've got all the gear. It might be a really fun time."

"What's the big deal? Is that your question?" Fanta sounds pissed and Maxine knows she's blown it. "It *is* a big deal, Maxine. Playing Harold's guitar is a very big deal to me."

"But why keep all that equipment if you never play? All his stuff just sits there taking up space in your apartment."

"I don't want to talk about it."

Maxine lowers her voice. "I'm just saying it's been like, five or six years."

"It doesn't seem that long to me."

Fanta puts the phone down in her lap. Despite the appearance of being a sparse, no-nonsense woman, her apartment is much like Freudian Slips, piled floor to ceiling with boxes, record crates, trunks, and garment bags. Years of her life mildew in stacks. Fanta wonders if she crammed all this stuff into her life to prepare for being alone. She spots wood rot in the corner and it's like a punch to the sternum.

"All right," Fanta resigns. "I'll try." Then she hangs up the phone and closes her eyes.

Goddamn you Harold, she thinks.

Maxine grumbles, but helps Fanta load her van. Getting the Triple Rectifier head stacked on a 4x12 Marshall cabinet out of the depths of the closet isn't easy to manage. Fanta is thin, but wiry, and does most of the work. "Do you really want to bring all this gear?" She responds by standing in front of the van with her arms folded. Maxine shuts her mouth.

The other girls are already waiting at Powder Keg. Squeaky is content to use the rehearsal kit, but brought her own kick pedal, cymbals and snare drum. Kitty has an ancient Carlsbro bass combo. As Maxine and Fanta settle in, Squeaky practises press rolls, *Brrrr-ump, brrrrmp.*

Maxine patches the microphone into the old PA system in the corner. "Oh great," she gags. "This is a stinky fucking mic. Testing...one two three...this sure is no fun for me...." The microphone breaks up and crackles from too many drops on the cement floor. "I think this XLR cable might be fucked," she says, walking around the room. "I'm getting feedback from every corner!"

Kitty spends the next twenty minutes tuning her bass. When finished she jumps into the discussion of musical styles. "I listen to hardcore," she says. "Deathcore."

Squeaky tightens a lug on the snare drum. "Oh yeah? Well I'm into Gruntcore."

"Ha-HAH!"

"I like everything," Maxine says. "Cow-punk, girl garage, fifties rockabilly, greasy R&B..."

"You need some kind of direction," Fanta says. "Cohesion."

"Why?"

She answers dryly, "It *helps,* Maxine."

"Let's just play some rock and roll," Squeaky says. She starts with a simple kick, just providing the beat, then a double kick, once in a while a few fills, keeping it steady. Kitty tries a few times for a bass line before she gives up.

"FUCK," she wails, "I fucking hate these strings." She tries again and locks in with Squeaky's groove. Kitty plays bass with her fingers, which is harder than using a pick, but she thinks it sounds better.

"Nice," Squeaky encourages. "Keep it going."

"WHAT?" Kitty's amp is up far too high and the feedback is uncontrollable.

They stop, then start again. Squeaky lays down a filthy 4/4 groove. This time Fanta begins to pick a little melody. Kitty gains some confidence with a rumbling bass line. It goes on for some time and then Squeaky quickens the tempo. Fanta adds a dirty rock riff. It's obviously something she practised before. Kitty messes up, and causes a train wreck. Everyone starts playing something different, not knowing who to follow. Fanta turns her back on them and goes into a corner. "Give me a few minutes," she says.

Squeaky swipes her forearm across her sweaty face. "Nice, Fanta," she exclaims. "Holy *fuck!* Those are some nagging little hooks."

"Yeah," Kitty agrees. "She can really play the shit out of it." Fanta places her fingers carefully on the frets and shifts the guitar. It's nice to be out of her room, she decides. She hasn't felt this good in some time. They go over what they have again and again. Maxine throws in a few "Yeah yeahs!" and "All right, all rights!" then sits cross-legged on the floor to try and write some lyrics.

Fanta brought Harold's pedal board, though she never learned how to use the effects. She messes around with reverb for a bit then retunes her guitar and goes back to picking out melodies. All the music lessons Harold had given her come back, and the memory of those endless hours practising bar chords is still buried in her muscles.

They start again and Squeaky throws in a couple double-bass fills and crashes the cymbals. From her wide smile it's clear her happiest moments are behind a drum kit. Fanta

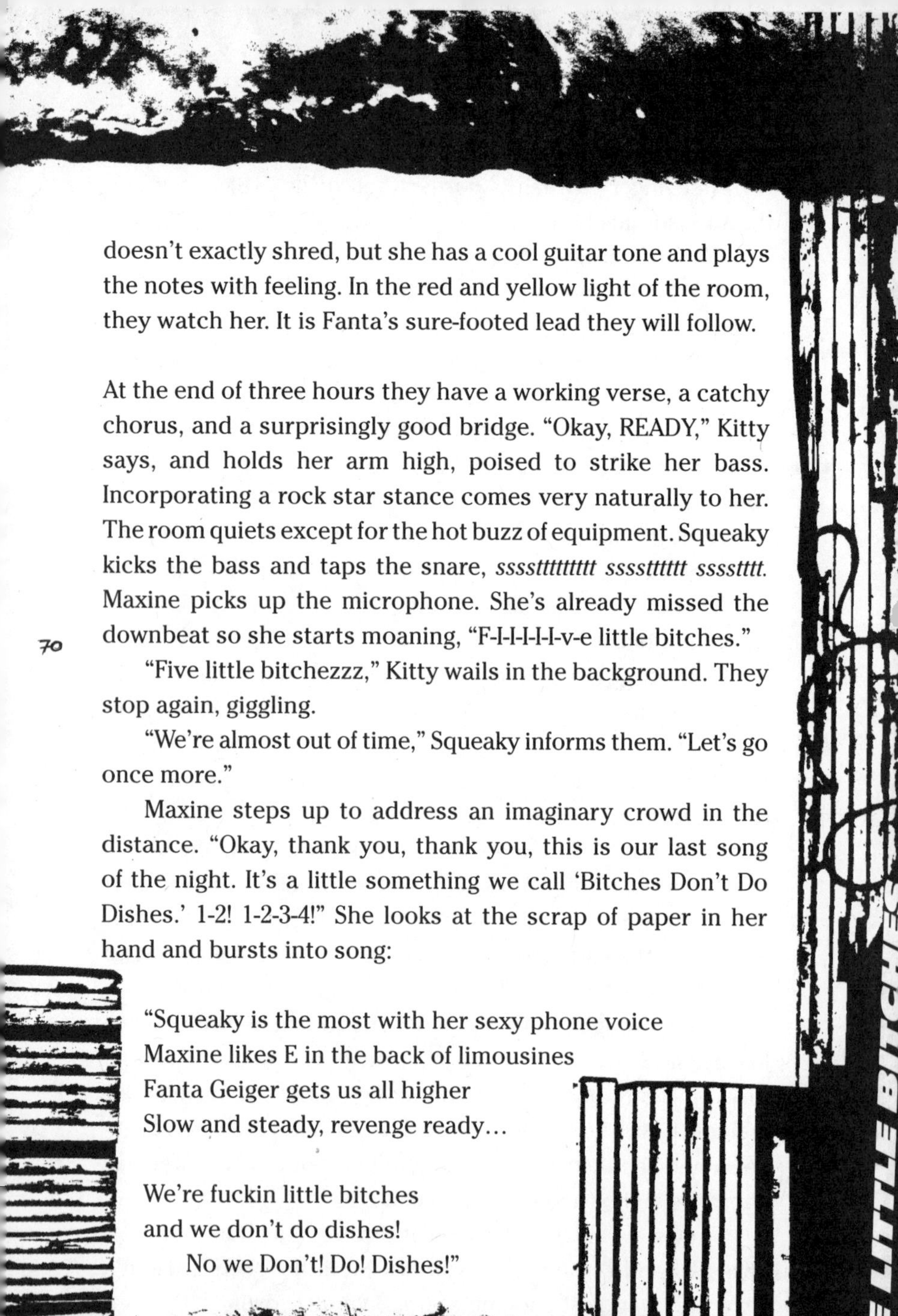

doesn't exactly shred, but she has a cool guitar tone and plays the notes with feeling. In the red and yellow light of the room, they watch her. It is Fanta's sure-footed lead they will follow.

At the end of three hours they have a working verse, a catchy chorus, and a surprisingly good bridge. "Okay, READY," Kitty says, and holds her arm high, poised to strike her bass. Incorporating a rock star stance comes very naturally to her. The room quiets except for the hot buzz of equipment. Squeaky kicks the bass and taps the snare, *ssssttttttttt ssssttttttt sssstttt.* Maxine picks up the microphone. She's already missed the downbeat so she starts moaning, "F-I-I-I-I-v-e little bitches."

"Five little bitchezzz," Kitty wails in the background. They stop again, giggling.

"We're almost out of time," Squeaky informs them. "Let's go once more."

Maxine steps up to address an imaginary crowd in the distance. "Okay, thank you, thank you, this is our last song of the night. It's a little something we call 'Bitches Don't Do Dishes.' 1-2! 1-2-3-4!" She looks at the scrap of paper in her hand and bursts into song:

"Squeaky is the most with her sexy phone voice
Maxine likes E in the back of limousines
Fanta Geiger gets us all higher
Slow and steady, revenge ready…

We're fuckin little bitches
and we don't do dishes!
No we Don't! Do! Dishes!"

At this point the song slows down and Maxine sings with a comical baritone: "We just use a haaaaaammmmmer…" Fanta fumbles during the bridge and quickly recovers. The song picks up again and Maxine shimmies like a dervish on speed. In the dingy practise room she commands their attention.

"Kitty drinks all day and wants to get laid
If we go to Montreal don't expect us to call
Only Squeaky can *parlez francais*
And this is what *WE* say…

We're fuckin little bitches
And we don't do dishes!
No we Don't! (*clap-clap*) Do! (*clap-clap-clap*) Dishes!"

The song goes into double time for the last minute, then Squeaky crashes the cymbals and they're done. Maxine tries to catch her breath. The series of snap kicks at the end took the wind right out of her.

As they leave the rehearsal space and walk into the cool night air, each girl has different thoughts. After hitting the drums for a few hours Squeaky's arms shake with exhaustion, but she's clear-headed and lighter inside. Kitty runs through a catalogue of songs she wants to cover. A music video plays in Maxine's head in which she's the star. It's been on a loop since age eleven.

Fanta says nothing, rubbing her knuckles. It's the same feeling she used to get in winter, when each day was covered in ice, impossible to survive because she had to walk so slowly.

BIO

NAME: Fanta Geiger AGE: 37

OCCUPATION: Guitar player, vintage store owner

BIRTHPLACE: Dusseldorf, Germany

PREVIOUS BANDS: None

INTERESTS: Simone de Beauvoir, Vali Meyers, Gaudi, Angela Davis, vermouth, iggy Pop circa 1984, The Strand

EARLIEST MEMORY: disillusion regarding Santa

QUOTE: "Long is the way, and hard, that out from hell comes up to light."

FANTA GEIGER

Fanta's Bavarian parents were proud of their heritage. Her father was an engineer and her mother scrubbed the house and made strudels. Unleashed dogs, smokers, and bad credit made her hysterical. If a guest came by unannounced, Fanta's mother would excuse herself to go clean the bathroom. She refused to shit in public toilets. From a young age Fanta found her exasperating and sad and unbearably claustrophobic.

There had never been anything childlike about Fanta Geiger. By high school she was far ahead of the other kids, who swivelled their heads at her in the hall. All in black, she stood out in a sea of denim and pastels with her orange eyelashes and pale skin, her sad but generous mouth. When teachers called on her she was not afraid to give the right answers. She had a quiet sarcasm that didn't translate well to those around her.

Music and art were everything to Fanta. Her record collection ranged from Iggy Pop to Lene Lovich to Genya Ravan. Her favourite artists sang about being an outcast, they burned in it, made an inner circle of something odd and unique. Fanta experimented with different looks—the androgyny of Ziggy Stardust, East Village bohemian. Most were pieces from thrift stores she reassembled on her mother's sewing machine. If people were going to single her out, she would give them good reason. Her best friend, Les, shaved his head except for a long piece he bleached blonde and combed in front of his left eye.

In the fall of senior year, as Fanta was driving her VW bug to school, a van sped through an intersection while running a red light, and slammed into her.

By the time she got to the hospital, the pain was inhuman. The last thing Fanta remembered was worrying about her Physics test. As she lay in the emergency room, other patients cried out in agony around her. Hate surged in her heart. They'd finally broken her. A nurse checked her vital signs, and then stuck a burning IV into her hand. Another came with a shot and Fanta faded out again. The nurses who had administered her morphine became Fanta's deities.

Her legs were crushed. In the rush of activity around her, Fanta understood she was being sent to surgery to piece her broken legs back together. They wheeled her on a gurney to an operating room that was brightly lit and very cold. Strangers in green uniforms attached equipment to her. A doctor leaned over and gave words of encouragement. He smelled like he'd eaten eggs for breakfast. Someone placed an oxygen mask over her mouth. The air in the mask tasted tinny and metallic. Then she was floating upwards, to heaven, on a calm white cloud.

Fanta spent weeks propped in her hospital bed, hooked to an IV, a catheter, and drainage tubes running from the sides of her legs. The nurses gave her shots of blood thinner each day and inquired about her bowel movements like they really cared. Her knees had been rebuilt with plastic and metal implants and were the size of bruised cantaloupes. When the nurses changed the bandages, Fanta admired the incisions. A row of staples held each wound closed, like she'd been implanted with large zippers. After a few weeks these were pulled out. The scars looked like giant red worms embedded in her skin.

During the months of rehabilitation it took her to walk again, Fanta finished her last year of school by a correspondence course. When she came back to write her provincial exams, her legs still hurt, and she used a cane. Certain girls fawned over her with cloying sympathy. As usual, boys ignored her.

None of that mattered to Fanta. By this time her scars had changed again. They were soft and pink, raised in defiance, magnificent.

Fanta was twenty-four when she'd met Harold Dixon in Pinky's Laundromat. She'd received a Bachelor's Degree from an Eastern university, but it was all she could do to endure her classmates running through the tree-lined campus with their idio-anarchy. She had recently moved to Vancouver, and was currently in a phase of sewing baby doll dresses in camouflage and tiger prints, and pairing them with coloured tights. There were plastic splints she wore in her shoes, and she walked with a limp when tired. Though a stranger wouldn't know it, on the day Fanta met Harold she was in a good mood. The sun shone in her neighbourhood and her bones didn't hurt.

Inside Pinky's Laundromat, she saw a neighbour from her building crouched beside the dryers, drinking beer with a friend. Fanta had bags of material to wash for her boss. She worked in an exclusive boutique, for a woman who let her sew outfits to sell in the shop. It was a great job except the owner kept a bottle of white wine under the counter and peed into a bucket in the back because the toilet didn't flush. The workday often ended with Fanta's drunken boss falling over in her platform shoes or driving into a building.

Her neighbour said, "Fanta, this is Harold Dixon." She assumed Harold's broad smile came from inebriation. He gave her a flyer for his next show. Nothing he said impressed her very much. When her laundry was in the washer she declined their offer of a beer and left. The men she met could not handle her dismissive self-reliance. Fanta was content and cold in the city alone. She liked how the continuous winter rain drove the weak ones mad.

One day she came out of her building and found Harold Dixon waiting for her. He wore a porkpie hat and a Hawaiian shirt underneath a blazer. She was on her way to get coffee and agreed he could come. They talked about a recent art show (pedestrian), emo music (soundtracks for writing suicide notes), and the shared slice of pecan pie (noteworthy). Fanta ignored the rude server and on the way home gave a homeless man in a wheelchair five bucks. Harold confessed he was a chronic masturbator and Fanta acted like she hadn't heard.

Harold Dixon played guitar and was the most talented member of a mediocre band with a screaming teen following that embarrassed him. He also liked to take photographs of old pickups and animal skulls. When he tried to take pictures of Fanta she put up her hand.

"Let me see your face," he'd plead. "At least give me an eye!" Over the next few weeks Harold took her to unusual places: an abandoned rail station, an abattoir. They shared a certain rare sensibility and a taste for decay. But Harold had a playful side, too. One day he showed up at her apartment with a rubber frog. "We're on assignment," he said. They took photographs of the frog propped up in the window of a coffee shop with a smoke in his mouth, on a magazine rack at a porn store, in the gutter beside an empty liquor bottle. The last photo was the frog in the bathtub with Fanta in red light.

The time spent with Harold was enjoyable, yet Fanta remained reserved. Only when he left did she relax and feel content. Off came her clothes, shoes, earrings, the entire costume. She couldn't wait to wash her face and pull back her hair and really see herself again. But Harold began to stay longer, and when he played his guitar, Fanta felt dreamy and full of bliss. Aside from a wide range of painkillers she'd been prescribed, she'd never come close to those feelings again.

Harold loved the scars on Fanta's knees. Together they wished on dried turkey bones and he put her red hair into tiny braids. His rudimentary sense of humour smoothed out her jagged edges. She bought him silk boxers, bags of licorice whips, foreign beer. He rubbed her legs when it rained and played melodies she'd inspired. Harold's feet smelled like popcorn and he had crinkles beside his eyes when he smiled. Some mornings it surprised Fanta to wake up so happy.

At Harold's shows he introduced her around with pride. Although she didn't like his band's music very much, she maintained a spot at the front of the stage and withstood the sharp elbows of the young fans Harold referred to as "teen poodles." When he was recording or on the road, Fanta puttered at home. The whirr of her sewing machine comforted her. Unlike most people, she enjoyed being alone for long periods of time. Her cat, Mr. Kibbles, was all the company she needed. She didn't exactly miss Harold when he was gone, but when he came home it felt like she was part of the world again.

While on tour, Harold was evicted for not paying his rent, and moved into Fanta's apartment. She bought a bigger bed and the first night he crawled in he said, "I'm gonna cuddle you a new *asshole*!" Fanta cut her red hair into a short, angled bob. She was in a period of sewing twenties-inspired ensembles. Harold wore a stylish brown fedora. They attended book launches, record releases, photo exhibits, swap meets. At every occasion, they were impeccably dressed for each other.

Harold went on occasional drinking binges. Anything could set him off: bad restaurant service or the plight of the polar bear. Fanta alone could console him. He'd creep beside her in the middle of the night, bloody and remorseful. "I'm so bad, Fanta," he'd sniff, "but really I want to be good." Fanta made Harold tea when he was hungover and salty cheese biscuits from scratch. He had a good memory and listened to what she had to say. They liked being together and agreed it was a fine and happy life.

The following year Harold's band put out a new album to mediocre reviews. The teen poodles who'd bought their CDs were fickle and had moved on to the next sensation. The tour was downsized to smaller venues. Some shows were cancelled all together. The band members used their own money to make an earnest video that became a viral laughing stock. Slowly the group fell apart. Harold became very depressed. Without an album to work on or a tour to plan, he didn't know what to do with himself.

The band had made Harold a lot of money, but little had been saved. He liked cigars and good booze and thick cuts of steak. Aside from sporadic checks from the band, he didn't have any income besides occasional work at a printing shop. Fanta took care of the rent and bills, like she'd done for herself before Harold. She would do anything to see him as happy as he'd once been. They didn't have much money for entertainment so Harold showed her chord progressions on the guitar. Fanta had long, nimble fingers. He seemed even more depressed when she caught on so quickly.

Over the winter Harold sat on the couch, miserable. His artistic side did not flourish with spare time. He began to have late nights at the computer. When Fanta went to work, he stayed home and jerked off. Downloading porn became more than a hobby. Her boss closed the boutique, so Fanta started working at a vintage clothing store, and got a second job, as a hostess during weekend brunch at an upscale eatery, that destroyed her soul. She thought of Harold on the couch while her customers shovelled frittatas into their gaping mouths. For her birthday, he'd put twenty dollars on the phone bill. When Fanta showed her annoyance he'd said, "Well, I put it in *your* name."

Often she came home and found Harold at the computer, sweaty and naked, beating off to porn. Despite his manic look he denied being high. Fanta couldn't be sure. He kept the lights dim and rarely went outdoors. Over time Harold sold his camera and lenses, then his acoustic guitar. Fanta also cleaned houses and would come home from work so exhausted she barely had time for a glass of wine or a joint before falling asleep. Life with Harold became a joke that had gone too far. One afternoon Fanta realized Harold hadn't left the house for almost two weeks. When she pointed it out, he complained about the rain. With his long johns and cardigan he looked like an old man. "You can't just lie here," she said. "At least play some guitar." His Gibson SG sat in the corner, out of tune and untouched. He'd once bragged it was the same guitar used by Jimmy Page, Angus Young, and Frank Zappa. Harold examined it like a foreign fossil. Fanta had detested people like him in the hospital, the ones that always complained and reeked of self-pity.

Harold said the rainy days caused depression. Her suggestions for him to form a new band, exercise, or develop a hobby were met with ludicrous excuses. He promised once the sun came out, he'd be better. It occurred to Fanta there was nothing romantic about him anymore: abrasions on his dick from constant wanking, and toenails an unacceptable length. The bedroom smelled of cigarette butts. One night the comforter caught fire when Harold fell asleep smoking. After they put the fire out, Fanta ranted. Instead of listening, Harold decided it was a crucial time to reboot his computer.

After another exhausting day, Fanta lay in bed, reciting the capitals of countries. She dreamed of seeing Greece, Argentina, Madagascar—places she and Harold would never visit. Fanta tossed, unable to sleep. Harold hadn't woken up when she'd come home, and his snoring from the couch was intolerably loud, like he was screaming through his nose. Her legs ached, feet sore from standing. She'd been helping customers all day and was sick of working with difficult people.

Fanta got out of bed and stood over at him. In the dark room her mind blossomed with rage. Finally she turned on the light. Harold kept snoring on the couch. She had a sudden urge to throw his belongings out the window and smash the guitar. Fanta pictured the broken bridge like a snapped spine. The Gibson was his most valuable possession, and she could never do that to him. Instead, she gathered his dirty socks and underwear and empty cigarette packs she'd asked him to clean up numerous times. His mess covered the bedroom floor and now crept toward the living room. She kicked it all into an enormous, foul-smelling pile. Besides the guitar, everything else he owned was in the pawn shop. Fanta opened the window and threw it all out. She couldn't tell if she had feelings for Harold anymore, and it was only this that moved her to tears.

In the kitchen she filled a coffee mug from the tap. Fanta stood over Harold, considered a moment, and then threw cold water in his face.

Harold yelped and bolted upright. Fanta ran back to the bedroom. "YOU CUNT!" he yelled and shoved her onto the bed. He looked around and screamed, "WHERE THE FUCK IS MY STUFF?" Fanta lay in stunned silence and pointed out the window. He rushed out, slamming the door. For the next twenty minutes she watched Harold scour the street. Finally he came back upstairs waving a cigarette pack. "You're lucky I found this," he said, locking himself in the bathroom. Fanta pulled a jacket over her pajamas and put Mr. Kibbles in his carrier. Luckily her coworker Maxine had gone to Mazatlan for a week and left her the key to water the plants.

Many times at work the next day Fanta had to stop from calling Harold to apologize. He was at such a low point in his life. She'd never cared about the success of his band or the money, but his confidence had suffered. Their fight took the strength out of her legs and she was irritable and slow-moving all day.

For the next week Fanta stayed away. She spent a lot of time listening to music and crying in the bathtub. It wasn't clear to her if Harold would miss her while she was gone. Finally she gathered her things and went home. In the apartment, Harold lay sleeping on the couch. There were more pawn tickets on the coffee table. They'd been steadily piling up over the last few months. She went into the bathroom and sat down on the toilet. On the edge of the sink was a glass pipe with a bulb at the end burned black. Fanta stared at it a long time. In the cupboard she found more speed pipes in his shaving bag. It all made sense—how Harold's checks disappeared so quickly, his constant masturbation and odd sleeping patterns. She cringed at herself for believing Harold when he'd said he spent so much time in the bathroom because he liked to read Chinese philosophy in the tub.

Fanta kicked the corner of the couch with her boot until Harold woke up. Then she was at a loss for words, so she threw the house keys at him. They bounced off his forehead. Fanta fled from the building, but halfway down the street she stopped and went back to the apartment. He had the chain on the door and wouldn't let her in.

When she returned the next day, Harold would still not open the door. "I'm sorry I hit you with the keys," she said truthfully. Fanta abhorred violence. He let her in, and sat on the couch, uninterested. The pipe and a lighter were out on the coffee table. Fanta asked a lot of questions and he had no answers. She took down his photos of her and cried. Harold did not. Finally, he crammed his knapsack full of clothing, picked up his pipe, and left. After so many years together, their breakup was much less dramatic than she'd expected.

Over the next few weeks, Fanta got his guitar and amp out of the pawnshop. There were a lot of things she wanted to say to Harold, but he never came back. The phone didn't ring. She thought he'd at least ask for his guitar but he didn't.

Five months later she saw Harold again. She'd heard he was living with a girl who did Internet porn and was rumoured to be a junkie. Harold was thin and unshaven, sitting at the bus stop. He looked as if his bad habits had got the worst of him, despite a worn, blue blazer and jaunty scarf tied around his neck. Scabby and shabby, he at least tried to keep some style. For a terrible moment all the love she'd once had for him came rushing back.

"Oh, how wonderful to see you, Harold," she said, dripping sarcasm. "You look *fantastic.*"

"Oh Fanta," he said. "It's so good to see you too..." When he reached out to hug her, she stepped away. His eyes were pinned. "Hey, will you lend me twenty bucks, Fanta? Just until tomorrow?"

"I got your guitar out of the pawn shop. It's been sitting in the living room for months. Go ahead and sell it, I don't care."

His face changed and he was the Harold she'd once loved, the one who'd held her arm when they crossed an icy street and rubbed oil into her long pink scars. For the first time she saw his misery, even regret. "No, Fanta," he said. "I want you to have it."

Fanta put her earphones back in. If Harold said something as she walked away, she didn't want to hear it.

A few weeks later Fanta bumped into her neighbour at the grocery store, the one who had first introduced her to Harold. They stood with their grocery carts in the dish soap and toilet paper aisle. Her neighbour said Harold was in bad shape. No one could get through to him. There was a rumour he'd been busted at Pinky's Laundromat, trying to steal quarters out of the washing machines.

“I’ve got to go,” Fanta said, swinging her cart. “I need cheese from the deli. Oh, and olives, too.” She filled her cart with pickles, crackers, chocolate, nuts, and apricots. Her legs hurt, but with each step she made it home. After the grocery bags were emptied, she pulled out Harold’s guitar from the closet and strummed it a few times. Then she went to bed.

The bad dreams began: Harold dead-eyed at her window, his rotting corpse beneath the bed. Fanta recalled how she’d enjoyed being alone when he went on tour. She imagined they were still together and Harold was simply on the road. It worked for a moment until her stomach burned.

Fanta had changed the locks after Harold left, but often imagined she’d see him on the couch when she came home from work. It was an odd, but comfortable scenario. Every time the phone rang it might be him. Fanta didn’t have many close friends and thought it was Harold when she heard knocking late one night. But when she opened the door it was her neighbour, pale and red-eyed. He gave her the news that Harold had fallen asleep at a friend’s house and never woken up. His last words had been, “What a comfortable pillow.”

Fanta sewed her own dress for the funeral. She received many compliments on it. A long time passed before she enjoyed solitude again. She played Harold’s guitar every night, until her fingertips began to shred.

Wreck Beach

Squeaky's phone rings early morning after a Friday night jam session. They'd been up late working on their newest song, "GHB OD," based on Kitty's previous weekend. Squeaky had sharpened a sick drum solo using only a bass drum, two toms, and a wooden snare. Afterwards a celebratory drink turned into a dozen sloppy beers.

"I am *so* sorry," Maxine croaks. "I don't want to be up now either, but I'm going to Wreck Beach with Fanta. Last night you said you were into it."

"I made a plan to go to the nude beach with you and Fanta? Damn, I was drunker than I thought."

"We're supposed to meet some vendor about selling beach hats. You still want to come?"

"Okay, but I'm leaving my bottoms on. I don't wanna get sand up my poon."

The beauty of hanging out with Maxine Micheline and Fanta is that they do things Squeaky would never do on her own. After a shower she sits on the window ledge in a pair of plaid boxer shorts, smoking her weed pipe while drying her hair in the sun. It's early May, but already very hot. She looks out at the blue-grey city. North is a losing view. She watches a crackhead jerk down, grab a Q-tip from the gutter, and put it in his mouth like a cigarette. Then Fanta's white Chevy van turns the corner with Maxine's head out the window. Her bleached hair shines like yellow fire in the sun.

"You look like a little kewpie doll sitting up there," Maxine calls. "I want to pay you to come and dance on my coffee table!" Squeaky smiles and shoots her the finger, then grabs a beach towel and heads downstairs.

She arrives home late in the day, sunburned and sandy-bottomed. Paula's bike blocks the front hallway and Paula's in the living room, furiously sucking on a bong. Squeaky drops her beach bag on the floor and falls on the couch. "Whew, I'm beat! I went to Wreck Beach and saw a lot of penises that looked like buttons. How was your day?"

"We were supposed to go for a bike ride."

"Maxine called early and she and Fanta came to get me. I figured you'd sleep late since Izzy was here last night."

Izzy is an older skater that Paula has a hopeless crush on, encouraged by his occasional texts for a booty call. Squeaky has known Izzy for years through a skate crew. He's a good guy and told Paula straight up he didn't want a girlfriend, but Paula is insistent that one day he'll change his mind.

"He took off early. I've been depressed all day."

"Bummer," Squeaky says, relieved she'd been at the beach.

"Oh, and Rocket came by."

It's like Squeaky's been hit with a cattle prod. "Rocket?" She'd heard he was working in a call centre and dating a seventeen-year-old. Rocket is a grizzled thirty. He had called once before, but Squeaky didn't answer. The only way to get over their relationship was not to see or talk to him and it was working. "Rocket hung out *here*?"

"I bumped into him on the street, and he wanted to say hello, so I invited him in to smoke a joint. I called, but your phone was off. All we did was talk about you. He says that—"

"I don't want to hear it," Squeaky says sharply. "Don't discuss me with Rocket. He's my *ex*-boyfriend. I don't see him anymore for a reason. If you want a friendship with him that's your choice, but leave me out of it."

Squeaky walks over, grabs her bong, and then marches down the hall to her room. Rocket is on her mind, to her immense irritation. She opens her door and yells at Paula, "And quit smoking my weed!"

Growing up, Squeaky had girls for friends, but many of them ended up sleeping with one of her brothers. She longs for a code of solidarity, but feels suspicious of her roommate. Paula never hung out with a boy without putting his dick in her mouth. She often leaves her dolphin-shaped dildo in plain view. Once, Squeaky went in her room to borrow a book and saw it on the nightstand, covered in dried mucous flakes.

As long as they'd lived together there was a revolving door policy for boys in and out of Paula's bed. Squeaky now wonders at the mix of bipolar potheads and unattractive co-workers that Paula brought home. Her roommate didn't seem to have a type—she had sex with anyone and looked at it as a learning experience. Squeaky once admired Paula's open attitude, her inability to feel shame. Now it all seems like a louche charade. She doesn't know how much longer they'll be roommates, and feels nostalgic, like it's the end of an era. For a while they were close, like only two single girls can be.

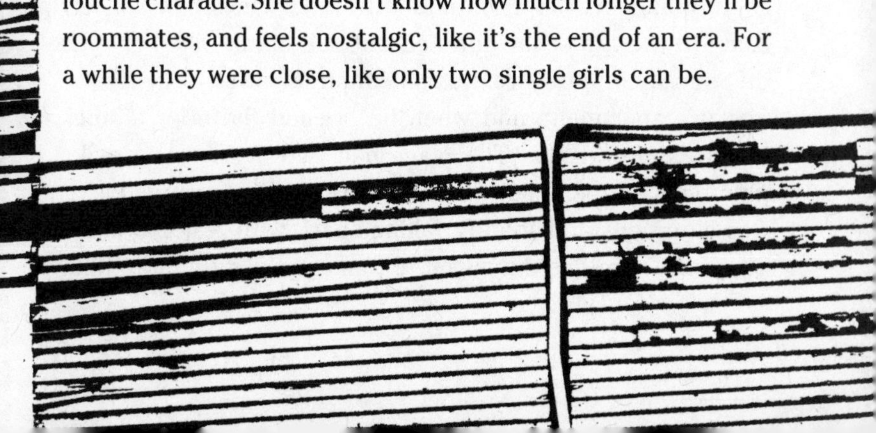

Hating Paula Grubler, PART 1

Squeaky and Paula Grubler had been casual acquaintances for years. They first met at a going-away dinner for a mutual friend who was leaving to hike through Tibet. Occasionally they were at the same birthday party or orphan Christmas. At a rock show Paula let her cut into the beer lineup, and complained about her living situation. Squeaky had just moved out of Rocket's band house and into a cramped bachelor apartment she hated. The girls exchanged numbers. When the friend came back from Tibet, they saw each other at a dinner in his honour. Paula gave Squeaky her number again.

A few days later, Squeaky was riding her BMX in an industrial area to get a transmission mount for Andre. She passed a dusty junk shop with an "Apartment for Rent" sign in the window. Curious, she locked her bike and went inside.

The store was owned by an ancient man named Detroit Johnny and his mute Filipino wife. The wife's nose barely came to the top of the counter, but she didn't take her eyes off Squeaky in the store. Detroit Johnny showed Squeaky the upstairs apartment, and when he opened the door a stack of boxes fell on him. The place had two bedrooms, creaky plumbing, and jammed windows covered by dusty blinds. It was enormous and shabby, falling apart, with real character. The rent Detroit Johnny wanted was only slightly more than what Squeaky paid for her entire apartment. She went home and found Paula Grubler's number. They gave Detroit Johnny a deposit the next day.

When all the boxes were moved out and the apartment cleaned, the girls were amazed by the high ceilings and stained hardwood floors. It was a real find. They painted the kitchen a psychotic chartreuse. There wasn't much in the neighbourhood. Two large windows in the living room gave a northeast view of a busy intersection. There were one or two daytime hookers and a whole lot more at night.

Paula Grubler did morning bong hits to get through her tedious job in a furniture warehouse. She shoplifted herring and mini-cheeses from the supermarket, and collection agencies called often. Paula believed most of her problems stemmed from peeing in her pants in kindergarten because she was afraid to ask for the bathroom. She'd worked as a barista at a huge coffee chain until being fired for stealing beans. Her biggest success was with a dog-walking service, until one pooch was killed by a garbage raccoon. She went to an art college for one term, and then used her student loan money to go backpacking in Thailand. When she returned, she took a random job at the furniture warehouse. The apartment she lived in was too expensive, so she moved in with Squeaky Ladeucer.

Later that night, Paula knocks on Squeaky's door. "I got some more weed." Squeaky inspects the bag and nods. Their fight is officially over.

They go to the upstairs fire escape with the pot pipe. Paula pulls out the baggie, sticky bud flat from her back pocket. She sniffs it with a delirious look. When the bowl is packed, she takes a hard drag, looking out at the city lights.

"If it bothers you, I won't hang out with Rocket ever again," Paula promises. "Your friendship is more important." Squeaky believes her. Even though they argue sometimes, and Paula does weird and questionable things, Squeaky loves her. They help each other scrape by each month, riding their bikes and smoking dirt weed, or paying for one movie and sneaking into three.

Squeaky asks, "What's on the burner for tomorrow?"

"I'm going for a mani-pedi."

"Mani-pedi? What's that? It sounds like a French race car driver. *And coming up on the inside, it's Mani-Pedi!"*

Paula examines her fingernails. "It's a manicure and pedicure."

Squeaky raises an eyebrow. Paula is a tomboy, even more so than her. She does a quick check; Paula's facial hair is still unkempt. "What made you decide to do that?"

"Izzy likes girlie-girls. And I want him to like *me*."

"Isn't it better to be yourself? I mean, it just seems like less work."

Paula shrugs, then picks up the pipe and lights it again. "I want to go to Mahone's and watch the game. Will you come with me?" Along with her dabbling in oil self-portraits and building bird feeders, Paula also follows a variety of sports on TV.

Before Squeaky can say no, Paula pouts, "You never hang out with me anymore." It's true—since the party on Punk Street Squeaky and Paula haven't spent much time together. And now with the band starting to gel with their sound and style,

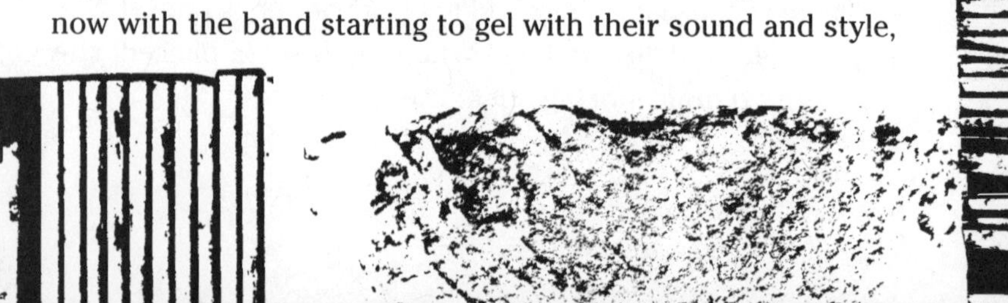

they practise more. When Squeaky's shift at the bakery ends, she usually hangs out at Freudian Slips. It's like a clubhouse, where girls meet up to share information, pass on the word.

The sports bar is exactly what Squeaky expects. The table of men beside them loudly hit on the waitress.

"Are YOU on the menu?"

She works her way through a bowl of peanuts. "Paula, this is a terrible place."

"I know, but check out that high definition!"

One of the drunken men squeezes between the tables and Squeaky bumps him by accident. "Hey," he says, "this one tried to grab my ass!"

Squeaky looks him up and down. "WHAT ass?"

When the game is over, Paula is belligerent. She squats outside the bar and pees on a random car. Then she and Squeaky take off on their bikes, chortling. At home, they smoke a joint and debate blueberry pancakes versus waffles for breakfast. If it rains tomorrow, they agree to stay in their pajamas, all day.

5B

Five Little Bitches

The back yard of Fanta's apartment building catches the last bit of sun. Feral cats roam the tangled underbrush. For the last few weeks the girls have been looking for a permanent jam space with no luck, and everyone's discouraged.

Regular rehearsals seem to be paying off. Squeaky's solid backbeat is a perfect complement to Fanta's simple but effective riffs and no-frills power chords. Kitty can slap a cool bass line on anything. They have a few covers and three originals they keep rearranging: "Bitches Don't Do Dishes," "GHB OD," and "2-Drink Drunk." There is a spirit of camaraderie and trust that makes it easy to share ideas. No one is afraid to be ridiculed or feel vulnerable. They can't afford to keep renting a room at Powder Keg, and don't want to lose their momentum. When Squeaky saw Tony King about another tattoo, he knew someone who might rent out the basement of her house for rehearsals. Now they are tense, waiting for the call.

Maxine reclines on a lounge chair, biting her nails, while Squeaky does bunny hops on her BMX. "Hey," Kitty says, "I think I just got my period. Does anyone have any cunt sticks?" Fanta winces and tosses her the apartment keys.

"Even if we have to stay at Powder Keg, it's not that bad," Squeaky says.

"It's not that bad if all you need are three-inch amp fuses and some downers," Maxine replies. "We've got to get *on* this. We can't even decide on a name!"

"Hey," Squeaky perks up, "what about The Mumps?"

Maxine shakes her head. "That's taken. How about Red-Headed Stepchild?"

"Red-haired people are *weird*," Squeaky teases. When Fanta hears this she curls her lip in a mock snarl. Everyone has noticed a change in her. She's even laughed at a fart joke or two.

"We should call ourselves Moose Knuckle," Maxine says.

"Who's we," Kitty jokes, "you got vag mites?"

"There's not much cachet to the term 'moose knuckle,'" Fanta replies dryly.

"I like The Gennies." Kitty wiggles her eyebrows. "As in someone touching *my* gennies."

Maxine adds, "Seven Days Red?"

"Those are all terrible. Not terribly funny."

"Okay then, Fanta, what would *you* name a band of four hot bitches who are tough—"

"With two *Fs*!"

"—intelligent, and fucking rock?"

Fanta is silent for a moment. "Wet Leather."

"Jeezus, that's actually pretty good."

Squeaky's phone rings and she moves toward the back of the yard. "Hello? Oh yes, Tony said you might call..."

"Here little puss-puss," Kitty chirps and chases another meowing cat into the bushes. "C'mere, you little fuck!"

Squeaky comes back and says, "Listen up...we got ourselves a new jam space."

"Hot damn."

"Hot *dog*!"

"Where is it?"

"It's not even that far from here. It's the last house on Punk Street." Squeaky looks at Maxine, "Apparently, the owner is an old friend of yours."

"Who is it?"

"Her name is Rosie. Rosie Stone."

During the walk over Maxine nervously prattles on. "Jeezus, I can't believe it's been, like, over a goddamn decade!" She pulls a mirror from her purse to recheck her appearance. "I've known Rosie since high school. We were best friends. I mean, we did everything together. We were roommates for *years*."

Squeaky asks, "So, what happened?"

"We were living together and worked at this club. She started dating our boss, Julian, and doing a bunch of shitty drugs. After she moved in with him, we had a big fight, and stopped being friends. No one's seen her in forever. I heard she got into porn. I heard she made a film under the name Madeleine Mudflaps! Can you imagine?"

"Who *cares*," Kitty says. "Everybody's gotta make money. If it's a good jam spot, let's take it."

"Don't get your hopes up. This could be a total gong show."

The address is an old two-storey house beside an empty lot. "Hey, I know this place," Squeaky says. "It used to be the Pointed George band house, and also the Curious Sticks. It's always been a rock 'n' roll halfway house!"

Fanta sighs. "At least they didn't tear it down and build a condo."

They clamber noisily up the driveway. Kitty bangs the knocker and moments later a tall, elegant woman opens the door. She wears a blue sundress and her caramel coloured hair cascades down her back. Maxine sees nothing of her former best friend. Rosie looks strong and healthy and serene.

"Maxine," she says. Neither moves for a moment. Then Rosie reaches out and they hug each other real tight.

"When Tony told me some girls wanted the basement for a practise spot, I honestly wasn't sure. But then I heard you were in the band, Maxine, and I was so surprised and pleased." They are sitting in the sparsely furnished living room after having been served drinks on a tray. It's too surreal for Maxine, who can't believe Rosie is serving her lemonade, right on a goddamn *tray.*

"I'm doing renovations, so it'll be noisy upstairs, but that shouldn't matter." Over the years the hardwood floors have splintered and the bathroom ceiling bulges plaster.

Maxine blurts, "What the hell? You do *renovations* now?"

"How much do you want for rent?" Kitty asks.

"How does a hundred per month sound?"

"That sounds pretty damn generous," Squeaky says.

"Well, Maxine's my oldest friend."

So much is changed in Rosie that Maxine is stunned into silence. She hasn't seen her since their final blowout, when Rosie was a drugged-out mess. Now she is poised, fit, seemingly untouched by their frenzied youth. Incredible, Maxine thinks. Rosie is the girl who gets everything.

"Old friends," she says without conviction. "We haven't spoken in ten years. This whole time you've been living here and we've never *once* seen each other? Unbelievable! How is that possible?"

"Well, I'm kind of a homebody."

"You used to be a real mess."

Her eyes flash and Maxine feels a flush of triumph, until Rosie answers in a quiet voice, "I'm not the same person I used to be, Maxine. A lot happened in those years I don't care to revisit."

Maxine can't wait for the story.

Rosie invites them to stay for dinner. The girls help in the kitchen except Maxine, who downs a glass of wine, then pours another and goes on the porch to smoke. Her mood darkens when she hears Rosie laughing. She grabs her purse and opens her compact to freshen up.

During dinner, Maxine, now in too much makeup, talks about her childhood. She is drunk and tells Rosie dramatically, "When I think how as a teenager you read my journal, I feel that is rape!" The room goes

silent. Someone at the end of the table giggles. She's pretty sure it's Kitty, who takes a drink. Everyone takes a bunch of drinks.

Maxine passes on dessert and complains about how fat she's become, despite her thin physique. When she leaves the table to use the bathroom, Rosie says, "Yes, I can see her ass really *exploded!*" Kitty howls. When Maxine comes out of the bathroom it's obvious she's heard. Her face is red and she starts talking again, too loud.

Franky Sparrow

Summer gently passes into fall. The pools shut down, trees change colour. Every Thursday and Sunday night the band meets to play music in Rosie's basement.

Though friendly with each other, Rosie and Maxine do not resume their former closeness. Too much time has passed; it's as if they once spoke a common language, now long forgotten. Squeaky gets along especially well with Rosie, and likes her calm, gentle energy. Sometimes after practise Squeaky prepares her a meal or whips up a quick snack. One night, riding home late from Rosie's, Squeaky sees a gig poster for Fire Chicken and decides life couldn't get any better. Her secret crush is back in town.

Franky Sparrow plays guitar in Fire Chicken, a local band with punk leanings and a heavy sound paired with whimsical lyrics. They enjoyed a modest hit with "6th Grade Thong." Fire Chicken's joker rock had thrived on the large independent label Skat Records for years. Back when Squeaky lived with Rocket in the band house, Franky Sparrow was among the revolving roommates. Franky made her laugh, and was the only bright spot during the last miserable months with Rocket.

Then Fire Chicken had gone to Austin to write and record their next album and, when Franky came back to town three months later, Squeaky and Rocket had broken up and she'd already moved out. Rocket soon left the band house too, and Franky Sparrow got two new guys to live there. Nerf was on welfare and stayed on the couch smoking his speed pipe. The other one worked on a road crew for the city and spent his free time locked in his room watching porn on his computer.

He wrote in giant black felt on his door, "STAY OUT OR I'LL PUNCH YOU IN THE FUCKIN' HEAD!"

Franky Sparrow had been a guitar tech and roadie for years before forming Fire Chicken. They hit the European circuit a couple of times every year, and had also toured Australia and Japan. It was fascinating for Squeaky to hear what life was really like on the road. When she went to pick up her mail, she always brought Franky Sparrow bread from the bakery and treats for his cat, Puddles.

One day she stopped by the old place to say hello and Nerf answered the door, looking upset. He was a small man with bad skin and prematurely grey hair dyed a sick shade of green. "Puddles got hit by a car."

"What? My god! Poor Franky."

"The guts were squashed all over the road," Nerf added.

"Does he want company?"

"You can try." Franky Sparrow looked like an unbalanced, buzzed-cut bruiser, but Squeaky knew he was a sensitive boy with good manners. She didn't find him menacing at all and knocked gently on his bedroom door.

From inside Franky rumbled, "WHHHHAAAAT?"

"It's Squeaky. I'm sorry about Puddles."

The door opened and Squeaky could tell he'd been crying. Franky sat down on the bed and described the thump and finding Puddles dead in the road. The car hadn't even stopped. "I'm gonna hunt that driver down and snap his neck," Franky threatened. "And then throw the body in the bushes. See how *he* likes it."

"Remember the time she chased that pit bull out of the yard?" They laughed and Franky recounted how once he'd caught Puddles in the garbage with a red beard and spaghetti sauce eyebrows. Then he put on some music and they stretched out on the bed.

After a while, Squeaky got a strange feeling in the bottom of her stomach. Unlike Rocket, Franky smelled like a man; aftershave and tobacco and sweat. She had a strong desire to pull off her pants and ride his face.

"I've got to go." She sprang from the bed and immediately regretted it. Franky gave her a long hug goodbye. She and Rocket were broken up but still fucking, and Franky and Rocket were friends. Squeaky considered herself to be loyal, but there was a heat in her belly the entire ride home.

It's Friday night and Fire Chicken is playing at The Sewer, one of the few places left in Vancouver for punk and metal bands to play. Squeaky drinks warm-up beers at home. She is wearing mascara and has even taken off her ball cap. Franky is on her mind—how much she likes his bad tattoos and long eyelashes and crooked teeth.

Squeaky taps her foot and checks the clock, waiting for Paula to get ready. Finally her roommate emerges from the bathroom. Her foray into grooming has produced a painful result; one eyebrow is tweezed smaller, and her hair is curled in flyaway brown bits. By the time they get to the bar, there is lipstick on Paula's teeth. The opening band has already finished, and Fire Chicken are about to play. Since the bar is packed, Squeaky stands on a table to see the stage.

When Franky comes out she gives a two-fingered whistle. Fire Chicken rips into each song with their distinct sound: rapid-fire bass and guitar; a thunder blast of drums; amusing verses sung through a brutalized larynx. Fans thrash at the front of the stage, slamming into each other, and exchanging jabs and bruises throughout the entire sonic overload. Squeaky pushes to the front for the encore, risking a few elbows to her face. Franky sees her and grins. When the show is over he jumps off the stage and gives her a sweat-covered hug.

"Squeaky! What's happening, little mama?"

"Hey, Franky. Just wanted to say hello. Great show." Everything out of her mouth seems idiotic.

"I gotta break down my gear, but stick around till I'm done, okay?" Squeaky beams and gets another beer before last call, then waits by herself as the lights come on. Paula has already left with some hammered fool with mouth foam.

Franky joins her at the bar. "So, Nerf got us evicted."

"How?"

"He found out that his ex-girlfriend cheated on him when they were going out and threw a two-by-four through her bedroom window." Franky takes a long swig of his beer. "So he split town and the rent didn't get paid. I'm homeless, but only for three weeks. The new album is almost mixed, and then we're back in Europe for a couple of months." Franky is on tour so much he doesn't keep a regular job, but sometimes works on a painting crew or clips weed when he's in town and needs cash.

"There's room at my place," Squeaky offers. "You can stay on the couch."

"Really?"

"It's a pretty big apartment. I've got a roommate but I'm sure it'll be okay. She has people over all the time." Paula once brought home a drunken boy who mistakenly tried to crawl into Squeaky's bed. She kicked him in the chest with both feet, propelling him into the hallway. Another time Squeaky went to the laundry room and found two street kids camped on a blanket. Paula had let them in, and it wasn't even raining.

"I might take you up on that offer. You won't even know I'm there," Franky promises. "Hey, do you still talk to Rocket?"

"Never. We don't hang out anymore." Squeaky tries to give him a meaningful look, but isn't sure he notices.

On Sunday night after practise, Squeaky rides her skateboard home from the bus stop and wishes Rosie's house wasn't across town. Franky Sparrow had phoned and will be sleeping on her couch for three weeks. She plans to make him a late dinner of cheesy macaroni with herbed biscuits and sweet butter. At the apartment she runs up the entire flight of stairs and rips off her sweaty shirt. Soon she is whisking cheese sauce at the stove.

She hears the *plink* of a beer cap hitting the kitchen window. Franky is standing on the sidewalk, and she comes down to help with his bags. "It looks way worse on the outside," she says, leading the way up the rickety staircase.

Franky comments on the comforting pumpkin colour of the living room walls. He's brought two six-packs, and Squeaky nervously takes a swallow of beer that spills onto her lap as he checks out the living room. A gigantic collage is spread on the floor, photos of models combined with penises, vegetables, army tanks, and balding white men.

"What IS all this?"

"That's my roommate's. It goes through the kitchen all the way to her bedroom and up the wall. Paula went to this expensive art school. This is what fifty-thousand dollars in tuition gets you."

Franky examines the collage between slurps of beer, a dubious look on his face. "Hmmmmm," he offers, non-committally.

"If you step on it, even by accident, she'll get hysterical. Take a look." They follow the collage as it continues on into a bedroom that has an odd, pungent odour of old food and sweaty feet.

"It smells in here," Franky sniffs, "like rotten grapefruit and old socks."

"More like KFC and semen."

They go back to the living room. Franky flops on the couch and drains his beer. "Where should I put this?" he asks, waving the can.

"Oh, anywhere near the overflowing garbage is fine."

"Where's your roommate now?"

"I'm not sure." She doesn't want to tell him they just had a dirty dish war, and that lately Paula has been slamming doors and cupboards, yet denies anything is wrong.

For the most part, Squeaky thinks of herself as an easy-going girl. Having grown up with brothers she finds the things Paula does, like waxing her legs and leaving fuzzy strips all over the bathroom, more puzzling than anything else. Paula's mood swings depend on which boys she currently likes, and their status is in constant flux. Efforts to get laid have resulted in forays into rock climbing, birdwatching, and now, extreme collaging.

The Filipino man in the apartment down the hall begins to shout at his wife. It happens a few times a week, and when the parents aren't home the old grandma screams at the kids. Squeaky puts dinner on the table and Franky wolfs his food like a man who hasn't been fed in days.

After dinner they crack the other six-pack and listen to music. She tells him what happened with Rocket. Franky says, "I dated a couple of girls who got jealous when the band went on the road. I'm not into the hassle anymore."

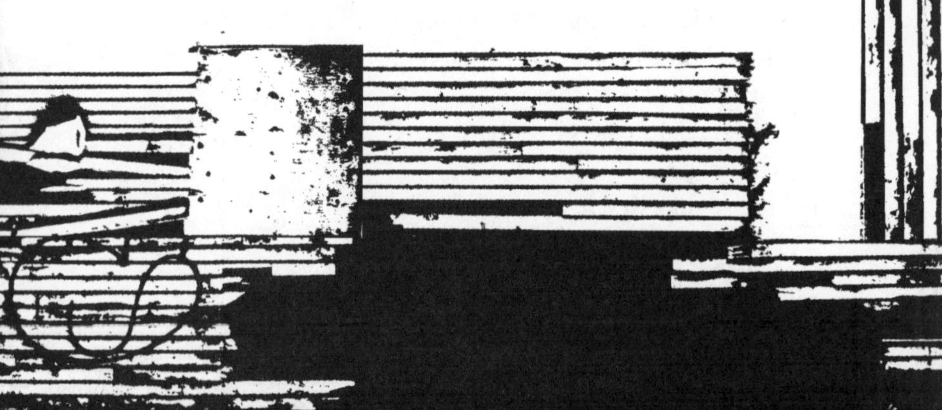

They are sitting cozy on the couch when Paula comes barrelling into the living room. Squeaky makes the introductions.

"Oh my god, I'm a huge fan," Paula gushes. "I love your song, y'know the one, 'Loved you for so long-long, since your 6th grade thong-thong!'" She begins to dance clumsily around the coffee table, shaking her ass. When she stops there is silence. Squeaky gets Franky a pillow and blanket. They say goodnight and go to bed.

Most mornings Franky is asleep when Squeaky leaves for the bakery, but sometimes he goes into the suburbs early to clip weed, folding his blanket neatly on the couch. He also does the dishes and takes out the garbage and once even cleaned out the tub after showering. From his clipping job he brings home weed, which makes Paula Grubler happy. Everyone likes this new arrangement. Franky turns Squeaky on to music she's never listened to before, like XTC and Mink DeVille and Durango 95.

Without a boyfriend, Squeaky enjoys having no one to answer to, or undermine her confidence, or take up her time with stuff she doesn't want to do. And yet, she has a massive crush on Franky Sparrow. They spend a lot of time hanging out and laughing, giving each other affectionate little pats and punches. She wonders if Franky doesn't like her a little bit, too.

Each morning Squeaky peeks in at Franky sleeping on the couch. She wants to curl up with him so badly it makes her cunt ache.

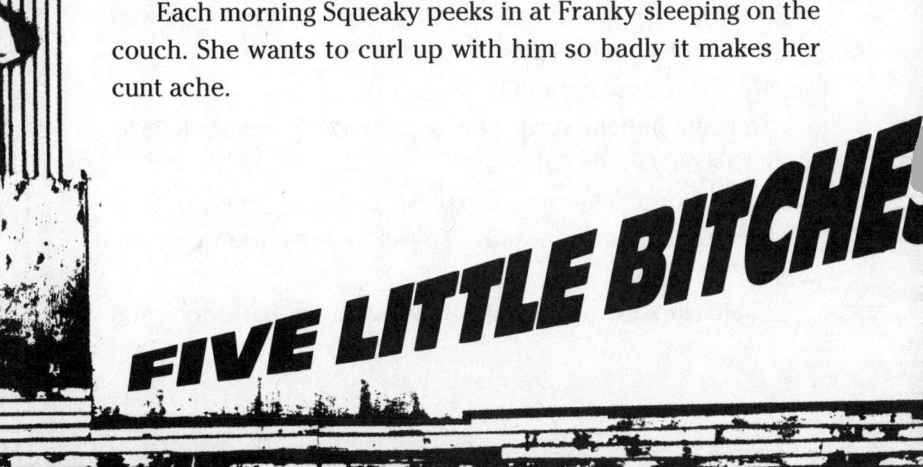

Hating Paula Grubler, PART 2

Squeaky messes up the timing on her ride cymbal yet again.

"I'm SORRY," she laughs. "My mind's not in it. Do you know what Franky said to me last night? He said I was a snot-nosed little bitch, and he wouldn't have it any other way!"

Everyone forgives her because they've never seen Squeaky act so earnest and cheesy before. It turns out Maxine knows Franky Sparrow from a fling years earlier with Tex, the singer of Fire Chicken. No one is surprised by this information. Maxine's been around.

The girls are jamming non-stop, and Wet Leather is beginning to show consistency. There is a growing understanding of the dynamics in their ensemble. Kitty and Squeaky lay the pavement for Fanta's chords to tasty leads. Maxine can hit the high notes—she has trouble holding them, but there is a wild enthusiasm that permeates the vocals. So far their lyrics are mostly about drinking and fucking.

Squeaky's phone rings. She looks at the screen then turns it off. "It's only Paula," she says.

Kitty says, "That she-beast isn't coming over, is she? Last time she came to practise she sat in the corner creepin' on me."

"Nah, she's giving herself a Brazilian in our bathroom. You

know, I always thought Paula had more interesting things to do than rip hot wax off her patch," Squeaky ponders.

"Grossies!"

"Are we set up for tonight?" Fanta asks. Rosie is going to bring her computer and a microphone to the basement and record their songs.

"Are you kidding?" Squeaky says, adjusting her wristbands. "Rosie's the most organized girl I've ever met."

"Yeah," Maxine says, "but she sure wasn't like that when *I* knew her." It bothers her how everyone has gotten close to Rosie except her. She plays with the microphone cord, lips pinched. "Hey, does anyone want to take a break and go to The Sewer for a drink?" It's the local bar where she often culls boys from the herd.

Kitty agrees. "Somebody buy me a whisky!" She has dark circles under her eyes. If there's a reason for not sleeping, she doesn't let on.

"I should call Paula," Squeaky says. "She was upset this afternoon when she found out Izzy didn't invite her to his birthday party." It's hard to convince her roommate it would be easier to get over Izzy if the two of them just stopped fucking. Squeaky remembers those nights with Rocket, how they clung together as the love drained out. "I guess I should invite her out, too."

Kitty snorts. "Sounds like someone has a case of the 'Guess-I-Shoulds.'"

"Well, she's been bummed out lately."

They've heard the story before. During drinks at The Sewer, Squeaky forgets all about that call.

They've been down in the basement for hours, playing the same three songs over and over. "Okay, one more time." Everyone looks at Fanta and groans.

"You don't think we can do a better version than that?" She is the one who encourages them to keep going when they lose the beat, pushes when they keep flubbing the same part in a song. They're recording off the floor with the levels set beforehand. Everyone agreed they wanted it live, instead of each laying down a separate track and having it assembled on the computer.

"Let's do 'Bitches,' again," Fanta says. "And Squeaky, slow it down this time."

"You're telling me to slow down? *You* start the song."

Rosie burns the disk and they race upstairs to the stereo. The sound is raw and loose, but there's an authentic grittiness. Everyone bobs excitedly, and when it's over they take it outside to crank in the van.

Back at home, Squeaky can barely contain herself when she plays Paula and Franky the rough recording of three songs: "Bitches Don't Do Dishes," "Cold-hearted Woman," and "Whatever, Trevor."

Franky says, "I'm impressed." It sounds like he means it and asks to hear the disk again. "The drums are fuckin' great."

"You really like our music? What would you say if you didn't?"

"Luckily I'm not in that predicament." Franky picks up his guitar and leaves the room. Squeaky can't stop smiling.

"I left you a message earlier," Paula accuses. "You didn't even call back."

"Oh, shit. I meant to phone you."

Paula sighs heavily. "I wish *I* was in your band." Squeaky gives a look across the kitchen table, her excitement dribbling away. *Here we go again*, she thinks, another tedious episode.

"Whaddya wanna do," she says, trying to curb her annoyance. "Be our backup singer? A go-go dancer?" For a moment she's afraid Paula will take her seriously. They both know she has a terrible singing voice. Right now there is a perfect balance of chemistry within the band, a familiar easiness and comfort. There is no room for Paula in Wet Leather, no space to be made. When they're in the middle of a song, everyone feeling the same groove, nothing they do is a mistake.

Squeaky changes the subject. "Hey, that song 'Whatever Trevor' is about this guy Rosie used to know who would only go down on her if he put a pair of rubber Spock ears on first. True story."

"I don't think Rosie likes me."

"No, she's just real cautious of new people. I think she went through some bad shit in the past. Rosie's a really generous person. She even put a mattress in one of the upstairs rooms if we want to crash out after practise." It had somehow become Kitty's personal space of crumpled gig flyers, dirty socks, picks and pennies scattered across the floor.

"Maxine doesn't like me. Neither does Kitty."

Squeaky finally loses her temper. "Jesus, Paula! With that attitude the real question is why anyone *would.*"

Paula sulks away and slams her bedroom door. Squeaky debates going to apologize, but she just wants to sit and enjoy her songs without any drama. Down the hallway Franky plays guitar in the living room and, as if following the Pied Piper, she heads that way.

The Indian summer is long gone, and everyone's tans have faded. The day after her argument with Paula, Squeaky helps Rosie bring in zucchini and squash from the garden. She's quiet as they work, with Paula still on her mind.

What she'd said last night was true—neither Maxine nor Kitty did like her very much. Maxine claimed to know a girl named Wanda who'd beaten up Paula Grubler in high school for blowing Wanda's boyfriend during the spring formal.

Squeaky doesn't want to go home and see Paula, but Franky is there and leaving next week on tour. After helping Rosie hang the new curtains Fanta sewed for the kitchen, there isn't anything left to do so Squeaky says goodbye and rides her skateboard to the bus stop. At home, instead of Franky, she finds Paula's door open and Paula moping on the bed. Squeaky is startled to see her wearing thick purple eye shadow and bright lipstick. "Wow," she says, stunned into forgetting they'd argued. "That's quite a look."

"I went to film the making of Izzy's graffiti mural. He doesn't care how supportive I've been of his urban beautification project." Paula's spirits are low because, despite the hard work with her video camera, he didn't want to come over and fuck her. She complains that it's Squeaky's turn to wash the floors and they have a petty squabble over the cable bill, then both go to their rooms and slam the door.

Someone is cropping out and Franky gets Squeaky a Saturday of clipping weed in the basement home of a suburban grow-op. She's worked for her brother Leon in the past during big orders when he couldn't find enough people to trim the bud. It's her day off and normally Squeaky hates to clip weed, hunched over a table covered in marijuana stalks, scissors stuck to her gloved hand. This time she jumps at the chance to spend a whole day in a basement with Franky Sparrow.

Over the course of hazy, gruelling hours, they ramble—about heroin, and the Vietnam War, raccoon attacks, dwarf porn, and their opinion of what it would feel like to be sucked into a black hole. In the back of a minivan on the ride home, she and Franky sit close together, stinking of marijuana leaf. His tour starts in just a few days, and he spends most of his time rehearsing with Fire Chicken. Soon she won't get to see him at all.

Paula's door is closed when they arrive home around midnight. In the living room they sink onto the couch together—it's a debatable hazard of the job that after many hours of clipping, excessive amounts of THC absorb through the skin.

"I'm ripped," Squeaky states matter-of-factly, "completely lit up."

"Me too."

"Thanks for bringing me to work, Franky." The lights are dim and they sit close. Squeaky gazes up at him.

"I'd do anything for you," he says. "You know that, right?" Then Franky puts his large hand on her shoulder and strokes her collarbone with his thumb, just once.

Something is understood between them.

The next evening Franky is off at practise. Paula slouches into the kitchen as Squeaky chops yams to go with the lamb chops and port au jus, French green beans, and chocolate mousse for dessert.

"Heya, Paula. How you doing?" She's in a great mood and plans to make Franky a dinner to remember.

"I'm okay." Paula looks tired and rubs her eyes. "I had a crappy day. People at work are jerks. And you guys kept me awake laughing last night."

"Sorry about that."

"I saw the two of you sleeping on the couch. Did you guys fuck?"

Her tone makes Squeaky glance over. "Uh…we just kind of rubbed up against each other and passed out."

"That's it?"

"It feels like we want to go further, but are afraid to ruin the friendship." Squeaky had crawled into her own bed in the early hours, horny and wrapped in her sheets, thinking about Franky lying on the couch while cursing her cowardice.

"Where's he now?"

"Practise." Squeaky begins to finely chop sweet onions. She's giddy and can't stop her feet from kicking.

Paula sits down heavily at the table. "So, you two really didn't do it?"

"I told you. We giggled on the couch in the dark for about three hours and fell asleep."

"Just fuck him."

"It's a timing thing. I've got this feeling that we'll get together *one* day."

"It's just sex. It's physical."

"Hey, ease up. It *isn't* just sex with Franky anymore. I really like him. I don't want to mess it up." Squeaky's voice begins to climb. "What's your problem with that?" When Paula says nothing, she turns on the stereo.

She's almost finished cooking when Andre calls. He has free tickets to a UFC fight and needs an emergency babysitter. His girlfriend is a rowdy redhead who used to strip under the name Brandy Snifter and has a toddler from a previous marriage. Squeaky knows they don't get out much, and though she wants to stay home and wait for Franky, she agrees to come over. It's only one train stop away, so she grabs her deck and skates to the station. When she gets to her brother's place, he's sporting full fan gear, waiting at the front door while his girlfriend hurries around the apartment.

"Thanks buddy," Andre says. "I owe ya." He looks at his watch and bellows, "Babe, let's GO!"

The girlfriend rushes back to the bathroom, waving a hairbrush. When they leave, Squeaky does the dishes and checks on the baby, then crashes out watching TV. Andre and

his girlfriend get home shit-faced in the middle of the night, so she decides to stay and sleep on the couch.

In the morning Squeaky wakes just as the traffic starts to rumble. It's barely light when she rides home, already feeling it's going to be a good day. She walks into the apartment and decides to peek at Franky on the couch. Maybe she'll go in and crawl on top of him. It makes her wet to think of it.

She opens the living room door, but Franky isn't on the couch. She surveys the room. There is a case for a movie called *Hardcore 84* on the coffee table and when Squeaky pushes play the screen shows a man fucking a large-breasted woman from behind. An empty tequila bottle sits on the coffee table. The couple on the TV groans. Squeaky wonders if Franky is out clipping weed, even though it's so early. Then she freezes. His sneakers are beside the door.

Her bedroom is empty and so is the bathroom. Squeaky goes down the hall and stands in front of Paula's door. She's heard that sound every day for three weeks—Franky Sparrow snoring.

Squeaky pushes open the door a crack. Franky is sprawled on the end of Paula's bed. He wears a T-shirt and socks, nothing else. Paula Grubler sleeps naked beside him, breathing with her mouth open. Her orange dildo lies in her gently curled palm. Squeaky goes back to the living room. On the TV, flesh slaps wetly. She walks out the front door and down the stairs on to the street. She looks up at Paula's bedroom window. The idea of Paula and Franky waking together makes her stomach burn.

In the empty lot, she finds the perfect rock. She stands on the sidewalk then arches her back and hurls it dead centre through Paula's window. The glass shatters. She's always had a good pitching arm.

The Last House on Punk Street

The last house on Punk Street was built by the husband of Mrs. Clara Thornton. She lived there fifty-two years before being moved into a complex for seniors where she promptly died. Mrs. Thornton's son was happy to unload the East Van eyesore at the bottom of a dead end lane. It had been a crash pad for different bands over the years. The first time Rosie Stone saw the house, she vowed to reclaim it from years of neglect.

Besides the holes in the walls and floor, a broken toilet downstairs, and an ancient furnace on the edge of collapse, the structure was solid. Coffered ceilings and wainscot panelling lent the dingy rooms an air of elegance from a bygone time. A curving wooden staircase wound to the second floor, and then a tiny set of stairs led to the attic. When the workmen left, Rosie rented a sander for the kitchen floor, mended the fence, and had the two rusted cars towed from the backyard.

At thirty-four, Rosie had begun to notice wrinkles at the corners of her mouth and the sides of her fingers. This did not make her afraid of aging, only more conscious that time was passing. She longed to have a garden and a yard, a comfortable chair on a porch.

So she'd cashed in her stocks and used her savings to pay the principal, negotiating a decent mortgage. The large bedroom on the second floor had its own ravaged balcony, and she chose this room for her suite. There were two small rooms on either side, and a rust-stained bathroom with a claw-footed tub. The main floor had a large living room, kitchen, another bedroom, and a back porch. Rosie found it quaint: the ancient gas stove, the scent of lemon oil on the hardwood floors, and that beautiful staircase which she spent a month refinishing. Out back, blackberries grew wild beside the fence.

At first, the extra space made her uneasy, and she was relieved when Wet Leather began to practise there. Though she wanted to forget her old life and the person she used to be, Maxine is there to remind her. Rosie thinks it might be a good thing. Her world seems much bigger now.

The girls help her with odd jobs: painting baseboards, pulling weeds, ripping up old carpet. Sometimes she and Maxine finish each other's sentences, and then are overly polite and cautious of each other. But Rosie looks forward to practise nights and seeing the girls. She has a glass of wine or two with them, never more. Fanta brings her design books and records. She enjoys hearing recaps of Kitty Domingo's absurd antics, and adores Squeaky, who, for Rosie's birthday, baked an elaborate devil's food cake with whipped cream and chocolate icing.

When Rosie opens the front door and sees Squeaky after finding Franky and Paula Grubler together, her small hands twisting and mouth trembling, Rosie invites her to move in on the spot. Squeaky breaks down in grateful tears. For dinner, Rosie simmers mussels in apple cider vinegar and cilantro, a meal for Squeaky's broken heart. From that night on, it never feels like an empty house again.

Andre comes over a few days later and insulates the attic room for Squeaky. They put in a closet and paint the slanted walls. She refuses to go home until Franky Sparrow leaves on tour. She is too miserable to eat. A broken record in her head won't switch off: it's over with Franky before it even started. And Paula—it hurts worse to think about her.

One morning there is a note from Paula in the mailbox. "Dear Squeaky," it begins, "I know you must be feeling emotions. Some of these emotions might be anger, fear, hurt, and embarrassment. These feelings are like a bag of bricks. You need to put it down or one day you will trip…" Squeaky stops reading and rips up the rest. Paula has a penchant for speaking in lame psychobabble. She calls the furniture warehouse and asks, "Is Paula in today?"

"Yes, just a moment." Squeaky hangs up.

The October afternoon is cloudy. Fanta drives her van, and the girls go to work on the apartment. Squeaky sees that Franky Sparrow's things are gone and the window has been replaced. They pack up the kitchen and move the bed and TV. Squeaky takes the stereo and coffee table, too. It gives her a grim satisfaction to see the apartment bare.

The girls finish moving Squeaky upstairs and have just sat down when the house phone rings. Rosie answers. "Hello? Who's calling please?" She looks at Squeaky with her hand over the receiver and whispers, "It's Paula."

When Squeaky shakes her head, Maxine grabs the phone. "She doesn't want to talk to you. Don't call here again, skank. No, you heard me. *Skank*!" Maxine puts the phone down with disbelief. "That bitch just hung up on me!" Then she sees the look on Squeaky's face.

Fanta unfolds the newspaper and sits down at the large round table. A pot of oil for popcorn sizzles on the stove. Rosie has rented a lowbrow comedy she hopes can cheer up her friend.

Squeaky pushes up her sleeves and begins washing dishes. "Hey," she says. "I can't tell Franky who to be with."

"She's not too loyal, is she? The number one rule between girls is thou shalt not fuck your friend's boyfriend," Maxine states. "Or ex-boyfriend."

"And especially not the guy your friend likes," Kitty adds. "What a dog dick!"

"Not a woman down for the cause," sniffs Maxine.

Squeaky hopes it won't be a whole night of discussing her

ex-friend. Besides hoping Paula's skull cracked open from the rock, Squeaky really doesn't wish her any harm. She simply wants to push a giant red button that will evaporate Franky and Paula from her memory.

"You've been talking about Franky Sparrow non-stop for weeks." Maxine's speech is punctuated by popping corn. "Him and Paula getting together seems pretty…slimy."

"I liked him, and he didn't like me. He likes *Paula*."

"As if," Kitty interrupts. "She's got a big fat beaver."

"It might be something he regrets," Rosie says softly. "We've all made mistakes."

"I'll bet she has a smelly PUSS!"

Squeaky says, "Okay, guys."

"…turd gurgler…" Kitty mumbles, putting a cigarette in her mouth. "…scummy little shit…"

"Maybe we should watch the movie," Rosie interjects.

"…human gag reflex…"

"He's an asshole," Maxine says. "And she's a cunt. They're not that far apart."

Squeaky looks at the ceiling and then bellows, "ENOUGH!" The room goes quiet in a heartbeat. She continues rinsing dishes. "Sorry," she mutters, "I just don't want to think about it anymore."

Fanta rattles the newspaper and changes the subject. "Hey, listen to this personal ad. 'I met you last Wednesday on the waterfront. You gave me a bite of your pork bun. I liked your beard. Let's meet.'"

Kitty is confused. "Is that some kind of code?"

"Personal ads are the last bastion of the disconnected and over-horny."

"Fanta, if you had to write a personal ad, what would it say?"

"I'd go with something simple like, 'Coffee? Cocktails? Anal?'"

The girls roar with laughter, but Squeaky doesn't smile. She stands at the sink washing dish after dish after dish.

ROSIE STONE

Mornings in the house are a ragtag jumble. Squeaky and Kitty thump downstairs to the kitchen where Rosie is making fresh orange juice. She wears denim overalls with tennis shoes and a men's cotton shirt. "Good morning, ladies."

"Good mor-ning, Ros-ie," the girls reply in schoolyard unison.

"You two have any plans for the day?"

"Nope."

"Nah," Squeaky shrugs, "how about you?"

"Attacking the wild rhubarb." Rosie pulls on a pair of gloves with such determination it makes them laugh.

She recently cut inches off her long caramel locks and dyed her hair dark brown. It makes her cheekbones stand out more and her eyes seem even bigger. Rosie hides her perfect tits and high round ass in oversized shirts, never leaves the house without sunglasses or a hat shielding her face. Rosie is a beautiful girl who doesn't like being noticed. She detests nightclubs and bars. They once dragged her to karaoke, but when they signed her up for a song, she was mortified for days.

"It's Tony King's birthday," Rosie adds. "I'm making him a special dinner tonight."

"Ooh," Kitty says, "as in 'special sauce'?"

"Rest assured, I don't want to know what that means. Will you gals be around for dinner tonight?"

"We're going out, right Kitty?"

"No we aren't. I'm totally broke and—*Ouch*. Why did you just kick me? OH. Yeah, yeah, right," Kitty grins. "No, we're definitely going out tonight."

"Don't feel like you need to stay away."

"It's no problem," Squeaky assures her.

"What's up with you and Tony?" Kitty takes a bite of toast and chews with her mouth open. "You guys make fuck or what?"

"He's just a friend," Rosie answers. "We were neighbours for years. The only reason I have the job at King City is because of him." She tells them how, after once admiring Tony's full sleeves, he gave her a tattoo on her arm with no ink so she knew how it felt.

Kitty persists. "You really don't like this guy? Haven't you noticed his massive boner for you?"

"Yeah, he obviously really likes you."

Rosie removes her gloves and leans against the counter. She looks uncomfortable. "Maybe you already know…well, I figured Maxine told you a few things about my past."

"She kinda mentioned some stuff," Squeaky admits vaguely.

"I'll sum it up: I was young and stupid, dating a rich loser, and basically a drug addict. In that situation, doing fucked up things seems natural. We made some porn, like every couple does. Only my ex sold ours and started a production company. I was so out of it I signed all my rights away."

"That's horrible."

"Well, I did sue him. The settlement paid for most of this place."

"Right on," Kitty jokes, "it's the house that fuck built!"

"So, my point is that I'm not looking for a man anytime soon." Rosie pulls her gloves back on and heads to the garden.

Her reluctant career in film began during her last year with Julian. After Maxine ended their friendship, everything spiralled. Rosie got into a routine of coke to go up and pills to come down, on a steady diet of booze. Julian didn't seem to mind, as long as she kept him entertained. Mostly this meant watching her have sex. They trolled the Internet and she invited men home where Julian had installed several peepholes and a hidden camera. But he was a libertine with escalating demands. Soon he wanted to be in the same room, jerking off. Weekends turned into drug-fuelled fuck parties, mostly with his friends who were heavily into crystal meth and GHB. There always seemed to be a camera rolling. If she balked, or didn't show a believable amount of enthusiasm, Julian withheld his attention, money, and more importantly, drugs. He knew eventually she would do what he wanted. They lived in a glass penthouse downtown, surrounded by people, and she always felt alone.

Things came to an abrupt end on Julian's fortieth birthday. He rented out the Vancouver rugby club for the evening, and wanted a live sex show. Rosie found herself doing coke in the locker room with a group of men.

She counted them: seven. Tonight he expected real bang for his buck. The locker room smelled like she remembered from high school: urine, sweat, and fungus. She gulped down a salty cap of GHB and immediately did another line.

"I'm gonna have a shower," someone said. "Anyone care to join me?" But he only looked at Rosie.

A few days after the party, Julian broke up with her. He hadn't been around much, but she was so stoned on pills that she barely noticed. Having never been dumped before, it made sense to be presented with a large settlement cheque. Always the businessman, Julian had a pen and contract ready by the time the doorman came to pick up her bags. Standing at the front door, in a miserable state of withdrawal, Rosie signed the papers. She'd been distracted by all the zeroes.

At first it was difficult for Rosie in her own apartment. She didn't know how to change a fuse or light the gas stove or how much it cost to take the bus. There were no friends to call, and she considered reaching out to Maxine, but too much time had passed. Elsa was living in a villa somewhere in Italy. She hadn't seen much of her mother in years.

Rosie developed a routine. She slept late in the mornings and then walked down to the corner for the newspaper. In the afternoons she went to a matinee or read library books. If someone commented that she looked familiar, it set her heart racing. The film from Julian's birthday, *Madeleine Mudflaps*, became a bestseller for Vixen, Inc. She went blocks out of her way to avoid people or places she knew. It was preferable to stay home and have things delivered. Slowly she felt like a ghost in her hometown.

Tony King lived in the apartment above her. The first time they'd met was when his sink overflowed and she had to pound on his door in her pajamas. He was always friendly, chatting on the staircase when he passed, and once in a while they borrowed items from each other: coffee filters, a plunger, the laundry key. She was grateful for human contact besides the landlord and mailman. Tony brought her cupcakes for her birthday, and soon they shared an occasional meal. He had a face as ugly as a Halloween mask and Rosie made it clear they would not be dating. It had nothing to do with his looks. She'd had boyfriends all her life and didn't think she needed another one.

In grade school, little boys had given Rosie unwanted kisses between the two trees in the playground they all used as a pretend prison. They'd left presents in her desk, pink-jewelled earrings and bracelets that turned her wrist green. At school dances they'd slobbered across her neck during slow songs. Men would whistle and make propositions from car windows. They'd leer if she crossed the street or crossed a room. It was a relief to have Maxine at her side, Maxine who never did anything quietly. What Maxine lacked in finesse she made up for with volume and style. Rosie had learned more from her than anyone.

Rosie began to visit Tony on her walks. It surprised and relieved her that none of the guys at the tattoo shop knew about her porn career. She didn't mind going to the store when they needed cigarettes or coffee or chewing gum. Her Spartan lifestyle didn't take much to maintain, but she liked the company and accepted the job to answer the phone and book appointments a few days a week.

Tony had a lot of loyal customers who sat hours for him. They liked his artwork and he was popular at King City. He watched out for Rosie from afar. None of the guys in the shop were allowed to mention her fuck films. Word on the street grew that anyone who messed with her was dead meat.

Tonight Rosie plans to make a simple roast chicken and potatoes. When Tony knocks on the door, she lets him in. She notices he's wearing a new shirt. He looks tired and kisses her on the cheek.

"Long day at the shop?"

"Yeah, sorry I'm late. I had to finish a cover-up on a guy who had a tattoo of a Hershey's Kiss with his wife's name on it."

"That sounds romantic."

"Not really. It looked like a big turd with a name tag on it."

She laughs. "Go sit and relax." Tony is thrilled with the presents she has for him: an engraved flask and video game he wanted.

They sit and catch up. "There's a lot more stuff here now," he says, looking around. "You really got a full house. How's it working out with Squeaky living here?"

"It's pretty smooth. Kitty crashes pretty much full-time too."

"*That* one's a handful," Tony whistles.

Rosie works away on the cutting board. Kitty does leave her crap all over and treats the house like it's her personal party pad. She's their wild little sister, and gets away with a lot.

"I just admire the way those girls bulldoze into any room, no matter what the scene. They don't care what anybody thinks. It must be nice to have that kind of freedom." She glances over at Tony. He knows about her past and Julian, but swore he'd never seen her films. It's occurred to her before that it might not be true. There doesn't seem a right way to ask this, so she keeps chopping carrots.

He goes into the living room and when it's quiet for too long, she finds Tony asleep on the couch. He's barefoot, in jeans, with his black bandana pulled low over his eyes. She sits on the edge of the cushion and touches his rough-looking hands. Since moving out of the apartment and only seeing him at work, she misses him.

Tony opens his eyes as she straddles him. Her tongue is cool in his mouth as they kiss. When she pulls away, he pulls her back, trembling.

After they fuck for the second time and eat the burnt chicken, they lay together in drowsy contentment. "I've loved you from the first time we met," Tony says. Now he's pretty sure his heart is gone for good.

Franky Sparrow Returns

The harder the rain fell that winter, the easier the music came.

They play loud and fast on those short, dark nights. In Squeaky's attic room the cold outside doesn't matter. Time has not eased her feeling of betrayal or the sick feeling in her gut every time she thinks of Franky or Paula.

Squeaky sometimes reads Paula Grubler's horoscope to monitor her movements. Every rumour she hears fascinates and appalls her. There are snippets here and there: Paula puked behind a tree at a Christmas fundraiser; she'd gained a ton of weight; she'd shit on someone's front lawn at a party. Every day, no matter where Squeaky is, Paula Grubler gets on her nerves.

In the middle of a frozen January evening, Maxine comes over to the house in tears, throwing herself across the couch.

"The pipes in my apartment burst again. And my landlord's cat got into my room and clawed my favourite pair of leather boots! Bwah-waaaah!"

"Your apartment flooded last month too," Rosie says, marking the spot in her book.

"I know! I need a new place to live," she bawls. "My boots are ruined. BWAH!"

For most of her adult life, Maxine had lived in one shitty apartment after another. This one was particularly bad. Every week she brought a new complaint of smelly hallways or silverfish.

"I HATE looking for a new place to live."

"Me, too," Rosie commiserates, and goes back to her book.

Maxine is jealous that Squeaky and Kitty moved in. She hates feeling left out. Not to mention, if she lived there the band could practise even more often. They're getting good—Maxine knows it. They could really *go* somewhere.

She sits up and wipes her eyes. "I could stay *here.*"

"Oh?"

"There's more than enough room. And half the band is here already."

Rosie thinks uneasily of the years she lived with Maxine: the shit-show parade of boys, diseases, poverty, excessive drugs, and numbness. They'd been reckless, with an easy habit of finding trouble. Rosie doesn't want to go back to the way things were before. She'd been the supplier, the one who took Maxine along to dinners and outings she'd never be able to afford. But the issue was never money. It was that Maxine believed she'd been entitled to what everyone else had, and more.

"Okay," Rosie hesitates. "Let's give it a try."

The next morning they load Fanta's van with Maxine's red velvet chair and opium bed. She takes the small room on the main floor beside the kitchen, adding details of white fun fur and leopard print, even hanging up a disco ball. Then she decides to christen her new bedroom. The girls are sitting at the kitchen table and can hear her flirting over the phone.

"You gotta come and check it out. It's the Maxi Pad. My mom's asleep. Wanna come over and make out?"

"Dude, get some new pickup lines," Kitty scoffs, piling more pasta onto her plate. "You realize we're going to have to soundproof that room, right?"

With the newest addition of Maxine and her belongings, the house seems glutted with shoes and CDs and bath towels and a general, lived-in mess. There is foot traffic all day, with gossip, laughter, and complaints. They are always together: preparing elaborate dinners, crammed into the living room for movie nights, throwing birthday parties. Outside the house the girls move in a protective pack. Their term of affection or encouragement is an enthusiastic “You fuckin’ little *bitch*!”

It’s a week after Valentine’s Day. Franky Sparrow stands on the porch at the last house on Punk Street. The sound of loud music shakes the windows. Rosie opens the door when he knocks. “Can I help you?”

“I’m Franky Sparrow. I heard Squeaky lives here. Is this her band? They’re great.”

Music blares from the basement:

“WE ARE COMING TO YOUR TOWN
TO DRINK YOUR BEER AND PARTY DOWN
INVASION! INVASION! INVASION!”

Franky asks, “Can I go check them out?” Rosie hesitates, then opens the door wider. When he lumbers down the basement stairs the girls trail off. Everyone looks at Squeaky.

“Hi Franky,” she says, striving for nonchalance. She puts the sticks down, but doesn’t move from her throne behind the drum kit. Seeing Franky makes her nervous, and the sick feeling in her stomach returns. Maxine scowls and Fanta gives a neutral nod. Kitty goes for a beer from the mini fridge.

“I just stopped by to say hello. Do you guys mind if I sit and listen to another song?” They all turn to Squeaky again.

She shrugs. “I don’t care, as long as it’s cool with everybody else.” Franky settles onto a milk crate.

“This is a song about a guy,” Maxine announces. “It’s a little something we bitches wrote called ‘Whatever, Trevor.’” Clutching the mic stand with both hands she looks back at Squeaky and counts off by stamping her foot. “Let’s go…1 and 2 and 1-2-3-4!” Franky watches Squeaky pound the toms in an explosive flurry, staring at a space above his head:

Whatever, Trevor!

“As soon as you left
My life got better
Now you want me back?
Here’s a building, take a header
(boom-boom-boom-boom)
Whatever, Trevor!

You could get it up
But never went down
Your breath smells like a sewer
in the worst part of town
(boom-boom-boom-boom)
Whatever, Trevor!”

During the bridge, the heavy bass riffs turn into funk and the tempo playfully slows into a soulful groove. Franky is surprised at how good Wet Leather have become in the past six months. They play a unique, stripped down meat-and-potatoes rock, with killer hooks and catchy melodies. Fanta’s lead on the song blows him away. He asks how many more songs they have.

“Five more originals,” Maxine says. “And they’re *all* good ones.”

Squeaky says, “Come back when there’s a second show.”

“You should record a demo. Shop it around. I’ll bet you chicks get signed.”

Maxine wears dog tags, shredded zebra leggings, and an army jacket, with purple boots. With her dark lipstick and white-bleached hair it’s a formidable look. She puts her hands on her hips. “Chicks?”

“Oh, sorry. I mean *ladies*.”

Kitty pipes up, “*I* sure as fuck ain’t no lady!”

Squeaky tries to bring the conversation back around. "Yeah, I think we're ready to record something."

"Studio time costs money," Fanta counters, "which we don't have."

"Yeah, even at a dump like Powder Keg. It's always about money and we're broke-ass."

Maxine rants, "BULLSHIT! Fuck money. Rock 'n' roll is my church. It's my salvation!" Everyone is impressed by her outburst.

"If you guys get a few more songs together, you can open up for Fire Chicken the next time we play here."

"Yeah, sure." No one believes him. Squeaky walks Franky Sparrow up the stairs to the front door. "How long have you been back in town?"

"About a week. I'm staying with Nerf."

"Oh yeah? Seen Paula much?"

"I haven't seen her since I left town. Squeaky, I'm going to be totally honest with you. I didn't fuck Paula. I have *never* wanted to fuck Paula. That night you stayed out, I came home shit-faced and walked in on her in the living room watching porn. Getting busy with her dildo, y'know? Then she had my pants down and gave me a blowjob. That's it."

"That's *it*," Squeaky says. "Hmm."

"There was never any attraction there. I was fucked up and passed out in her room."

Squeaky is glad he doesn't mention the broken window. She opens the door and looks out to the road. The streets are thinly covered in snow, a cold rain beginning to fall.

"Who cares," she shrugs. "*I* sure don't."

She hopes it sounds light, but it didn't come out that way at all. The look on his face makes her stomach sink.

"I'm impressed by your trash drumming," Franky says, walking down the porch stairs. "You hit really hard. For a girl."

"I hit hard for anyone."

She slams the door loudly to prove it.

Good Kitty Gone Bad

Kitty Domingo doesn't like to be alone. Her earliest memories are of the commune, surrounded by broken people who dropped out of the world, women who shaved their heads and changed their names to things like Starlight and Aurora Celeste. Artists impress Kitty. She thinks it takes guts to write. It takes guts to spend your days alone in a studio, sculpting a hunk of clay, or practising an instrument for hours. Heroin had given her that kind of confidence, to talk to strangers or sing on the street. She feels a kinship with cripples, especially musicians. Kitty Domingo has seen the worst of many things, which is why she ends up with Myron Belleveaux.

Myron became fat after beating a decade-long crystal meth addiction. Now his only pleasure comes from walking his two pit bulls or having the occasional crack hoot in the bathtub. He plays drums, guitar, and saxophone and is the replacement singer for a resurrected punk band whose lead singer overdosed years earlier. Myron is always out trying to flog his band. Through what means Kitty doesn't know, he keeps his filthy blond hair in stupid-looking spikes, and his two pit bulls live in his car so he always smells faintly of dog shit.

Kitty is at punk rock karaoke one night, stealing drinks and engaging in escalating warfare. Myron is one of the few people able to handle her combative state. When the bar closes he lures her to his place with a bottle of lemon gin. Myron has a tiny dick. She lets him put it in her ass because she knows it won't hurt.

In the morning, Kitty wakes up and barfs from her hangover. Then she lies on Myron's couch and watches rock videos. Kitty has no feelings for Myron and steals his cigarettes when he leaves the room. He asks if he can see her again. Kitty says no, offended. She has a boyfriend, after all.

Spring begins to creep in. It's late morning and Maxine uncurls from one of the large chairs on the back porch and stretches to put her feet on the railing. The streets move fast in the distance, but the garden is warm and quiet. Birds chirp from somewhere deep inside the gathering of leaves. The feral cat that lives in the lot next door gave birth to three mewling kittens under the porch. In the upstairs bathroom the shower runs. Yesterday Kitty got the results of her pregnancy test. It's more upsetting this time, since it will be her second abortion.

Kitty shuts the water off and joins Maxine on the porch, wet hair dripping. "You worried us when you didn't come home yesterday."

Kitty had tumbled in sometime during the early hours. She pulls up her too-big jeans that are obviously not from her closet. "I went to see my mom. And then I fucked my boyfriend. Figured I'd get in a few free ones."

"Which boyfriend is that?" Kitty is back with Jasper Sparks, but gives a coy shrug. Maxine has to laugh.

Then Kitty sinks down in a chair. Her cute nose, baby-blue eyes and wide smile belie her unhappiness. She can go easily from euphoria to inflamed violence to cavernous depression. "I can't fucking believe I'm pregnant. Again," she adds darkly. "It's next Thursday, and there better not be any of those Christian pro-life ass-heads out front. Or I'll clear a fucking path right through the middle of 'em." She smacks her palm with a fist for emphasis.

"Have you ever noticed how most of those people are too old to have kids or even take care of one?"

"Or else they're a bunch of stupid dudes who don't have a fucking clue!"

Kitty's mood swings again and her blue eyes fill with tears, startling Maxine. "*IS* this wrong?" She thinks of how Myron Belleveaux smells like dogshit, his gnawed fingernails and lack of hygiene. "No. I refuse to be tied to some loser for the rest of my life! Goddamn little fuck trophies." She stands up. "I'm going to the beer store. Wanna get drunk with me?"

"I have to work."

"Quit your job!"

When Kitty leaves, Maxine calls Squeaky at the bakery and fills her in. "Do you think she's really okay?"

"Sure. I've known her a long time. Kitty's a tough one."

"Her mother's taking her to the clinic. What's her name? Jasmine?"

"Jewel," Squeaky corrects. "She's a nurse, it'll be fine. Hey, if Kitty wants to get fucked up because she's pregnant, I can't blame her. She's been through a lot." Kitty will tell anyone about shooting heroin and living on the streets, and then the years it took to get clean.

When she isn't playing music, Kitty seems lost. She hates being alone and makes a boy follow wherever she goes.

It's early in the afternoon when Kitty returns, considerably drunk, with a full forty of malt liquor. Maxine is in the same spot on the back porch, having put off going to the store to unpack boxes.

Kitty uncaps the beer. She has a peculiar look on her face. "Where the fuck *is* everyone?"

"Rosie stayed at Tony's last night. She's probably at King City. Squeaky's working until three. There's a shipment in from Toronto at Freudian Slips. I have to go help Fanta... eventually." Maxine tilts back to face the sun. It feels too good to move. She opens her eyes to look at Kitty. "Did you tell the father?" Then she closes her eyes again.

"Jasper is the father," Kitty says, but isn't as confident as she sounds because of the night with Myron. She is pretty sure they didn't use a condom.

"What was his reaction?"

"Who *gives* a fuck?"

Maxine doesn't know what to say. None of them are unbiased. Sometimes she wondered if growing up without a father had warped her ability to trust men. Even Fanta, who was so pragmatic, had never dealt with the pain of Harold Dixon. They are hard, scarred women, unable to survive the world otherwise. Maxine has seen the devastating wake of a broken heart. Love affairs were good for two songs, one in the beginning and one at the end. But still, it pains her to see a young girl so disillusioned.

Kitty turns somber. "The last one wasn't a big deal." She chugs more beer and belches. "Like the worst nightmare rag cramps ever."

"We know how bad *those* can get."

"But I wanted painkillers and the doctors wouldn't give me anything 'cause I used to do heroin. Now they've got a pill you just take home and shove up your cooch. My friend bled for like, three weeks."

"I had an abortion when I was fifteen. It's just a clump of cells right now, like a sea monkey. Half the size of your pinky nail."

"Did you feel guilty after? Did you…you know, regret it?"

"No. Just relief it was out of my body."

They sit for a while and say nothing. Finally Maxine breaks the silence. "Well, I've got to unpack boxes. But I'll come back as soon as I'm done." They both know Kitty has a hard time being alone. "Are you going to be okay?"

"Sure," Kitty answers with doubt.

When Squeaky gets home later that day, Kitty has passed out upright on the couch. She pokes her with one finger, delighted. Kitty wakes up at the clunk of a bottle hitting the coffee table. Squeaky asks, "Have you met my friend, *Jacques Daniel*?"

"OH MY GOD, YOU'RE HOME, I LOVE YOU! I could only find coolers in the fridge. Goddamn bitch pops!"

"I heard the news from Maxine. How are you doing?"

Kitty considers. "Gettin' fucked up. Wanna get some coke?"

"Well, I guess we know whether you're keeping the baby or not."

"You got any money? Make the call."

"Yeah, that's what you need right before an abortion. A distracting ego trip."

Kitty's eyes narrow. "What the fuck do you mean by *that*?"

"I mean, just from a health point of view, is it a good idea? Remember the last one? You got really sick afterwards."

"FUCK THAT! It's gone next Thursday!"

Kitty puts on Slayer, "South of Heaven." It's her favourite song.

By six o'clock in the evening Kitty is completely ginched. "Daaaaaddddyeee," she says in a baby voice, "can I pwease have some more rye?"

"You're so twisted it's almost a style point." Squeaky laughs, mixing drinks in the kitchen.

Maxine comes home and right away dives into the gram of coke. She cuts a line and snorts it loudly. Kitty does another then bellows, "This shit is prime time!" She picks up her bass, shouting for everyone to listen. Maxine bounces up and down on the lumpy couch.

"This cocaine is too speedy," Maxine jabbers. "Do you guys think so? Cuz I do. Oh my god, I really do. It's gonna kill me to come down. Coke makes me want to poop…forever!"

“Coke and GHB is a way better combo. But I’ve seen people do shit like hump footstools in the middle of a party in a G-hole. Damn, not only is this brat sucking my resources, it’s making me horny.”

“You heartless bitch,” Maxine says, smiling widely. “You’re delirious.”

Squeaky fires up the bong. “Are we going out tonight?”

“Yeah,” Kitty says. “You’re buying.”

After more drinks, Kitty becomes maudlin, then annoyed. “You know, I should’ve just stuck with the big purple stick.”

“Huh?”

“My vibrator,” she says. “What, did you think I put a tree branch up my vagina?”

“Jesus, Kitty! I’m trying to finish my mashed potatoes.”

They stop talking when they hear a key in the front door. Rosie walks in, and surveys the room with obvious chagrin.

“You’re finally home,” Kitty says. “Want a line?”

Rosie perches on the arm of the couch. “No,” she says. “I can’t. It will put me in a very bad place.”

“Ah-ha-HAH!”

Squeaky winces. “Kitty, she’s serious.”

“Oh. Sorry.”

Everyone watches Rosie, who looks unhappily at Kitty. “Honey, you do what you need to. I understand. I really do. But I’ll be staying at Tony’s.” She says goodbye and they feel even worse when she tells them, “By the way, I found another condom in the washing machine.”

When the door shuts, Maxine carves another line. “It’s so weird. In the old days it was Rosie who had the drugs. And trust me, *she* always wanted more. Now she’s got one gigantic stick up her ass.” Rosie goes to bed at a reasonable hour. She gardens and subscribes to *International Air* magazine, stays on top of who buys and sells mineral rights. She actually finds these things interesting.

"Yeah, what a snob," Squeaky says testily. "Who *wouldn't* want to sit and grind their teeth with you all night?"

A cab drops them off near the dingy bar. Two young men smoke out front. The smell of stale beer wafts into the street. "Hey ladies," one says. He has a skinny mustache and wears a tracksuit. "Come in and have a drink."

His pimpled friend catches Squeaky's eye and she looks away. "Bitch," he mutters.

"Fuck off, you little puke," Kitty snarls.

People rudely push past. Kitty is cynical on the street, but when bums talk to her she's always a little bit sweet. A toothless man in a doorway cackles, "I like my women like my toast—with a crusty bottom!"

In the bar Squeaky buys a shot of Frangelico for Kitty, who downs it and gags, "That shit tastes like monkey jizz!"

"I'm trying to expand your tastes."

"Shut up and gimme more of those mud drugs!"

Kitty Domingo is a hit with the boys all night. "Buy me some tequila," she demands. It brings out her fiendish side. She drops a lit cigarette into someone's hoodie and watches it smoke across the room. Kitty crackles with intensity and they can't stay away. Boys love girls like her on the downward spiral. There's no other ride quite like it.

They squeeze in at a table and check out a couple across the room. The man whispers to his Asian girlfriend who cries openly. Maxine says, "Look, he's breaking up with her!"

Squeaky goes to eavesdrop. When she comes back she says, "Nope, they're in love and she's leaving the country."

"Fuck," Maxine says. "That never even *occurred* to me."

"I wanna see Jasper," Kitty demands with drunken rancour. "Lesh go meet him. This party is over except for the hippies dancing." They try to talk her out of it. Kitty insists she'll go alone, so they call a cab. Some guy hits on her as she stands outside smoking. "You want me?" Kitty screams. "I'm BLIND! I'm not even fucking here!"

The next day's hangover is a bad one. Kitty opens her eyes and pieces of memory drift in on painful clouds of shame: lurching through the crowd at a crazy angle before wiping out the bouncer; throwing wine on someone's shirt at a party; telling the cab driver he smelled like dog shit; smashing a bottle in Jasper's kitchen; later crying to someone on the phone. Kitty wakes up a few hours later still drunk, cuts her foot on the broken glass, and pukes while sitting in the bathtub. She wonders who's mad at her and what she said to Jasper. He isn't around and she goes back to bed groaning. A few hours later she gets up again.

Jasper sits on a chair in the kitchen. He has his hoodie pulled up and glares as she limps to the bathroom. Kitty shuts the door and sits on the toilet wearily. Her face is yellowish-grey, eyes bloodshot. She tries to comb her hair and gives up. Finally she goes into the kitchen.

"You were a real crotch last night," Jasper tells her.

"I'm sorry. It's the hard liquor."

"You always say that."

"It was shots of tequila and cramps!"

"Well, next time I'm gonna be with the nice girls who drink beer."

Across the table Jasper folds his arms. It amuses her—until this point he'd worshipped her. Kitty stares back, sizing him up. He will forgive and love her again, she is sure. Just then her belly rumbles and a belch erupts. It's loud and she can taste it. Jasper looks at her with revulsion, like he's never really seen her before.

Kitty has a sinking feeling she just lost the war.

After the procedure the following Thursday, Jewel drops Kitty off on her way to work. The ghost of a free-loving hippie remains in the gentle creases of her face. When Kitty is nestled under a blanket on the couch, Jewel hugs Rosie and says, "Thank you for taking care of my child." She long ago gave up hope that her daughters survived their childhoods undamaged.

Kitty sleeps for a few hours on the couch while Rosie reads by the window. She is touched by Jewel's genuine love and concern for her daughter, something she never saw in her own mother. She feels protective of Kitty, even more so than before. When Kitty stirs beneath the comforter she asks, "How are you, honey?"

"The cramps are really bad," she whimpers. "They wouldn't even give me any codeine to take home because my chart said I was an addict. Those fuckers...*ow*...*ow*..."

"I'll call Tony," Rosie says, getting up. "If anyone can get you some painkillers, it's him." That's a whole conversation left unspoken. Long ago they decided some parts of his life were better not discussed.

Kitty closes her eyes. Warm clots of blood ooze into the diaper between her legs. Thoughts of Santana, her stupid dead Catholic ex-stepfather, fill her head. He would've said she was going to hell for this. The only time he tried to make her go to church Kitty threw a tantrum right in the aisle and never had to go back. The thought makes her chuckle as she drifts back to sleep.

Tony shakes her. "Wake up. Rosie called me. She said you needed some pills."

Kitty rubs her eyes, disoriented. She sits up, shirt hanging off her shoulder. "I am...I am. Whaddya got?"

He hands her a bottle. "These are 8 mg dilaudid. Don't take more than two pills every four hours. Got it?"

"You want me to remember *what*? It takes me years to remember a postal code!"

"I'm serious. Don't fuck around."

"OKAY. Where's Rosie?"

"She went out to buy groceries and rent you some movies. I'm supposed to wait here and make sure you're all right." It is clear Tony does not want to babysit. He knows Kitty's reputation for trouble. His friends in the party scene stay away from her on purpose.

"Thanks for getting me these," Kitty says, now demure. "You got a lighter?"

"You better not cook that."

"As if there isn't stuff that *you* do and don't tell Rosie about."

Tony grabs her arm. "If you bring up that shit around her, I'll kick your goddamn ass."

Kitty's stomach seizes up again.

Fanta's van pulls into the driveway. Rosie had called, stuck in traffic, to see if she could go check on Kitty. In the living room she feels an uneasy tension between Tony and Kitty. For a moment Fanta prickles with dislike. Then the phone rings, and she walks into the kitchen to answer it. Tony slams the front door on his way out.

"Hello?"

"Is Squeaky there?"

"No she's not. Is there a message?"

"It's Franky Sparrow."

"I'll tell her you called." Fanta hangs up and goes back to the living room, handing Kitty a takeout container. "I brought you a burger. I figured you needed the iron."

Kitty is ravenous. "Fuck, this looks good. I'm gonna eat the shit out of it!" After two bites she lies back on the couch and holds her stomach. Then she says in a small voice, "Fanta, do you wish you could go back in time and do things differently?"

"Absolutely. I'd repack for my holidays."

"That's it?"

Fanta senses Kitty is dealing with larger issues she can't put into words. "There is a certain wisdom only gained from living."

"My god," Kitty says. "That totally gives me hope."

She's so sincere it melts Fanta, just a little.

The next day it rains all afternoon. Downstairs, Fanta plays her sad guitar. Kitty thinks it sounds real nice. For once the rest of the house is quiet. Squeaky sits on the living room floor with old issues of *Mojo* spread out. The phone rings and she gets up. "Don't answer that," Kitty begs. The phone stops ringing then starts again so Squeaky unplugs it.

Through the bay window is a slice of the seaport, the orange cranes and distant mountains a dark blue. On the couch Kitty lies pale-skinned and morose, still bleeding. "Squeaky," she says. "I feel really bad right now. Tell me something good."

A pained look crosses Squeaky's face and then she smiles at her friend. "I remember the first time I met you. I came home and you were drinking beer in my living room with Jasper and Rocket. Right away I paid attention. We were friends by the end of that six-pack. When I heard your laugh, that crazy *Ah-HA-HAH*...it killed me. You were dressed like a gothic farm boy, remember? You told me you'd spent your laundry money on banana splits. Sometimes we're like little kids, dazed by the big city lights. You *are* a good person. It's just easy to get caught up in all the noise."

Kitty smiles and her eyes shine. The music plays low and for a moment she forgives almost everything.

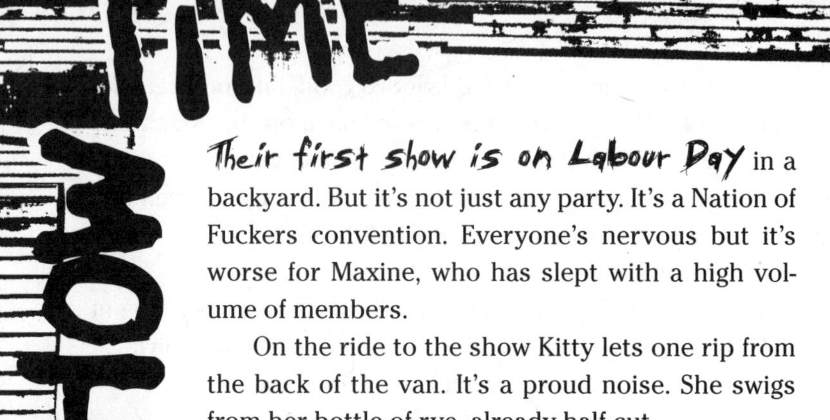

Their first show is on Labour Day in a backyard. But it's not just any party. It's a Nation of Fuckers convention. Everyone's nervous but it's worse for Maxine, who has slept with a high volume of members.

On the ride to the show Kitty lets one rip from the back of the van. It's a proud noise. She swigs from her bottle of rye, already half-cut.

"*Why* did we agree to play at this party?"

"'Cause we got asked to," Squeaky responds. "Besides, it was time to get out of the basement."

Maxine bites her bottom lip. "I hope there'll be some hot guys there."

"It'll be alcoholic dudes with low self-esteem," Kitty jokes, "so in other words, just your type."

"And don't give away all our records just to guys you want to bone," Squeaky adds. They have a proper EP, but not many copies, and plan to pass out only a select few tonight. It was put together by a guy they know who records bands in his house, and he only charged them for the pressing fee. It was hardest for Squeaky, since the drums had to be played front to back, unlike the guitar and bass, which could stop and start.

"Oh, lay off," Maxine snipes. "And gimme some more of that." She grabs the bottle from Kitty and takes a long, burning swallow. "Is Jasper going to be here tonight? Or are you guys back off again?"

"Nah, he's not coming. He's selling mushrooms at some rave."

"People still go to raves? Now that's a demographic that didn't age well."

"We're playing with The Disrespectors tonight. Has anyone heard their CD?"

“I hate that band. All the songs are about bitchy girlfriends. They suck!”

“Their album is called *Fresh Boobs*. That says it all right there.”

“And the singer’s name is Bryce!”

“So what?”

“Pay attention—every Jesse is born bad and Bryces are sexual deviants.”

“That’s bullshit.”

“It’s a scientific *fact*.”

They pull up at the house and there’s already people hanging out of windows and crowding the lawn. Squeaky whistles as she slides open the van door. “It’s going to be a big one tonight.”

At least a hundred dudes in denim mix with Kitty’s crusty punks, customers from Freudian Slips, various restaurant crews, and the boys from the tattoo shop. A small stage has been built in the backyard. It will later be dismantled and the wood used for a half-pipe.

Even Fanta seems ruffled. “Well,” she murmurs, “*this* is a new realm of terror.”

“So what, it’s our first backyard party,” Maxine prattles, “next we’ll be playing in a club, then headlining the club, and then—”

“—Selling out arenas,” Rosie says, joining their group. She’s wearing cut-offs, tube socks, and a T-shirt with *Wet Leather* in big letters across the front. She pats Kitty on her back soothingly. “Are you girls nervous?”

“Not really. I just want to shit my pants!”

“Tony gave me the word. You can start whenever you want.” She helps them move the amps and cabinets, and before they can even set up the crowd starts to heckle.

“I’ll make sure Tony keeps the boys in line.”

“We can handle it,” Maxine says, shooing her away. Rosie hustles off the stage to a round of whistles.

The girls attempt a clumsy sound check. Whoever is in charge of the Fisher-Price equipment shuts off the canned music. The girls face the crowd. Maxine is wearing leather pants and adjusts her mirrored sunglasses. A few guys laugh skeptically. She lets the noise swell around her.

“C’mon Tits, let’s see if you can play.”

“I’m getting a chubby.”

“Show us your *wound!*”

Maxine says grimly, “Your dink’s gonna shrink when *we* get done with you.”

Behind her, Fanta slouches in black pants, black shirt, and Ray-Bans. Kitty nervously rocks back and forth on her feet, wearing a denim tuxedo. She sees a friend in the crowd and throws double devil horns. Squeaky twists her ball cap, and adjusts her wristbands, mouth dirty with freckles.

Catching Maxine’s nod, she counts them into “Invasion.” It’s a false start. Kitty hits a few bad notes and stops. A few people scoff, but their friends in the crowd cheer them on. Squeaky cracks her drumsticks and they start again. This time it’s good. She can see that the people standing up front are smiling and moving their heads. Some guys even start low dancing, spilling their cans of beer. At the end of the song, they steam right into “GHB OD” and “Whatever, Trevor.” Maxine uses the mic stand like it’s a stripper pole and gyrates against it, aware of the guys in the crowd trying to catch her eye.

She’d insisted on a slower song next, a country punk ballad that Squeaky is against. Having been to these parties before, she knows The Nation of Fuckers like loud, aggressive rock. It isn’t going to work—the crowd is too amped up. But to her surprise, when Maxine begins to croon everyone quiets:

Drove 50 miles to see that boy
Drank a bottle of whisky outside his door
He said I wasn't his kind no more

It's hard to be good
when you love a bad
bad ba-a-a-d man

I held the gun, waited cold in his truck
Thought of all the other women,
He'd already fucked

It's hard to be good
when you love a bad
bad ba-a-a-d man

When he said, "I don't want you here"
A long winter started
That's lasted five years

It's hard to be good
when you love a bad
bad ba-a-a-d man

Women in jail kill time
braiding their hair,
I dream of dresses I'll never wear

I'm a cold-hearted woman
but he's a cold
cold cold ma-aaaan...

The audience of red-faced drunks is enraptured. From their wild applause Maxine knows they're in her hand. She can take them anywhere. It's the best high she's ever felt.

"We're Wet Leather, and this is our last song. It's for all the girls out there who are fuckin' little bitches." Fanta starts the intro into "Bitches Don't Do Dishes." A few tough girls push their way to the front and soon there is a row of them twisting. Maxine struts around the tiny space of stage as Kitty whips herself in mad half-circles. They blast their way through the song, and by the end the girls in the crowd are singing along:

"We're fuckin' little bitches,

And we don't do dishes!"

It's like a switch is flipped, and the show is over. Maxine takes a bow, chest heaving.

The howling crowd demands more. Fanta is first to bolt off the stage. "We gotta play an encore," Kitty says. "They fucking love us!"

Squeaky scrambles out from behind the drum kit. "Dude, those are the only songs we know!" Kitty throws an arm around her shoulders and they walk off together. Only Maxine is left onstage. It surprises her to look around. It seemed she'd been singing to a much bigger crowd.

The girls load out their gear, refusing offers of help from various fanboys. Rosie joins them with an armload of beers. They stand at the van, discussing the show, ignoring enamoured bystanders. The set was fifteen minutes, but only seemed to last five.

"Let's get back in there and get drunk," Kitty says, though she's already quite smashed.

"We shouldn't leave the van here with our gear," Fanta says, shutting the back doors. "I'll drive it home and come back."

Maxine is doubtful. "You promise, Fanta? We have to celebrate."

Fanta has no intention of coming back, but this is the easiest way out. The stress of getting up on stage took a lot out of her, more than they know. Playing is one thing, but standing around to listen to flattery and back-slapping is quite another. Her bones hurt and she wants to lie on her couch. She honks the horn and the girls all wave goodbye. Loud music and laughter drift from the backyard, and they return to the party, swaggering in like rock stars.

Though still suffering from a hangover, the next evening Squeaky remains elated from their show. She's in the kitchen cooking spaghetti puttanesca—a whore's sauce with capers and peas. Maxine had brought home some guy from the party with long toenails. They know this because he sat barefoot on the couch all day and only left when they started to vacuum him. The phone rings and Franky Sparrow's voice is the last thing she expects.

"Hey, Franky," she says warily, stirring the sauce with the phone to her ear. "What's going on?"

"I'm calling from our tour bus."

"Tour bus?"

"Okay, I'm on a cell phone in a *van*. What are you doing?"

"You mean right now or what am I doing in general?" The awkwardness between them reminds Squeaky of the time Maxine asked a waiter if they knew each other, then realized they'd once fucked.

Franky laughs. "Whichever."

"I don't know...playing music, working, hanging with my girls. Why?"

"So, Wet Leather is playing gigs now."

"Yeah," Squeaky laughs. "Our first show will be hard to forget. It was last night, in Beaver's backyard."

"I heard you guys killed it."

"How'd you hear that?"

"I keep myself in the know. Word is you kicked ass."

Her cheeks flush. "Yeah, it went pretty well."

"So then you girls have enough songs for a set?"

"Sure..."

"Hold on," Franky says. He muffles the phone then comes back. "Well, Squeaky, I'm about two hours from Banff. Listen to this." He explains that the Party Micks, the band they are touring with, dropped out because the guitar player broke his hand punching a wall. Fire Chicken has no one to open for them. "I talked to the guys and if you want, Wet Leather can come on board."

Squeaky is floored. "What? Are you serious? You're asking if our band wants to tour with *Fire Chicken?* You guys are way outta our league!"

"Who says?"

"Wet Leather has only played *one* gig."

"Trial by fire. Our booking agent can call the promoters and tell them to find an opening band, or we can show up with our own. I'd rather give my friends the shot."

It feels good to hear Franky call her a friend. It hasn't felt that way for a long time. Squeaky protests weakly, "But we're not much of a draw. We don't even have a real CD."

"So what? Burn some copies and sell them cheap. It'll help you out if there's merch. You're not gonna make any money on this tour. Our guarantees in Canada aren't that good."

"I have to talk to the band. You're sure the guys in Fire Chicken are cool with this?"

"Are you kidding? They'll love you chicks."

"Fanta hates being called that."

"We'd rather have you guys. I mean girls. Er, ladies."

"Don't hurt yourself."

"And you don't have to show your appreciation with sexual favours," Franky says. "But it's encouraged."

"Only if we don't use a condom."

"You filthy girl."

The warmth in Squeaky's stomach moves downward, but she focuses on band business. "So what's the plan?"

"We play Banff tonight, Innisfail tomorrow—"

"Where's that?"

"Some shit town in Alberta so Fat Ricky can see his kids, then a show in Calgary, but there's already enough bands on that bill. So, you'll need to meet us in Regina…in four days."

"Four days! That's not much time."

"I'll call back in an hour."

Squeaky hangs up and runs into the living room, where Fanta, Rosie, and Maxine are listening to Kitty, who is splayed across the couch.

"I thought of a new job," she tells them, "I'm gonna be a stylist for the recently deceased. My tag will be 'Dying in Style.' I'll make sure you've got a nice coffin and that your hair and nails are done professionally. Just because you're dead doesn't mean you can't—"

"Listen to this," Squeaky interrupts. "Franky Sparrow just called and offered us a tour with Fire Chicken."

"Huh?"

"What?"

"WHAAAAAT?"

"Their opening band fell through. They invited us to finish the Canadian tour. We have a show in Regina in four days if we want it."

"I don't fucking believe this!" Kitty leaps off the couch and erupts in a spastic dance.

"Well, we won't make any money. But think of how much fun it'll be."

"Let's do it," Maxine says. "I'm ready to leave *now*."

Kitty gives her two high-fives. "Yeah, baby! Me too."

"No," Fanta says, shaking her head.

The noise in the room stops at once. Maxine cries, "What? Fanta, why NOT?"

"A tour with Fire Chicken? I never signed on for that."

"Are you *serious?*" Maxine is nearing hysteria. Without Fanta they don't have a band. It's not even their van.

"What about work?"

"We run our own store. That is the fucking beauty of being your own boss."

"I'm pretty sure I can get time off from the bakery," says Squeaky. "If I can't then I'll quit. It's just some job. I want to play music, not make goddamn cheese scones the rest of my life."

Kitty squints at Fanta in disbelief. "Fuck YEAH! Why are you playing in a band if you don't want to tour?"

Fanta knows this is the beginning of a trajectory that will change them, and from this point on things will never be as easy. She'd seen what the business had done to Harold Dixon. One day they would long for these simple times, picking out little melodies in the basement before it got taken out of their hands and finally fell apart. But it's Maxine who sways her. It's the way her voice cracks when she begs, "Fanta, *please*."

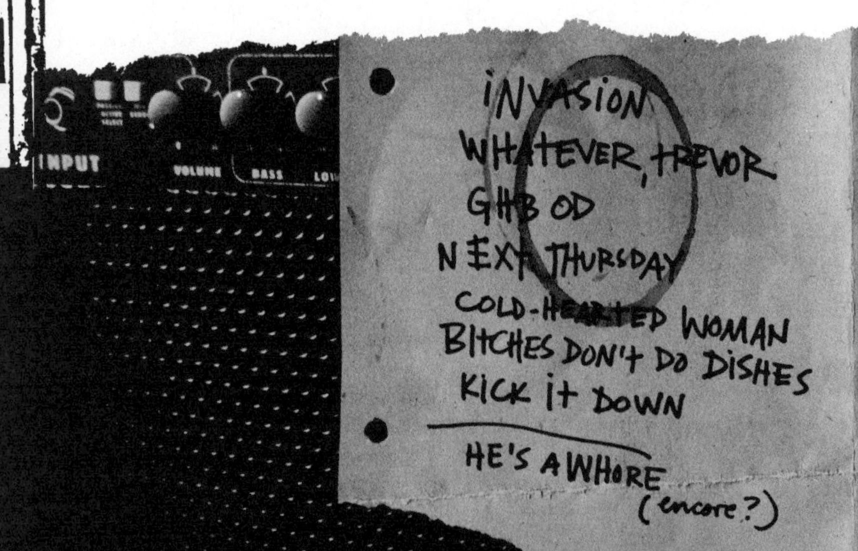

They will have thirty-five to forty minutes on stage. Fire Chicken's booking agent forwards a list of Wet Leather's dates, load-in times, contracts, and directions to each venue. It is called the Book of Lies.

"I hope the van makes it." Squeaky pores over road maps spread across the floor. "These are some brutal drives."

"Let's rent a motor home," Kitty says.

"That's a little out of our league. We're more in the price range of an ice cream truck."

Rosie has created a Wet Leather website and put everything online: bios, tour dates, even tablature. She tapes up a box of burned CDs and bundles stickers with elastics, watching the whirlwind around her with a detached fondness for the reckless girl she used to be. It isn't envy for her friends, but the energy and excitement of Wet Leather that makes her wistful. They are creating an impact on the world, and she has nothing to leave behind. The closest thing is her love for Tony King.

"Only me and Fanta have a license," Squeaky says. "We really need another driver. Why don't you come with us, Rosie?"

Kitty kicks up her leg in agreement. "Yes! You're our main bitch!"

"That's a great idea." Fanta is relieved. So far the biggest obstacle has been finding an acceptable cat-sitter for Mr. Kibbles, but she knows the tour won't be easy. Rosie is good with paranoid potheads and crying drunks, which will be useful for this trip. It can take a lot to handle Kitty or Maxine on a bender.

"Well, I do work for cheap—in fact, nothing."

Only Maxine opposes. "The van's already crowded with band members."

"So what," Kitty says. "Rosie can bang her ass on the tambourine."

There is a rigid look on Maxine's face. She knows it's petty to feel this way, but she doesn't want to share this tour with Rosie. For once she refuses to be stuck in her shadow.

"She's right," Rosie sighs. "It's probably not a good idea. But thanks for trying to include me." Rosie leaves the room, and when the screen door bangs shut they know she's upset. Everyone frowns at Maxine.

"She's got a lot of skills we could use," Fanta says curtly.

"Like what? Showing her cunt for money?"

Outside, Rosie hears it all.

Fanta honks the horn. It's early in the morning, and the girls scramble out of the house with their packs. The Chevy van has an extended back crammed with gear, and it's a tight fit. Kitty rips through her knapsack. "Fuck! Why can't I find my fucking *everything*?"

Kitty Domingo, despite what most people believe, is often paralyzed with insecurity. They are all anxious about the shows ahead of them. Squeaky sits in the open side door, tapping her drumsticks. Two little girls ride slowly past on their bikes, gawking. The air is electric and cracks with possibilities.

It's an unusual crew: tough little Squeaky, a five-foot menace in a too-tall world; Fanta's eyes intense like a childhood fever never left her; pretty Kitty, a lumberjack princess on the verge of petulance; and noisy Maxine, thrumming with lunatic energy. Nothing can get in their way. No man can take them down. The van doors slam, and they're off.

The Canadian Tour

Outside the suburbs of Vancouver, the smell of manure from the rich farmland creeps into the van. They drive further on to an arid valley with orchards and wineries, past rocky, charcoal-like hills with trees growing up the sides, and then wind through dense, rugged forests with bright red trees dying from the pine beetles. The van chugs up into mountain ranges that slope down into the golden cattle land of Alberta. The open road is like a grey tongue, unfolding.

Inside the white whale of the Chevy is a private universe. Each girl has her own place. Fanta and Squeaky sit up front and each drive for three-hour shifts, swapping CDs, maps, and water bottles between them. Maxine takes up the middle seat with her long legs, sprawled like a grand odalisque. In the very back Kitty has carved out a hamster nest, and stretches out between duffel bags and road cases with contentment. Kitty Domingo, they learn, has the uncanny ability to sleep through any kind of noise, in any position. Her behaviour devolves at rest areas, and she terrorizes truck stops. Late in the night they stop at a fleabag motel outside Lethbridge. The girls drink a bottle of warm Baby Duck in plastic glasses. Fanta, road-weary, falls asleep at once.

The next day Squeaky drives into the stripe of pink and blue on the horizon. She slows at a solitary white church with a roadside Jesus and Mary to give passing blessings. They take this as a sign to pull into a highway diner for breakfast. As they sit waiting for their pancakes and fried eggs, a man in short shorts, studded belt, and shaved legs swings through the restaurant, dual charm bracelets on his ankles. It's early morning and the sight makes them smile until they hear one trucker warn, with clear malice, "You're in the wrong place, pal."

They burn joint after joint as they burn through the plains. The heat of the Prairies is a slow scorch on empty stretches of flat road. Squeaky can't get used to the absence of mountains. The cracked earth in Saskatchewan goes on forever, and the dry grass gives the land a deserted feel, like nothing could ever grow here. Even the buildings are flat and close to the ground, with no god to encourage their spires. Kitty declares, "Saskatchewan is the sound of the loneliest fart ever heard."

They drive into Regina, past signs for Holiday Inns and Arby's, following directions to the industrial part of town. The bar has a familiar smell—spilled beer, sweat, dirt that's remained in dim corners for decades. Lugging her cases inside,

Squeaky passes Maxine, who is losing her cool with the bar manager. Since they're the opening band he doesn't think they need a full sound check. Squeaky's stomach sinks. The sound will be terrible if they get everyone's levels in line check.

"Listen, sweetheart," he says, a mid-thirties metrosexual fraying at the edges. Maxine's jaw clenches, her smile stiff. "If there's time after Fire Chicken gets through *their* sound check, fine. If not..." the manager's voice trails off and he shrugs. "They ain't coming to see you anyway."

"Wet Leather will be the biggest band to ever play here." Maxine says with a confidence that does not seem at all manufactured. The manager appears to reconsider, and at that moment Kitty runs in.

"Bathroom, bathroom," she screeches. Having just woken up, her hair stands up in odd black puffs and her jeans are so dirty there's a sheen to the denim. "Goddamn, where's the can? I gotta throw down to brown town!"

The bar manager is startled. Kitty takes off, holding her ass in a bunny hop as Maxine sighs, pointing, aware she's just lost some bargaining power. The manager gives a dry chuckle, but there's nothing humorous in it. Exhausted from the drive, Fanta sinks into one of the dark booths. She wants a shower, clean clothes, a nap, hot food. Discontentment rolls off her in waves.

Through a door in the back and up a rickety staircase is the band room. There is a tub of beer on ice, as well as a table with three bags of chips and a bowl of crackers in single packets. Maxine is the first one there—all she has to move is a microphone. "Some hospitality," she says from the locker-sized bathroom. She peers at herself in the mirror, rims her eyes with more black liner. "Kitty will go through that beer before the show even starts!" They are silent as Fanta shuffles up the stairs and looks around. Every wall surface is covered in graffiti—band tags and drawings of cocks, mostly deformed. She stretches out on one of the old couches, eyes closed.

The thought of putting on a bad show upsets Squeaky. She worries that the monitors won't be loud enough. Kitty tends to turn her amp too high, and if she can't hear the guitar or vocals it throws off her timing. Not to mention Kitty always breaks her D string which takes her forever to change.

Kitty finds her way upstairs. She opens a beer then shoves two in her shoulder bag. "Hey, that booze is for Fire Chicken too," Squeaky tells her. Kitty makes a face. "Man, you are *such* a brat."

"A little Bukowski cherub," Maxine agrees. Her voice is hoarse from nervous chain-smoking. Loud voices and laughter float up from downstairs. Fire Chicken has arrived, and Squeaky says they should go hover near the soundboard and make sure they get a turn.

Fanta heaves to her feet. "God," she says. "It's been a long Tuesday."

"There she is!" Franky Sparrow lifts Squeaky off her feet in a hug. When he puts her down she shuffles her sneakers, looking pleased. Then Franky introduces the girls to the rest of the band. The bass player has burgundy hair and a long scar down his spine. He is tall and moves like a three-legged cat. Rumour has it Jonah once did a backflip off the drum riser, but now gets so drunk he tends to fall off the stage. In most of the band photos he's wearing a bandage or some kind of splint.

"Hey, girls," he smiles, handsome despite his missing teeth. When he offers up the bottle of vodka wheedled from the bar staff, Kitty lunges.

The singer, Tex, is older, wears sunglasses indoors, and is impeccably polite. He gives each of them a perfunctory handshake. Pushing fifty, he is equal parts historian, visionary, raconteur, and bully. There are metal plates in his head from a severe motorcycle crash and lightning storms drive him to lunacy. His fists are the size of small hams.

Last is Fat Ricky, a skinny, stoner blonde, heavily tattooed and involved in several pending paternities. Fat Ricky has adoring women in every city. He gives a toothy grin, tightening his snare. "I see you givin' me eyes," he says to the girls as a means of introduction.

They move the cabinets, put the heads on top. The stage emits a buzz; cables to amp heads, mics up, everything wired to the band. There's nowhere to go before showtime, nothing to do but wait and drink the hours away.

The room is a red haze of heat.

Behind the kit Squeaky feels the rush as she counts in, bass drum kicking. The crowd is full of ragged Saskatchewan punks and tough-looking Indians. She can see boys with bare chests, dripping sweat at the front of the stage, three deep from the opening band. The rest of the room is blackness. Maxine puts her high-heeled boot on the monitor and strains forward. Her voice climbs up and down, robotic then melodic:

"Invasion!
Invasion!
Invasion!"

Kitty attempts mid-air splits. She runs across the stage to Fanta, and then jumps back, whipping her neck. The kids scrutinize each band member, but Fanta seems to puzzle them, with her flawless solos and detached insouciance. *C'mon Fanta,* Squeaky thinks, *Give it up a little*.

They maintain an onslaught of energy through every song. Kitty lets loose fast, growling bass lines, while Squeaky savages her drum skins. At their Girlschool cover finale, the

crowd sounds ready to rampage into the streets. And then, Fanta breaking through the wall she keeps around her, drops to her knees with a wince, and then arches her back into the song. The band knows it's a mock performance, a lampoon of the rock star cartoon, but it works. There's even sweat in the ass crack of her pants.

Squeaky can see Fanta straining and she hits the toms harder, her mouth a tight O of concentration. Then Maxine takes a running leap off stage. There's a flash of fear for a moment as the crowd surges forward like ticks on a teeming beast. Squeaky pictures Maxine's clothes getting torn off, earrings ripped out, strangled by the microphone cord. It can happen. But the crowd flips her easily back onstage. Squeaky crashes the cymbals a final time and the set is over.

They fucking killed it.

September 12, Winnipeg, MB

The Royal Albert has long been a punk landmark, a transient hotel in the middle of Winnipeg, an inhospitable city where the elements conspire to make the people as tough and unyielding as the land.

After last night's show in Regina, the guys in Fire Chicken were full of congratulations and welcomed them on board. They also warned that the crowd at the Albert could get pretty wild. Crammed at a table in the back near the bathroom, the girls form a protective half-circle. Tonight it's a grimy-looking mix of metal heads, committed punks, drunks, and a mental patient or two. At a table in the middle of the room, some chick bounces up and down on her boyfriend's lap.

"I doubt she'll be able to keep that pace up for long," Fanta observes dryly.

"Let's invite them up onstage to do that during our set!"

A string of pale blondes single-file into the bar and head straight to the bathroom. A drunken older woman with glasses and frizzy brown hair stumbles through the crowd revealing a sadly wrinkled décolletage. "Who wants to get punched in the face?" Someone flicks beer at her and she screeches again, "WHO wants a PUNCH in the FACE?"

An overweight guy at the next table agrees. She clocks him in the mouth and staggers away. "Oh my god," Maxine says. "Are you okay?"

"Yeah," he smiles, teeth bloody. "I liked it."

Kitty pipes in, "How 'bout a kick in the balls then?"

No one knows what to expect when they climb onstage,
but at the first guitar lick the crowd ripples in response. With each song the noise thunders louder. The Winnipeg crowd knows how to have a good time. "Don't slow down," Maxine tells the sweaty mob of fans clumped in front her. "You're gonna LIKE this one!" The audience stands slack-jawed and glassy eyed, waiting for her to wind them up again. She nods at Squeaky, who stomps on her bass pedal and kicks them into gear:

"GHB OD! GHB OD!"
I woke up and smelled like pee
GHB OD!"

During the solo, Maxine stands to one side, rocking out. The chick who'd been riding her boyfriend manhandles her way up front. She jumps into the fray and is shoved into the wooden stage, grabbing at Maxine's leg for balance. Maxine lands on one knee, and tries to salvage the move by doing a half-roll off the stage into the girl, wiping out on the beer-slick floor. The girl smacks her head hard on the side of the speaker. She stands for a moment then wobbles back to her table. Someone pulls Maxine up, laughing and fist-pumping with a bloody nose. She doesn't feel a thing.

The sky above the parking lot is black and gold and midnight blue. There is a smell of concrete cooling, pollution, and manure. No crosswalks slow the traffic that moves like the herds of bison people once believed were endless.

Maxine has been befriended by a haggard stripper with shitty coke. Their friendship will last as long as the drugs. Wet Leather seems to attract waifs and strays like strange prizes. When the bar closes, everyone else goes upstairs to their hotel rooms, but Maxine does lines with the stripper in the back of the bouncer's van. She can't get any coke up her bloody nostril, but keeps trying. Her knee doesn't hurt anymore, and when the drugs run out the bouncer pulls out more.

He asks Maxine, "Are you Croatian? Croatian women and Russians have good legs. I'm a leg man. But when you move upwards to the face, sometimes it doesn't look so good. It's like they've had a hard life. I like big women. Big like Vikings." He shakes the tiny bag of coke at them and says, "Hey, why don't you girls make out?"

At 6:17 a.m. the sun is a big red disk alone in the sky.

It's not cheap to fill the Chevy's tank, and Wet Leather gets $150 for each show, no matter what Fire Chicken's guarantee might be. The girls work out a $15 per diem for food, booze, and cigarettes. The rest goes to gas. Each venue is supposed to provide a band meal or a buyout for dinner, but if the bar doesn't set up a hotel room they'll have to drive to the next town or sleep in the van. At this point there's no question it's about the music—they're barely surviving.

There is a mound of scrap paper Kitty has pulled out of her bag, the numbers of potential boyfriends. After hours on the highway she's restless. She wants a long smoke break in a country western bar, a beer and a shot, not a five-minute pee stop. Fanta tells her, "We'll stop in Dryden. It's about a hundred kilometers."

Kitty swears. "That's too *long.*"

"Patience is a virtue."

"Okay, I'll try that virtue thing." She's silent for a moment, then says, "Fuck it, I'm gonna kill someone."

Fanta feels the miles wear on her, then shifts back into a smooth ride. Despite her misgivings about touring in general, she doesn't mind long stretches in the van. Squeaky is a great co-navigator, a dependable girl behind the wheel. She's a typical muscle bitch, analyzing every tick of the engine, checking the oil and tire pressure at each stop, even standing tiptoe to wash the windshield. At a rest area Kitty tears around the parking lot making odd honking sounds.

Back in the van, it's Squeaky's turn to drive. Maxine climbs into the passenger seat.

"Shotgun!"

"Fanta's my co-pilot."

"What, you think I can't read a map or a road sign?"

"Okay," Squeaky sighs. "Whatever."

Maxine buckles up her seatbelt. "I tried to get my license once, you know. But when I went in to take my road test, they gave me this old crabby lady as my examiner, and I *knew* she was going to fail me as soon as I saw her shoes…"

Squeaky tunes her out and focuses on the road. Frequently Maxine's lengthy narratives lack a punchline or plot. Squeaky's never met someone so uncomfortable with silence. Chattering on, Maxine tosses her cigarette out the window mid-sentence.

"NO!" Squeaky yells at her. It's the first time they've seen

her lose her temper. "Don't *ever* do that! How the hell do you think forest fires get started?"

"Jee-eezzz, sorry Squeaky."

"Goddamn city kids," she grumbles.

For a moment, a ray of sun busts through the cloud circle like the fucking eye of God.

September 13, Thunder Bay, ON

A city beneath a storm cloud. Clusters of churches line long strips of highway with pawnshops and thrift stores. Each band gets two rooms at a motor hotel down the street from the venue. The numbers are written on the doors in felt pen. One room has mould growing in the shower. Much of the artwork appears stolen—the screw holes are all different sizes. It's an off day, with no show until tomorrow.

The adjoining bar features lesbian karaoke night. Squeaky comes in for off-sales, and stays for Maxine's Patsy Cline number. Afterwards she watches her flirtatiously accept all drinks offered.

"What's the deal, Maxine? I didn't know you were into girls."

"I've tasted pussy," she shrugs. "I like cock better."

Squeaky takes her beer down to Franky's room and sits crowded beside him on the bed. She never wants to leave this spot. The room might be full of bed bugs, but when Franky squeezes her leg it feels like she just caught a snowflake on her tongue. Her crush on him is back in full effect. While they work through the six-pack, karaoke songs filter down from the bar—they can hear Maxine and Tex in a sing-off of escalating decibels. Franky and Fat Ricky trade tour stories, each one more absurd and repulsive than the last, like the time Jonah had the runs and shit into a box backstage, or the decoy sweat martini someone actually drank.

They see Fanta pass the door of the room, wet with rain from her walk along the lakeshore. "Hey," Squeaky calls, "come and hang out."

Fanta pauses in the doorway and declines a beer. She understands having a few to liven up before a show, but not getting so messed up on their day off. No one is interested in seeing different sights. It's become clear that just because they're in new cities, doesn't mean they do anything interesting.

Kitty lurches into her. "You smell like an AA meeting." Then Kitty spills her drink all over Fanta's shoes.

"Watch it," she huffs. "Kitty, can you even *remember* the last time you were sober?"

"No, but I can't remember the last time I was drunk, either!"

Thunderstorms rock them all night.

September 15, Highway 17E

The fog is dangerous, full of murder. There's a sour stink in the van. A bath right now is worth thousands, and Fanta wonders how she will be able to stand the tedium and delirium of the same bar, the same set, night after night. The van: beer cans, ashes, garbage under the seats, dirty shirts, ripped maps, rolling wine bottles.

Fanta appreciates the architecture of the common home in the endless motion of changing landscapes. This two-lane highway has not been kind, but she tries to remain optimistic. *Wawa, Sault Ste. Marie, Blind River, North Bay*. Endless towns full of people with uneventful lives. At the shows the kids faces all look the same. Sweating, contorted, savage, grotesque, open-mouthed in the blue and yellow lights. Fanta's dreams are of broken glass, in the colours of a Toulouse-Lautrec painting.

But right now she feels at home driving down the dark highway, Neil Young on the stereo, the miles softly passing by. Fanta remembers how Harold once told her she had a heart of gold. She'd said no, there was a black streak in it, and he had replied, "Well, you have a heart of gold to *me*."

Fundamental changes occur, she thinks, when you finally grow up.

Sound Check

"I can't hear anything up here!"

"I think the battery in my wah is dead."

"Can I turn my amp up?"

"C'mon, just show me the chorus one more time!"

"Where's my gaff tape?"

"My bass amp took a dump. It's FRIED. The standby button flashes red and now it's green and red."

"Why does the back stage reek like salami?"

"Are we done here? Are we good?"

September 16, Toronto, ON

Maxine flings her clothing across the hotel room. The entire floor is hidden beneath her costumes, the bathroom draped with wet undergarments like a bombed lingerie shop. Tonight she can't decide between a lime green puffy crinoline with a dog collar that just fits around her waist; a fur bra with a matching skirt and red patent laced boots from the sixties; or a girdle garter, like a sausage miniskirt that had been dyed black but turned midnight blue.

They did an early sound check and now have a few hours to relax, take showers, or wash their clothes. Squeaky has a friend in Greektown and takes Kitty out with her. She wants her to see more of the city than just the hotel and bar. Fanta needed to rest, and props herself against the headboard observing the hurricane that is Maxine, changing into yet another outfit. Fanta ponders that, while Maxine claims Wet Leather is simply about rock and not sex or gender, she now wears a sheer top with Big Gulp stickers over her nipples.

"I'm nervous about this show," she says, twisting to see her reflection in the floor-length mirror. "Toronto is sooo cosmopolitan."

Only five shows in and already Fanta sees the common trait of lead singers—the desperation to be adored and the need to please. Artifice has begun to impede her natural spontaneity. Maxine tells the same repertoire of jokes in each practised pause, recites anecdotes and scripted song intros.

"Everything doesn't have to be a construct, Maxine." Fanta puts down her book and sits up. "Especially when it panders to the lowest common taste. To be unique is true beauty. When you just let go of what you think you're supposed to be, it's corrosive and fierce and magnificent."

Maxine points to her pasties. "So, too much then?"

They are picked up and driven to the show. Toronto is a flat city on a grid, like a giant international airport. The CN Tower looks like a syringe, and Kitty has a sudden urge to get high. Coke is easy to find on the tour, but she likes the down.

While the other girls are oblivious to it, the city gleams for Maxine. Everything from camera angles to her hemline is based on strategic placement. She doesn't want to have sagging skin and a soft belly, creeping close to forty and just hanging on. Right now, it thrills her to be the scene-maker, that she has the ability to create thunderclouds of chaos. Men buy her drinks, offer compliments, lavish attention on her. She's a star whether she's onstage or in a back seat, the brightest light in the skyline. The great gulps of neon roll over her real easy, open-mouthed, dreamy.

The hipster crowd is there to see the opening act, two beardos and a shaggy-haired keyboard player in neon leggings. Headbands are *de rigueur*, as are anti-fashion eyewear and mullets. Despite the heat, many hair farmers are wearing scarves and ironic cardigans. One has even committed to dark sunglasses the entire evening. As Wet Leather threads their way to the stage, the audience inches forward. A couple of people nod and a few brave souls even clap. Fanta plays some quick notes and adjusts the gain. She is wearing men's trousers with suspenders and white flats. With her skinny angles, she has a hip androgyny the kids approve. They cluster and fawn at her side of the stage. She's bewildered and hides behind the long fringe of her red hair.

None of this matters to Maxine—she will win them over tonight. She regrets her choice of body stocking and sequined cape. Then again, it's her personal circus, and the carnival can't exist without her. The stage lights heat her blood and time seems to slow. She takes a deep breath and begins the show.

September 17, Sherbrooke, QC

The Theater Granada is a building too grand for their dismal set. Wet Leather barely elicits a response. The kids stand and shift through "Invasion" and "Whatever, Trevor" with blank looks, clutching their phones. Kitty is convinced the bass sounds like shit, puts one finger in her ear and scrunches her face. "Turn me UP," she yells at the soundman. A few people dance, but most aren't willing to commit to a band or song they don't know. Kitty couldn't be more bored, and rails against them with disgust.

"If you're just going to sit and stare, why dontcha go to a movie instead?" She takes swig after swig of her bottle, the look darkening on her face.

"My friend thinks you're gorgeous," a girl tells Kitty after the show. She points to one of the boys milling in the crowd.

"Oh, yeah? Well if he thinks I'm so gorgeous he can walk his *own* ass over here and tell me that." Kitty packs up her lunky bass, cord dragging behind her. Right now she just wants to get backstage and pour another drink.

After a few plastic cups of vodka, she stumbles out to the front of the club and runs straight into Maxine, who is chatting up two boys in identical punk uniforms. Kitty weaves with a plastic container of pasta which Fanta has forced on her, and chews with her mouth open while trying to follow the conversation.

"Sherbrooke is sooo gorgeous," Maxine enthuses. "It's like historical buildings don't just dot the city here and there like at home, it's the whole town..." The two French boys don't seem very interested.

"Discharge," Kitty interrupts, reading the patch on one boy's hoodie. "WHAT'S THAT? The stuff that comes outta your dick?"

They laugh nervously and Maxine ignores her. "No, really," she persists, "what's it like to live here?" With effort, Kitty remains quiet for the next minute.

"The scene 'ere used to be good," one of the boys says, "but now it is dead."

Kitty belches and throws her container of takeout pasta in the street. The little French punks pretend to be horrified.

"Pick up de gar-bage."

"Don't just leave it there for the rats and street cleaners," Maxine chastises. "That's *rude*."

Two men start yelling and pushing each other. Kitty does a sharp careen over to investigate. She smashes a bottle on the street and just as suddenly the crowd breaks up. Maxine is still chatting up her two cute fans, debating whether to invite them back to the van. She wants head, but they're so baby-faced she'll probably just give them a CD instead.

Everyone's attention is diverted to Kitty, who begins dancing a sudden, messed-up Charleston. "Wait, wait, wait," she says, going faster, "it's the where's-your-pants dance!" She swings her legs and flaps her arms on the spot, crazed. Finally she stops, panting. "There," she tells the crowd, "that's all you get."

The two boys can't take their eyes off Kitty. "Preddy cool gurl," they agree in their heavy French accents. Annoyed, Maxine goes back inside.

She joins Squeaky, who sits at a table with a ginger ale, going through a folder of receipts. Each band takes a rotating night at the merch booth, hawking buttons and CDs. An earnest fan's attempt at conversation is met with pained replies as Fanta holds up various T-shirts.

"Look, he's trying to hit on her! Good luck, man," Maxine scoffs. "Fanta stands for fucked and never touched again." Squeaky closes the folder and wordlessly pushes away from the table.

At bus call Maxine is irritable and ugly. She has cramps and takes three of Fanta's painkillers. They sit and ache in her stomach. Two hours to Montreal and a feeling like bad weather keeps following her. The van pulls hard to the left and in the darkness they hear Squeaky curse in her French patois. Maxine leans against the cool window, quiet for once. When she falls asleep she dreams of her grandmother's home and a rotted brown garden destroyed by snow.

There's a gay pride parade in Montreal and the van can't get to the venue. The streets are blocked off for crowds of men in leather harnesses, theatrical drag queens, and dykes on motorbikes. Dance music pumps through the air as Tex tries to navigate the trailer down the narrow streets. The female police officer standing at the barricade refuses to let them through. "The unmitigated audacity!" Tex declares. After numerous failed attempts to get near the venue, Squeaky jumps out to help. Tex's face is a frustrated purple.

"S'il te plait, donnes nous une coupure," Squeaky pleads. *"Je te donnes ma parole."* She swears they will unload the vans and

then park somewhere else. It will save having to move tons of equipment down several uncomfortable blocks.

"*Tasse-toi,*" the officer commands, and lifts the end of the barricade. Squeaky jumps into Fire Chicken's van, which smells like dirty socks and potato chips. "Hustle it," she says. To her annoyance, Maxine has crammed in too, and is practically sitting on Franky's lap.

Fat Ricky shoots the finger in the officer's honour as they pass. "Why don't you lick my pouch?"

"Actually," Franky says, "it's not that easy to get someone to lick your pouch."

"Yeah, it is. You pull down your pants and put your bag by their face, and when they smell salt they just staaa-aaart lickin.'" Fat Ricky tries to push Squeaky's face near his crotch and she elbows him away. "Get lost, butt-cheek!"

The van moves at a slow crawl. "I love this city," Maxine says. "You can't toss a quarter without hitting a strip club or a church." The smell of greasy fries wafts through the window. "Oh my god, I hate that smell! I once worked at this fish 'n' chip restaurant and the boss would yell, 'Make it swim! Make it swim!' because if you put on too much batter the fish sinks in the oil and you have to get it out—"

"There's the club," Squeaky says. "Coming up on the right."

"—and I was so glad I quit, because I always smelled like grease. That's why I hate fish 'n' chips. Then I started dating this really cute little rockabilly boy but he was eighteen and I was thirteen so sometimes, y'know, it was kind of weird."

The van slows to a stop. Maxine looks at Franky. "I'm totally not hitting on you, but you have beautiful eyes."

"This is IT," Squeaky says loudly.

They slide open the door and jump out like commandos.

In a park across the street, Maxine watches Fire Chicken do a live TV interview. Squeaky is out buying drumsticks and Fanta has gone to see Notre Dame Cathedral. Half-asleep, Kitty closes her eyes to the sun, lets it leech the sickness from her skin. If it weren't for Maxine, it would be relaxing to lie on the grass, listening to the fountain and the birds and distant house music.

"Why should *they* be in charge? Look at them," Maxine nudges Kitty, pointing to Fire Chicken. "Their whole gender is mesmerized by anything...*jiggly*. It's ridiculous!"

When she slops wine on the grass and screeches, Kitty rolls over. "Give me some of that," she says, grabbing the bottle. With Maxine, it's easier to just give in.

Wet Leather is halfway through the set when a girl gets on stage and does a jittery, maniacal dance. Fanta and Kitty look at each other then burst out laughing. It's a good moment. After a minute or two the girl dives into the crowd. Almost at once she pulls herself out of the pit like a creature from a tar pool. She's sweating profusely, with quasi-dreadlocks and striped arm stockings, and performs her spastic dance again before belly-flopping off the stage once more. The next time around Maxine joins her in jerking tandem. It's like *Flashdance* on patchouli-flavoured crack. The band manages to carve an entire instrumental passage in the middle of it. Derisive laughter and applause fill the air. The crowd is charged by the spectacle, and it's a powerful thing to create. The adrenaline lasts all evening.

Fire Chicken hits the stage and Tex, in his boots and ten-gallon hat, isn't sharing the spotlight. When the dancing girl climbs up for their set, he tries to shove her off. She grabs his hand and bites it. The bouncers drag her off the stage, shrieking and kicking. To his credit Tex finishes the show, but goes to the hospital as soon as it's over.

September 18, Montreal, QC

Fanta feels at home on this island, as if the long steel bridge jolted her from a deep slumber of winter dreams. She leans over the balcony of a hotel room at the Lord Berri, on Levesque and St. Catherine's street. Rumour is the Stones stayed at the St.-Germain. She pictures Marianne Faithfull and Mick clutching each other in the fog on cobblestone streets; Janis Joplin blowing Leonard Cohen in the Chelsea Hotel. His song "Famous Blue Raincoat" plays in her head:

Yes, and thanks
For the trouble you took from her eyes
I thought it was there for good
So I never tried....

There will be no love stories in this room, tonight. Everyone's out at the discotheque, but Fanta wants to stay in.

"We were on fire last night," Squeaky announces, as the van rolls on. "Our band was Foghat rad!" She pulls a shirt out of her bag, sniffs it, and then chooses another.

Kitty yawns with boredom, then reaches behind her and punches Maxine on the arm. "Punch bug, no return!"

"If you hit me again, I'll hit you twice as hard. Got it, Kitty? I don't fucking play like that! What are you, fucking eight years old? How'd you get so lit up? Jeezus, you're *cooked.*"

Everyone is sleep-deprived and surly. "Anyway, we had a good rhythm going last night." Squeaky tries to lighten the mood. "I think for the first time Wet Leather had the better show. It's too bad that girl took a bite of Fire Chicken."

"It's not *that* bad," Maxine smirks. Sometimes Tex makes her feel like he's doing them a favour by letting them on his stage. She's equally insulted that he's never hit on her, despite their decades-old tryst. She's smoking too much and unscrews an empty pickle jar to drop yet another butt inside.

Kitty is riding shotgun as Fanta drives into Quebec City. "Hey, slow down, Chief," she yells out her window as a car zooms past. "Hey, Chief, where's the fire?" Maxine giggles, and her irritation at Kitty dissolves.

The van is like an isolation chamber. Once Maxine and Kitty are let out, trying to get them back inside is like herding kittens. The two of them were tight from the start. They laugh at the same things, dislike the same people. Kitty is Maxine's favourite windup toy. Onstage they perform best to each other. Kitty pulls flamboyant moves with such raw enthusiasm it deflects attention from her barely adequate bass lines. "Kitty Domingo," a critic of the band will later write, "is the very best of the mediocre."

Fanta asks for quiet as she navigates the tapering streets. It seems like a European city here with the old architecture, cobbled roads, chic little French girls. At a bus stop, they watch two teenage girls sitting cross-legged, chalking sidewalk graffiti so intently that they let the bus pass.

September 21, Quebec City, QC

After loading out the gear, the girls croon drunken blues in the alley. A nearby resident protests, "*Ferme ta guele tabernacle!*"

"*Ecoutes puis apprecie,*" Squeaky laughs.

Kitty screams, indignant, "I'm just trying to live my LIFE!"

They are exhilarated. What seemed a dud of a show revved up when Maxine gave a series of snap-kicks in gold Lycra. Soon there was a floundering pit. Then the kids started stage-diving two at a time. They gave Maxine flurries of hugs before back-flipping. Even Fanta was amazed at the rabble. It felt like watching the circus burn.

"No one wants to put their hand in the water and grab the fish," she sums up, "but once someone does, everyone wants to club it."

The sky cracks and rain begins to pour. There are a few fans gathered around the van, and trying to move around them is like swimming through mud. Their after-party goes off with a round of Irish car bombs. Someone gives Kitty a beer, but she's so drunk it drops before reaching her mouth. When the glass shatters on the cement she blindly grabs the nearest guy and yells, "If you were a bitch I'd knock you the fuck out!" On the way back to the hotel Kitty demands to stop for poutine, which she later pukes up in the elevator. Then she stumbles down the hallways, knocking artwork off the walls.

When the manager comes to the door, she is already passed out. They try to defuse the situation, but then Kitty sits up and vomits into her pillow case. The manager kicks them out of the room, and everyone packs their bags, grumbling. Squeaky is especially mad. Franky had invited her to his room to watch TV, but instead of hanging out with him now she has to drive to the next town and sleep in the van.

They've only been on the road twenty minutes when Kitty calls sleepily from the back. "Can we stop? I need to pee."

"Scissor it, bitch!" Squeaky hits the gas. "It's going to be a long night."

September 22, Trois-Rivières, QC

This is the city where she was born, and Squeaky hums a homesick little melody, taps a few beats on the seat. Kitty starts blowing into a wine bottle. "Good, good," she says. "This is a little tune I like to call 'Rag Fart.'"

Years of sweat and spilled booze have oozed through the floorboards of the club, changing the chemical makeup forever. The owner leers at Maxine's leather miniskirt, ripped fishnets, flimsy tank top, red bra underneath. They make fun of his soft gut just beginning to look absurd.

"Fuckin' muffin top," Kitty dismisses, tuning her bass as a cigarette dangles from her bottom lip. Two green lights shoot against the backdrop. From the stage they eye the empty room—stained carpet and oily, red banquettes.

When the microphones are up they start sound check. The soundman working the board says through the PA, "Drums." Squeaky taps the kick pedal and the voice booms again. "Don't hit it like a little girl. I said I want to hear DRUMS!" Afterward, as she walks by the soundman, he winds a cord so fast she trips. He has a long beard and looks like a biker. When she swears, he tells her not to stand there.

Fire Chicken have already gone to eat and the girls group outside the venue, calculating their dinner money. A party has started in the parking lot. Boys keep trying to breach their circle with loud come-ons, a few putdowns. Kitty finally loses her temper and explodes, "Can you please FUCK OFF somewhere ELSE?"

They eat greasy pizza and walk back to the club with little energy, then spend two hours bored backstage. It's impossible to pump up for the show. The vibe isn't good for them from the start, and Squeaky can tell it's strictly a Fire Chicken crowd. The room is blue with smoke and lights, and clears considerably between their songs, making the acoustics even worse. The monitors feedback and they struggle to hear themselves, slugging through every song. Finally, the set is over. They go backstage and complain about the soundman. For some reason, in the wait before Fire Chicken's set, he plays the Russian military anthem, which pisses Franky off because it fuels the absurd rumour they are a white power band.

When Fire Chicken starts, the pit becomes a churning wave of metal spikes and raised fists. Squeaky watches the kids, how their faces change as Fire Chicken play. Some of them have the kind of night in a small town that changes the direction of their lives by precious millimeters.

September 24, Moncton, NB

"Did you fuck Jonah, Kitty?"

"NO!"

"Just tell me. I walked by Fire Chicken's van last night after the show and thought I heard you guys."

"I didn't, Maxine. I don't *want* to. I wouldn't fuck him with YOUR cunt!"

The tour has worn them all down. The edges are rounded, and their most elementary humour comes out. It's the second-to-last show of an epic but exhausting two-week adventure. Then there's the long drive back, which no one wants to think about—Kitty clawing at the windows and Maxine's constant complaints.

Everyone pools their money for a decent meal before the show. They sit in T-Bone's steakhouse, and decide to share the lemon cream halibut and maple butter salmon. Kitty hasn't puked up the three double Caesars she's downed, but she's close.

"I can't believe the tour's almost over," Squeaky says glumly. She will miss living out of each other's luggage, opening the door to a motel room and the four of them rushing to claim a corner. Driving into a new city, playing the songs they wrote together, conquering a room full of skeptical strangers. Not to mention she won't get to see Franky Sparrow every day.

Maxine says, "*I'll* miss the shows. When you play rock 'n' roll, you're not thinking about sex. All you're thinking about is rock 'n' roll!"

"That must be relaxing for you."

"Oh, check out Jokey Smurf."

"I wanna buy FIRECRACKERS," Kitty exclaims.

"I'll miss these social interactions," Fanta sighs. "I really will."

They can't tell if she's being sarcastic or not.

The show is in a small nightclub, but draws a huge crowd. Standing at the microphone Maxine greets them with her usual introduction. "Hey, New Brunswick. We're Wet Leather and we like to fucking PARTY!"

Kitty grabs the microphone and slurs, "We like to *fuck!*" The band is a panel of worried faces. Squeaky kicks them immediately into "Invasion," then "Whatever, Trevor," and "GHB OD," one right after the other. A preppie gets up on stage, but instead of diving just drops lamely into the crowd. "Come on," Kitty shouts. "Tits to the pit!" A surge of girls push forward.

Maxine slaps their hands. She loves the feeling of winning over the room. Before every show the anticipation makes her want to puke, but now she's calm, sharp but relaxed, swallowing up the sound of her own voice bouncing back from the walls, thriving on it and the energy it elicits. Right up front, two punk girls in asymmetrical haircuts study her every move. Maxine holds the notes red-faced, so the cords stick out on her neck. "All right, all RIGHT, ALL RIGHT!" There's adoration and envy and lust in every gaze. She thinks, *I could fuck anyone I want in this room, tonight.*

Backstage, two determined groupies float between members of Fire Chicken. Squeaky is unimpressed. "Spandex," she murmurs, "dressing skanks since the eighties." After the gear is loaded, Fat Ricky, Jonah, Franky, and then Squeaky squish into the groupie's car. Somewhere, there's a party. Kitty piles in across laps in the backseat. She's not one to get left behind. Fanta has a few stern words with the driver, then demands Squeaky's room key. No one ever wants to bunk with Maxine for good reason—she's making out with a random fanboy she'll end up fucking loudly in the hotel room.

On the ride to the party, Squeaky can't believe her good luck. She's sitting on Franky's lap with his arms around her. Every bump makes her ass grind into him. He squeezes her as the car stops at a deserted-looking house with blaring music. A few people are clumped in a kitchen party. Everyone follows Fat Ricky and Jonah around; they're the ones with the coke. When two wasted girls begin a shrill burlesque, Franky hands Squeaky a beer and says, "Come sit outside with me."

On the busted-up porch they smoke a joint and talk about random things, like Franky's first guitar, an Ibanez with lots of low action. Squeaky says, "I really owe you. And the other guys, too. It's been a great few weeks. Thanks for taking us on."

"Hey, we'll be opening for *your* band one day."

They discuss the tour, their best shows and whose van smells the worst. Suddenly Fat Ricky bursts onto the porch. "Dude," he says to Franky. "You gotta come and see this." He rushes back in the house. "Bring something to fuck this chick with!"

Franky and Squeaky raise their eyebrows at each other, and then follow Fat Ricky to a room down the hallway. On a bed one of the Moncton groupies is spread-eagle, moaning as some guy pumps a Red Bull can in and out of her. Jonah sticks his cock near her mouth and she grabs it, sucking greedily. Someone else holds a video camera.

Squeaky walks out of the room and back onto the porch. Franky follows her. "Stay if you want to," she tells him.

"Nope," he says. "Not my style."

"I'm gonna split."

"I'm coming too. I'd rather hang out with you."

They look at each other. Squeaky feels shy and asks, "Can I have a sip of your beer?" Franky hands it over.

"Squeaky, you wanna go back to my hotel room?"

"Ummm....*yeah*."

They take Kitty with them in a cab, and turn her loose in the hotel lobby. The hallway to Franky's room smells like carpet cleaner and old food trays. At his door, Squeaky hesitates. She knows if she goes inside they're going to fuck. Lust is simple to understand, but what else is between them lies murky and undefined.

Franky says, "Are you coming in?"

She hangs *Do Not Disturb* on the doorknob behind her.

September 25, Halifax, NS

After load-in, there are a few hours before the show. Kitty heads to a pub with the guys for beer-battered fish and chips. Maxine stays sleeping at the hotel. Only Fanta and Squeaky explore the city. They climb to the top of the old citadel, and for a long time just look out at the cold, black water.

Fanta shivers. Halifax makes her think of broken ships on the rocks and sailors lost at sea. "Imagine what it would be like to just slip into the undertow."

It's the end of September, but there's a winter chill ready to settle in their bones. Squeaky puts her arm around her friend, who accepts it, and they breathe the salty air. "It's been harder than I thought," she tells Fanta. "The long drives, hours of waiting, no food, no sleep, the bad shows, everything. But we got this far, and that's something." Squeaky's breath puffs out and flutters her bangs as she speaks. She won't know what to do tomorrow night without her kit to strike and trap case to pack.

"I just wonder where all this will leave us."

"You mean when we're old? I'm going with the suicide retirement plan. Or maybe a heroin addiction, I can't decide."

Fanta stares over the water. Squeaky hugs her again and says, "Sometimes things only make sense in the moment."

It's the last show of the tour, and the fanboy from Moncton has followed Maxine. He trails her around the bar, but she's not into it. "He's too young," she complains. "*And* he watches football." Already she's looking for someone else. Fanboy corners Kitty on her way to the band room.

"Where's Maxine?" he asks, smooth-skinned and innocent. "Why won't she talk to me?"

Kitty has no time for the lie, the charade of false agreements. "She's probably figuring out how to avoid you," she shrugs.

Backstage they can hear the demands of the rowdy crowd, but it's anticlimactic. The last thing they feel like doing is performing. There's no sense of anticipation or giddiness. Everyone knows what they're doing tomorrow: driving back home to normal life and work. It's like the end of camp. The camaraderie of strangers forced to party together every night is a bond formed only under rare and specific conditions such as these.

Squeaky drums on the back of a chair to warm up. Maxine and Kitty chug their drinks. Fanta rubs her knuckles, cracks her wrist. It's time to go on.

The stage lights burn through Maxine's hangover. She's still sore from her all-night fuck-fest of mediocre sex, and gives a hollow, "Hey Halifax. We're Wet Leather." Fire Chicken stays in the band room, finishing the last of the good beer.

Squeaky starts with her *Kick-tom-boom, Kick-tom-boom, CRASH CRASH CRASH* opening, hitting the drums with rhythmic fury. Fanta plays an effortless lead, and now there are cool-looking fractures in her guitar. It's a twelve-bar shakedown, and Kitty assaults the bass with her signature grimy sound. As usual, a few males without shirts beat against each other at the front of the stage, vying for their attention.

"These chicks can shred!"

"Shit yeah, Nitro!"

Maxine loses the momentum with a lackluster "Cold-Hearted Woman," in which the crowd thins out to buy more drinks. She grabs her water bottle off the drum riser and takes a long swallow.

"Kick it up a bit," Squeaky tells her. "It's the last show."

"I *know*," Maxine snaps. "I'm doing my best. Do YOU want to stand up here and sing?"

"It's all you, Titsy Gallant."

Kitty overhears. "Ah-ha-HAH!"

During "Bitches Don't Do Dishes," Maxine musters some enthusiasm. She finally forgets her fatigue and sore booze belly.

"We're fucking little *BITCHES* and we don't do *DISHES*!" Maxine rolls around the stage with real demented flair. She knows she looks good when she sweats. Fanta stays the silent centre of the storm, uncompromising, her guitar an instrument of mayhem, of control.

Everyone hangs backstage after Fire Chicken's set. The vibe is melancholy and the last of the free booze is gone. Fanta is nearly drunk. "Those tequila shots were vulgar." She shakes the hair out of her eyes and attempts to refocus. Kitty flirts with Jonah in the corner, grabs his face as if to kiss him on the lips, then quickly turns his head and plants one on his cheek. Then they begin massaging each other. Tex tries to charm Maxine, who isn't having it.

"A few years ago I was hot for you," she tells him, "but now I got your number."

Kitty confirms, "Y'all are never getting laid! Well, except her and Franky." She points to Squeaky, who can't hide her smile fast enough. "I knew it! You two are slurping genitals, I can tell. Why are you trying to keep it a secret?"

Just then a tall, older man strolls into the band room. He's wearing an expensive watch and skate shoes, and has silver in his sideburns. Tattoos twist up and down his arms. He glances around, assessing the room.

"Eddie Camaro," Jonah says. "Hey, man!" They slap palms. "Good to see you, man. When'd you get here?"

"I had to be in Toronto for some meetings. Thought I'd catch the last show. Good numbers on this tour." Maxine and Kitty are like frozen deer on the highway.

Eddie Camaro is the original guitar player for the legendary Green Meat, one of the first bands in the West Coast punk scene. After a decade he quit, and released two solo albums that every punk owns. Then he gave up playing music and founded Skat Records. In the days of dwindling sales, Skat Records still make a decent profit as an independent label. Eddie Camaro puts out the bands that the true punks love.

"Hello, Squeaky," he says, extending his hand. "Eddie Camaro. I run Skat Records."

"Nice to meet you," she murmurs shyly.

"I'm Kitty!"

Eddie shakes her hand, too. "You know, you're playing with one of the best drummers around."

"You're tellin' me? I'm just trying to keep up."

"I'm a *huge* Green Meat fan," Maxine interjects. "But, I mean, I really liked your solo stuff, too." Star-struck, she touches him with an outstretched arm, and then makes bowing motions like he's a shrine. Everyone cringes.

His manner is friendly and relaxed, unpretentious. "Franky speaks very highly of this band."

He asks Tex and Jonah to give him a few minutes. When they shut the door it's quiet without the raucousness of bar noise filtering in. Eddie Camaro has an intelligent face and dark eyes, almost black, a weary yet knowing look. His voice exudes calm authority.

"I like your sound. Stripped down but catchy songs, that's good. A Thin-Lizzy-meets-Poly-Styrene kind of thing. Fucking great guitar leads. The vocals aren't quite there yet..."

"I know, I know, right?"

"...but some of the songs aren't in your key." Maxine deflates then beams when Eddie says, "There's a definite stage presence."

"THANKS! Oh my god..."

"All the way to the kit. I fucking love it. The fact it's still raw and unpolished really showcases the guitar. You should think about recording your album with Skat Records."

Kitty blurts, "But I don't even have a decent amp!" Maxine gives her a withering look.

"I've been interested since Franky sent me your demo." Eddie sits down and opens a beer. "This industry has gone belly up. CD sales are way down, and everyone's had to scale back. What you've got now is these corporations buying up big bands, with contracts that give them control of not only the music but the merchandise, back catalogues, everything. So after they spend multi-millions on the big names, they don't have anything left for new bands. If you're a smaller outfit it comes down to touring, word of mouth. Grass roots in the digital age. But let's face it, there's not too many women doing what you're doing. If you're interested—"

"We ARE!"

"Then why don't you come to New York for a few days? Franky offered to drive your van back and I'll fly you home. We'll talk more, and, if you like what I'm saying, we can look at a contract."

"Look, Mr. Camaro," Squeaky says. Everyone is surprised. She's the easygoing beat-keeper, not the first to complain. "I don't want it to be a big deal, like some huge marketing push about us being an all-girl band. We happen to be chicks and we rock."

Eddie says, "Then just stay strong and true."

New York City

The noise is deafening the minute Maxine steps onto the sidewalk. A man selling sunglasses whistles when she passes. “Heya, Blondie, that’s a belt, not a skirt!”

“Whatever whatever,” she shrugs, strutting past. “I do what I want.”

The streets are liver-spotted with gum, and the September humidity lingers, relentless. Maxine stops for a pack of cigarettes at the corner newsstand and watches a large woman in tight pants, ass jiggling. Following her is an Asian man with mincing steps, eyes glued to her behind. Men in suits talk loudly on their phones, cars honk, stylish women halt taxis with ease. There are so many windows in this city, so many lives being lived behind them, right now, and in this minute Maxine’s part of it. She buys her cigarettes and swings her hips on the walk back to Eddie’s, unlocks three different doors to get inside.

Eddie Camaro's assistant Judy picked them up at the airport; Irish, sweet-faced, and sharp-tongued, she knows her way around the city. Eddie owns an apartment in midtown Manhattan, with an adjacent band suite. It is clean and comfortable, decorated with gig posters and old maps. Julie leaves them with directions to a restaurant down the street where they'll meet Eddie in a few hours. Everyone sprawls out to unwind.

"Hey," Kitty says, "what're we gonna do here? There's no TV!" Fanta throws up her hands in disgust.

At Cafe Andalucía, Guillermo, the owner, flirts with the girls even though he's in his seventies and complains of rheumatism. Self-portraits and paintings of women *in flagrante delicto* hang on the walls next to scenes of bullfights and charcuterie. Eddie orders plates of anchovies with olives, prosciutto, and fine cheeses. In the corner is a jukebox. Kitty borrows money to feed it, then sings along loudly to her selections.

Eddie asks Fanta, "Have you been to New York before?" He pours her another glass of Roja.

"Once, before the World Trade Center." While visiting her mother in Sudbury, she took a Greyhound bus to see her friends, who'd become high-rolling waitresses living in Brooklyn. "People seem kinder now, more willing to talk to each other. But I'm a stranger," she pauses, "and don't know if that's true."

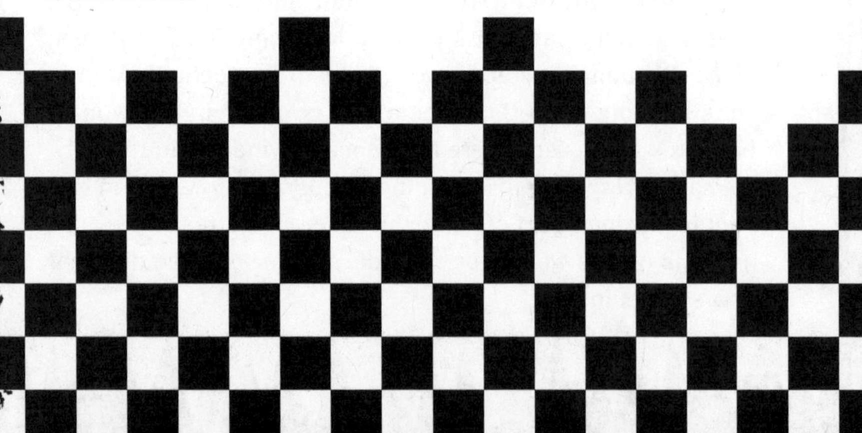

They have the next day to themselves until their business dinner with Eddie. They have little money and walk everywhere. Maxine falls into her stride in the city, the grinding noise her natural backdrop. Fanta is slow and determined, a map always folded in her pocket, while Kitty runs between them like an excited stray, barking the names of streets and subway stations. Back at the apartment, the girls change for their dinner meeting with Eddie Camaro.

The restaurant is a place Maxine has seen mentioned in her gossip magazines, so hip it has a one-letter name. A genteel woman asks if they have a reservation and then slips off their coats. Eddie waits for them at the bar. The room is softly lit and draped in rich linens, its patrons' heads in a constant swivel.

Maxine whispers to Kitty, who is finishing her second cocktail, "Those whisky sours you keep drinking are twenty-five bucks each." Kitty nearly spits up then discreetly slips a fork and teaspoon into her pocket.

"Don't worry," Eddie winks. "I'll charge it to the company."

They work their way through grapefruit-ginger scallop ceviche, Norwegian salmon, and Moroccan spice-rubbed lamb rack, with a white wine gruyere fondue for Fanta, the lone vegetarian. "I'll get right down to it," Eddie begins. "I want to produce your record and sign Wet Leather to Skat for a two-album deal."

Maxine's mouth is full and she nods with vigor. "MMM-HMMM!" Kitty and Squeaky slap palms.

"I'm not signing a multiple-record deal," Fanta says.

"Well, we don't want to put the time and effort into promoting a band who become successful then walk away after we've done the hard work."

"One album. That's it."

"We haven't decided that," Maxine says testily. "As a *band*."

"It needs to be figured out when you come to the office tomorrow and look at a contract."

"One album at a time or I sign nothing," Fanta insists. It would be great to have a quality recording, but she won't commit herself, on paper, to anything for too long. She continues eating her golden beet carpaccio as if she hasn't said a thing.

The next day it's so hot they feel like the melting rooftop tar. Maxine steps out into the street to whistle for a taxi, wiggling inside her push-up bra. A car stops at once. "Fifth Avenue and 17th Street, drivah." She's already developed a faint Queens brogue.

The city overwhelms Kitty Domingo. It makes her nervous and fidgety. "Do we know where we're going? I don't want to get crimed." Squeaky calms her down by calling out Times Square marquees in various accents. They arrive at the Skat Records office, and after being announced by security, they ride the elevator to a bright, open office of buzzing cubicles.

Judy comes out to greet them looking frazzled. Her red corkscrew curls are awry, not her usual polished look. One of her fake nails is missing. "I'm trying to quit smoking," she whispers. "I don't think I want to live anymore."

She leads the girls up the spiral staircase to Eddie's office, directs them to the soft leather sofa and chairs nestled around a walnut table. After giving them each copies of the contract, she gently refuses Kitty's request for a tequila sunrise.

"Read through this and Eddie will be in shortly to go over it. Then hopefully we can celebrate. God, I think I'd commit *murder* for a cigarette right now!"

After struggling with the law jargon, they elect Fanta to read the contract and tell them what it says. While they wait for her to finish, Maxine opens the window. Exhaust fumes and noise balloon upward: horns blaring and shouts of angry pedestrians. She picks a random window and wonders: Who lives there? How do they make their money? What are they doing? What's the worst thing that ever happened to them? She looks at the hundreds of thousands of windows and it's overwhelming.

"Well, Fanta?"

"The contract offers us ten thousand dollars to start—"

"Ten GRAND," Kitty squeals. She bounces in her chair and then stops. "Wait, is that good?"

Fanta continues, "The advance gets paid back out of our sales, which they call *recouping*. Skat puts up the studio time to record our album, and pays the expenses such as the pressing and art department. They guarantee negotiable tour support." She flips back the pages of stapled papers. "Meaning the more money we spend on tour, the less for us at the end. There's no signing bonus." She looks at Maxine. "And it's a record by record deal."

It irks Maxine to hear satisfaction in her voice. "Okay, but do we get to keep the rights to our songs?"

"No, the label has all the rights, forever. They also get to use our material in other projects, such as Skat Records compilations and videos. And there's no mention about creative control except that each song, and the album as a whole, has to be approved by Skat Records before its release." She brushes the hair out of her eyes and shrugs. "It's not a deal with the devil. I'm sure this is standard stuff for a label this size."

Maxine will sign anything. She's nearing the end of her thirties and believes this is the last chance for a music career. Looking below at the crowded streets—tourists, cons, cripples, CEOs, street vendors, socialites, thieves—she wants them all to know her name. "Let's do it," she says. "I'm in."

"Me too," Kitty says. "Who else is gonna pay *us* to make a record for them?" She picks up the contract and throws it down again for emphasis. "Hurry and sign it before they change their minds!"

"We have to pay it all back," Fanta warns. "It's not free money."

"Let's sign it—in *menstrual* blood."

"Why do you have to say things like that, Kitty?"

"I don't want our songs to get fucked with too much," Squeaky says. "That whole part about their approval makes me nervous."

"Fuck that! I'll be a slave babe. I can't *wait* to sell out!"

Kitty cracks them up and they're still giggling when Eddie comes in. There is a bemused look on his face when he sits down and asks, "What's the joke?"

For the next hour they go through the contract, point by point. Kitty struggles to pay attention. She gives up and makes noises to herself until it's time to sign her name.

"But you have to understand something, Eddie." Squeaky curls her small fists on the table. "There's a whole vibe to Wet Leather. Our music is the kind you play when you're drinking a bottle of tequila on a Saturday night, getting so drunk you become a whore. A *cheap* whore. You know? Music that makes you get rowdy, gives you the balls to quit your job. Not some watered down Auto-Tune and Beat Detective crap. Our music is the real deal, because *we're* the real deal. So I'm sorry, but our first priority is not making hits for the radio."

Maxine interrupts, "Not that we don't *want* to have a hit song on the radio..."

"If we sign the contract, then realize we don't like the direction it's going and quit, what happens then?" It terrifies Squeaky to think of putting out poppy mall-punk hits people would ridicule, especially her brothers.

The leather chair squeaks as Eddie leans back. He's treated them well but they know he doesn't run a successful record label by being a nice guy.

"Typically," he answers, "we'd sue you into the stone age."

Julie comes in with glasses on a tray. Soon the sounds of popping champagne corks fill the room.

In Eddie's small courtyard, Squeaky grills vegetable skewers and steaks thick with chipotle saffron. There is a bottle of Glenlivet on the round glass table from which they toast every ten minutes or so. Eddie has to leave soon for a flight to San Francisco, where he splits his time. Skat Records has a recording studio there as well as in Colorado. Wet Leather is booked for three weeks of studio time mid-January, which gives them almost four months to work on the songs for their album.

Eddie lays down his napkin. "That was a fantastic meal," he compliments Squeaky, who gives a modest shrug.

"I can't believe we have to leave New York tomorrow," Maxine sighs. There is a feeling in her gut like she belongs here and shouldn't go home. Eddie has gotten them invitations to the after-party of a movie screening, and she heads to his bathroom to check her hair. When she comes out she notices a black and white photograph on the wall. It's a grainy photo of a pretty brunette, smiling sadly at the camera, as a much younger Eddie holds her close.

Maxine jumps when he clears his throat from the doorway. "Sorry," she apologizes. "I was just leaving the bathroom and...who's in this picture with you?" She wonders if that's the infamous girl Eddie wrote his first album about. *Spider Songs*. It's a little piece of a punk rock icon, and Maxine's hoping to hear the story.

Eddie studies the photograph with a tender look. "She would've really loved your band. Maybe that's why I'm pushing

for you girls to succeed." The light drains from his face when he says, "I lost her a long time ago."

The car arrives to take Eddie to the airport. "I'll see you in a few months," he says, and gives them each an affectionate hug. Back in the band suite Maxine stands at the mirror, holding her stomach.

"I feel bread-plugged," she moans. "I ate too much, and I have a potbelly in this dress."

"Potbellies are the new washboard abs," Kitty says. "Just like ass is the new pussy."

Outside they wait for a taxi and a couple of kids in mini-gangster gear push past. "Check out the junior juice," Kitty points, so enthralled she is nearly run over by a cyclist. "Holy shit, that missed me by a cunt hair!"

The party is at 21st and Lexington. They give their names to the doorman who consults his clipboard then lets them inside. In the lobby a bejewelled woman yells in Italian at an older gent who sits on a plush purple love seat. The party is in a two-level apartment with checkerboard marble floors. The men are in tailored suits, while the women wear expensive gowns and grip designer handbags. Black and white light bulbs, thousands, cover the ceiling.

"I hate it when I overdress for these things," Squeaky says. She's wearing sneakers and a hoodie. Kitty has barbecue sauce on her shirt.

"Fuck, I need a drink," Maxine hisses. "I feel like a gang of idiots. And Kitty, don't you dare roll a slut butt from the ashtray!"

A manicured fop approaches Fanta at the bar, asks what she does for a living. "I sell toilets." He quickly slinks away.

Drinks are expensive and they warn Kitty not to steal them. Squeaky lights the joint in her pocket and the star of the movie comes over. "I smelled something and *knew* it was you." Her mouth is agape. "Can I have a hit of that?" He is even more gorgeous in person, his shirt the most dazzling white she's ever seen. After handing back the doobie, he kisses her hand and saunters away.

"Jeezus, did you see that? Squeaky actually swooned."

"Nuh-UH!"

The girls stiffly try out poses. On the other side of the room there is a small cluster of fawning women around the movie star and his brilliant white shirt. He looks stoned and bored. Fanta asks, "Do you hate this, Maxine?"

"Nah, I hate to love it."

Kitty interrupts them, demanding a tampon. "You should invest in some of your own," Maxine scolds, trying to hand it to her with discretion from her purse.

"These are SLIMS. I need a bigger rig!"

"C'mon," Squeaky says. "Do you guys really want to stay at this party? Let's go somewhere I can afford to get gnarly."

"Deal breakers with dirty asses," Kitty says, too loud. "I hate these shit-cocks!"

"We'd better go. Kitty's already at Stage Four!"

Maxine doesn't want to leave. She's never been to a party like this before. Who knows who she might meet? With reluctance, she follows the girls, who swing loud and untouched through the crowd. She loses them at the impasse of a couple that won't step out of her way. He's a slick-haired, suited man, and she's a bony, overdone blonde.

"Oh my *god*," the woman titters, as her date cranes to peer at Maxine's tight dress emblazoned with a dragon, the mouth of which ends at her crotch. "They let *anyone* in these days."

Maxine hurries after her girls. She isn't ready to be here. Yet.

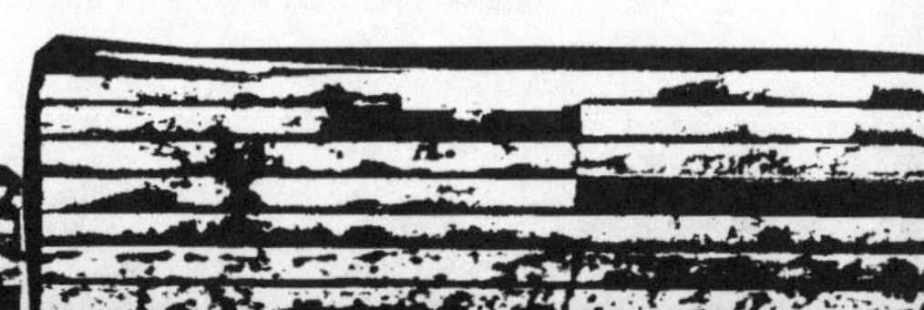

Maxine opens the front door already feeling like a has-been. The tea with pot butter and handful of morphine pills for the five-hour flight got her home, but her nerves are long since shot. It's depressing to be here, back in her old life of work and debt. She sags for a moment, trying to adjust.

Squeaky pushes past her into the foyer. "Rosie baby," she calls, dropping her bags. "We're home!"

Rosie comes out of the kitchen and gives Squeaky an affectionate hug. "I've missed you." She looks at Maxine and says hello, but her tone is cool.

"We called from New York," Squeaky says. "Did you get the message?"

"You signed with Skat Records. It's fantastic news."

"That's right," Maxine says. "We're going to be *HUGE*."

Rosie wants it to happen for them. Wet Leather's music gives her back the lost memories of her youth: of being out in the sun in a bikini, drinking beer, sand in her shoes, cute boys in the next room, bases loaded, being part of a crowd when everyone shares the same moment. She doesn't doubt Maxine will find the notoriety she craves, but it will come at a price. It's not just her talent that will take her far. And Maxine will go all the way.

Rosie's smile borders on pity. Maxine decides it's the last she'll ever look at her that way again.

After a run to the grocery store, Squeaky prepares a returning feast of chicken mole, cornbread, and flaming tongues of roasted red peppers. Fanta went directly home and Kitty has gone to see her mom. It's just the three of them, and there's too much food. Squeaky pours a round of strawberry, pineapple, and jalapeno margaritas. Rosie declines. The house is quiet as they finish their plates.

"I called a bunch of times from the road. How come you never answered?"

"I've been sick lately," Rosie smiles. "I'm pregnant!"

They don't have to ask if she'll keep it. Squeaky squeals and jumps up to hug her. "Well, aren't *you* a fuckin' little bitch!"

"Congratulations," Maxine says, but it's not completely sincere. She feels envy, turmoil, regret. When they were young *she* talked about wanting kids, never Rosie. Already Maxine can picture it: Tony moving in, their perfect child, a fairytale wedding, and then Rosie popping out a whole fashion line of adorable tots. Maxine excuses herself and stays in the bathroom a full ten minutes. On the way back Rosie pulls her aside.

"When the baby comes it's probably better you don't stay here."

"How about I leave right *now*?"

Rosie shrugs. "Suit yourself."

"Well, here's to looking at the bottom of the goddamn glass once again. What the fuck am *I* supposed to do?"

"This is what you do, Maxine. You stand up and move one foot and then the other and then you go."

Fanta is happy to be home, alone again. She eats noisily, wears unflattering and comfortable clothes, breaks wind, smokes joints, and talks to herself. She demands a month off from dealing with anything band-related. When they call, Fanta won't answer or return messages. It doesn't matter that Maxine is depressed about business at Freudian Slips, or Rosie's raging hormones. Fanta doesn't even go out on Halloween. If they leave her alone for one month, she promises to write the music they need for the album. Maxine doesn't want to lose any momentum, but lyrics are the last thing to be added so there isn't much she can say. In every way they need Fanta more than she needs them. Four weeks pass and on Thursday night she shows up at Rosie's with her guitar, just like she promised.

It's early November and not raining, so Squeaky fires up the BBQ for baby-back ribs and Dijon egg salad, a dinner in honour of Rosie's pregnancy.

"I'm glad you're having this baby. Otherwise we'd be eating egg drop soup. With charred tomato calamari."

"Borscht," Maxine laughs. "With the sour cream bleeding in. Followed by a lovely cayenne pepper tea."

"And cave cheese," Kitty adds. They groan in disgust.

Rosie is wrapped in a shawl on the rocking chair, with her hair in a side braid streaked with amber. She wears a flannel shirt and thick woollen socks, and has the easy smile of a contented woman. Looking at each of them she says, "It seems so long since the last time we were all together." Maxine left most of her furniture and hasn't been back since the fight that nobody mentions.

"We gotta stick together," Squeaky says. "Four bitches is one thing, but with five you can take over a country."

Fanta asks, "Boy or a girl?"

"I'm into raising female warriors," Rosie says. "Forget lions."

Kitty is self-elected DJ and plays The Muffs and The Raincoats and The Slits and The Gits. They sit down with Fanta after dinner to go over the money Wet Leather made from the tour minus expenses. It seems they just broke even. Kitty does some calculations and comes up with an absurd figure. “Nice work,” Maxine says. “Did you skip math class to sit in the smoke hole?”

They go downstairs to practise, sadly aware they’ll have to find a new jam spot once the baby comes. It’s a familiar jumble of cables and crates. Everyone turns on, plugs in, and fixes their levels. By the middle of the fourth song it starts to come back.

Fanta sets about teaching a new arrangement to Kitty. “I’ll just noodle,” she says.

“Anyone can noodle. Learn the song.”

For a while Maxine sits and listens to Fanta, how patiently she teaches. When Squeaky begins to fiddle with the lugs on her drumheads, Maxine goes upstairs. Rosie sits in the kitchen with a cup of tea and a crossword, looks up then back down when Maxine slinks in.

“Look, I’m sorry for how I acted before the tour. I was a jerk. You forgive me, right?”

Rosie puts down her pen. “You say hateful things and apologize and then it’s okay? That’s negotiable.”

“Yeah, but then *you* kicked me out! I had to go live with my mother.”

“I gave you seven months’ notice.”

“Still…”

“You couldn’t live here with a crying baby. It would drive you nuts. It’ll probably drive *me* nuts.”

Maxine erupts with staccato laugher and says with relief, “So have you, like, bought a crib or anything?”

“No, we’re going to keep the baby in a drawer.”

“Do you love being pregnant? I heard you get hemorrhoids. Is it weird to have something growing in there? I mean in your belly, not your ass.” She babbles on, and Rosie wonders if fame is her only aspiration. She’d once been that lonely, too. Thankfully, downstairs they call for Maxine.

Fanta has shown Kitty the song basics, and now has to teach the melody to Maxine. She plays it through once then slows it down. Kitty runs her fingers along the fret board, popping the strings. They try to come up with some lyrics but nothing flows.

"Why don't we just leave it as an instrumental?"

Maxine has been scribbling on a notepad and jumps up. "No, I've got something. And Squeaky, slow it d-o-o-o-wn." She rattles the paper in her hand and belts out with her raspy voice:

"Get your shit together
Or get the fuck on out
Get the fuck on out!"

"Your frustration
Is gettin' aggravating
So here's an invitation
To the local bus station
To get the fuck on out
Get the fuck on out!"

"Gee, what are we gonna call *this* song?"

"Hmmm," Fanta replies ponderously, "perhaps something along the lines of...say...*get the fuck on out*?"

"You got anything better?" Maxine barks. "No? Then let's take it from the bridge." They straighten up and sing like raunchy choir girls in perfect key:

"Get your shit together
Or get the fuck on out
Get the fuck on out!"

Christmas flies past and they decide to play the new songs live before heading into the studio. They get a Friday night gig at The Sewer. Rosie, who in Maxine's opinion is overly protective of her ballooning gut, has refused to come down to the show for fear of flying elbows.

The Sewer is filthier than any bar they played on the Canadian tour, and doesn't even have a backstage area. In the women's bathroom there are broken tiles and rotting wood over the dirt floor. One stall has a sheet of blue plastic for a door. In another, the toilet seat is rimmed in shit. In the very last stall a girl retches. Maxine leans over the clogged sink and puts on more lipstick in the mirror. *Hey, Vancouver*, she thinks, *I'm home*.

Wet Leather wait to play, cramped on the ramp that leads to the stage. The singer of the opening band pulls out her enormous tits and wags them at the crowd. Fanta and Squeaky watch, appalled. The barely dressed backup singers are tuneless, clearly there for show. During the songs a drunken grey-hair gets up to join them, lifts her skirt and gyrates at the crowd.

"Nice ass," Kitty comments. "It looks like a pancake with a rip in it."

She spots Paula Grubler in the crowd, wearing a studded leather jacket and wielding a gigantic purse. "Mother-cunt," Kitty says, nudging Squeaky. "I can't believe she showed up!"

"This is me, letting that butt nut roll right off my back."

Kitty makes a face. "Where's Franky?"

"He has to do a clip tonight. Hey, we should find Maxine. We're up next."

"Ah, there's lots of time. She's probably in the bathroom, emptying her turd holster."

Squeaky decides to get some fresh air. She likes to go outside and check the vibe before a gig. Outside she says hello to a few acquaintances, makes small talk. Then she hears a familiar voice. Rocket walks over, and she already knows what he's going to say.

"Squeaky, can you put me on the guest list?"

It's hard for her to look at her ex-boyfriend and believe she'd once been so hurt by him. He looks wrinkled and grey, with the unhealthy pallor of an addict. She remembers his bad moods and ill-humour that lasted right until the day she'd left.

Then Rocket had cried and they'd fucked and he'd told her that he loved her. But still he wanted her out.

"My guest list is full. Sorry."

"Oh, come on babe…"

"I never gave you a hard time about anything. I never once made you feel bad about our breakup." Squeaky doesn't have to say it loudly because they both know it's true.

"I know," Rocket answers uneasily. "Thanks, babe."

"So the least you can do is pay ten bucks and not swindle into my show. Okay, *babe?*"

Squeaky turns and heads back inside. After she'd moved out, Rocket had come over with a box of things she'd left behind, including a pair of underwear that weren't hers. Seeing him is a reminder of all the ways her dating life has drastically improved.

When it's their turn to go on, Kitty curses the soundman. "This is some decrepit shit, dude." She scowls at the crackling switches. Her gear is so thrashed her patch cord is taped to the side of the bass head.

"This must be Vancouver," Maxine yells, stepping to the microphone. "I can smell the ROCK!" Fanta wonders if she can sound any more generic. They start the first song and it's sloppy, but the crowd of drunkards loves it. Kitty Domingo gets huge cheers from her fan base here tonight. She's come a long way from the days of straining butts out of beers.

The room smells hot with an undercurrent of electricity. Each song takes on a life of its own, reflecting the atmosphere of the crowd. The set is tight and seamless until the start of their new song, "Next Thursday." It's about her abortion, and Kitty attacks her bass strings with a jagged-toothed aggression, hitting all the wrong notes. Maxine tries out a new wave falsetto:

"I never wanted a
fuck tro-phy,
I just wanted
you to love me..."

Kitty thrashes away, knocking over the mic stand. A moment flashes from those bloody, pain-hazy days: sad music on the radio upstairs, hot water running as she sat in the bathtub, killing her baby. The song changes into a grinding, deathcore refrain she spits at the audience:

"Next Thursday is taking too long
Next Thursday this creature is GONE!"

The crowd throws the violent energy right back. Wasted punks slam each other and knock against the stage. One of them pulls out Maxine's microphone cord then Kitty breaks a string. They wait for her to change while Fanta plays the familiar opening to an old Guns N' Roses song. It's a joke, but everyone loves it. "C'mon Fanta, shake it," Maxine encourages. "Rattle those bones!"

During the next song, Squeaky looks out at the crowd and sees Paula Grubler squished up front. Rocket rubs up behind her. Paula gives her a smile and even waves. It's so startling Squeaky messes up the tempo and overcompensates. Fanta turns and makes eye contact, and she quickly recovers.

After the encore, Squeaky throws her sticks into the crowd and goes out back to cool off. Her hair is dripping with sweat. It wasn't a great show, musically, but she figures that happens with new material, and thanks a couple of fans. Going back inside, she notices Jesse, from the Nation of Fuckers, sitting at the bar. He's still got his unfortunate beer gut and ridiculous mustache. She also knows he's friends with Rocket. Squeaky hops up on the stool beside him.

"Hey, Squeaky," Jesse says, punching her arm. They've always been cool with each other and often compared hockey teams. "That was a great show. You guys have really improved since the Nation of Fuckers convention."

"Thanks, man." Squeaky cuts right to it. "So, how long has Rocket been with her?"

"Who?"

"You know, the one he's with now."

"Oh, you mean Paula?"

"Yeah...PAULA."

Jesse realizes he's done something wrong. "Don't ask me anything else," he pleads. "I can't incriminate myself."

Squeaky apologizes and he buys her a shot. The whisky sloshes in her stomach. She hasn't talked to Paula in well over a year, Rocket even longer. It shouldn't matter if they're together but it bugs her anyway.

Then Jesse spots Maxine. "Hey, girl! You looking for a mustache ride?"

The last time Maxine had seen Jesse was when he'd taken her to the Nation of Fuckers clubhouse and ditched her. She stops and juts out her hip. "I'd watch it," she warns.

"Does that mean you don't wanna swab my knob?"

"Bouncer!" Maxine snaps her fingers and points to Jesse, who quickly hustles his ass away.

Squeaky is incredulous. "That was a little excessive, wasn't it?"

"No. He can't talk to me like that."

"Who pissed in *your* bannock? Jesse made a bad joke. That's nothing new for him. When you do shit like that to someone, it gives us *all* a bad name."

"Thanks for having my back," Maxine rages. "You should be sticking up for me, not acting like a two-faced bitch!"

When the soundman takes down the microphones, Squeaky unscrews her cymbals slowly, spends an extra-long time removing the rack toms off the stand and the legs off the floor toms, putting everything into their bags and cases. When she's finished, she sits at an empty booth, still upset from Maxine's outburst.

Just then, Paula Grubler comes and stands at the edge of her table. It's the worst timing. She looks the same except for bigger hair and a nose ring. It appears she's even had some success with mustache removal. There is a hopeful expression on her face.

"Hello Squeaky. Can we talk?"

"I'd like not to know you," she snaps. "Can we please start *now*?"

Paula Grubler's eyes fill with tears and she lowers her head. Squeaky watches her walk away with the feeling of destroying an enemy, only to realize how much you miss hating them.

The mohawked promoter, a fat blonde with booze nose, tells them the cash box has been stolen so they won't get paid. Maxine storms through the club, ranting, demanding apologies and free drinks. Only one tour and she's used to getting what she wants.

the Studio

There are four people living full-time in a three-room studio, a small, industrial space with no windows. Only Fanta makes an effort to bathe. It's January in San Francisco, it's raining. It doesn't seem like a good place to be.

"You can't hide behind the fig leaf of punk rock forever," Eddie tells Kitty from the control room, when she messes up a walking bass line for the sixth time in a row. Nothing comes easy or fast, but what they have down so far is good.

There are two rooms in the universe that matter right now: the studio and the control booth. Down the hallway is the living space: a kitchenette, stained circular couch, and a triple-level bunk bed. A glass door leads to a small outdoor slab of concrete. It's a cramped space and Maxine, even more than Kitty, is climbing the walls. She tells a few painful jokes and says, "How am I doing? I'll be here all night."

Fanta plays her tracks over and over, through different amps and guitars. There is an endless tuning of strings and tweaking of delay and reverb. Eddie loves the power chords she's built into every song, and gives her distortion pedals to try out. They mess with the flanger box, even a phaser. Lixie, the engineer, is concerned over diminishing studio time. She pushes up her glasses worriedly. "What if it's not done?"

"Who comes in next, Far from Finished? Bump those guys back a week," Eddie shrugs. "No big deal."

There are all-night music and drinking sessions, followed by Squeaky's pre-dawn feasts: paneer pizzas with lotus chips, avocado and cashew enchiladas, ratatouille with whole cloves of garlic so they won't get sick. When the band wakes up in the early afternoon, it starts all over again. Each song is taken apart and re-tuned, dissected from vocals to drums. Everything gets thrown in the mix, and they play in and out of what the other is doing. This working environment requires them to drink pomegranate mojitos, cases of beer, and hot chocolate with Irish cream.

The record will take a few months to mix and be released in spring. Eddie Camaro sends Maxine for singing lessons to learn proper breathing techniques and not blow her voice out so often. Eddie is the right producer to enhance their sound. Everyone likes the direction he's taking while honing their songs. He changes the arrangements and brings their musical style together with the right amount of polish. They've finally got the right amps matched to their guitars.

Eddie watches Squeaky in the studio as she thunders through the drums. "I'm impressed she can play along to a click track. Not everyone can do that." Squeaky is a tiny, two-armed orchestra all of her own.

Maxine hangs in the console with him as he goes over levels. "There's so many buttons in here it's like being in a rock 'n' roll spaceship," she says. Eddie doesn't respond, and she has begun to feel like he encourages everyone but her. When Fanta heads into the studio next, he raves over every note she plays.

"Listen to that," he says to Maxine. "She can take three chords and make them really *mean* something."

"What about me?"

"Drums, guitar, bass, and then vocals."

"I mean, do *I* have what it takes?"

"I'm backing this band the whole way."

Her voice becomes husky when she touches his arm. "Your opinion means *a lot* to me."

Eddie flicks the intercom. "Oh, that's a sweet chord," he says.

As a band, they feel an urgency that wasn't there before. There had been a long period of songwriting and rehearsals in Rosie's basement that led to this recording. Only Fanta remains unaffected. She's written her solos and knows what she's going to do. The simple assembling of notes is chosen for their effectiveness. Fanta likes everything to be useful and compact. She doesn't care for guitar layering, and prefers a raw sound. They soldier through daily recording sessions and cut the basic tracks.

Kitty is confined to the living room, plugged into a tiny practise Marshall. There are times when she wants to slip out, see if she can find some black tar. San Francisco isn't her town, but dealers on the corner all look the same. There are too many things to think about now: having a publicist and booking agent, doing promotion and press. The music she plays is based on anger—chaotic jams. Sitting in the studio and discussing each song dissects it to death. Kitty wonders if she went out and got some heroin, how long it would take for anyone to notice.

Eddie tells her to get ready, she'll be up next. He'll get the right sounds out of her bass no matter how long it takes.

They go out for some air and drive through Chinatown. A woman walks into traffic and nearly gets hit by their van. "Watch it lady," Kitty yells out the window. "This ain't Tiananmen Square!" She wants to be dropped off in Berkeley, where she knows some old Gilman Street punks, but the girls refuse. Everyone is keeping a close eye on her.

"Hey Kitty, I forgot to tell you Jasper called while you were in the booth. Twice."

"He's a Pisces and I'm an Aries. That fishy fucker is always trying to put my fire out!"

"I'm so sick of hearing about Jasper," Maxine grumbles. "Put a sock in it."

"Why don't you put a COCK in it?"

There's remarkably little dissension within the group, but it happens. "We're making progress," Squeaky says, but uncertainty belies optimism. All day Maxine has been in a dark mood. Her vocals are the last to get recorded and it's wearing on her. She is wearing the Face—mouth turned downward and a thunderstorm scowl. It could take hours of cajoling for her to relent. When the van stops, she opens the door and stomps off.

"Fucksake," Kitty groans. "What's she mad about NOW?"

"Next Thursday is taking too long..."

"Next Thursday is taaaaaking too long..."

"Next Thursday is taking too looooooong..."

"Yes! That's it! That's the one! Excellent! Now, one more time."

Lixie has been recording bands at Skat Records for almost ten years. Compared to other groups, she says Wet Leather is far less organized, but way more fun. Squeaky asks her how the album's going. "What happens between you guys comes out in there," she says, pointing to the studio. "And there's a strange mix tonight." Lixie believes most things are geographically determined.

"I'VE GOT IT," Kitty screams as they sit on the circular couch, brainstorming album titles. After a few shots and a bump, her volume is on eleven. "BORN WITH BUSH!"

"Interesting," Fanta responds. "I like the socio-political subtext, as well as it being a comment on the sexualization of young girls."

"HUH?"

Squeaky says, "I like it, too."

"We're probably not going to think of anything better," Maxine adds.

"Do we all agree?"

"*Born with Bush* it is."

"Born with Bush, ALL *RIGHT!*"

The control booth is like a sensory deprivation chamber. It's the best place to sleep if one wants to be without sound or light, and Kitty's favourite spot besides the top bunk. With four girls in this environment, solitude is hard to come by. When Lixie gets to work, she laughs at Kitty's rumpled hair. "Shut your fuck before I kick you in the man-pussy," she says, half-heartedly.

Today the plan is to work on tracking vocals. Squeaky makes a lunch of mini-burgers and polenta fries while everyone sits in front of the TV, waiting for their turn in the booth.

"This is fucking painful," Maxine complains. "*How* expensive is studio time? And they're just using Pro Tools."

Squeaky nods. "There are so many turd polishers. It's sucked the soul right out of music—out of everything." They agree it was easier when Wet Leather made their demo playing live off the floor. If a guitar went out of tune they were stuck with it, but the shitty sound had a certain appeal. Eddie wants this Wet Leather album precise and meticulous.

"Lixie says we have an interesting dynamic."

"No kidding. You can't tell me other bands work like this," Squeaky says, and throws a mini-burger at Kitty, who catches it in her mouth with a snap.

"That's it," Eddie says over the studio speakers. "You're done."

It's five a.m. and they've finished backing vocals of the last two songs: their cover of "Kicking it Down" and "Whatever, Trevor." Eddie and Fanta added a whole new verse:

"You snort lines and discuss
your numb nose
then wonder where all
the time goes
Whatever, Trevor."

Eddie has booked Wet Leather on a summer tour with Fire Chicken across America. "You're tough enough to handle it," he says. They've proved themselves during the last crazy few weeks—eating, drinking, playing music in a three-room studio. The less resilient would go mad.

The girls also meet their publicist. Her name is Adalita Medina and she works for Skat Records Canada out of the Toronto office. She is a tiny, tough Chicana who once terrorized an entire Mexican village for three weeks on peyote. Adalita has the ageless look of a woman who has spent her life enjoying it. Her three sons are named after kings and eat potato chips for breakfast. They are the smartest kids in their grade.

They learn this and more during a night of drinking with Adalita that ends in a bar in Oakland. Adalita is staying nearby, and says goodnight. They promise to go back to the studio after a final drink. Tomorrow the girls are driving home to Vancouver. Fanta went to bed hours ago.

The red-haired bartender has thin lips and entertains a group of white wannabe gangsters. Kitty stomps past in her big black boots and one of the guys says, "Why dontcha come over here and sit on dees nuts?"

A skinny woman asks Maxine for beer money. "I only need a dollah," she begs. Maxine makes a beeline for the bathroom. The skinny woman drifts away, muttering.

Squeaky waits at the bar to order a final round.

Sudden loud voices make everyone turn. The posse of white boys is closed in a tight circle, and there's some sort of commotion in the middle. When it breaks they see that one of the white boys has the skinny woman in a headlock. He's punching her in the face. Squeaky grabs a bottle off the counter and pounces on a goon. He picks her up then throws her to the floor like a rag doll.

Kitty bellows and runs in. A man punches her in the chest and then breaks a bottle over her head. The bathroom door opens and Maxine launches herself, kicking, and lands one square in the first set of balls. She picks up a chair and throws it in shock. Other patrons just stand around watching. The last ranting white boy is wrestled out the door by his friends. Squeaky has blood on her face and Maxine demands the bartender call the police. "We're fucking pressing charges," she screams.

"That trash bag was mouthing off," the bartender says. "Those guys are my friends."

"CALL THE FUCKING COPS!"

Everyone from the bar pours outside. When the police arrive Squeaky has a bloody towel against her head. One officer questions them, and the bartender, then some witnesses. A second cop talks to the glaring white boys posturing across the street. The skinny woman is put into cuffs, despite her swollen and bruised face. She is known to police.

"BULLSHIT," Squeaky says, shaking with fury. Maxine puts a protective arm around her. The bartender substantiates the claim that the woman provoked the fight.

Kitty says, "You fucking disloyal cunt whore!"

"Easy," an officer warns.

"We need a cab," Squeaky says. "I wanna get the fuck out of here *now*."

America: Paradise, Devoured

They survive the beginning of spring in Vancouver: icy rain and grey sky for miles. Eddie sets up a video shoot for "Whatever, Trevor" in a warehouse with a couple of built-in sets. The concept is a performance piece, with dramatized scenes of each band member. Trevor is being played by Fat Ricky. In Maxine's vignette, she tries to get Trevor's attention by wearing lingerie and satin mules, but he's too busy watching the game on TV. Kitty gets to trash and spray-paint a Honda. Fanta's scene is in the boudoir, filing her nails with boredom as Trevor tries to seduce her. Squeaky pretends to throw him out a window when she finds him partying with other girls, including a pregnant Rosie. It takes a weekend of filming and they hit every mark.

Adalita is in town and takes them out for dinner. She gives the girls little flurries of kisses. During the expensive meal, she pulls out her blackberry three times. According to her, *Born with Bush* shows tremendous progress, and she's set up interviews for Wet Leather at different points along the upcoming American tour. They may also be filming segments for MuchMusic and MTV Canada. The industry is still run by men, and she warns them to use their tits strategically. She tells them, "I like my women smart and my men stupid."

One night Fanta gives Maxine a ride home from work. Neither says much and they quietly listen to the radio. "Whatever, Trevor" comes on and Maxine shrieks and cranks the volume. "OH MY GOD! That's us! That's us on the fucking radio!" Fanta is so excited she pulls the van over.

It's a poignant moment that could only happen once. They're glad they have each other to share it.

June heats up and it's time for the *Born with Bush* tour of America. The girls are flying to Boston to join Fire Chicken, who just finished the southern states. Wet Leather will only be going out for a month. Eddie Camaro doesn't want them to burn out early on the road. The band declined a tour manager, but now they wonder if a month will be too much for Fanta to handle.

Rosie lumbers out to the porch to tell Squeaky goodbye. The baby is due in a few weeks, and Tony King has already moved in. It's bizarre to think Rosie will have a child before the tour is over. They give each other one last hug. The blue pompom on Squeaky's hat droops as she climbs in the cab.

She picks up Maxine on the way to the airport. Squeaky gives a low whistle when she emerges lugging two giant suitcases, a carry-on, and an equally enormous purse. The sky is a yellowish white, about to storm. If it's an omen, no one knows what it means, but as they drive south the sun burns off the cloud cover.

At the airport, the Customs lineup of miserable looking travellers snakes around the room. "This tour is gonna be great," Squeaky says. "Not like last time out when we didn't know anything. These songs are solid." She pulls out the *Born with Bush* CD and looks at the liner notes again. It feels good in her hands.

Maxine applies unnecessary lipstick. "Listen Kitty," she says. "I was thinking that for the first while, maybe you shouldn't get so drunk. I mean, weren't you surprised that Fire Chicken wanted to take us on the road again? We had so many shit shows I thought they couldn't stand us!"

"I never do *should*," Kitty says. "I do things because I want to or I said I would."

Maxine snorts. "Hey, if you've got a romantic notion about yourself, why not give it all you've got?"

An American flag hangs limply on one wall. The girls are tense, even though they have the expensive P2 permit needed to play shows across the border. "Oh god, what if we have to go into the special room? I heard they make you squat over a mirror."

"Kitty, sshhh..."

"What's next, a urine test? A chest x-ray?"

When the officer finally stamps their passports he says, "You ladies have a nice trip."

Everyone begins to talk at once. "We're not ladies," Kitty says. "Maybe ladies of the evening!"

Fanta grabs her arm and gets her moving, fast.

After an uneventful flight, they pick up the rental van. The first show is in Cambridge. They're surprised to be playing such an uptight, pretentious college town. Squeaky guides the rental van down the alley behind the bar and parks beside the Fire Chicken van. She gives a quick check in the side mirror. Kitty and Maxine storm inside.

Tex kisses them formally on the cheek, like a punk elder, but they can tell he's glad to see them. The bands are sharing a backline, and onstage Jonah tunes his guitar. He waves and gives a cheery hello. "Hey girls! We missed you." Everybody hugs. Fat Ricky emerges from the can with a young girl sporting tattooed angel wings on her back. After the hours spent cooped on the plane, Kitty is rambunctious and wrestles him to the ground, laying a vicious kick to his shin.

Franky Sparrow and Squeaky hold each other longer than anyone else. "Little mama," he murmurs in her ear. "I couldn't wait for you to get here."

He gives her a look. She gives it right back.

The bar is filled with sporty casuals and button-downs, useless bored males unimpressed by four women. Some guy tries to heckle Maxine. "OOOhhh, play a love song."

"Honey," she says, "It'll take more than a love song to get *you* laid!"

The audience doesn't quiet down when Maxine introduces Wet Leather, but she holds her voice strong and clear. The scattered applause after the first song only makes her try harder. The band backs up Maxine with pride. This is what is admirable and brave about her.

Squeaky cracks every rim with flair. It makes a difference that Franky Sparrow is watching from the wings. He places a towel and a beer where she can reach them. All through the set they sneak peeks at each other. When the last song is over she lopes offstage and they're out the door at once.

In the back of the Fire Chicken van, they kick off their shoes.

"It's hot in here," Squeaky says, undoing her bra.

He does a double take. "Have you *always* had those?" They kiss long and wet, whisper sweetly to each other. He pulls off her panties and keeps his face between her legs. Squeaky can't stop her moans. They rock the van when they fuck.

Franky has barely wiped off her stomach when Fat Ricky throws open the doors. He keeps staring until Squeaky nails him in the head with her shoe, then closes them with reluctance.

Franky pulls her close to cuddle. "Rocket cried to me many times about you." She makes a farting sound with her armpit. He pinches her nipple and she squeaks.

Steve is a quiet punk with a dog collar and a red birthmark that covers his face. He offers to let everyone crash at his house and both bands agree to take offers of hospitality—the less money spent on tour means more at the end. The punks that live with Steve all take an immediate shine to Kitty Domingo, who will flirt, drink their booze, do all the drugs, and ruin friendships in the process.

She stays up all night, fiending. The next afternoon, when the van is packed, she can barely move. As they pull onto the highway she says, "My god, I'm so drunk my mouth is sweating."

"We have a show in five hours and you're still fucked up," Maxine gripes. "What's *wrong* with you?"

"What's wrong with YOU," Kitty snaps. "Besides Daddy's cock up yer chute?" Maxine puts on her earphones in disgust.

Kitty is sad and torn, sitting in the front seat in the cool air. All she wants to do is drink whisky. Crawling into the back and sleeping is the only thing that can save her. She goes with the whisky, instead.

June 12, New Haven, CT

They are determined to have a good time even though they're in Connecticut. The uninspired décor of the bar they play is the number 9. It is, after all, the Nine Bar. "Hello chairs," says Maxine to the nearly empty room. The stage is so small Kitty jumps up on the counter for a solo. Naturally, she falls off. Fat Ricky goes home with the bar waitress and fucks her without a condom.

Franky and Squeaky have been all over each other since Boston. He asks if she wants to switch it up and ride with Fire Chicken. "Hell yeah," she says. "Get me outta this tuna can!"

"I'm coming too," Maxine says, and swaps seats with Jonah. In the back of the van Squeaky stretches out happily and puts her feet on Franky. After pulling up her socks he says, "Everything about you is so tiny and adorable." He holds up Squeaky's size three sneaker. "You've even got cute feet." Riding shotgun beside Tex, Maxine makes a clucking sound of disapproval. If she isn't getting laid, she doesn't like to be reminded that other people are.

They hum along to the stereo, burn with the sun through the window. "Come here. C'mere, c'mere, c'mere," Franky says, like a four-note phrase. He pulls Squeaky close against him. "I think you should kiss me."

In the front seat, Maxine keeps on clucking.

They are stopped at a gas station when Squeaky runs back to the van, waving a phone. "Rosie had a baby girl last night! Her name is Mabel Marlene." Everyone offers congratulations, and when the phone is passed to Maxine she says a few quick words. Then she curls up in the van and puts her earphones on, staring out the window.

It's hard for her to comprehend that Rosie is now a mother. While she's glad her sides no longer ache with envy, Maxine feels something missing from her own life. The white lines break up thoughts of the boys of her youth, what she'd meant to any of them. The years had been full of affairs that seemed to last just long enough. Now Maxine wants to love someone like her life depends on it. Those feelings never last on the road more than a night.

June 16, Pittsburgh, PA

Filtering into the 31st Street Pub are girls with full sleeve tattoos, pierced faces, and brightly dyed hair. Backstage, Maxine puts on a bondage top and leather pants, then changes again nervously. She drinks more than she can handle—showmanship and spectacle tenuously linked at the centre of each performance.

Wet Leather maneuver their way to the stage and pick up their instruments. A wall of burly punks forms at the front, jostling each other. Midway into the set Maxine asks for a beer, and a bunch of men lunge at her with their plastic cups upraised. She takes one and drains it to a chorus of cheers, lets the remainder run sopping down her chin. The band waits until she's ready to begin "Lucy's Lost her Knickers."

"They call her a bitch
A slut, a whore
It's just a name
What's one more?'

They call her 'skinny bitch
with no tits'
Why does it always
come to this?

$1.00 x3 Litres water
$2.99 Six pack Old Milwaukee
$3.49 1 box tampons
#4.59 1 bottle Advil
$0.50 x2 bars chocolate
$0.99 1 lighter
$3.99 1 pack Marlboro Red
$3.99 1 pack Camel Lights
$0.50 1 pack cinnamon gum
$6.00 Tittle-Tattle Magazine
$3.49 Vaseline
$1.50 Kleenex
$1.29 2 slushies
$0.75 1 stick Beef jerky
$2.75 1 box breath mints

Lucy's lost her knickers again
Whoa
Lucy's lost her knickers again
Whoa Whoa
Lucy's lost her knickers again
Oh no…."

Afterwards there is a party at the promoter's home. It's a bungalow decorated entirely in Tiki, with an open bar in the living room. Kitty is shit-faced and exuberant. She has the best night of her life with everyone she meets, and it's a gruelling pace to keep up. Maxine flirts with the promoter on the bamboo loveseat despite his kilt and Hawaiian shirt ensemble. When he lights her cigarette she comments, "Smooth."

"No," he says. "I'm a little bumpy."

"Want to go to your room?"

"I can't. I have to be up early tomorrow."

"Let's just have an orgasm." Maxine licks her top lip. "It doesn't have to take all night."

"If I do, what's going to happen next Wednesday?"

She's baffled but he refuses. Finally she storms outside. Squeaky is sitting on the lawn with a beer and Maxine flops down beside her. For the next ten minutes she analyzes his rejection.

"So…*what* are you upset about?"

"You're just pretending to listen," Maxine accuses. "You're just sitting there wondering when Franky Sparrow's coming back." Squeaky shrugs, takes a long pull of her beer, and looks up at the stars.

Abandoning her on the grass, Maxine goes inside for a round of tequila shots in the kitchen. Some fat guy standing by the fridge has a hole in his black spandex pants and pulls his dick out. Maxine shrieks with laughter and pretends to grab for it.

In the morning she is jolted awake. It feels as if she passed out under a slab of concrete. Her makeup is itchy and she's sore all over. The last thing she recalls is the fluorescent kitchen lights and some fat guy flashing his penis. There is a vague memory of puking in a laundry hamper. A baby wails upstairs. Maxine finds a smoke, takes a shit, and then creeps out of the house with a lone scavenged beer.

June 18, Columbus, OH

Kitty pegs the club immediately. "Rockabilly," she says. "It's where old punks and skinheads go to die." As they straggle in, the bartender looks on in disbelief. Squeaky and Fanta go to a laundromat down the street with their sacks of filthy clothes. They're the only white girls there, but no one cares.

Maxine sits at the bar with a glass of Scotch. An elderly gentleman in a threadbare suit and dapper fedora bought her drink. For all she knows they could be related. The old man tells her, "This used to be a good neighbourhood. Before they moved in."

Maxine is intrigued. "Who's *they*?"

"The niggers."

She slides off the bar stool, disgusted. Later, when Wet Leather attempts a sound check, the bar is already full of guys with shaved heads wearing braces and boots with white laces. They stand and watch with their arms folded. One flabby monster sporting bushy muttonchops looks a few IQ points below village idiot. The girls finish the first two songs to no applause. During the silence someone in the front says, "I hope your pussy smells better than your feet."

By the time they get to the scrappy thrash of "GHB OD," Kitty is jumping and falling, doing crazy neck whips and spins on the floor. When the village idiot starts dancing, the rest soon follow. Within minutes the pit looks like a boot party. The girls push through the set and get off the stage as soon as possible.

Franky is right there, waiting. Squeaky wears a trucker hat, hair in pigtails, and her mascara came off in black streaks when she played. Her white undershirt is wet with sweat and sticks to her. It's a look that works. "You've really been showing off your tits lately," Franky tells her. "I like it. Let 'em speak for themselves!"

She goes to the van to change, and as she opens the door Franky grabs her from behind. No one's around so she grinds her ass into him. He's hard. They climb into the van and Franky spreads her legs, goes down on her in the backseat while people mill around outside, then they fuck spoon-style real quiet and tight.

Later on, as Squeaky is managing the merch table, a pimply boy in Doc Martens and suspenders tries to initiate conversation. "You shouldn't go outside alone."

She snorts. "Yeah?"

"It's not safe." His insincere smile shows crooked brown teeth. His hand snakes out and squeezes her breast.

"What the fuck?"

"Oh sorry," he says, then reaches out and gropes her again before disappearing into the crowd.

Just then Maxine comes over and Squeaky tells her what happened. "Do you want to tell Franky? You know he'll punch the guy out."

Squeaky pictures a brawl, flying glass and bloody fists. Franky could get hurt, badly. Her feelings for him are more than just scrambled porn. "Fuck it," she says, and walks outside to cool off. The night clouds look spread across the sky like icing.

No one wants to stick around when the show is over, and they decide to find motel rooms outside of town. As they pull out of the parking lot, Fanta stops the van. In the circle of the headlights down the alley, a group of skinheads punch and kick another one on the ground. She turns on the high beams, but the men continue. "Should we stop?"

"Drive," Squeaky says. "We don't know what he did."

The skylight has faded in the west like a yellow bruise, the moon rotten in the middle.

June 20, Kalamazoo, MI

The show is at a cavernous brewery with disgusting beer and underage kids sporting black Xs on their hands. A rabid fanboy corners Maxine and tells her he planned to hang himself last month until he listened to Wet Leather. He explains his black eye and various scrapes are from throwing himself through a kitchen window. Maxine only pretends to listen. She's busy watching J-Dub, the cute guy selling T-shirts for the opening band, Puddles to Paradise.

"Excuse me," she says. "I need to go deal with this merch situation."

The fanboy pleads, "I'll wait right here. Come back..."

Maxine tries to convince J-Dub to do a line of coke with her, but he professes to be straight-edge. "It'll just make it so we can get to know each other better," she persists. "We can open up more."

"Umm…I have to use the bathroom."

"I'm going to the can, too!"

The fanboy dominates the space in front of Maxine for the entire set. A crazy light burns in his eyes, and while it's impressive that he knows all their lyrics, he screams them with unnerving intensity. He keeps trying to climb onstage but each time Kitty pushes him back with her foot.

Fat Ricky has a Kalamazoo girlfriend, a sloppy top-heavy blonde who invites everyone back to her place. While following the Fire Chicken van Squeaky teases, "I think Fat Ricky sleeps with even more groupies than you, Maxine."

"Maybe. I'd like to take a look at his numbers. But I've seen him with some real mutts."

Fanta sighs heavily. "You subscribe to a tepid sort of feminism, don't you?"

"Just 'cause *you've* never had a cock within an inch of your face."

They pull up to one of many buildings in a long row of identical townhouses. The sloppy blonde is generous with the beer and tokes from a pop can pipe. There's a game of dice and dollar bills. As usual, Squeaky and Franky Sparrow disappear together.

Somehow the fanboy makes it to the party. Maxine tries to avoid him while keeping her eye on J-Dub, who sits in a dark corner talking to a pink-haired girl in a cardigan. People begin to pass out in random spots. The fanboy keeps putting his arms around Maxine on the couch. "Cuddle up with me," he begs hoarsely. "Pleeease."

"NO," she says loudly. She looks over at J-Dub, who motions for her to join him. The lights are off and a while later Kitty comes in.

"Hey Maxine," she whispers. "You got a condom?"

"No."

"What? Fuck you."

Maxine has one in her purse but she's under the blanket with J-Dub and doesn't want to move. Then she's reminded of Kitty's last abortion and reluctantly gets up. She looks for her in the apartment and outside but Kitty's not in their van or Fire Chicken's. When Maxine tries to go back in the building, it's locked. There's a row of buzzers but she doesn't know the apartment number or the name of the sloppy blonde. The only thing to do is sleep in the van. It's cold and starts to downpour. An old lady in a pink housecoat watches from the porch as Maxine squats by the back of the van to piss.

In the morning they come out and find her shivering in the cold. Maxine had gone to the wrong townhouse; the front door was unlocked the whole time. J-Dub hooked up with the pink-haired girl. They stop at a deli and Maxine waits in the van. When she finds out there's mustard on her sandwich, she cries.

They can tell Fanta is in pain from the stiff way she moves. She tries to be nonchalant and cool, but each movement is economical. Her bones ache, and everyone pools their painkillers to take care of her. It's Squeaky's turn to drive, but she has a migraine from last night's shitty blow. She puts her head down, cap low, so they can't see she's about to start crying. It's not an option to ask Fanta to take her shift.

"It's okay," Franky tells her. "Don't try to be a hero." He drives the van while Squeaky sleeps off her headache in the back.

Kitty, in the van: "Fanta, will you spellcheck my postcard to Jasper?"

Pause. "This sentence needs a colon."

"Colon? Who uses a colon? The last time I used a colon I was taking a dump!"

There is nowhere for them to stay in Chicago and luckily Tex knows a fauxhawked programmer at the radio station who agrees to let them sleep on the floor. Their interviews are set up for a morning talk show at seven a.m. Squeaky and Maxine walk to an all-night drugstore. Tampons and Advil are in short supply. A woman with a stroller stops and asks them for some money. Her baby is hungry. There's a blanket pulled up but they can tell it's a doll wearing a tiny baseball cap. Squeaky gives the woman ten dollars.

The woman loves their accents. "You're Canadian? I'm cool with Canadians. Where you from?"

"Vancouver."

"Where's that?"

"Near Seattle."

"Seattle? Where's that?"

Squeaky asks where she can buy some pot and the woman says to meet her in that spot in one hour, but neither one is going to show up.

"You're a fool," Maxine says, as they continue walking. "That wasn't a real baby."

"You *think*," Squeaky replies with sarcasm. "So what, maybe it's one less cock she'll suck tonight."

"If it was a white doll in there, you would've only given her a dollar." They argue about it the whole time they sit in the rock 'n' roll McDonald's.

Back in the studio, Fanta gets the only comfortable spot, the couch in the green room. Everyone else crashes on the carpeted studio floor. Franky Sparrow makes a nook for Squeaky and him, covers her gently with the blanket of his jacket.

Maxine gets up and leaves the room, rolling her eyes. In the waiting area she pulls two chairs together, and wakes a few hours later, foul and shaky.

"Heeey-hey! This is Snack Davies and today on the morning show we're talking to WET Leeeeaaaaather, a hot new band from Vaaaaaaancouuuver, CANADA! And, if I may say, it's a *pleasure* to see four lovely ladies here this morning! Yes, that's right, for those of you who don't know, Wet Leather is a rock and roll quartet of WOMEN! O-*KAY* ladies, just a few questions before we play your song...What's it *like* being in a girl band?"

Kitty: "It's like being in a boy band who man-struates."

Maxine: "Do you ask *them* that question?"

Fanta: "It's a constant reaction to the misogyny that masquerades as rock 'n' roll tenets."

"Whoa, we got a live one here!"

Squeaky: "Snack, is that your real name?"

"Now girls, this is your first time touring America. What's it like for you here?"

Fanta: "I'm glad you asked that. I used to think this was a country of killers—all that power and arrogance. But that's who you are politically, not as individuals—"

"—Oh-KAY, for those of you just tuning in, this is WET Leeeaaather with the first single from their debut album—ho ho—*Born with Bush*—ho ho ho...this is "WhatEVER, TREVOR!"

It cuts to the song and they take off their earphones.

"You girls are on fire! Hot!"

"Sure. Like a case of barely contained crabs," Fanta says dryly. She pushes the microphone away. "I am *never* doing this again."

The girls go prowling through record shops and vintage stores. Passersby eye them with interest: Squeaky's skull tattoo, biceps, and wristbands; Fanta in motorcycle boots and shorts displaying her scarred knees; in a surprise move, Kitty wearing sneakers and an actual skirt; Maxine in a puffy crinoline number and fake ponytail, complete with toe-pinching red heels. One guy turns right around in a circle. Someone else takes their picture. A security guard at the Art Institute says, "Walk slowly so I can enjoy the view."

Chicago feels like a great town, nothing but good luck. Then a screaming man runs down the middle of the street with plastic bags over his bleeding bare feet.

It's time to get back on the road.

June 23, Madison, WI

"Stop it, Kitty!"

"I'm crop-dustin,'" she says, ripping another series of wet beer farts. "It's Wisconsin! Besides, that's what you get for missing the turnoff for Grandpa's Cheese Barn." All the girls are in the van and everyone's happy at the same time, teasing each other, cracking jokes. They're making good mileage and decide to detour and sit on the Mississippi banks. Everyone spreads out on blankets, watching the river run. Maxine opens the newspaper.

"Did you hear about this lawsuit? Man, it was so much easier when you could just fuck your teacher." She begins to read aloud but they aren't paying attention. "Listen! Hurricane Jade is approaching. It's time to start working out. I wanna be fit for the apocalypse. I don't wanna be all messy and whining and dying!"

No one says anything. Maxine hates it when they don't pay attention to her and finally quiets. For some reason, she thinks of the time her friend Mel's family took her to the lake. After lunch, Mel and Maxine had rowed the dingy to the other side. There were no outhouses across the lake. They had to poop. Each had selected a wooded area. Back in the water, Mel said she'd covered hers with a big rock. Maxine said she did too, but she hadn't. It didn't even cross her mind. She'd left her shit out in the open and run away.

They sleep the rest of the afternoon beside the peaceful Mississippi. It's late when they wake and construction on the road causes further delay to the show in Madison. Speeding down the highway they pass an RV with a bumper sticker that reads, "Man + Woman = Marriage." The driver is an old, lonely-looking dude. When Maxine gives him the finger he seems surprised.

When they arrive, Fire Chicken is on their second-to-last song. A large woman with huge tits dominates the space in front of Tex, waving her meaty arms in the air. Kitty jumps up to join them for "6th Grade Thong." Tex is resistant at first but she finds a way to work herself in.

He is furious they missed their set. There is a band meeting later so he can rant at them. Fanta points out they only have two drivers. He looks at her exhausted face and relents.

"And *I'm* getting a cold," Kitty tells him. "You dipshit!"

"Okay," Tex says. "You girls get a hotel room tonight and I'll drive to Kansas City for you tomorrow. Everyone could use a good night's sleep."

"Great," Squeaky says, "I'll ride in your van."

Franky is outside waiting for her. "It worried me when you were late. I hoped you guys would get here earlier...well, I hoped *you* would."

In the back of the Fire Chicken van there is an extended space behind the last seats, used as a cramped sleeping area. Squeaky grabs her bag and curls up here with Franky. The stereo is on and he sings to her as they drive down the highway. She can see his smile in profile and unzips his pants. He rolls over as she strokes him and pulls down her jeans. Squeaky rubs his cock against her wetness. They fuck hard and silent in the darkness as the van keeps rolling on.

June 25, Kansas City, MI

A border town of decaying roads and railroad tracks, Kansas City creates a feeling of people left behind. Squeaky steps aside for a toothless black man with palsy who smiles, despite his shell-shocked face. It's another all ages gig, a medium-sized crowd of teens with huge, coloured mohawks. The kids in Kansas City, Missouri wear their punk feathers like plumes to attract the few others like them.

Maxine's voice is raw. She sings the lyrics and adds a few spasmodic dance moves, but the songs lack energy. The whole set is loose and uninspired. It's embarrassing for Fanta, who is the only sober one.

A young fan stands stiffly up front. The way the boy
 thumps his fist over his heart with such conviction moves her. When you're young, Fanta thinks, your rage is so clean and uncomplicated. He gives her clarity in the moment that she wills herself not to forget.

The bands are invited to stay at someone's ghetto mansion. Kitty is drunk and howls for coke—she's sure someone has a line. She takes over the stereo but doesn't finish a song before she yanks off the record and slaps on another.

Franky grabs Squeaky, sauntering past, and tells the guy he is talking to, "Can you believe how fucking cute she is?"

"Yes, yes," the man says, giving her a glance. "But as I was saying about your guitar playing—"

"Do you have any idea how good *she* plays drums?" Franky pushes her forward. "And check out that rack!"

The man looks at Squeaky. "Are you Turkish? You have a sharp nose."

Franky takes her hand and leads her away. They find an empty room on the second floor and yank each other's clothes off. "Don't let me like you too much," he says. "I mean, unless you want me to."

"Huh?"

"Oh, who am I kidding? I love you."

Squeaky's smile is radiant. "I love you, too. Now fucking nail me to the wall, baby."

Hours pass for Fanta in another stranger's home, two thousand more miles to go. This room has dark red walls, and she pets the old cat sleeping on her lap. A man in a halo brace and the cat are her companions for the night. No one else bothers to talk to her. Fate has not brought her here. Fate is a drunk driver crossing a yellow line. Her situation now is nothing but poor choices and dumb luck. She tells the man in the halo brace about the coldness in her country, the slow death of broken promises. Her eyes are like the centre of the fire. The man with the broken neck is the only one who listens.

June 28, Tempe, AZ

The desert invades them. White people, tanned and unsmiling, guns displayed in holsters, beige dogs dreaming of the ocean. They forget the broken fan belt in Fort Collins, have already washed the great salt plains from their skin. Here in Tempe the garbage stinks, the tap water undrinkable.

It's so hot in this anemic college town that everyone has a collective migraine. They play an uninspired set for the ASU crowd. This is the third-most-visited campus for Playboy recruiters. The air is dry and drunk students howl, dumb and rich, looking to fuck or fight under the black desert sky.

In a bathroom stall, Fanta writes:

"Hell is other people."

—Sartre

Checkout time again at another motel. Everyone mills around the parking lot like usual. Middle-aged women walk by, clutching their purses tighter. Tex lies on a blanket on the grass with his transistor radio, beer in hand, cowboy hat over his face. Squeaky and Jonah take turns doing kickflips on her skateboard, while Fat Ricky is busy networking his cyber friends. Franky is still in the motel restaurant, where Maxine bickers with Kitty over who owes for extra bacon on the cheque.

Only Fanta observes the fat woman eating McDonald's in her car while reading a TV guide. She tries to imagine where this woman might live. A place where the walls are nicotine yellow, and the TV stays on all night.

A clean ocean breeze blows over the highway to Santa Cruz. They arrive in the middle of the night and wake up to a wide stretch of beach. In a public restroom the girls put on bathing suits, scrub their feet in the sink.

Fire Chicken has a friend in town named Metal Jay. After a breakfast of burritos and bong hits, they caravan with Metal Jay and his friends to a surf spot. "Cook it up, brah," the boys in the water yell. After a while Metal Jay takes them to a calmer spot. He lends Squeaky a board and she paddles out. Everyone watches as she rides the foam all the way in.

Back on the beach she flops on a towel next to Franky. "Look at you," he admires. "I didn't know you could surf."

"My brothers and I used to go all summer." As she says this, Squeaky misses them. Franky's fingertips trace the scars on her arm. She tells him she got them from Andre, who'd once thrown a cactus at her while babysitting. Squeaky had worn long-sleeved shirts for a week. They'd told their mother the cat had knocked over the cactus. They had a silent system of justice in their house. It was how they liked it.

Suddenly she is jolted from her reverie. Kitty is out too far, and she's not a strong swimmer. No one else notices the waves are dragging her further. Squeaky grabs Jay's board and runs into the surf.

"KITTY!" she screams.

Squeaky's arms push down while the waves push up. The board has just been cleaned with gasoline, and she slides around on it like an ice cube. She panics when Kitty's head disappears under the water. Then Kitty bobs back up, flailing and choking. Squeaky reaches for her and grips Kitty in a death-lock, pulling her onto the board. She sidestrokes to tow them back to shore.

Kitty staggers up the beach, heaving. "I'm foii-iine," she swears, laughing too loud. They had almost lost her. Squeaky pushes the board into the sand and then collapses, shaking, knees weak with fear.

That night, her near-death experience has little effect on Kitty. Behind the smoke machine she feels like she's licked the whole plate clean. Kitty has broken hearts in bathrooms, burned so hot and fast with strangers. The sound of the crowd rises up from the floorboards, a familiar song of rebellion and longing. Their piercings and brandings and split tongues say: *these are the times we are from.*

Maxine is in another volatile mood. "You were too fucking sloppy tonight, Kitty." They cram in the backstage room after the show. Near the end of the tour it's becoming increasingly difficult for them to negotiate Maxine's random hostility.

"*Sor*-ry."

"Hey, ease up," Squeaky protests. "These California kids are happy little beach stoners. Who cares?" Even if it's true, she doesn't expect Maxine to come down on Kitty like that.

Most of the time they read each other easily, and no one fucks up enough to throw everyone else off. If it happens, it's easy to recover. "We still put on a good show."

"*I* care! It's happened more than once this tour. Remember falling off the bar in New Haven? Look, I'm not accusing—"

"You're not accusing me," Kitty interrupts. "You're bringing *evidence* of how I fucked up. Don't start acting like we're all your employees."

"Screw YOU!"

Maxine slams the door on her way out. Everyone's used to her exits and watch unfazed, but inside Kitty trembles. *Fuck it*, she thinks. *I'm getting high.*

Later: she has to push and push and finally the needle goes in.

The rain gathers above as they head north. Kitty is gravel-voiced, scratching herself and rubbing her nose. This irritates Maxine, who is snippy and self-involved. It's an unpleasant ride. It crosses Fanta's mind, once again, that all she has to do is quit.

She enjoys playing guitar, but the songs aren't that difficult or challenging. Wet Leather could hardly be used as a springboard to a higher level of understanding or discourse. Maxine's milieu is closer to prostitution than poetry. She'll never get it. Fanta imagines sharing a hotel room with her for the next ten years, listening to those grim, determined orgasms. A worse reality is watching Kitty Domingo disintegrate. She's skin and bones already.

But Fanta looks over and there's Squeaky in her trucker hat, arms loose at the wheel. Her legs barely reach the pedals but she's not anyone to mess with. There's even a toothpick between her lips. It makes Fanta smile. This is why she stays on, despite the constant turbulence. She is drawn to women not afraid of alleyways. And there aren't that many, anymore.

Foul-Mouthed Wet Leather Just Want to Potty

Maxine Micheline, the lead singer of Wet Leather, is a force to be reckoned with. I'm waiting for her after their sold-out show at The Fillmore. These four Canadian women crank out such tough, over-amped rock, I don't know what to expect in person. Finally Maxine emerges from backstage. Immediately she is approached by a squat, unattractive fan. I watch her do three shots with him in quick succession (he's buying). Maxine is a natural flirt, artfully manipulating her audience. She stumbles to my table and introduces herself and bass player Kitty Domingo. Both are highly intoxicated, knocking over glasses as they shove in the booth. The following is a transcript of what transpired:

Underground Magazine: Maxine, I see you've brought another member of the coterie.

Maxine: This coterie could kick your ass, starting from the smallest one up!

Kitty: Jeezus, so this is who writes that shit.

UM: Let's talk about *Born with Bush*. It's a ferocious first album that proves you're more than pretty girls with power chords.

Maxine: Thanks!

UM: While most of your songs contain, at least in part, a wall-of-thrash assault, there's also the country-tinged waltz of "Cold-Hearted Woman," and the sing-along girl anthem "Bitches Don't Do Dishes." How do you define your sound?

Maxine: We don't. What's the point?

Kitty: Don't try to box us in!

UM: You've just finished an American tour with Fire Chicken, a band well-known for their epic vices. Any interesting experiences with them you can share?

Kitty: Maxine had an experience with one of them last night. He had so much pube you couldn't tell the difference between his cock and balls.

Maxine: Kitty, don't say shit like that.

Kitty: Ugh. (waves hands in front of her face) You got some mints or something? You're hali-casting bad!

Maxine: Shut up!

UM: Given your style and sound, one would assume Wet Leather is a hard-partying band.

Maxine: Fanta never gets drunk. She gets hammered on guitar.

UM: Do you have regular jobs when you're not on tour?

Kitty: I'm a fluffer. No, wait! Say I just work a bad attitude.

UM: It's been said "It's not how well a band plays, but how well they tour." Life on the road in close quarters destroys many bands. How do you combat this?

Maxine: Our routine is resisting routine.

UM: Would you call yourselves feminists?

Both: Uh…*Duh*.

UM: What is the driving force behind the music you play?

Maxine: Hold on. I want this answered in an eloquent manner. (She drags over guitar player Fanta Geiger and repeats question) Take it away!

Fanta: We're surrounded by death, disaster, every kind of malfunction. This generation is spoon-fed the easiest thrills. When nothing has any meaning, the sickness of irony sets in. From great despair comes revolution, and the spirit of that is rock 'n' roll.

UM: Any advice for your fans?

Fanta: Make your own stories. Live your own life.

Maxine: And if you plan to fuck your way into the music business, aim high. Don't mid-level!

UM: Maxine, that's an interesting costume. Describe it for us.

Maxine: I call it hospital chic. It's a dress Fanta made from a clear shower curtain, and I'm bandaged underneath. Approximate facsimile available at Freudian Slips in Vancouver, BC!

Kitty: Don't hit on her. She's still trying to get the taste of the last one outta her mouth!

UM (aghast): No, I would never.

Kitty: Then go snort coke off someone's dick!

I could go on describing the epic sound of Wet Leather, how Fanta shreds with a seemingly effortless phrasing, or how tiny Squeaky Ladeucer gets a massive sound out of her kit. Or Maxine's raw stage show, enticing in its questioning of power schisms. One could speak at length on the ebullient vulgarity of Kitty Domingo, but why bother? The tales will grow to be legendary. This is Wet Leather. They don't care who you think they are.

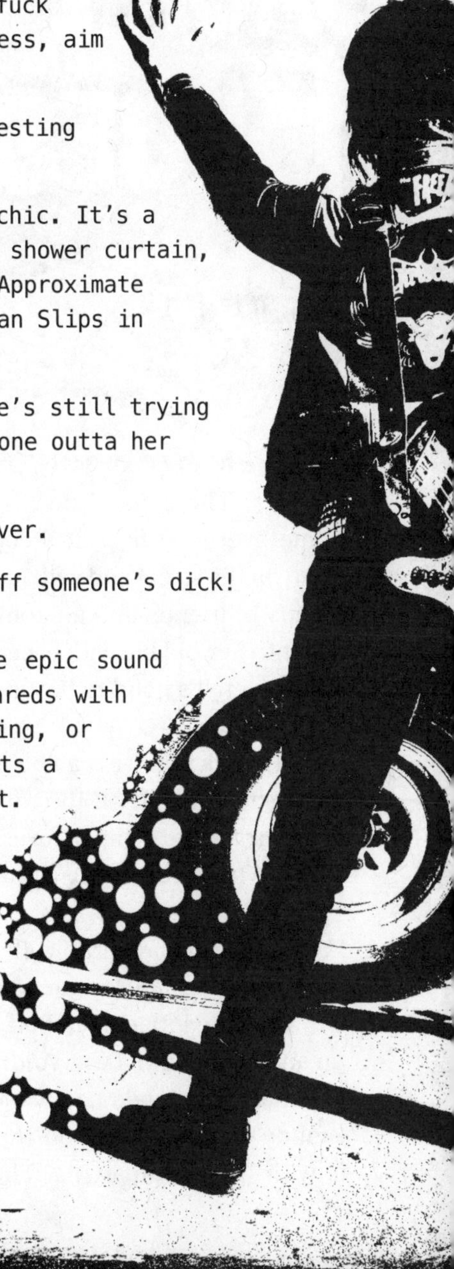

Back Home Blues

They return to Vancouver and the taste of salt under their tongues. There have been some powerful changes. Once home everyone feels it. People they don't know recognize them on the street and call out their names. Strangers demand tokens of friendship and souvenirs. It is only Fanta that can slip into her old life with ease. She basks in the solitude of her apartment. It's good to be alone.

Kitty is back in town, calling up the old debts that need to be paid. She nods off on the toilet, feet on the tile floor, a sour smell from the night before. It's not a surprise to wake up alone. What's surprising is that it bothers her at all.

"You're like my favourite guitar," Franky tells Squeaky. "It took a while to fully appreciate you."

They are lounging in bed, relieved they don't have to get up and hustle into a van. Andre has given Squeaky the keys to his apartment while he finishes a construction job up north. Brandy Snifter is back on the BC strip circuit and the baby is with the grandparents. This gives Squeaky time to figure out where to live. Rosie says she's always welcome in her old room, but she has a baby now. It's a little family, and Squeaky doesn't want to intrude.

Franky has been by Squeaky's side since the end of the tour. He doesn't have much but gives her what he does: a band patch, a silver skull belt buckle, a ball cap with a beer logo. It's only a few weeks before he leaves to tour Europe once again. Squeaky sleeps with her arms folded above her head. He thinks it's adorable when she snores. Their time together is extraordinary, delicate, obscene. It is a long July of hot yellow nights.

When Franky leaves there is a heavy space in her stomach. She drops him off at the airport and misses him before the doors even close.

Maxine stands on the porch and lights her cigarette with defiance. Rain or shine, she is cast outside. She smokes and looks at the sky. Off the road she has to deal with broken teeth and bill collectors. Getting older, the knocks hurt more. It frightens her to think of losing her looks. She is reminded of her grandmother, once a great beauty, decaying and dismissed. Laughter spills out of Rosie's house. Through the window the candlelight burns.

It frustrates Maxine to mark time until Fanta agrees to practise. She demands distance from the band after the tour. They work alternate days at Freudian Slips and never see each other socially. Without the band, they don't fit into each other's lives anymore. Even when they jam, it's the same thing: Squeaky lays down the rhythm, then Fanta shows them what to do until Kitty locks in. Sometimes Maxine can't find her place in that arrangement. She misses her cues. What guts her is how Fanta is so nonchalant about Wet Leather, and it's Maxine's entire world.

Squeaky has organized the baby shower, but no one really knows what to do except munch the canapés of mini-quiches and mushroom *duxelles*. They toast Rosie with grape juice in wine glasses. Maxine is not into these kinds of gatherings, and sneaks looks at the clock. She can't stand the smell of baby powder and baby shit and old milk. Predictably more beautiful than ever, Rosie's hands fold over her belly like a radiant eastside Madonna.

"Open your presents," Squeaky says gleefully, and hands her a crinkly parcel. "This is from Franky and me." Rosie tears back the paper. It's an AC/DC bowl and bib set.

"Adorable!"

"Cuuu-uuute!"

The present is passed for everyone to see. It goes around the circle and when it gets to Maxine, she pretends to snort coke from the spoon. She examines the next gift of fuzzy blankets with boredom and the tiny shoes fail to move her. She is handed a beanbag crocodile and says, "Great, the baby will choke on *this*."

"You know, I can't figure out what's worse," Squeaky says, looking pointedly at Maxine. "Getting older and losing it, or staying in the same place and hanging on."

"Squeaky," Rosie asks quickly, "how is it for you with Franky on tour again?"

Kitty pipes in. "You miss that greasy dude!"

"Sure I do."

Maxine arches an eyebrow. "Now that you're not on tour with him, do you ever think he'll cheat on you?"

"I try not to get tormented over hypothetical scenarios. Unlike Rocket, who tormented me with reality."

"Oh my god, you guys, I forgot to tell you I have a stalker!" Maxine can barely contain herself. "He keeps coming into Freudian Slips to ask me out—"

“Is this one from your international network of barnacles?”

“No, some random dude.” She huffs, “I’m like, you are a nerdy guy and yes! you deserve to be liked, but no! you cannot be obsessed with *me*.”

There’s nothing for a moment except the crackle of wrapping paper being gathered. They are surprised it’s Fanta who says, “I think if you do find someone to love, it makes life a little nicer.”

Kitty lights up a cigarette and is reprimanded at once. She is sent out to the porch. “I forgot the house is non-smoking because of the baby,” she tells Maxine, who follows her out. “That *beastly* little baby.”

“Yeah, I hope she takes after Rosie,” Maxine smirks. “Honestly, would you ever fuck Tony King?”

“What? I’d rather mount a birch tree.” Kitty throws her cigarette over the railing. “Bleeech! This shit tastes like walrus.” Maxine collapses with giggles. Only Kitty Domingo can make her laugh when she feels this blue.

Kitty is sneaking around with a crusty punk named Spitboy. He makes Maxine think of the soap scum after washing a sink full of dishes. Kitty blows off rehearsal and no one sees her again for two weeks.

Maxine is furious when Kitty skips her third practise. “Jeezus,” she fumes. “Is she still bailing on us to bounce back between those two turds?”

“Who,” Squeaky asks, “Jasper and Spitboy?”

“No, I mean Bullshit ’n’ Idiot.”

“I’ll talk to her.” After practise Squeaky goes to see Kitty, who is back living at her mom’s. Over the years Squeaky has made her chocolate mousse after bad haircuts, matzo ball soup for colds. Kitty respects her like a big sister. The look on Squeaky’s face says everything.

"I'm not asking what you're doing but you gotta stop fucking around. It's affecting the band. Understand?" Squeaky doesn't know if Kitty is using again, and if Kitty's wrongly accused, it will turn ugly.

She waits in the living room while Kitty talks to Spitboy on the phone. "Yeah, that's right," she tells him. "I let Jasper throw one in me for old time's sake. So *what*?"

That is the end of Spitboy.

They play a summer festival, a private party on a boat, and a triumphant return to the Sewer. A photographer from a music magazine arranges a photo shoot in a scrap yard. Maxine poses dramatically in the middle of every frame. *Born with Bush* is getting decent reviews. There is relentless promotion on radio and talk shows. Adalita has a lot of people for them to meet.

On Labour Day they are booked to headline at one of the biggest clubs in Vancouver. As they sit in their very own dressing room, cold bottles of beer laid out in ice for them, Maxine can't stop talking. "Jeezus, can you believe this," she says, tapping her leg nervously. "Can you fucking *believe* this? I used to be a waitress in this club in my twenties. I got stiffed for drinks and the bar manager tried to feel me up after every shift."

"A year ago we played the Nation of Fuckers convention for free," Squeaky muses. "It's kind of unbelievable we're getting paid four grand for a single show!"

They put on their laminated passes and are led to the dining area and catered buffet. Maxine squeals when she sees a carton of milk labelled "Wet Leather." There are six hundred people here to see them tonight. She can't stop talking excitedly and couscous falls out of her mouth.

"You eat like a goat," Kitty tells her. She takes a swig of Raven Cream Ale. "Man, I missed this beer. The thought of all that crappy American swill I drank on tour makes me wanna gush."

Squeaky's brother Andre is there, also. He's a big guy with a handlebar mustache and *Helloween* written in black marker on the back of his faded denim vest. Squeaky takes a big puff of his doobie and coughs. "Is there tobacco in this joint?"

"A little bit."

"A little bit? How about if I beat you up a little bit?"

"I don't mind tobacco in *my* joint, Andre." Maxine winks and pats the seat beside her. "Come sit by me." When Squeaky fires off a warning look, she titters.

The crowd reacts to Wet Leather with head-shaking abandon. A few scattered maniacs howl, some idiot barks like a dog. The smoke machines begin and Maxine slithers back and forth across the stage, long legs encased in black leather. It's a seductive sight. She headbangs and gives the audience devil horns and flicking tongue, but her stage banter needs work. "Welcome, Heshers of '82! You're gonna like this one:

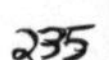

"Gramma's got a tramp stamp,
She used to be a doll
And still hangs out down at the mall
Along with several children
She didn't want at all

The boys wanna get in
But you don't know where she's been
when Gramma's got a tramp stamp
Gramma's got a tramp stamp
OH YEAAAAAAAH!"

Wet Leather is offered a two-month European tour, opening for Kids Killed by Cars, a prodigal punk band who sold out years earlier. After he ripped off everyone who worked for them, the singer is the only original member left. The new stuff mostly sucks but their name draws a crowd. Despite the fact that Kids Killed by Cars play uninspired crud punk, Fanta wants to go to Europe, badly. She'd play with almost anyone to get there.

The band is booked to leave Vancouver mid-September, in the last good days before solid months of rain. When Squeaky gets the confirmed tour dates her stomach drops. The band flies out three days before Franky Sparrow returns home.

She goes to Freudian Slips to see Fanta. "I can't believe I'm going to miss seeing Franky by seventy-two *hours*," she complains, beating her tiny fist on the counter.

"You and your boyfriend are both in bands. If you want to play music for a living, you'll have to accept touring."

"But it's so unfair." Squeaky tries to shrug it off and peers into the jewellery display of belt buckles. But her chin trembles.

Fanta continues to steam polyester. She wants to be sympathetic, but the thought of seeing London, Paris, and Berlin is too exciting. "Rock 'n' roll giveth, and rock 'n' roll taketh away."

"Fanta, I could seriously punch you in the balls right now."

Kitty waits out her time before the tour lying on Jasper's couch, underwear greying, watching Led Zeppelin videos and chainsmoking cigarettes. Jasper has a bag of speed, the good shards that are hard to find nowadays. She'd rather get some heroin and finish packing—at least then mundane tasks are doable, even enjoyable. But she can't start the tour strung out. She throws a few things into her pack, adds another dirty dish to the mound beside the sink.

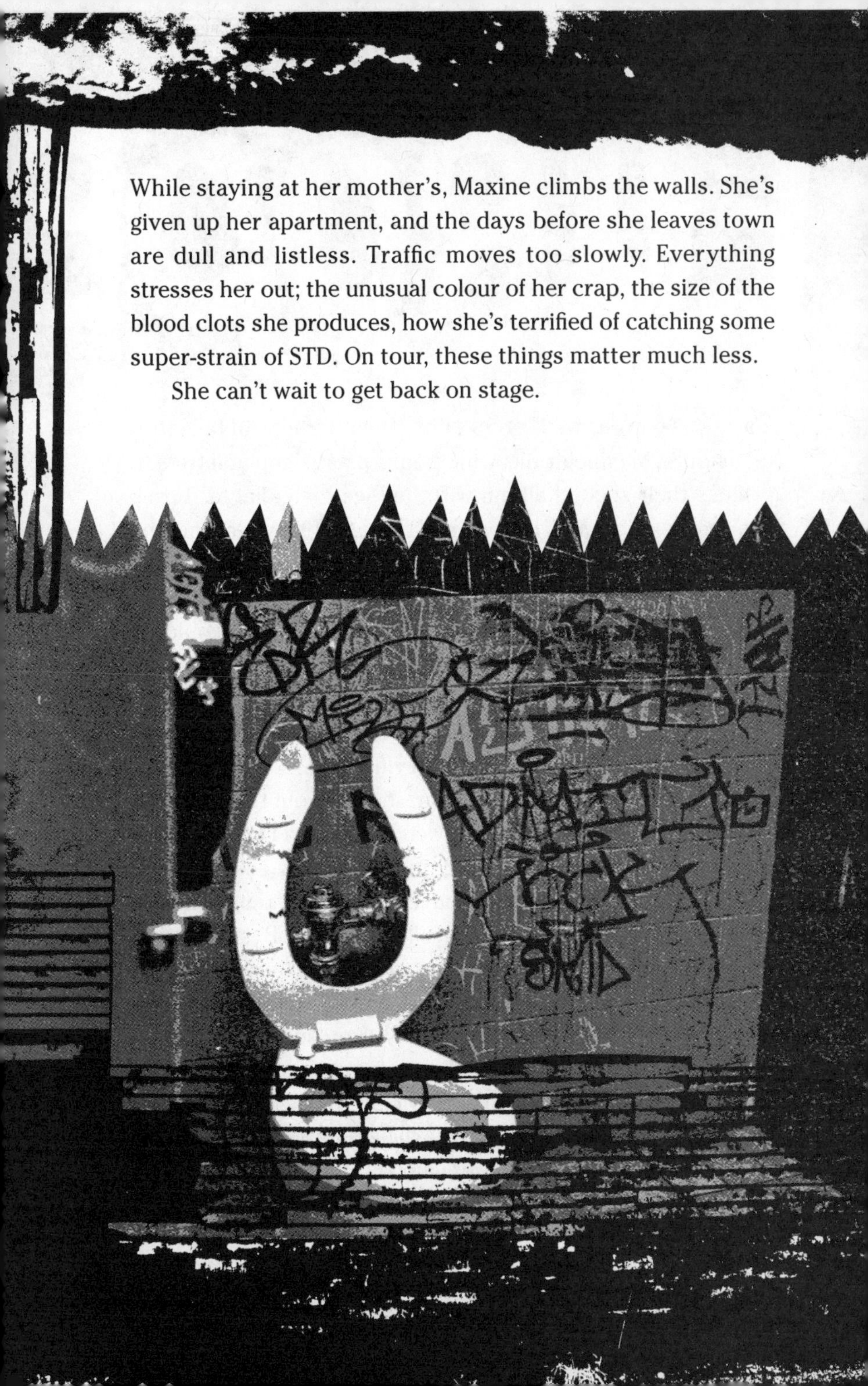

While staying at her mother's, Maxine climbs the walls. She's given up her apartment, and the days before she leaves town are dull and listless. Traffic moves too slowly. Everything stresses her out; the unusual colour of her crap, the size of the blood clots she produces, how she's terrified of catching some super-strain of STD. On tour, these things matter much less.

She can't wait to get back on stage.

EUROPE

The plane ride to Frankfurt, then Berlin, will take thirteen hours. Maxine drinks wine from a plastic cup and tries to discuss their second album with her seatmate, Fanta. Terms like *legacy* and *efficient record distribution* float around the conversation. "I want our next album to be songs that get women through bad men and bad breakups."

"I get it," Fanta says, trying to nap. "Songs that could be your personal anthem."

Kitty has taken three sleeping pills and snores with her head thrown back. Two small children begin to scream. "Great," Maxine groans. "They're trying to harmonize."

From her overstuffed carry-on, she pulls out the latest rag they're written up in, examines each photo for a litany of flaws. It's her first glossy, full-colour picture. She's getting more publicity as the singer. Editors have heard of her reputation for excess, and request her specifically for press. Besides being the frontwoman, she's the one who will give the best quote, the juiciest sound bite. Maxine has never been shy with a microphone thrust in her face. She knows to pose mouth slightly open, arms akimbo. The band has entered into a silent agreement with this, though Squeaky is embarrassed by Maxine's tits-for-tips exchange, and Fanta dislikes anything that detracts from the music. It's only Kitty who truly doesn't care. If she has a pill or a few lines then everything seems just fine.

The rust-haired woman coming towards them in Tegel airport looks like an angel. Didi is tall and stunning, with a charming Danish accent. She wears a leather jacket with tight black jeans and knee-high boots, a silk scarf around her neck. "Somefing tells me you are the band," she says, glancing at Kitty's backpack sewn with dental floss. "I am finking it must be you!"

Didi's husband, Wolfgang Kellar, runs Skat Records Europe. Usually when bands come to Berlin, they stay at his office, but an anti-fascist punk band from Italy is there for the night. Didi drives the girls to her home in Kreutzberg, an area known as a retirement community for old punk rockers. The apartment is large and bright, with thick animal skins across the couch. Helmut Newton photographs cover an entire wall. Fanta admires a watercolour series of females boxing. "It was women who built dis city after the bombing," Didi informs them. "All the men were dead."

She invites the girls out for some Berlin nightlife. Everyone but Fanta wants to go. She is too travel-weary, but appreciates how Didi's hospitality fills the room. "I'd like to stay and have a bath," she says. "Would that be okay?"

"Sweetheart, I fink dat would be fantastic!" Didi pulls out towels and containers of bath oils. When they leave, Fanta sits and waits for the faucet to fill the world's tiniest bathtub. She thinks how this woman has given up her whole apartment to a stranger, how she only knows punks to be this kind.

That night, for the first time in years, Fanta dreams of Harold. They are standing on a roof, beside a broken spiral staircase. In the dream he warns her of the missing steps. There is no sound but she knows he's protecting her.

She wakes and feels the burden of a country full of ghosts, with too much memory to bear.

They have two days in Berlin to rehearse, and Wolfgang produces everything on the list of gear they sent him:

2 short patch cords
6 sets standard gauge round wound bass strings
2 speaker cables
4 twenty-foot guitar cables (right-angled)
20 packs D'Addario XL-10 guitar strings
2 packages Jim Dunlop one millimeter picks

Wolfgang is a large, gruff Berliner with a menacing pompadour. He is a fifty-something punk from the generation of squatters, jumping over fences to take a shit. Eddie Camaro has been friends with him since the eighties, when Green Meat used to tour with Wolfgang's own band, Mega Colon. The bass player was notorious for defecating onstage and kicking his crap into the audience. When Wolfgang started his booking agency, Eddie sent him Fire Chicken, who became his first successful band. Sometimes, if Wolfgang likes the group he is promoting, he will go out on the road with them, but mostly he books bands and runs the office in Berlin.

Didi is the one who takes care of the musicians, and is a den mother to visiting girlfriends who follow the boys in the band. She speaks four languages and has many songs written about her. With rusty hair, pointy ears, and twinkling eyes she looks like a fox. She tells them how Danish girls have fear and respect for the sea. Their cities are a thousand years old and their language too difficult for Swedes. They believe Didi when she says, "I tell you girls, I fink nuffing is going to stop you."

Fanta wakes up to the sounds of traffic and kids playing, just like at home, but the noise is bicycle horns instead of cars, and the children scream to each other in German. She sits at a nearby cafe drinking fresh ginger tea and enjoying a small cake. It's chilly today, and inside her pockets her fingers ache.

While the other girls go shopping, Wolfgang takes her on a tour of the city. Fanta would rather see a bombed-out church, the burned remains of a train station, and chunks of the Wall covered in graffiti art. Wolfgang shows her an old shopping mall taken over as a squat, and the posh district where, in the eighties, he threw rocks and smashed store windows with hundreds of other angry kids. They cleaned out the parliament, which still had Nazi sympathizers. It's the reason the punk anti-fascist movement became so strong.

There are the socialist tenement blocks of the east, and wide boulevards built by the Russians, who loved to parade. The many parks are former bomb sites where buildings once stood, and children now play in castles made with logs. This is Fanta's homeland, and she feels most deeply the heaviness of history and shame. In others parts of Europe they can talk, even make a joke about the war. Not here. Never here.

16.9.A. Koblach

"FUCK YOU, AUSCHLOCK!"

Someone throws a plastic cup of beer at Kitty. It drips down her face. Having recently learned the German word for *asshole,* it features heavily in her vocabulary. She screams louder as more cups fly. One hits Fanta on the truss rod of her guitar, but if it bothers her she doesn't let on. She walks over to Kitty and says, "Keep your cool." It is clear this is the way the crowd shows affection.

The show is in a small Austrian town hall. While timid at first, the teenagers now shove, elbow jab, and kick one another. The promoter is a hairy, middle-aged man with a mild trace of eyeliner. He leers at Maxine from the side of the stage, while beside him his drunken child bride gyrates, tits displayed in an elaborate leather holster. The child bride prances onstage and whips Kitty with her long, bleached dreadlocks. Kitty wraps her hands around them and slings her offstage. Behind the drum kit Squeaky howls.

It's the first show with Kids Killed by Cars. Squeaky is a fan of their first album, *Struck*. They aren't very friendly and she'd hoped they'd travel with more style. The drummer didn't even want to strike his drums after sound check, but the stage was too small for her to set up in front.

Kitty slips in a puddle of beer and goes down in a bungled heap. A couple of guys from Kids Killed by Cars watch from the side of the stage, in their skinny ties and sunglasses, stone-faced.

The girls adore their tour manager, Friedrich, who jumps onstage to help. He is a wiry, toothless German with a tattooed skull. He once visited Vancouver and enjoyed the abundance of cheap drugs and roomy dumpsters. Besides running the merch table and wrangling belligerent musicians, he also drives Wet Leather in the Highway Tiger, an extended BMW van with a flat screen, GPS, and a small bunk above the back seats. After twenty-odd years on the job, Friedrich can procure any kind of drug and knows the best rub-and-tugs in Europe. For every road malady, he has a cure. He lived in Los Angeles for ten years and worked with the biggest acts in the business. Squeaky figures he must have seen five thousand rock shows, and doesn't expect Wet Leather to impress him.

With Kitty extricated from the cords and upright once again, she hangs back at the drum kit. When Squeaky and Kitty bounce off each other, the energy is like two little kids at Christmas. Even though Kitty hits her share of sour notes, her natural exuberance is thrilling to be around. Squeaky's not thinking about impressing Friedrich anymore, or the guys in the other band. She's trying to figure out where Kitty's going next.

When they come offstage, the guys in Kids Killed by Cars aren't impressed. "You played ten minutes too long," one of them complains.

Friedrich won't hear it. "Shut de fuck up. Who shit in your fucking brain?" He gives Squeaky a high five. "Yuh, you play pri-tty good show." She's over the fucking moon.

17.9.A. Vienna

The birthplace of Mozart and Hitler. Fanta explains that during the Ottoman Empire, the Muslim Turks were once at the gates of the city. Because of this, Austrians are notoriously racist, and it makes her think of her mother. Fanta says nothing else.

The show is in an old slaughterhouse called Arena. After years of squatting and bloody battles with police, the punks got the city to give in and let them keep it. Black and white photographs of dead punks hang in memorial. Now there's a building for sleeping and a big communal kitchen, a bar, and a sloping lawn with a stage for outdoor shows when it's warm. A new building attached to the slaughterhouse even has an elevator. The girls sit and wait in the courtyard on splintering picnic tables. Above them the slaughterhouse smokestack looms empty. All the animals have been burned.

They follow Friedrich through the maze of hallways to the stage. Fanta's guitar herds them forward. The flashing lights show the massive audience all the way to the back. It's the biggest crowd they've played, and eight hundred people stare at the band, expectant. Maxine freezes at the microphone. This has never happened to her before. The band can see her throat working but nothing comes out. The crowd begins to murmur when the silence lasts too long.

Fanta steps to the microphone. "Hallo, du hast Vet Leather!" She nods to Squeaky, whose kick drum jerks Maxine into action. They guide her one note into the next, and then she's working the stage like always. Unlike North American crowds, the mix of kids and grey-hairs waste no time enjoying themselves. The middle of the floor is a spinning pit. The sea of punks may not be able to translate all the words, but they come together on a boot-stomping gut level.

This is what Fanta's been reaching for, the harmony beneath the grit of it all. Brainsick strangers united through song. She leans over the monitor and offers her guitar. They've never sounded better—Kitty is nearly sober and razor sharp, and Maxine hits every note with perfect pitch. There's a thrill to playing music when it's pure and unpolluted. For once she doesn't feel part of a giant charade. The crowd is a dark mass, and to Fanta, they glitter.

It's a long wait at another border crossing in Eastern Europe. Squeaky sits on the grass with Gruesome Gary, the bass player of Kids Killed by Cars. He's Ecuadorian and Italian, the pin-up of the group. There is also Contagious Kenneth, the screamer, and Doug Do Not on guitar. Drywall Paul, who plays drums, doesn't get a cool nickname. "You're a pretty decent beat-keeper," Gary comments. "You don't see a lot of chick drummers that can actually *play*."

Fanta overhears this, and it irritates her when Squeaky laughs. She goes to wake up Kitty, who is sleeping in the back of the van. "Get up and get your passport," Fanta orders, after trying to gently rouse her for several unsuccessful minutes.

Kitty scrambles out of the bunk, disoriented, and pulls up her hood to sleepily join the line outside. She had been dreaming she held a baby with very long nose hairs.

Drywall Paul asks, "What the fuck country are we in, anyway?"

"Hopefully it's a place where the special goulash isn't made with horse meat," Maxine says. "That totally made me puke. It tastes like corn!"

"This sure ain't the world of boyfriends and burgers back home," Squeaky agrees.

Doug Do Not whines, "I don't know if tonight I want to have a shower *before* the show or after."

"Maybe after," Friedrich says. "Dat way if someone sucks your pee-pee, you make it nice for dem."

At the next gig they unload their gear and drink in the band room with the promoter, a strong-jawed blonde who has brought them food from home: dishes with pork, lamb, veal, paprika, garlic, and plum brandy. The promoter is unhappy about the turnout. "Six or seven years ago there would be hundreds of people at a show," she says, "now there is maybe seven. No one has any money; no one wants to pay."

"Fuck it," Kitty says. "Can we get any coke?"

"Oh no," answers the promoter. "It would take many days of notice, just to sit and wait for the..." she searches for the right word, "wanted man."

Most nights they get back into the van and head to the next city as soon as the show is over. The only constant in some of these places is the same ghastly clientele. As Wet Leather works through the set, the front row of boys clumsily paws at their legs. Friedrich keeps pushing them back. He can barely contain the overzealous males when Maxine thrusts her hips, singing:

"I'll tell you what I'm gonna do,
kick it down, kick it down,
KICK IT OOT!"

The audience shows their appreciation in the pit. From Fanta's vantage point on stage left, she watches men pound each other in the crowd. A woman joins in and they pound her, too. They seem to find such joy in this violence. Though, when someone falls, everyone rushes to help them back up.

Then the set is finished and glaring lights come on. The promoter herds the girls back to the band room where they are asked to remain until the bar closes. They load the gear and get into the van and everyone is gone again.

20.9. CR. Zagreb

Everything starts to go bad in Croatia. While driving through the city, they see rotting houses and punctured roofs, shelled buildings. The girls take shower shifts in their room at a grand old hotel which echoes with emptiness. Dinner is in the ornate dining hall, all the food and wine gourmet. The elderly server wears a faded suit with dignity.

The venue Wet Leather is set to play looks like part of something that was once a school. It's packed with kids. People stand on side tables and some guys loudly sing a football anthem as their girlfriends roll their eyes. There is no real backstage so Fanta sits down at a table with two smiling girls.

Mina is a petite brunette with sharp cheekbones and speaks the best English. She says, "Croatian women are beautiful and cold. They are dangerous. And Croatian men are pussies." After the emancipation, women began to get jobs and make money, become independent. Now their society is run by women. Eva, her friend with sparkly pink eye shadow, agrees.

It seems okay for Fanta to ask what it was like to live through a war. Mina says, "The alarms went off at night and everyone had to run to the basement. Parents became dead inside and passed that deadness on to their children." She says she saw three bad things that affected her. "But," she says, "only three."

All Fanta can do is entertain them with a forty-minute set, and promises to give all she's got. Mina and Eva stand right up front and clap as she fingers the opening phrase of "Invasion." The vocals never materialize. Maxine keeps missing her opening, and they stop and start again. Squeaky keeps the beat steady while Fanta downstrokes. Her wrist starts to hurt.

It startles everyone when Maxine suddenly blares, "WhoooAAA-AAA-OOH-WHOOOOA-OOH!" It goes on for an impossibly long time. If Maxine does coke before a show she rushes through the set, if drunk she's too loose. Right now it's a bad mixture.

"I'm gonna say this in Englishhh, so you can all understand. I wanna HEAR SOME NOISE," she bellows. "Louder, louder, come *on*. FUCK YOU!"

A plastic cup bounces off her shoulder and then a water bottle whizzes past her face. She threatens to walk off the stage. The crowd buzzes like angry hornets.

They huddle around the drum kit for a quick conference. "Uh-UH," Maxine says. "Fuck this. They're *throwing* shit at me." She crosses her arms. People begin to jeer.

Fanta looks over and sees Mina and Eva's disappointed faces. "Maxine, get your ass to that microphone and start the goddamn song," she warns. "If I have to walk off this stage, I'm gone for good."

She means it.

In the van on the first tour the girls listened to each other's music, gossiped, discussed the shows, told jokes, had sing-a-longs. Now everyone crawls into their corner with earphones on, or stares at the TV screen. Squeaky pines for Franky, Kitty pines for heroin. Fanta withdraws further.

"Can you keep it down," Maxine complains from the bunk. She has a violent hangover from the night before. "Just because you're talking loud doesn't mean you're saying anything."

"That's the pot calling out the kettle," Squeaky mutters. They're still mad about the embarrassing show and ignore her. Fanta finds Maxine's mini-stardom obnoxious, and the *SHBLATT, SHBLATT* sound of her spitting out toothpaste puts Squeaky irrationally on edge.

"I mean it. I need to sleep! *I'M* the one who has to get up there and sell these songs. *I'M* the one who has to entertain. All you have to do—"

"Maxine, you're like a seagull," Squeaky interrupts. "Always shitting or squawking."

"That's really rude."

"Okay then...how about you're like a sand dollar no one wants to pick up?"

"You're calling me a sand dollar? Why? Are you saying I'm washed UP?"

"*Some*body needs to get a sense of humour."

Maxine has a stubborn streak a mile wide. She bitches until the next stop.

24.9. CH. Winterthurn

They are surprised by the crowd of crusty Swiss shit-punks in the parking lot of such a clean country. Backstage the girls mill about while Kids Killed by Cars do their sound check, which is moving with brisk Swiss efficiency. Contagious

Kenneth's girlfriend has joined the tour, an aging Lolita with a boob job and thick legs encased in fishnets. She refuses to acknowledge the girls in the band, and there are loud displays of affection with Kenneth whenever one of them walks by. It creates unnecessary tension as she watches Wet Leather with suspicious eyes.

Squeaky has seen first-hand how certain women wear down a band. They hang around broke, drink all the booze, and are so proprietary over their men toward female fans, it creates endless psychodramas.

They look up when she enters the band room. "Hello," Squeaky says. "How's it going?" The girlfriend flashes an insincere smile, grabs a handful of crackers, and stalks out.

"Well, *she* sucks," Maxine shrugs, picking through the requisite meat and cheese platter. She crams chunks of bread into her mouth, followed by squirts of condiment tubes. "Whatever, Team Cankles."

Besides access to hygiene, the hot button issue in the band is that, if left hungry too long, Maxine will get downright hostile. Getting properly fed is the biggest problem for everyone—scavenging backstage, trying to find restaurants near the venue, not to mention vegetarian fare for Fanta. It's understood the opening act gets the scraps.

Maxine swallows. "You know what else sucks? The fat guy in their band—Drywall Paul? *He* hoards all the good snacks! And then I heard that on their rider they get vodka, Red Bull, and Jagermeister before every show. AND five pairs of socks. *Excuse* me? If they get five pairs of socks why do they all reek of foot odour? Has anyone smelled their van? And how come none of them hang out with us?"

They have begun to notice that Maxine is becoming more tightly wound every day. Moments of anxiety overwhelm her. She often gives creative excuses to mitigate a possible poor performance. “I have these weird foot cramps,” she says. “This shitty beer is giving me diarrhea.”

The increasing attention she receives only compounds her problems. The tour has become her personal parade of debauchery. She talks about who she fucked the night before while flirting with unattractive waiters over continental breakfast. She scouts guys as soon as she gets to the gig, and chats up any available male. If she doesn’t get some kind of action after the show, the night is deemed a failure. Then she climbs back in the van and starts all over again.

> “Kids Killed by Cars were here and fucked yer boyfriends!”
> “Good, now you got herpes too.”
>
> —backstage graffiti added by Kitty

Maxine lounges in the hotel room in her underwear. “Oh my god, that man is so hot. Franz? Fritz! I hope I gave him the right hotel name. Kitty, wake up and listen! He made my lady parts tingle.”

“I’m trying really hard not to vom right now.”

“Kiss my auschlock.”

“How about if I make you lick my fist when I pull it out of your ass? I’m trying to fucking sleep.”

“Jeez, sorry.”

“Smell the glove.” This makes them erupt into giggles.

“Maybe the guys in Kids Killed by Cars have gone tour gay,” Maxine muses. Kitty, now drunk and jovial, laughs into her pillow.

“Oh my god, YES! Tour gay. *BRAP*,” she burps. “Ah-ha-HAH!”

“And who the fuck ever said those guys were hot? Drywall Paul looks like John Candy in *Stripes*.”

“YES! OX. Let’s call him Ox from now on. Like, ‘Hey Ox, how’s it going?’ A-ha-HAH! Ox!”

When Kitty starts snoring, Maxine turns off the lights, mulling over the boys in the band. Kenneth is out since his girlfriend is visiting. There's Paul, but he's fat, and she's not a chubby chaser. Doug Do Not has stubby fingers she dislikes, and he didn't take off his shoes the first two weeks of the tour. His feet are a soft, rotten yellow. Gruesome Gary is the prettiest one and holds his bass like Sid Vicious, but he's young, and handsome in a way he doesn't know yet. He says he loves a girl back home, but that doesn't matter. Not tonight.

Maxine throws back the covers. All she can think of is a cock, or two, anything to shove inside her aching cunt. She pulls on a dress and heads to the door, stumbling through the darkness.

28.9. B. Brussels

Belgium is a country left in the dustbin of history.

01.10. D. Trier

The Highway Tiger breaks down near a squat outside Trier. It used to be a monastery that became an army garrison during the war. There is graffiti of aliens, Madonnas, and flying skateboards. It will be hours until Friedrich has the van fixed. No one complains about the downtime.

The girls go sit by the river, and then take the cement path that leads into town. Squeaky rides her skateboard, doing lazy carves. Fanta says, "Did you know, the Romans used Trier as a vacation spot when Italy became too hot in the summer?"

They know she gets excited by these historical points, but no one's in the mood for it. Kitty has blisters on her feet and as they pass the ruins of a church she grumbles, "I HATE looking at old shit!"

They turn a corner into an open square. A group of crusty street punks drink by the ancient Roman fountain. Even a ten-year-old with tattoos has a beer. Squeaky lends him her skateboard and he rides around the square, and they practise grinds on the stone steps where Roman nobility once stood.

The sun slowly fades on the red granite cliffs as they walk back to the van: thin Maxine, bleached hair growing over her grimy neck; Kitty's skinny legs and high-top swagger; Squeaky rolling between them. This moment is a snapshot in Fanta's mind.

03.10. NL. Amsterdam

Filthy brown water in the canals and hordes of atrocious Americans. Luckily the club is only a few blocks from the Backstage Hotel, where each unit is decorated like a dressing room. There are butterfly clasps on the headboard, even a road case footstool. Maxine smokes weed from a coffee shop and becomes so paranoid she refuses to go onstage, even though the show is hours away. "I'm serious," she states fearfully. "I've lost all feeling on the left side of my *ass!*"

Squeaky tries to figure out what time it is back in Vancouver. It's hard to find a phone, a helpful operator, or the country codes. She heads down the street and plugs euros into a payphone. Kitty follows along and sings in a pinched Buzzcocks falsetto, slapping her hand against her thigh:

"No Ass! No pants! Looking shitty walking down the strass-suh!"

Kitty hasn't called home, not to anyone, even her mother, even once.

It's a long drive from Potsdam to Frankfurt, through the strange dichotomy of castle ruins juxtaposed with signs for McDonald's, tiny villages in open fields beside eight-lane highways. The flat Dutch landscape puts them to sleep.

They stop for gas and Fanta is appalled to see Squeaky taking pictures of the Polish hookers working the truck stop toilets. "What, you live in East Van and have never seen a sex trade worker?"

"I'm in Europe. These are new, exciting hookers!"

"Sometimes I think you could stand to be a little more sensitive to women, Squeaky." Fanta looks at her sternly.

"What?"

"Yeah, I totally agree," Maxine quips. "You treat guys way better than girls!"

Squeaky's face goes red. "No I don't. Well, if I do, it's because I have three brothers. I grew up around guys. There's less drama and gossip with them."

"Oh, there's just as much. I was on tour with Fire Chicken, too."

"Whatever, Fanta. You act like you're so above everything, but really you want to be involved. You just can't lighten up."

Hearing Squeaky and Fanta argue upsets Kitty. Maxine finds her behind the gas station, with the sleeve of her hoodie against her nose, a glazed look on her face.

"What the fuck, are you huffing brake fluid?"

"Er....Ah...Guumph."

"Jeezus Kitty, don't let that out. Fanta's hanging on by a thread as it is."

She takes Kitty by the arm and they climb back into the van.

05.10. NL. Venlo

A Sunday night in a small town just across the border from Germany. It's a thin crowd and Wet Leather plays a dull, uninspired set. After the show the girls go back and hang in their separate hotel rooms. Squeaky trips while drunk and cracks the toilet with her foot. Fanta fights a cold. Nothing much interesting happens.

17.10. F. Bordeaux

The bar smells like centuries of piss and failure. For dinner the promoter gives the bands baguettes and cheese. Ten people come to see them. At an outdoor café, Squeaky finds a pubic hair in her cheese crepe. There is a pickup show in Dijon tomorrow. Hungry and tired, they load the gear and keep driving.

20.10. E. Barcelona

The Catalans are loud and love to laugh. They welcome Wet Leather at the show with a raving reception. The steaming

room is packed to capacity. Maxine and Kitty spend their per diems on a bag of cheap and abundant coke, and hang backstage, sniffling.

"I love the European way of living," Maxine says, grinding her teeth.

Fanta makes a concentrated effort to get along with her bandmates. "I agree. It's the way they immerse themselves in culture and history. We come from the land of the great forgetters. I mean, our cultural epoch is 'Introducing…yam fries!'"

But Maxine isn't listening—she's spotted her conquest for the night. He's the last member of a German terror group, now tanned with a slight potbelly. His hot South African girlfriend doesn't intimidate her a bit. "I'm about to have a heart attack," she says, sidling over.

The next day the sky is gold and reddish silver, a colour rarely seen. No one appreciates this but Fanta, the only one not hungover for the eight-hour drive to Valencia. She rides up front with Friedrich, ignoring the bickering in the back. They're driving down the highway and it's raining and it's

Spain. Heartbreak feels good in this country. In the wide open space the tiny towns go by. Fanta doesn't bother to explain that this used to be forests, but the trees were cut down to build the Spanish armada. Then all of it lost at sea. It changed the landscape forever.

25.10. UK. London

The tour is more than half over, but morale is at its lowest. Everyone is sick and stinky, hungover from the continuous bottles of red wine in Spain. Kitty coughs like she has bronchitis, and Maxine complains of gut rot. Squeaky ups the ante with stink foot. Friedrich pulls a booger out of his nose the size of a cockroach.

At the window Fanta quietly watches endless stretches of green fields. It brings back the classic English novels she read as a teenager, of Victorian heroines and their tragedies. Soon the fields turn into tiny plots of well-tended gardens and desperate patches of green. Then the sky above London closes up and they settle into its darkness.

Fanta is bitterly disappointed to see nothing more of this city than the inside of the club and a dressing room.

03.11. UK. Edinburgh

A pub. A pounding disco. Ecstasy from a man named Chiclets. Another club identical to the last. The street shimmers as Squeaky uses up all her coins to call Franky and say she loves him. Maxine is reminded of her grandmother: steak and kidney pie, gentlemen in tweed, old ladies with umbrellas. For once Maxine finds everything perfect, even the fine rain that falls. But it could be the ecstasy.

05.11. UK. Stockport

It is fall in Northern England, but no one is kicking leaves down the sidewalk. Stockport is a grimy English town with a desperate feel. The crowd is old punks who look like they've had a hard time their whole lives. It's sweltering hot in the tiny hall, wall-to-wall sweating bodies. Squeaky demands a small fan beside her. She'll never make it through the show without it. In the middle of the set Fanta turns white and sinks to the floor. Friedrich runs over and carries her backstage. No one is sure what to do. Except Maxine.

"No problem, no problem," she says. "Our guitar player just isn't used to your English cider." She raises her glass, and the crowd cheers her back. Kitty and Squeaky look at each other. Fanta hasn't had a drink.

Maxine stalls for time. "Don't forget, there's merchandise for sale at the back. And by the way, we're Canadian, not American."

Someone calls, "Same thing, innit?"

"Sure, just like England and Wales." This solicits boos from the crowd. "Okay, then," she hurries on, "we're gonna do another song, this one's called, 'Cold-hearted Woman.'" It's the only one with sparse guitar that can work without Fanta. Maxine walks back to the drum kit.

Squeaky asks, "Is Fanta okay?"

"Play it," she hisses.

By the next song Fanta is back onstage. "Are you all right?" Squeaky yells, and Fanta gives a shaky smile in return.

There's a feeling here in this room, in this town, that anything resembling hope is long gone. Old Rosie cider has gotten Maxine completely pissed. Her timing is off and Kitty's bass lines couldn't be any clunkier. Everyone's frustrated they're playing perfectly into what already seems like low expectations of them. An old man with red booze nose chortles, "Sit on me face so I don't 'ave to listen."

Halfway through "Lucy Lost Her Knickers," a condom flies through the air and hits Fanta on the arm. It's filled with mustard and leaves a greasy yellow smear on her arm. Her face is hidden in the long fringe of her hair, impassive, but her shoulders stiffen. Squeaky is furious, and won't let Maxine attempt to banter with the audience. She kicks them one song right into the next until the end of the set.

Afterwards Maxine will simply say the show must go on.

07.11. N. Oslo

The van takes a wrong turn into the Norwegian backwoods, where the houses look made from gingerbread. Even the trailer parks are clean, uniformly spaced, with tasteful decorations.

Four shows to the end of the tour and Maxine stops loading gear. She sits on her ass, smoking, drinking expensive coffees, long nails curved like the orange talons of a terror bird. The girls grumble to each other about it. "Her shit is so far off the mark it's wrapped in cellophane in the toe of her shoe," Kitty says.

10.11. D. Berlin

They are back in Berlin for the final show. Some movie executives want to put "Bitches Don't Do Dishes" on a soundtrack for a teen sex romp that is sure to sell millions. Wet Leather will receive a one-time payment of six thousand dollars. A camera crew will be at the show tonight shooting footage for a video.

"I got a call from the manager of Rock Shoe," Eddie's voice crackles through the phone speakers. "They want Wet Leather to start right away in the opening slot of their US tour. All stadium shows."

"Oh my god," Maxine squeals. "That sounds like *money*."

"You'll have your own soundman, guitar tech, drum tech, a merch crew, even a guy working the lighting rig. Not to mention riding around in a ten-grand-per-week tour bus."

"Fuck me," Kitty says. "That's more than I made all last year!"

Squeaky thinks of Franky Sparrow, how she longs to see him. "Look, I'm not eager to get right back on the road. Especially with a shitty band I can't stand like Rock Shoe."

It's as if Maxine read her mind. "What, you'd rather stay home and work on your love gut with Franky? There's no *question* we should do it. Think of the money and exposure. Rock Shoe is huge right now!"

"Yeah, but Squeaky's right," Kitty says. "They suck *ass*."

"They really do."

"You'll have to make a decision soon," Eddie says. "Their manager has already called twice."

"Yes!"

"No."

"*N*o."

"Pleeeaaase Fanta. What do *you* say?"

Something has shifted within Fanta, and Maxine's entreaties have no appeal. Touring could be fun, but was hard work, too. Fanta has been everywhere and seen nothing. Despite the constant travel, she's only had a superficial glance of each city. She can't think of any reason to keep going. It crosses her mind that it wouldn't take that long for her and her bandmates to become strangers once again.

She shakes her head. "I'm tired, Maxine."

Kitty picks at the scab on her chin from another UDI—unidentified drinking injury. "Tell that manager to fuck off or we'll throw him down and piss on his cock." Eddie ends the call.

"I'm going to the S036 to get shit-faced," Kitty declares. "Who's coming?" No one moves, so she shrugs and walks out.

"This is bullshit," Maxine seethes. "I'm so fucking PISSED. We have to tour! A band proves itself on the road. You've got to *sell* it! You've got to be able to deliver it to the people!"

Squeaky says quietly, "I think if Kitty were given fifty grand she'd be dead in three months."

"Oh, *now* you've got all this concern for Kitty? What about me? You're only destroying my DREAM."

Maxine slams the door and Fanta stares after her. "Do you think she's incapable of being empathetic, or does she just choose not to be?"

"It's the great philosophical question of our time."

Neither one laughs.

Standing at the backstage curtain amid amplifier cases, Fanta watches Kitty stagger through the audience then stumble to her knees. She understands the forlorn life of an addict, but no one wants to see their friend in this shape, and Kitty is deaf to complaints. It doesn't matter if a hotel manager in Oslo has to spend three hours cleaning her blood and puke out of a room. To Kitty Domingo, that's a rock star.

With her hand on the edge of the dusty velvet curtain, Fanta wonders when it will all be enough.

By the time the band gathers to hit the stage, Kitty can barely walk. Maxine is infuriated. "Goddamn, you're really messed up."

"Oh shit. *Yurp*."

Kitty teeters to an exit door, leans over the railing, and pukes. When she's done she looks up and sees tiny puffs of silver clouds. These make her feel better. Her tongue darts in and out of her mouth.

Squeaky is concerned. "Are you okay, Kitty?"

"Blugh-UGH!"

"Getting fucked up really increases your quotability. Are you guys ready?" Maxine taps her foot. "Let's GO!"

"Hold on," Fanta snaps. "Just give her a minute."

"Okay, ready." Kitty throws a jittery arm in the air.

"Halle-fuckin-lullah. Here we go."

Maxine shakes her ass as she gyrates across the stage. There is a belt of fake bullets slung low over her hips. Squeaky hunches behind the kit and bears down. The only thing keeping her going is the bag of weed inside her kick drum. Maxine is already at the high end of her vocal range, and it's usually during this moment in "Bitches Don't Do Dishes" that she prepares to stage dive. To the room it looks like a spontaneous moment of pure energy, but the band knows her script. Maxine scans the crowd and zeroes in on the hottest guy she can find.

For Fanta, the last show is the worst yet. The mix that comes from the monitors is vicious and shrill. Not only is Kitty hitting the wrong chords, she's holding them obliviously. Despite the wild cheers, all Fanta feels is relief when it's over. Backstage are executives, fan club members, promoters, dealers, groupies—people in a constant buzz, all wanting something. Fanta doesn't know how many more introductions she can muster through. Everywhere she turns there's a camera in her face. Under the fluorescent lights of the dreary back room, the vibe is sycophantic. Everybody pushes to get closer, desperate for some kind of souvenir.

The end of the tour with Kids Killed by Cars will not create a great loss in their lives. Contact between the two bands stayed at a bare minimum. They decline a farewell drink with Wet Leather and go out on the town with Wolfgang instead.

Didi has come to the show, and they sit and talk with her about the tour.

"You get used to this lifestyle and then it ends like *this*." Maxine snaps her fingers. There are brown, puffy bags beneath her eyes. "It's like being in a car that slams to a stop."

"I can't believe we'll be home so soon. I'm only three boarding passes away from Franky Sparrow." Squeaky wonders if all the time apart has taken a toll. "Didi, if Wolfgang is gone for a long time on tour, when he comes back, is it like how it was before?"

"No," Didi answers. "Sweetheart, you have to practise being in love. Like anyfing else, it's a skill."

She hugs them all goodbye.

"Omigod, this is so awesome," Kitty says, but it isn't. She's not looking forward to going home, or the long plane ride, and has no intention of sleeping until then. Her face is sharp and rebellious, covered in grime. In a corner she snorts the last of the flap. "Shit," she says to no one. "Damn, my nose is burning."

She makes a move to sit beside the skinny blonde boy with a mouth—obnoxious, just how she likes 'em. His muttonchops are so big it looks like his ears are made of hair. This thought makes her laugh uncontrollably. The room is spinning full of people speaking a foreign language. After a while she realizes it's English. The boy asks if she's okay. Kitty pisses herself on the way to the bathroom.

When she returns, Maxine jerks her thumb at the camera crew. "Get a load of *her*. It's like watching a car crash and wondering if you're in it."

Everyone hears. Instead of sitting down, Kitty does a perfect swan dive into the glass-covered table.

The entire room jumps at the crash. A few people try to help Kitty, but she's rolling around in glass, cackling. Her blue eyes hold the storms of Jupiter. Fanta cuts through the crowd and pulls her up. Kitty's howls desist at once.

"FANTA, I LOVE YOU!"

She brushes the glass off Kitty's clothing and checks for cuts. "Listen to me," she says, cupping Kitty's chin to get her full attention. "You're too special to be a rock and roll cliché."

"What, you didn't think I was gonna die of old age, did ya?"

Fanta is exhausted. She's sick of the quarrelling and contention, the way the adulation has distorted them. Sometimes her legs hurt so much she doesn't mind the idea of sitting down forever. But that's not the worst. Kitty's falling apart right before their eyes.

"I can't do this anymore," Fanta says. "I quit."

"You're not quitting," Maxine scoffs. "We're all tired. Why don't you just go find somewhere to sleep and—"

Fanta opens her guitar case and pulls out the SG, the last piece of Harold Dixon. She holds it high over her head and smashes it on the cement floor. Finally it's just a mess of wood splinters and mangled strings.

"I LOVE YOU FANTA!" Kitty screams again.

Maxine asks the camera crew, "Are you *getting* all this?"

There's no spotlight, just Fanta's head high, walking out the door, not looking back. This is Fanta saying goodbye.

VANCOUVER, AGAIN

As soon as the plane lands, Squeaky calls Franky Sparrow. It doesn't matter that she's tired, smelly, dishevelled. She can't wait to see him. He doesn't answer his phone, and she hoists her duffel bag dejectedly into the taxicab, riding wet between the legs. The city spreads out like a filthy, untapped jewel. Excitement swells through her again. She will find Franky Sparrow. She has the numbers. At some point during this night, she'll be getting laid.

Fanta comes home to the same grime. Her apartment smells like sour smoke and old cat piss, and she walks to the bathroom over a film of cracker dust and dander. Mr. Kibbles is still here, his yellow eyes so decayed they look filled with broken glass. Decrepit and slow-moving, his breath smells of dead things. Fanta picks up the cat, and it gurgles in response. He has been with her since before the car accident, before Harold Dixon, before Wet Leather, before they sliced whole parts of her away. She looks at the junk piled around her apartment and realizes she didn't hoard these things to keep the world out. She did it because without all this stuff her life was empty. Fanta squeezes the burbling death-cat to her chest. It's time to put him down.

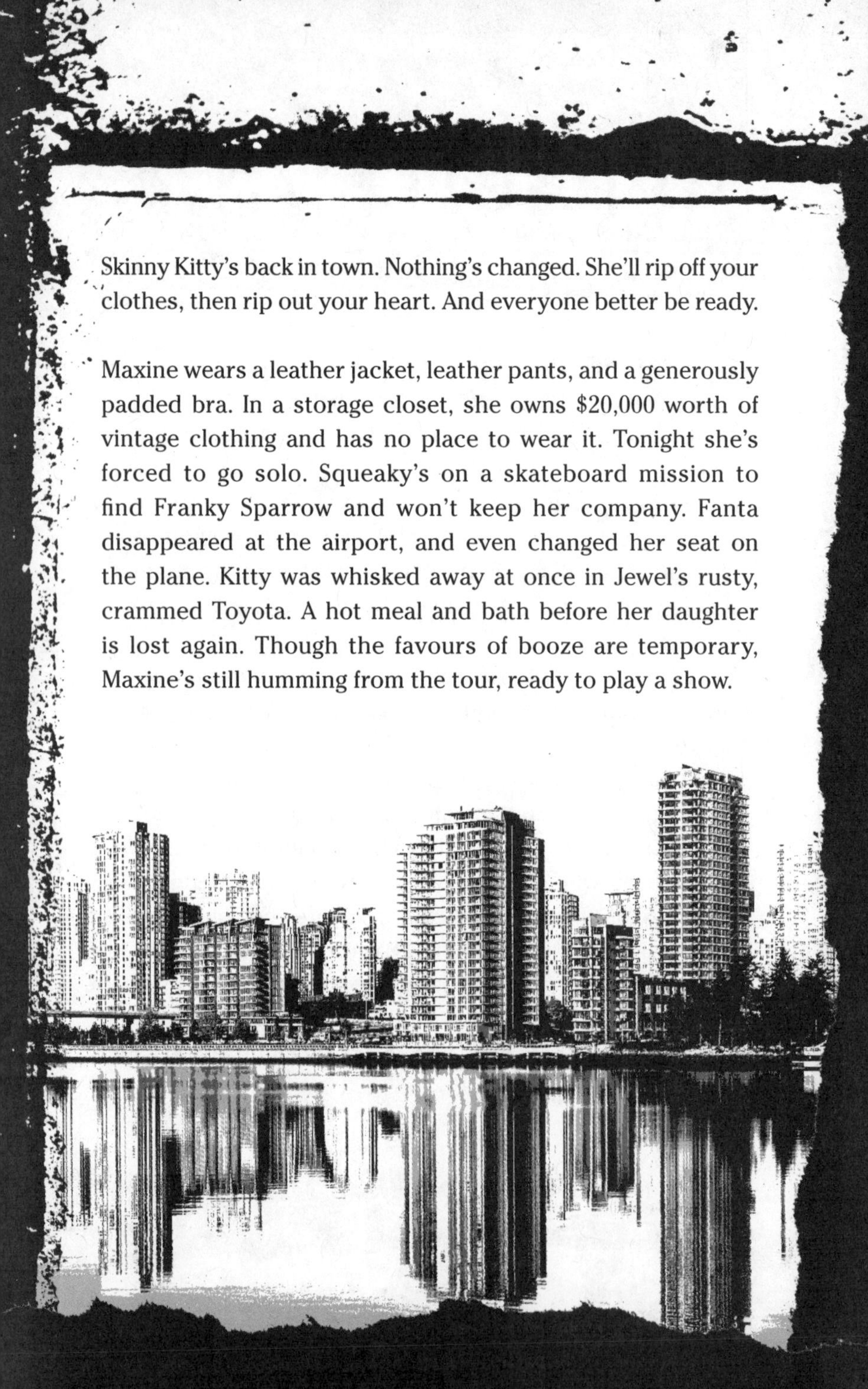

Skinny Kitty's back in town. Nothing's changed. She'll rip off your clothes, then rip out your heart. And everyone better be ready.

Maxine wears a leather jacket, leather pants, and a generously padded bra. In a storage closet, she owns $20,000 worth of vintage clothing and has no place to wear it. Tonight she's forced to go solo. Squeaky's on a skateboard mission to find Franky Sparrow and won't keep her company. Fanta disappeared at the airport, and even changed her seat on the plane. Kitty was whisked away at once in Jewel's rusty, crammed Toyota. A hot meal and bath before her daughter is lost again. Though the favours of booze are temporary, Maxine's still humming from the tour, ready to play a show.

Melancholy MAXINE

Maxine rents a house on the west side of town. It's in a trendy neighbourhood where people leave notes about each other's garbage and healthy-looking blondes bound up bike paths. It has a deck, a fireplace, even a dishwasher. Squeaky has nowhere to stay and Maxine invites her to move in. It doesn't seem like a great idea, but Franky has slept on Nerf's floor while Wet Leather toured Europe, and Squeaky needs a place to bang him on a regular basis. Maxine agrees to rent them a room for a month or two, until they find a place of their own.

It starts to sour the first day. As Squeaky unpacks boxes, Maxine flits in and out of her room. "Do NOT put that up," she orders, spotting a Fire Chicken gig poster. "I don't want to stare at Tex for the rest of my life."

"What, you don't like Tex now?"

"I never really did."

Squeaky shrugs and rolls up the poster. "Whatever."

"Have you talked to Fanta yet?"

"Nope."

"She left a note at Freudian Slips saying someone was coming next week to cover her shifts. What is going *on* with that woman?"

"Who knows? It's Fanta. You can't predict what might happen. Maybe she'll come back if you give her enough time." Squeaky hangs one of Franky's shirts in the closet. "For now, just move on to other things."

"Screw Fanta. She can be replaced."

"That's not true. It's not Wet Leather without Fanta. Don't you get it, Maxine?"

"What?"

"If we don't stick together, we're never gonna win."

Maxine decides to get drunk and buys a gram of coke to celebrate her new roommates. The first line leads to loud peals of song. The third drink and second line plateau at bawdy reminiscence. By the fourth line the booze is nearly gone, and Maxine wanders wasted around the house in a ball gown and high-heeled shoes. At the end of the night she's breaking glass and crying at the mess.

Franky has a high school friend in the neighbourhood who stops by. Chad is a professional volleyball player and registers surprise at meeting Maxine, in a gown and sneakers. She changed since her feet hurt.

"Chad, this is Maxine."

"Well, helloooo Chad. Tell me, what do you think of my dress?"

"Lose the shoes, dude. Total turn-off."

Chad brought beers they finish. Maxine offers him a line which he declines. Even though Chad's three inches shorter and not her type she asks, "You want to see my room?"

"I'm calling it," Squeaky says. "I've got an early shift at the bakery."

Franky jumps up. "I'll join you."

"Nighty-night, you two. I'm gonna stay up and entertain Chad-You'll-Be-Glad."

Squeaky washes her face and joins Franky in bed. She has just pulled up the covers when they hear, "Ooh, yeah, ooh YEEEAAAHHH…fuck me, fuck meeee…"

"Oh great, we're gonna have to listen to that all night."

"And that's just Chad. Wait till Maxine gets started."

They giggle in the dark, and cuddle closer. "You make me happy," Franky says.

"You too, baby."

In the background: "Fuck MEEE..."

When Squeaky gets home from the bakery the next afternoon, Maxine is just waking up. She comes into the kitchen in a short negligee, ass hanging out, and gulps a glass of tap water. "Dude, I'm so hungover. I need another eight hours of sleep."

"I didn't rest too well myself. Chad? That was a bit of a surprise."

Maxine laughs. "I know, right? The first thing I told him was, 'Just so you know, this will *never* happen again.'"

"Maybe he didn't want more either."

Maxine flings the fridge door wide. "Damn, there's nothing to eat. *Great.* I guess I have to go to the grocery store, even though I feel like total crap..."

"Well, I'm off to meet Franky," Squeaky says cheerily. It's a miserable November day and she buttons up her coat. "By the way, Rosie's been trying to reach you."

Since coming back from Europe, Maxine hasn't returned any of Rosie's calls, or even seen the baby. The more days that pass, the harder it is to go.

She gets dressed and drags herself to the grocery store in the worst possible mood. It's a sour coincidence she bumps into Rosie in the parking lot. Her old friend is stunning, as usual, with no makeup and glowing skin, wearing boyfriend jeans and a pea coat.

"Rosie! Oh god, how ARE you?" They exchange a clumsy hug. "How's the baby? Crawling like a marine?"

"You'd know if you came to visit," Rosie laughs, hair falling out of a casual bun. "I've been leaving messages for you."

"I'm sorry. It's been such a whirlwind, finding a place to live, and Squeaky and Franky moving in."

"Sure."

Maxine reaches over and pats her belly. "No more baby," she jokes. "Now you're just fat!"

“Cute,” Rosie says, arching an eyebrow.

“I’m kidding, you look great, really. Anyway, I’m totally babbling…we should get together and have lunch sometime, okay? Oh my god,” she claps her hands. “It’s freezing out here!”

“We need to talk about Freudian Slips, Maxine. That’s why I’ve been trying to reach you.”

“Huh?”

“Fanta asked me to be in charge of her stock when she left.”

“Left? What do you mean *left?* It’s been a couple of weeks. I thought she was just pissed off and taking a holiday.”

Rosie has already spent hours at Fanta’s apartment sorting through piles of vintage clothing, old records, sewing supplies, Italian handbags, Puccini. There were stacks of cracked serving platters in the oven, and trunks full of bathing suits with shot elastic.

“Well, I’m packing up what’s left at her place to sell in the store. Are you okay with me taking over her shifts? I’ll have to bring Mabel, too.”

Maxine clenches her jaw and looks up at the sky, braying in anger. It’s a loud, vicious sound that startles everyone in the vicinity. “WHAT the FUCK! Why is everyone trying to ruin my fucking *life*?”

She trips over herself getting away. Rosie’s mouth turns down unhappily, watching Maxine run into the store and hide behind a display of poinsettias. She debates following her, then thinks of Tony King at home with Mabel and puts the groceries in the car. Wet Leather comes through the speakers. Rosie turns off the stereo and drives away slowly.

After a bout of all-night drinking, Maxine looks almost dead. She left her bedroom door open and every time Squeaky passes by, her waxy skin and open mouth look corpse-like. Finally, Maxine gets up. She grunts at Squeaky and heads to the bathroom, unleashing unseemly groans. It's late November, and snow flurries dance outside the window.

When she comes out of the bathroom, her face is green. "Well, I would call *that* explosive diarrhea. And either I have an ingrown hair or else I got herpes."

"You don't have herpes."

"It's a really big ingrown hair then. Will you look at it?"

"NO!"

"O-*kay.*" Abruptly Maxine shifts gears. "Anything for lunch?"

Squeaky makes her a cheese omelette with onion and tarragon. With all the on-order cooking she's been doing lately, she should be running an underground restaurant. In the living room Maxine sprawls across the couch with her plate, despondently watching TV. Egg falls out of her mouth as she eats. Squeaky finds it hard to imagine getting back into a van with her. This is one hell of a depressive slide. Maxine's bleached hair stands up like the fuzz of an unhappy, newborn chick.

A postcard of an iguana:

"I am 8 degrees from the Equator. There is a yellow boat
moored in front of me, and long days to contemplate
the slowness of cats unfolding."
Love,
Fanta.

Maxine is pissed off once again, and it seems like her bad moods never subside. It bothers her how Franky and Squeaky stay in their room, smoking weed and laughing at private jokes. The only time they come out is to make runs at the refrigerator. "Why do you expect me to do your dishes," she shouts at him one night. "I'm not your girlfriend, am I? Or your wife?"

She storms out of the kitchen and slams her bedroom door so loudly it knocks a picture off the wall. "Damn," Franky says, shaking his head. "Three weeks of ragtime, and only one of rock 'n' roll."

The December afternoon is wet and the kitchen warm. Squeaky talks on the phone with her landlord, who says she and Franky can sign the lease tomorrow. It's a house on the east side they've been hoping to get. "We'll be moving at the end of the month," she informs Maxine.

Squeaky goes to the kitchen and begins rinsing dishes. She's glad to be leaving. It's not like the carefree days of living at Rosie's—all the shared feasts and hours playing music, strutting around in a proud pack. They were younger, less jaded, and every night seemed to last a whole weekend.

"It's for the best." Maxine is dejected but refuses to show it. "I really hate how Franky leaves his wet towel on the bathroom floor. And he never remembers to pull out the cans on garbage day." His whiskers stick to the sink, and she swears he pees on the floor.

"So…what's the problem?"

"It irks me that he doesn't do his share."

"Franky helps out in other ways. Besides, I always pick up his slack."

"All I'm saying is, if he fails here, here, here, and here, what does that add up to? The big picture."

Squeaky blows the hair out of her eyes loudly. "I'd drop this one, Maxine." She viciously abrades a burnt muffin tin with a scrub brush.

"Oh, guess what? I can't believe I forgot to tell you. It turns out my old drummer, Patsy Cakes, now manages bands. I think we should hire her."

"For what? We're not *doing* anything."

"Squeaky, are you with me or what?"

"You want to talk big picture?" She turns to face Maxine, hands dripping. "Okay, let's talk about the big picture of Wet Leather. Maybe if we'd had someone else instead of Fanta dealing with everything—finances, the driving, wrangling our asses—*maybe* she wouldn't have been so overworked. Rosie wanted to help us, for free I might add, but you had to say no and not let her come on tour."

"You're bringing that up NOW?"

"It still bothers me how you acted so shitty. And it's just another example of how Wet Leather was hindered by your personal garbage."

Maxine crosses her arms, eyes narrowed into slits. The moment does not pass easily.

After a few days of icy politeness, Maxine leaves to spend Christmas with her mother. She does not return for the rest of the month or answer her phone. As Squeaky packs her bags, she is filled with regret. It hurts to lose yet another friend. She thinks of Paula Grubler, so needy in her desperate couplings, how they'd once been so close. Even now, Squeaky just can't forgive her. She wonders how much of the trouble with girls is her fault: is she shallow, judgmental, cold? When the band fell apart, Maxine was lost and depressed. It just seemed easier to ignore it.

All her life, Squeaky hung out with boys. She likes their easy camaraderie, how they seem less prejudiced by emotion. Girls are flamboyant and passionate, put together with brilliance, but sooner or later she always pulls the loose seam. She loves Maxine Micheline like no other. The woman could really light a stage on fire. They'd once had each other's backs and were stronger for it. There's a deep friendship and shared history. They've seen the world together.

There are things she doesn't want to forget.

San Felipe is a quiet beach community that was once taken over by young people who'd flocked there to party. It used to be the last city at the end of the highway, but now it's an abandoned town on a side road. On the bus ride Fanta speaks to no one and buys the wrong ticket in Ensenada. The bus driver tries to make her pay double. She refuses, cursing the feeble guidebook Spanish, and the meekness of her mother. In town, she rents a small room. The sky is a purple, blue, and black, a colour she tries to find a sound for with her tongue.

In San Felipe, times are hard. The three-block town shuts down with the sun. Kids in cars with tinted windows cruise the strip. As a stranger, Fanta can only wonder at their world. Whole days pass when no one speaks to her, except for the man at the all-night taqueria. Sometimes she misses her girlfriends, but after the last months of tour noise, this newfound silence is paradise.

One morning Fanta builds a sandcastle and is happy for the first time she can remember. They are halfway through the four-day winds that come once a year. After that, they say, the sun will burn so hot.

The Rise of Kitty Domingo

Pretty pretty kitty in the city. It could be a whole song, that one line over and over. Back from tour she goes on another binge. It doesn't matter that Wet Leather is on the cover of a music magazine, or that the clip of her coffee table swan dive is heavily downloaded. Their music videos are in constant rotation, and strangers recognize her now. She doesn't like it. Inside of a squat, no one cares what she does or about the ugly twists of skin over her veins.

Kitty refuses to go to residential rehab. She swears there are bedbugs. People steal from her. Jewel fears her daughter burns so fast the world will lose her. And it might. Every time Squeaky sees her that winter, Kitty is a mess. In the springtime, when Jewel shows signs of a breakdown, Kitty agrees to a week-long retreat deep in the Kootenay Mountains. There is no smoking, no drinking, no drugs, no meat, no computers, and no television allowed. Because of this, Kitty Domingo hates her mother.

The property is miles from the nearest town. There are separate log cabins for men and women. Kitty arrives in the evening, as everyone is singing around a bonfire. She is appalled when they start chanting a prayer, and sits with her arms crossed. Somehow, she gets two mosquito bites on her face. Kitty can't believe this goddamn hippie hell.

In the morning someone asks her, "How did you sleep?"

"Great," Kitty answers truthfully. "What have you *done* to me?"

The women in her cabin consist of a bald ex-anarchist, now into gospel; an art history professor getting over a divorce; a Danish girl, very serious and questioning; and Mica, a beat-boxer who is studying to be a yogini.

After mandatory morning exercise, Kitty sneaks into the woods for a cigarette. At breakfast she checks out the older ladies who have shaved heads with grey stubble coming in. They are silent and austere. It fascinates her that one wannabe nun has curly brown hair all over her neck and chin. Later, Kitty is put to work stacking firewood. As she strips leaves from the branches, it occurs to her how everyone here is so keen on expanding their inner light, and all she can think about is what's for lunch. Kitty wants to drink, get high, yell, expose her bellybutton, and jerk off, all of which are forbidden.

Kitty's cabin mate, Mica, takes her to the nearby hot springs when work is finished. The sulphur in the water smells like hot egg farts, but it's peaceful in the woods with the melting frost. Mica asks, "How are you enjoying your time so far?"

"I don't know." Kitty makes an effort not to swear. "This kinda seems like a place where people hide out from the world."

"People do that in the city, too." Mica ties back her dreadlocks with a leather string. "They stay in their apartments, watching TV, avoiding each other." She casually gets naked before slipping into the water. Mica has no tits and a big bush.

"I dunno," Kitty says doubtfully. "The people here seem creepy, like they pushed some weird bliss button."

"They've spent years studying to become enlightened that way."

"Pfffftt."

Later that night Kitty hollers from the bathroom, "My shit stinks like goddamn *vegetables*!"

On the third day, Kitty runs away.

She trudges through the woods to the road and puts out her thumb. The first car that stops is a middle-aged lumberjack with a mustache and puffy vest. "Where to?"

"I need cigarettes. And a bar." Most of all she wants a shot of heroin, and if anyone can find it, she can.

"Climb in."

The man stops at a liquor store then drives to a deserted camping area. They sit on a picnic table. He hands her a bottle of rye and says, "I'll drive you to the bar when that's done." She takes a long swig and shudders. After a few more drinks, the man begins to play harmonica. He urges Kitty to sing but she refuses. "I was born with no urethra," he suddenly says.

"I'm ready for that ride to the bar now."

Back in the car, the man starts the engine and drives down the road. He leans over to turn on the radio and strokes Kitty's thigh. Slowly his hand creeps higher. Her pants are already unzipped. The man begins to rub between her legs, so excited he barely keeps his eyes on the road. Kitty makes appropriate noises as he moves his hand faster. They pull into the parking lot behind the tavern and she zips up her pants. "Thanks *Mister*," she snorts. He hasn't even noticed she's on the rag.

That's how the night begins.

Kitty wants to turn the day off but it's too bright. Her eyes are pinned, and she needs a cigarette. Her hands are shaking. This is bad news. She looks down an alley and sees a hundred miles.

It's a long trek back to the cabin. At some point, Kitty glances up, surprised. The clouds have never seemed so freaky before. She's only been high for a day, but her body remembers. Now she's back at rock bottom, dope-sick with no home, lying to people and losing everyone close to her. Fanta's long gone. She owes Squeaky so much money long overdue.

And Jewel's on Lithium, only one phone call away from being back in the psych ward again.

As she walks through the woods, it dawns on Kitty she can't live like this anymore. Some of what she's heard at the retreat has gotten through. The people here talk about forgiving yourself and the shame you feel, learning to accept your flaws. Kitty thinks she can do it. Maybe she even deserves it, too.

Maxine begins to date a man named Ron Pink. He's ten years younger and fucks her with great enthusiasm. They spend a lot of time in her opium bed. Maxine says she loves him, and it might be true. Ron has a gigantic cock and elaborate facial hair. He also wears a variety of odd-looking hats. It's kind of his thing.

Ron Pink also paints portraits of nude women, and asks Maxine to pose for him. It doesn't matter how long she has to sit cramped on a stool. She likes people to look at her. In the studio she forgets her many disappointments.

But when the portrait is finished, Ron stops coming by. He won't return her calls or emails. Maxine sits at her computer, staring at his photos, analyzing every message. One afternoon she happens to see him ride past on his ten-speed. He doesn't even stop to say hello.

She's at a show one night to see an electro-clash pixie rapper named Short Fuse, when Ron Pink appears at her side. "I *called* you," Maxine says. "Why didn't you call me back?"

"I'm having a dance party later," Ron says, evading the question. "Make sure you come over." He kisses her on the cheek and then disappears into the crowd.

She notices two younger girls staring at her. One snickers behind her hand to her friend. Maxine does a quick glance to her left and right. She looks back at the fresh-faced girls who are openly laughing. Maxine belts back her drink and moves near the front.

The entire show she looks for Ron and then spots him through the thinning crowd. He is talking to one of the young girls who'd rudely stared at Maxine earlier. Ron sees her watching, then he and the brunette scamper away. Maxine thinks maybe it's not a good idea to go to his party after all.

Outside she's relieved to find him smoking alone. "Hey," she says, trying not to slur or sway. "Hey, is that party still going on at your place?"

"Uh....I don't know." Ron Pink looks over her shoulder and takes a heavy drag of his cigarette. "I'm not *sure*."

"You don't want me to come over because you want to fuck that brunette. Right?"

He looks nervous and says nothing. Then he begins to gesture. "Well...I...."

The young girl appears at Ron's side. "I need a cigarette," she giggles, and pats down his pockets. He puts his arm around her waist. The girl stares at Maxine, while firmly pressing her body against Ron. Then she whispers in his ear. Ron pats her ass and nods in response.

"Goodbye," Maxine tells him. "The two of us will *never* fuck again." Ron and the girl laugh like she's made a hilarious joke.

It's a lonely walk home.

Maxine creeps through the Nation of Fuckers clubhouse in the early morning. A shirtless man snores wetly on the couch. She pukes in the shower while trying to sober up. Her stomach feels sick and loose, the soap burns between her legs. Suddenly the water becomes burning hot, so hot it scalds her skin. "Fuck," she screams. "Fuck fuck FUCK!" When Maxine turns off the shower there is laughter in the living room. This marks the winter of a slow decline.

Valentine's Day goes by with barely a blip.

Allen does her taxes, and then she does him. He wears sweater vests, has crisp sheets, and likes blowjobs in the morning. Most of all, Allen enjoys watching documentaries on plane crashes. He neatly folds his clothes when undressing. Maxine doesn't mind that they rarely go out in public, so it surprises her when Allen invites her to the suburbs to have dinner with his family.

On the train ride there, he informs her that his ex-wife will be at dinner. "That bitch really treated me like shit," he adds. Apparently three times a year she and her girlfriends had gone to Ibiza to sunbathe, snort coke, and cheat on their husbands. Allen's family are Russian Jews, and during dinner he and his mother argue in a variety of languages. The ex-wife is a brittle blonde who refuses to eat. She cuts the food for her pretty toddler into miniscule bites. As soon as the meal is over the ex-wife packs the toddler and leaves without once looking at Maxine.

Following the after-dinner coffee, Allen gets into an even louder argument with his mother. They are supposed to get a ride home, but he refuses. "It'll only take an hour on the train. I'm not going to be stuck in a car with that woman."

Maxine complains as she walks. Her feet ache in her heels and she sits down on a bench to rub her ankles. "I thought your family and I really hit it off."

"You don't know my mother. She wants to know why I don't have Jewish girlfriends. She thinks you're going to steal from me."

When they get back to Allen's apartment, Maxine is only mildly surprised when he breaks up with her. She spends a last night with him anyway. In the morning he fixes the bed so it's tucked and swept. No evidence left.

Maxine accepts a date from a man she meets online. On the first date he brings flowers. On the second he brings his kids.

That spring, Maxine moves into a high-rise apartment downtown. She begins to audition for TV shows and commercials, with little success. At night she paints her face and goes out alone. She prefers dim, expensive bars where no one says much of anything.

Her friends don't call to see how she is, and that makes her even more depressed. Squeaky stops by every few months with royalty cheques and residuals, but the visits don't last long. When Kitty got back from some weird commune, she moved into a sober living house for three months. They talk on the phone sometimes, but it's mostly about triggers, detox, and urine samples. It seems like Fanta fell off the face of the earth. And even though Maxine apologized to Rosie for the blow-up in the grocery parking lot, things aren't the same. They alternate days at Freudian Slips and coordinate work matters mostly through voice mail and notes taped to the cash register. Maxine begins to hate going there—the clutter, the dust, the smell of old things nobody wants. When summer ends, she decides to sell her stock and signs the lease over to Rosie.

Maxine leaves her house on a rare occasion to buy a carton of cigarettes. She's in the corner store with her hood pulled up, leafing through a magazine. The bell rings and two girls walk in. They are beautiful and young, smooth-faced and confident in their tube tops and feather earrings.

"Oh my god," one whispers loudly. "Isn't that Maxine Micheline?"

Her friend flicks her long hair and looks around. "Who?"

"You know, that singer from Wet Leather."

"Oh yeah, it is. Gawd, what happened to *her*?"

"I hope I look that good when I'm a walking skeleton!"

The girls clutch each other, laughing, and skitter around a corner to the back of the store. Humiliated, Maxine puts the magazine back, and quickly pays for her cigarettes without a word.

For weeks she lies on the couch with the curtains shut, watching TV. One afternoon Maxine wakes with a strange desire to see her grandmother. She takes a cab to the nursing home, which sits behind a massive condo development that used to be all trees. Maxine and her mother come here for Christmas and birthday visits, and it always smells of scrambled eggs and antiseptic. In the room her grandmother is propped up in bed, sleeping with her mouth open. Maxine creeps in and sits in a chair, watching her frail chest rise and fall. The funeral would be a tasteful, sparsely attended affair. The only ones who'd show up would be relatives wanting money. Anyone Maxine's grandmother once loved is dead.

The old woman wheezes on and on. Suddenly she wakes and smiles at Maxine, toothless and joyful. "Oh, it's you," she cries. "What a special occasion!"

Maxine feels better than she has in a long time. Then a gurgling sound erupts from the old woman. Her head shakes back and forth with palsy, mouth trembling. She lays back, eyes closed, and begins wheezing once again.

The taxi ride home uses the last of Maxine's money. She walks in and out of the rooms she lives in. Mouldy takeout containers on the floor, every dish dirty, an empty bed and an empty life. Instead of a lover sleeping beside her, there's a stack of tabloid magazines. Once she'd had her pick of men. Not anymore.

Maxine wants a family, but fears she's become too old. She can't find anyone to make her happy. Rosie is practically married to Tony King, and Squeaky and Franky are always together. It dawns on Maxine that no one cares about her now. All she'd had was Wet Leather, and their breakup is still so painful. What destroys Maxine is that her friends don't love her anymore. They never really had.

She finds the sharpest knife in the kitchen. The bathroom is bright and she adjusts the mirror. For a long time Maxine holds the blade to her wrist, her throat, her heart. Then she goes back to her wrist and slices.

It's early evening, and outside the pink and yellow lights begin to fade.

Black-Eyed Thursday

Fanta arrives from the airport, holding a bag of coffee beans and sticks of vanilla, and knocks on Squeaky's door. Her limp has gotten worse, but her cheeks are a dusty pink colour, and her hair is cut so Squeaky can actually see her eyes. Even the tops of Fanta's feet are tanned. They give each other a long, silent hug.

"A year passes like nothing," Squeaky says.

"So does two."

In the kitchen, Squeaky makes them vanilla pancakes with birch syrup and whipped cream. Fanta talks quietly about the tiny fishing village where she lives and no mail ever reaches. Limes and mangoes grow wild, and there are beetles the size of baby birds. The town's only payphone is on a road yellow with dust. No one there has ever heard of Wet Leather. "At night," Fanta tells her, "I listen to the howler monkeys scream."

Squeaky gives her the royalty cheques that Skat Records have sent. When it came to crediting songs, Fanta split everything into four equal parts, despite doing most of the writing. Everyone owns the same share of the music, and it's just another reason Squeaky loves her friend. They sit on the back porch and eat with plates balanced on their knees. The air smells like burning leaves and Halloween. Fanta asks, "How is she?"

She reluctantly opens the tabloid Squeaky hands her. On a back page is a photo of Maxine leaving the hospital, wearing sunglasses with her collar turned up and an ugly bruise on her cheekbone. Fanta looks at the magazine and says nothing.

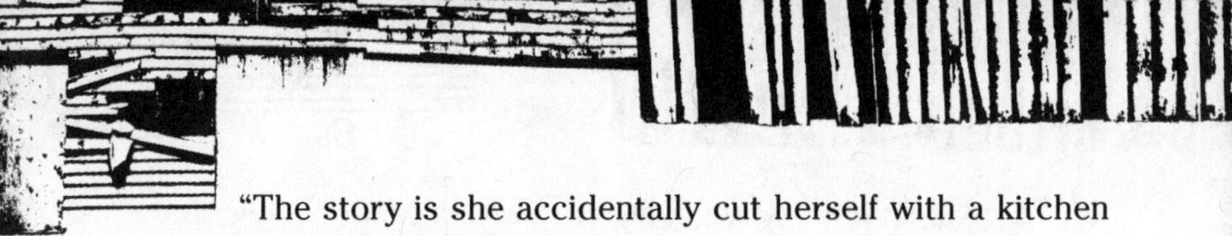

"The story is she accidentally cut herself with a kitchen knife while making dinner. Cutting carrots or something."

"Do you believe it?"

"I don't know."

"It's lucky she got to the phone first."

"I've tried to talk to her but she's pretty distant. If it wasn't an accident, I don't think she meant to go so deep."

They don't say anything for a while and then Fanta clears her throat. "What about Kitty?"

"She doesn't get fucked up anymore. Sobriety is a huge deal to her. We jam every once in a while, and she plays in a bunch of new bands. Whenever I call she's out on a bike ride, or at the gym, or off learning how to kayak. Kitty's nuts, but she's happy and crazy. Then there's Maxine, who's sane and sad."

"Can we see her?"

Squeaky has a wounded look. "Maxine's not accepting visitors. We abandoned her, Fanta. I saw her sliding downhill and all I cared about was Franky Sparrow. You split town, and that's cool, and Kitty's doing her own thing and that's really good, too, but there wasn't much left for Maxine. You know? She took it hardest when we broke up. Maybe it would help if the band got together and jammed with her again."

"Okay," Fanta agrees. "We'll play."

Squeaky insists Fanta come and see her new jam space. There's a mischievous look in her eyes. They drive to an industrial area in East Van and park in front of a nondescript warehouse. "This is it," she tells Fanta, getting out. "A space of our own. Chicks only."

"You rent this place?"

"Damn right. I signed a five-year lease." Squeaky heaves the door open with a flourish. "Welcome to the clubhouse."

There is an impressive living area with a sectional couch and animal skin ottomans. An impromptu art studio takes over one corner, along with a half-pipe Louie and his friends built. Squeaky's drums are set up on a low stage with a bunch of other equipment. Kitty's two bands also jam here—a death metal outfit called *Rattus Rattus* and the country-punk duo Cow Poke with her sister, Nadine. "Wet Leather can practise anytime we want. It's a long way from the days at Powder Keg."

"Does Kitty live here, too?"

"Sure, you know her, wherever her backpack falls. Or her dirty pants." Squeaky kicks a sock ball across the floor as if she's scored a goal. "Now, check *this* out."

She hits some switches and the back of the warehouse lights up to reveal a chrome-topped cocktail bar and cherry wood tables. Squeaky takes her on a tour of the kitchen: a walk-in freezer, an eight-burner with a flat-top grill and oven, a jury-rigged fan and ducting system. In the corner is an old Hobart dishwasher.

"It's my underground restaurant. I used my earnings from Wet Leather, but my brothers built most of it. Actually, living with Maxine gave me the idea. I call it 13C. It's the number of the warehouse."

The counters are spotless, the *mise-en-place* impeccable. She gives Fanta tastes of applewood-smoked salt, grains of paradise, Sri Lankan cinnamon. "People come for a six-course dinner and I set the price. I get lots of birthday parties and post-show band feedings. They can smoke weed or cigarettes and bring their own booze. I just did the wedding banquet for some newly married punks." Squeaky is booked solid for the next two months.

"An army marches on its stomach," she says.

THE REHEARSAL

Maxine waltzes into the warehouse an hour late. The girls are kicking back, messing around on their instruments. They stop mid-laugh when she walks in. Kitty rushes over and embraces her.

She was the only one allowed to come to the hospital. "Oh Maxine," Kitty had cried, leaning over the bed. "What happened? Why are you so sad?"

"Because I'm old."

"You're *not* old. You just gave up." Kitty had said it so emphatically that Maxine laughed.

It's a dreary evening and they watch her pull off her wet things. She notes Fanta's deep tan and short haircut, and gives a curt nod in her direction. Then she flashes the remaining bandage. "Don't worry," she says, waving her wrist airily. "It was just a stupid accident." Maxine's once-blonde hair is now a flattering jet black, and sticks up in angry spears.

"Good, 'cause right now you look crazier than a shit-house rat," Kitty snorts. Her fingers climb up and down her bass, playing riffs from reggae to funk to metal.

"Bend for a friend," Maxine grins, shooting her the finger.

When Fanta takes off her guitar and hugs her, Maxine remains impassive. She's gotten better at hiding her emotions. There are no more fantasies of private planes flying them to arenas, tropical photo shoots, or luxurious hotel suites. Now she's back at zero, starting with even less than before.

But Fanta keeps hugging her and finally she squeezes back. When Maxine feels Fanta's bony shoulders, the dark weight lifts in her, just a little.

Squeaky lays down a shuffle beat on the snare, and Kitty locks in with her juggernaut bass. The new Hamer with a tobacco burst finish unleashes Fanta's blizzard of notes. Maxine throws in her off-key, unhinged, exasperated growls. And somehow, it all falls into place.

ROSIE AND MABEL

The Wet Leather show is on a mild April evening. Tony King had objected to Rosie bringing Mabel with her. For the first time ever, they'd stood in complete opposition. Rosie shifts the baby at her hip and makes her way through the crowd.

Four hundred tickets have been sold and half that many kids stand outside the venue. Some are wearing homemade Wet Leather T-shirts, others hawk bootleg recordings. There are threats of a fire marshal coming. It's been a long time since Rosie's gone out and she wears a tight dress and booties, even lipstick. At the door the bouncer crosses her name off the list at once.

Backstage, she asks for Maxine. She misses her old friend, and figures the girls are probably somewhere huddled together, working out the dynamic, or else pulling each other's hair from the roots. Then she sees Maxine, strutting like a peacock in red leather, trailed by a camera crew. She is being filmed for a reality series about celebrities overcoming depression. "Hey Maxine," Rosie calls. "Look who I brought to see you."

"Oh Rosie, how *are* you?" Maxine kisses her, European style, on each cheek. She falls on baby Mabel with little gasps. "OOOOhhhh, cuuuuuuuute, cutie cute cute CUTENESS!" Mabel looks at her with confusion then reaches up and yanks Maxine's hair.

Rosie notices Maxine is sporting a new mouthful of expensive-looking teeth. Her face is unlined and smooth, as if all the character and history have been erased. It's also quite apparent her breasts are several sizes larger, and strain in two large mounds toward her collarbone.

"You're not staying for the show, are you? It might be too loud for the baby..."

"Yes, I think that—" Rosie tries to answer but a wave of fans sweeps Maxine away. Her words hang in the air and it feels like another perfect letdown. All Rosie's life she's never understood why some women were so unkind. Then she looks into her baby's face and knows what is right and true.

She wanders over to catering for a slice of watermelon. Mabel shrieks in delight, bottom teeth jutting out of her smile. Everyday Rosie takes her to work in Freudian Slips, where Mabel plays in piles of taffeta and chews silk ribbons. She settles onto one of the road cases backstage and waits to see her old friends. She wants to tell them how the other day her daughter said, "Mama, where does yesterday go?"

Squeaky circles the dressing room, feeling worse with each lap. The great Squeaky Ladeucer, she thinks, once the drummer for the epic Wet Leather, now limping toward the bathroom. She worries she might puke from exertion during the set. She can't eat before a show, but right now what she craves most is a good meal, maybe a thick steak or *poulet-frites*.

Franky Sparrow is out on a Canadian tour. Squeaky offered to fly him home for their concert, but he hates airplanes and didn't want to come. She calls his phone and he doesn't answer. For the past few days she's been mortified by the thought that she misses Franky so much she might suddenly burst into tears.

Before he left they argued in a Greek restaurant that smelled like an armpit. Franky ordered a pitcher of beer to himself like most people order a drink. Her raised eyebrows made him indignant. "You partied when I met you," he fumed. "What's different?" She excused herself and kicked a hole in the bathroom door, mostly by accident. What had changed was that she couldn't imagine life without him.

Franky Sparrow has a belly he calls good living. His lifestyle might kill him, but that won't stop the party. Squeaky worries about him now, especially the mornings he wakes up with a shot of Scotch. Sometimes the restaurant takes all her energy and she misses the old, carefree days. When Franky had left on tour with Fire Chicken, it felt like she shipped her troubled teen off to camp.

Squeaky wonders if she wasn't happiest playing drums in her band, before Franky Sparrow, with nothing but time. Franky pissed his bed until age eleven and hates to be alone. She loves him more than any boyfriend she's ever had. If they break up there isn't a chance they'll be friends.

Her phone rings. It's Franky. She chews the end of her braid and doesn't answer. It would be hard to be without him, but she could do it. The phone rings a minute later, and it's Franky calling again. She races back into the empty bathroom and ducks in, locking the door.

"Hi Franky."

"Hey baby…"

A girl giggles in the background and Squeaky has to clamp down on the urge to ask who's there. She's not even sure what city he's in. The sound of female laughter annoys her.

It occurs to Squeaky that she isn't so laid-back anymore. She and Franky are apart for long periods of time in which they used to thrive, but it's hard to be in a constant state of departing. When she was still touring they had an agreement they could fuck other people on the road. Neither ever did.

Franky asks, "You ready for your big comeback?"

"It's just one show, more like a trial run. But I really think we need more practise."

"Relax. Don't stress about it." She wonders why he can't just sympathize with her to which he responds, "Do you really want me to *help* you worry?"

They have been through some battles, but after a few jabs at each other, things always cooled down. Girls with coy voices don't call and leave vague messages. Franky Sparrow is a decent guy. They've seen each other through lost pets, disappointments, the deaths of distant friends. On the tour with Fire Chicken across America, she and Franky had fucked in alleys, shower stalls, gas stations. All they did that entire first year was screw. Squeaky longs for those days of rough glee.

"I'll call you back," Franky says and hangs up. Right now Squeaky is worried about playing a show with her fractured band and loses the last of her confidence when she talks to her boyfriend. Something in that tears her apart.

If they broke up, at some point they'd have to stop hating each other. There would be time for new interests and pursuits. She decides to start calling her brothers once a week, wherever they are, talk to them and their wives. Spend more time with her friends. She could really knock a few dishes out of the park with extra time in the restaurant.

Squeaky leaves the backstage area and works her way outside. Everyone wants to pat her back or congratulate her. She pulls up her hood and blends into the shadows. The fresh air feels good. There is a line waiting for tickets and she overhears a young guy say, "I hear these chicks are old."

"Old is not necessarily bad," says his girlfriend, cuffing the back of his head. Squeaky laughs then turns and runs directly into Paula Grubler.

"Sorry. Oh! Hi, Squeaky."

"Hello, Paula."

They stare at each other. Paula looks fit, and is wearing tight jeans and a Wet Leather T-shirt. Her hands are shoved in her back pocket, and she smiles hopefully.

"I really love your album. I play it all the time."

"Thanks."

Paula has such a genuine expression of relief it makes Squeaky feel bad for the years of ridicule. They'd had a lot of fun living together: midnight bike rides, breakfast bong hits, Halloween acid trips. Paula had always been up for adventure, and girls like that were hard to find.

"Well, I gotta get ready to go onstage."

"Wait." Paula grabs her arm. "I really want to tell you how sorry I am about everything that happened. But I never understood why you forgave Franky and not me."

Squeaky thinks it over and shrugs. "I took what I could carry." They look at each other for a long moment. Then Squeaky says goodbye and Paula gives a small, crumpled wave.

The bouncer lifts the rope to backstage. It occurs to Squeaky what a great life she has: her family, her friends, the restaurant, and even the crowd of screaming teenage girls here tonight. She used to think that without Franky, these things hardly mattered. Then it hits her. Without her girls, she didn't have anything. After all they've been through she'll never abandon them again.

The phone rings again and Squeaky holds it to her ear.

"Franky," she says.

Bitches Unite

Kitty sits with her miniature fender amp and plugs in. Her butchered hair has grown into soft black curls. Playing music had always gone hand in hand with having a few drinks, and those drinks never led anywhere good. But now she's happy to see things how they are, see people how they are. It's her first sober show. She is nervous and excited, and proud of herself for feeling this way—not being high and mushing her emotions into one monotonous groove so she wouldn't be scared. She goes to the bar for more club soda and lime juice. The bubbles make it seem like a real drink.

Maxine's stomach churns with nostalgia and nerves. Peeking out from behind the curtain into the audience, she sees a smattering of her past: jilted sluts, lowlifes, leeches, and enemies she feels compelled to impress. The time when forgiveness could have mattered is long past. Back in the band room the anxiety gets to her and she screams, "FUCK!"

Fanta flinches at the proximity of the screech, the certain shrillness that can only be found in Maxine's pre-show jitters. "What's wrong?"

"The sound here is gonna be *shit*."

Fanta has shadows under her eyes. It's been hard for her to adjust to the city noise. "Maxine, they do in-house sound here. It'll be fine."

"This better not be one of those shows where all I hear is guitars and no vocals and I end up screaming and losing my voice." She turns to Kitty. "How many times do I have to tell you? I have limited monitors. Turn your fucking bass down tonight."

"Relax," Kitty shrugs, collected and cool.

"They're filming this FOR MY SHOW!"

Kitty laughs. She can't help it. Hysterical people have always amused her.

"Hey," Squeaky says, "did you guys see Rosie?" She pauses and fishes around in her hoodie pocket. Inside is a rotting chestnut Franky gave her months ago that had fallen off their tree. "Little Mabel is adorable."

"I can't believe she brought her *kid*," Maxine spits.

The contempt in her voice makes something inside Squeaky snap. Everyone knows Maxine wanted to keep Wet Leather going after Fanta quit, tried to hire some session musicians to crank out riffs and put out a record herself. Eddie Camaro had quashed that idea.

"I'm so sick of this shit." Everyone looks at Squeaky.

"What?"

"I said, I am sick of this SHIT!"

The room instantly quiets. Even Kitty stops playing her bass.

"I'm not up on stage to shake my fucking hairdo. We can't even rise above the petty bullshit! What's the point? Can anyone explain why girls can't just fucking get along?"

Maxine opens her mouth then closes again. She pulls out her phone and scrolls through numbers of people who have called. It's easier than looking around the room.

"Remember the Kukoo's Nest," Fanta says. They all know what she means.

They were in the German Alps, in a town at the base of Hitler's mountain compound. The tiny club was called the Kukoo's Nest. They crammed on stage, Kitty bumping into

Maxine, their mics getting knocked over. When the boys crowd-surfed their feet scraped the ceiling. The crowd swelled to near danger. It was an extremely violent mosh pit, all male, but right in the middle of it was four girls, in tartan skirts and boots and patches. They kicked their legs and spun in a tight circle, arms around each other's necks for protection.

Dancing, just like that.

Fanta has never enjoyed hometown shows. The pressure and expectation are always too great. Tonight it's different. Standing in the wings about to walk onstage, she is reminded of Harold, and the patient hours he'd spent teaching her guitar. She had really loved him. It was nice to have that memory back again.

The energy and heat in the room are palpable. Coloured lights flash, cueing the start of the show. The girls clamber onstage to a loud assortment of cheers. Maxine steps to the microphone with a buzzing, familiar excitement. She wants to sum up, in a moving and eloquent way, how happy she is to be standing on this stage, in her hometown, how much she loves the gang of women behind her. The crowd watches with anticipation and she forgets everything she wants to say.

"Uh...Hey, Vancouver...I...I mean, we...uh..."

The seconds tick past. All the time Maxine spent with these girls swells over her again: those first awkward jams, how every sweaty hour in Rosie's basement counted. The tours across Canada and then America, in all their tattered glory. The first time she and Fanta heard Wet Leather on the radio. A bar brawl in Oakland. The crusty punks at the Roman fountain in Trier, the buildings still standing with bullet holes. Maxine looks back at Squeaky, sticks poised, who gives her an encouraging nod. Trying to find these words makes Maxine choke.

Then from the side of the stage comes the loudest cheer. "WE LOVE YOU MAXINE!" It's Rosie holding Mabel, who wears fuzzy protective earmuffs. She pumps the toddler's small fist at Maxine.

Maxine laughs as tears spring to her eyes, and she's careful not to smear her makeup. With a dazzling smile, she's back in action. She wraps herself around the microphone stand, projects her entertainer's voice to the back of the room. "I'm not going to stand here and talk all night—"

"I doubt that," someone mutters.

"—but I do have one thing to say. It's the only thing that matters, and it's what this show is about tonight. It's what *Wet Leather* is about. And that is...it's time for BITCHES to UNITE!"

She and Kitty start the call that gets the front row clapping first. "Bitch-es unite! Bitch-es UNITE!" The crowd takes it over the top. Squeaky backs them up with the kick drum, and even Fanta joins in. It lasts a full thirty seconds.

They open right up into "Bitches Don't Do Dishes." It's like the old days again, powerful and familiar, and they find each other easy in the flow. Kitty runs up to Squeaky and jumps backwards off the drum riser. She points her rumbling bass at the audience, picks out people and pretends to shoot them. Kitty Domingo, they say, really puts on a show.

Maxine holds the room with her lusty bar singer's voice, raw and seductive. Everyone's here tonight, even Eddie Camaro, who stands in the wings, arms folded, looking like a proud papa.

Kitty holds up her bass and finger-plucks, a comic sneer as she slaps and pops her strings. She carouses like an alley cat mixed with a city raccoon, tumbling around Fanta's side of the stage to make her laugh. She tears up and down the length of her bass, and then joins Maxine at the microphone, who slings an arm around her neck. Together they sing:

"We're fucking little bitches
And we don't do dishes!"

As the song ends Maxine holds her vocals. What is supposed to be a few simple notes ends up an extravagant arrangement. It's a glorious thing. When she stops and the applause dies down a drunken goon in front yells, "You look like ya got a nice CUNT!"

Fanta does a fast downstroke into the next song as Kitty rushes forward and punts his face. They keep right on playing.

They don't miss a beat.